Heaven Pays No Dividends

Heaven Pays
No Dividends

A *novel by*

Richard Kaufmann

Translated from the German by

Eric Mosbacher

New York · 1952

The Viking Press

Contents

Heaven Pays No Dividends

1 - The Golden Haze

Once upon a time I was very happy. In those days pears used to grow nearly as big as my head, and they were much juicier than they are now. People on bicycles towered high over me, I could ride on dogs, and once I actually ran underneath a horse. The air was clearer and purer, and I could be happy without smoking cigarettes; I was satisfied with inhaling the cool, clean air. Water tasted better too; it tasted as good as the air did, and I could enjoy it without diluting it with coffee or alcohol. True, life even then had its disagreeable or alarming features, such as snakes, and poached eggs on spinach, but they didn't occupy much of my thoughts, and I soon dismissed them. The sun rose earlier in the morning and shone all day, and when it went down I knew that it was time to go to sleep. At midday a golden haze hung over the land; the air was as golden as the age. I distinctly remember it.

I remember being in the garden overlooking the Rhine. It must have been spring, because blossoms kept falling into the glasses. Of course I didn't have a glass myself. In fact, by rights I shouldn't have been there at all, because the sun, in the strange way it had, had already set in the west in a canopy of red, blue, and violet, and the lamps had been lit. Our terrace was crowded with people. There were men in black coats, an old man in an alpaca coat—that must have been my grandfather—and then there were the women.

I have never seen so many beautiful women in my life. They wore light blue and pink dresses, padded and fragrant and smooth and silky with pleats and ruching and lace, and the loveliest colors imaginable—lavender, mauve, and ivory, delicate pastel shades.

I sat under the table, looking at the legs and listening to the conversation going on above my head. Sometimes I didn't bother

3

to listen, but just gobbled the food that was passed down to me, as if I were a little puppy. I can still see my father's face when he discovered me under the table, and nowadays, when I come to think about it, I can well understand his feelings. He was a typical gentleman of the old school; he had been in the diplomatic service, and during the First World War he had served in the cavalry. I think he must have held quite an important diplomatic post. I'm sure that never in his life had he sat underneath a table and gobbled tidbits passed down to him by a soft friendly hand. My father, as long as I knew him, was a tall man with gray hair, which later turned white. Sometimes he played billiards, and when he had nothing else to do he used to go to the Café Rohr for a cup of coffee—iced coffee in the summertime. There was an enormous number of people in our garden when my father seized me by the collar, hauled me from under the table as ignominiously as if I were a terrier or a dachshund, and packed me off to bed. My cries and protests were of no avail, and I had to leave in great haste. On my way up I could hear the conversation, so, of course, I stopped for a moment and listened.

"What a lovely house you have, Max!" one of the gentlemen said.

My father, either out of superstition or modesty, would not admit it. "There are plenty of lovelier houses in the neighborhood," he said, but he added, "All the same, I'm satisfied. It suits me perfectly."

"Yes, yes, heaven pays dividends, as the saying is," one of the ladies at the table said.

"You mean virtue pays dividends," another lady remarked. Everybody laughed again, and I laughed too. It was a happy time.

II

The woman who made the garbled quotation could only have been Aunt Yevgenia. She was not a real aunt, but one of my mother's school friends. After the war she had had to escape from Russia, and later, after my mother's death, she became our next-door neighbor.

Yevgenia had three daughters. Christine, the eldest, was blond, ambitious, and was always known as Kride. Josefine, her sister, was rather like her mother; that is to say, she was dark, had a full, round mouth and high cheekbones. The youngest was called Margarete, but at the time I'm talking about she couldn't have been born.

When Margarete was born Yevgenia sent her children away and came and stayed with us.

"Aunt Yevgenia has suffered a great deal in her life," my mother told me. "You must never ask her about what she has been through. It's painful for her to be reminded of it. So be a little gentleman and don't remind her of it!"

Good heavens, I was no gentleman! I went straight to Yevgenia and made her tell me all about her experiences, and I didn't have the feeling that she found talking about them painful in the least. On the contrary, she liked having an audience, and, as she had such a thrilling story to tell, I listened as attentively as if I had been in confirmation class. She stuffed my imagination full of exciting stories of revolution, murder, and escape from Russia, just as if it had been an empty chocolate box. When she had finished I made her promise not to tell my mother that I had asked her any questions about things she found it painful to be reminded of. She promised, but promptly forgot and told my mother about our talk, with the result that I got a thorough scolding.

But what can be expected of a boy who sits under the table, looking at people's legs and counting them, just for something to do, and contemplates the shoes, the small colored shoes of the ladies and the black pointed shoes of the gentlemen? Every now and then a hand appeared under the table with a praline or a piece of tart. I ate what came without bothering about who the owner of the hand might be. I was completely indifferent to the identity of my benefactor. I was very happy. I have searched long in my memory, but I don't believe I have ever been so happy. There was everything—company, security, incomprehensible conversation, and then that friendly hand—until my father's hand came down and grabbed me by the collar. . . .

III

My mother died young. She couldn't get over the fact that after the war my father, not content with giving up his uniform, which suited him admirably, declined to return to working for the Foreign Ministry. He was a lawyer by training; he had specialized in international law, and he had private means. But then something happened to my grandfather's shares, and we had to sell the house. It was an exciting time. My mother died, and we moved into the town. Soon afterward my grandfather died too.

I've only dim memories of the villa and its terraces over the Rhine. There were some wonderful hiding-places under the bushes in the garden and in the niches of the terrace walls, and you could watch the ships going up and down the river, and in the distance there was a big factory chimney, with its everlasting plume of smoke. But it was a long, long way away. Where we were there were no factories, only villas hidden in orchards and the bright foliage of the trees—aspen, ash, weeping willow, and copper beech. The whole hillside was covered with them.

The house had been my grandfather's wedding present to my parents. I think of it as a fairy house. I know that people still live in such houses. People who can afford them actually build such houses nowadays; there are certainly far worse things they could do with their money.

Early in the morning the river was covered with mist and haze; sometimes it was so thick that the ships were invisible; you could only hear their sirens. But then the sun drove the mist away, and you could see the blue or brown water again, and the green banks and the smooth roads, which from above looked like metal streaks; and you saw cars driving along them. You don't see such marvelous cars nowadays. Nearly always they were open cars, and the drivers wore caps and goggles and big gloves. Long before you saw them you used to hear them sounding their horns. The cars were by far the most romantic thing about the whole landscape. A ride in a car was the thing I longed for most.

This fairy-tale house had a gardener whose name was Thomas and a cook whose name was Josefine. The first time Yevgenia's second daughter, who was the same age as I was, came to see me, I asked her whether she was named after our cook. It was just as well my mother didn't hear.

It sounds heartless, but I think it was just as well that she died before we had to sell the house. It meant everything to her, and she was tremendously happy in it. She adored it—the room with the big, shiny furniture, as well as the music room with the white piano, at which she used to sit sometimes and play "When I Still Wore Frilly Dresses."

I remember it as clearly as if it had been only yesterday.

I think my father started having a better opinion of me after we sold the house and moved into the town. He had been wounded several times in the war, and at first he had to remain seated a great deal. Later he grew better. As he had traveled a great deal and knew a great many people, he settled down to writing articles, which brought in enough money for us to live on. We moved into a little two-story house in a pleasant suburb. It had a garden, of which we were allowed to use the front half.

Our part of the garden was planted with grass and bushes. In summer my father used to sit in it in a deck chair, reading newspapers and periodicals from all over the world, in German, English, French, Italian—heaven knows what other languages he knew besides. We had three rooms on the ground floor, and a bathroom and bedrooms upstairs. Yevgenia had found them for us. She had also found us a woman who arrived punctually every morning at half-past six, put felt slippers over her shoes, and moved about the house in them like a ghost. She woke me, gave me my breakfast, made sure I was properly dressed, and then got my father's breakfast. It was a tidy, orderly world. With what he earned from his writings to supplement his pension from the Foreign Ministry, I think my father managed to make both ends meet. He may also have had a disability pension, because of his wounds. But he never liked talking to me about money.

He was a modest man. His tie was always neatly tied, his collar was always clean; he had a gentle, pleasing voice, and he always walked with a stick, which he never put down. When anyone shouted or was violent or rude he only raised his bushy eyebrows slightly. In the evening he wrote articles, about politics and other things I didn't understand. His room was furnished like a cell; three of its walls were covered with books. I think he was happy in it. There were a number of periodicals that valued his opinions and paid him better than they paid their other contributors. My mother would have been very unhappy in those surroundings. She would never have got over our coming down to live in a suburb, surrounded by middle-grade officials, commercial travelers, and business people.

The back part of the garden, which was out of bounds for us, was used as a kitchen garden by the industrious Nissel family, to whom the house belonged. Herr Nissel was a Social Democrat and worked on the railway. He had built the house with his own hands, as he used to tell me every now and then.

He always repeated the words "with my own hands" several times. I used to look at his hands; they were red hands, with short fingers, but otherwise there was nothing very notable about them. But they had built a house, and that was something I couldn't properly understand. Why should one build a house oneself? What for? Why not employ a builder? In any case, there were plenty of houses for sale. Houses didn't die, they lasted for generations. That's what I thought to myself, but naturally I didn't say anything about it to Herr Nissel. Instead I admired him.

Frau Nissel's name was Martha. Every now and then she had furious outbreaks of jealousy, but otherwise she and her husband lived in peace. They had a son, who later went to my school. His name was Ott-Heinrich. The Nissels were not a little surprised that I didn't have a double name too.

But, in the long run, life would have been boring if Yevgenia hadn't come and opened her dressmaking business on the ground floor of the house next door. She made beautiful dresses, which she designed herself, and she had customers in the best circles. I had only to creep through a hole in the fence to find myself in another world. My father and the Nissels knew about the hole in the fence. Both disapproved of it, for different reasons, but they never said so, probably because they realized that it would have been useless to forbid me to use it.

IV

When you are young you are apt to take things as they come. The great thing is that there should be variety, and plenty of it. No change can be so bad that you can't get something out of it. When my father sold the house on the Rhine I think he was a bit worried about what I'd say. What with the large staff needed to run it and the garden, it must have been as big a headache as running a factory. It was all very beautiful, but quite useless; and on top of it there were the rates and taxes, and all the expense when he entertained. No, my father was not in love with the big house, and when I accepted our new home without complaint he was glad.

There are many things you don't understand till you've been through them yourself. My father was not suited to war, but he had spent over four years at the front in spite of that. War is a thing for stocky little men with thick heads and big chests. My father was tall, thin, aristocratic, though he didn't come of an aristocratic family. All his ancestors had had entirely useless occupations; for generations there hadn't been a baker or an artisan or a landowner among them. Men of my father's type ought to be exempted from the fighting services—my father could have been exempted if he had wanted to be. I don't know what the motive was that drove him to compete with men with red faces and huge fists who could carry a sixty-pound pack as if it were a matchbox, and shout at the same time. If he had wanted to he could have served his country honorably as a commercial counselor in Switzerland or Norway. That's what everyone who had the chance did. Because of my grandfather's connections, my father would have had no difficulty in doing the same.

My father was the most peaceable man under the sun. Not till much later did I understand how he managed to survive four and a half years in the trenches, putting up with hunger and cold and enemy shelling, and storming enemy trenches shouting "Hurrah!" —all for the sake of gaining two hundred yards of ground. He never spoke about his experiences. In our house talking about the

war was taboo. If a friend or acquaintance broached the subject
my father would grow quite quiet and knit his brows. He was far
too polite to say anything, but either in that way or some other
he always managed to change the subject.

I can still see him in my mind's eye, when he was troubled by
the fragments of a British mortar-bomb which he still had somewhere in his body, pacing the carpet backward and forward from
chair to chair, with compressed lips. At these times there was
nothing he would let anyone do for him, and it was best to pretend not to notice. Sometimes, instead of being troubled by the
bomb fragments, he'd have a bout of the rheumatism that he had
picked up in Flanders. Herr Nissel had also served at the front for
four years, but didn't suffer any ill effects. On the contrary, when
the war was over he built himself a house. My father sold a house.
That was the difference.

When the flood of war books broke upon the world—a new
war book came out every week, cheerful or bitter or heroic or
whining or cynical; there was every conceivable kind of war book,
ranging from bare reporting to witty essays about what it felt like
in the middle of a thousand-gun bombardment—I never saw him
read a single one of them. Sometimes I'd start talking about one
of the latest to appear, but he invariably dismissed the subject.

"Yes, yes," he'd say, as if thinking about something else. "I
daresay that's just what it was like."

"But you were in it," I'd say. "Tell me what it was like."

"I don't know," he'd answer. "It was dreadfully boring. But
sometimes it was fine. Particularly in hospital."

You can imagine how disappointed I was. He didn't have the
slightest touch of heroism. He had done what was expected of
him and was glad it was over, and that was all. Now he lived in
the little world he had built up for himself. The suburb we lived
in suited him. He didn't care in the slightest whether his new
neighbors were "beneath" him or not. The anonymity of his war
experiences survived in him. I sometimes think he must have felt
a bit like a fish out of water when he came home in 1918 and
found himself living in a house with a gay young wife who wanted
to catch up with all the things she had missed during the war
years, while all he wanted was to be left in peace, to think about

one or two things that had occurred to him during those years. From that point of view, our move to the suburb was an improvement in his circumstances and not the reverse.

In spite of his modesty he didn't do at all badly. He never had the experience of writing an article, hawking it about from editor to editor, and then having it left on his hands. Above all, he never had to call on a friend for help.

Fortunately he had enough friends and acquaintances who took pleasure in introducing him to editors or publishers. Once or twice a year he'd pack his old-fashioned leather case and go and see them all. When he came back and I met him at the station I could generally see in his face that he'd had a successful trip.

"Come along!" he'd say. "Let's go out and have a really good dinner. I've had to lunch and dine out with so many people, why shouldn't I dine out with my own son?"

We'd go straight from the station to the best restaurant in the town and dine à la carte, with a bottle of wine. He did all the choosing, and then he started talking about Hamburg, Vienna, Berlin, Leipzig, Düsseldorf, all the places he'd been to. On these occasions he was the most delightful host that could be imagined. Once we happened to meet Kride at the station and took her with us, and she agreed about what a delightful host he was. She was very impressed by all the names he mentioned.

"In Berlin we met Herr H., of the Globus concern," he said, and started imitating Herr H. and his pompous, inflated way of speaking. He stuck an invisible monocle in his eye and puffed out his lips as he talked.

"And what did you do?" I asked.

"I did the same," he answered.

That, of course, was a delightful lie. I knew perfectly well he had just sat there, looking on in amazement.

He pursued down to the smallest details the consistency with which he organized his life after the war.

"One thing we learned in the war was to do without all unnecessary kit," he sometimes said to me when we sat facing each other across the dining-room table in the evening. "By the end of the war we managed with very little kit indeed. It's only a matter of getting used to it."

So we "did without all unnecessary kit" in our house. We had only the bare essentials. When I come to think of it, our life in those years was rather Spartan.

Another lesson he had learned in the war was self-control. I don't think he was self-controlled by nature; he struggled all his life to achieve it. He told a story to illustrate this; he always told stories to illustrate his meaning.

"We had an old major who demonstrated self-control to us," he said. " 'When you're entering a trench under bombardment,' he used to say, 'the thing to do is to walk upright, calmly and without hurrying. Then you don't notice the enemy fire.' "

I was expecting an exciting war story and listened, goggle-eyed. But as usual I was disappointed. My father said no more, as if that was the end of the story, so I asked him whether he had taken the major's advice.

"Not a bit of it," he said. "When the enemy opened up we tumbled into the trenches head over heels. Only the major strolled along the parados, full of contempt for us."

"And what happened to him?"

"He got a direct hit from a field gun."

The art of self-control might have embittered my young life somewhat, but one day my father wrote a letter to the editor of *The Times* of London, to which he used to subscribe. The letter was a highly technical one about some question of neutrality or international parity. He explained it to me at dinner one evening. From the fact that he used his fork to help with the explanation I could see that he set great store by it.

"It's very important," he said. "I hope *The Times* will print it."

I hoped so too. Heavens knows his English was good enough.

The Times arrived six times a week in a flat wrapper. It generally stuck out of the letterbox at the garden gate. It had "Johannes Stamm, Esq." on it. So my father was an esquire, at any rate in the eyes of *The Times!* I was not a little proud of the fact.

One morning, after the letter had been sent, I awoke earlier than usual. I got up and went over to the window. It was summer, the grass along the paths was covered with dew, and birds were singing in the trees. My father, in his dressing-gown and slippers, was walking toward the garden gate. Generally he was a late sleeper. He bent down, picked up a twig, and threw it under the bushes; and he stopped for a moment and watched a redstart which was sitting on a branch and singing. Then he went on, opened the letterbox, and took out the post. My father glanced cursorily at the letters, put them in his dressing-gown pocket, and ran his eyes over the whole front of the house. As he couldn't see anyone, he put his thumb inside the wrapper of *The Times*, tore it open, took out the newspaper, and opened it. He had a typical way of opening *The Times*; he opened it in the middle and jerked it inside out. Then I watched him, motionless and tense for a moment, running his eye over the leader page. Then, with a second jerk, he folded the paper up again, put it away, put his hands back in his dressing-gown pockets, and walked back to the house. This time he didn't pick up any twigs. He looked like a big boy with iron-gray hair.

However, in the end, the letter was printed. Four days later it was answered on the same page by a member of the House of Lords; and eventually the *Deutsche Allgemeine Zeitung* in Berlin printed both letters in full, my father's and the English peer's, with an article on the subject by the editor himself.

After that life in our house grew quiet again. We reverted to the Spartan cult of self-control. Never again did I see my father in his dressing-gown in the garden early in the morning.

v

In the long run that kind of life might have grown a bit boring, because when you're young you can't live solely on school lessons, self-control, and porridge and milk. Fortunately Yevgenia lived next door.

Yevgenia, with her three daughters, her two seamstresses, and her fashion catalogues. Yevgenia, with her dogs and cats, her photographs, and her cushions. Yevgenia, with her samovar, which she kept going for eighteen hours a day. Yevgenia, with her extraordinary name, which nobody could ever spell. The intense, emotional, untidy, bewildering Yevgenia, with her mother-wit and her healthy common sense. Women like Yevgenia are the only kind worth marrying. True, after a fortnight you'd want a divorce. But that fortnight would last you a lifetime.

In Bulgaria they grow roses in fields in long rows. Women in bright costumes pick the blooms and take them to a factory, where the flowers are pressed to make attar of roses. A bottle contains the perfume of a whole field.

It was rather the same with Yevgenia. She contained in concentrated form the qualities of a whole regiment of women. She impressed everything with her personality, from the window sill by the door, where she used to put down her perfumed cigarettes and then forget them, to the latest sofa cushion her kittens had scratched and ruined. She possessed the *shirokaya natura*, the broad nature of the Russians, which one thinks of today in connection with the trans-Siberian combines and the Murmansk canal; and it was all concentrated into her tiny ground-floor flat.

It was utterly impossible to keep away from Yevgenia. She baked and sewed and smoked and cooked, and all the time she talked in that rather husky, foreign-sounding voice of hers. She nearly always wore a black kimono embroidered with green flowers, and she was continually going from room to room, scattering cigarette ash and snippets of sewing all over the place, mislaying patterns, forgetting appointments, pushing a cat that had gone to sleep on a rug out of the way with her slipper, scolding a dog, supervising her two eldest daughters in the housework, gossiping with the neighbors, and receiving the customers who besieged her house. She was a genius at dressmaking.

She and my mother had become friends at a boarding school in Geneva. Yevgenia had been as loyal to my mother as a bulldog. All that had been long before the war—in that golden age which was perhaps not really so golden as it seemed in memory.

Yevgenia came of a well-known family in central Russia, and relatives of hers had been influential officials in St. Petersburg. But *tempi passati*—all that was dead and gone. In 1908 Yevgenia had been sent from Geneva to Paris, where she had met an attaché at the Russian Embassy, a big, fair, broad-shouldered Russian, with whom she had returned to St. Petersburg. She had had two children by him. The first had been born before the war and the second at the outbreak of the war. They had a German name—

Josefine's and Kride's father had evidently come from the Baltic. The Balts fought on both sides in the war, as it suited them—at any rate, that's how it seemed to me. It also seemed to me that things went well with Czarist Russia only as long as they had enough Balts in the government. The Balts are extremely capable.

Yevgenia's husband had naturally fought on the Russian side. He was an infantry lieutenant and was killed, unpretentiously and almost as a matter of course, somewhere near the Masurian Lakes or on the Czech border. Yevgenia had certainly been very much in love with him. When misfortune struck her and the war was lost and the Revolution broke out, she fled from her native land. She went first to Italy and later to Germany.

All this threw no light on the birth of her third daughter, Margarete, who was born long after the end of the war, in 1923. This was an obscure period in Yevgenia's life. She had come to see us in 1922, when we were still living in our house on the Rhine, but then she had disappeared—to Paris, to North Africa, to Hamburg, nobody knew for certain where. She wasn't so badly off, because she had brought gold, jewelry, diamonds—the currency of refugees —with her from Russia. One can still live comfortably in Central Europe with a handful of diamonds.

Yevgenia never told us all that happened during those years, when she had traveled about Western Europe, still relatively young and attractive to men. Not even Kride, who was her mother's confidante, knew the whole story. Yevgenia was slightly shy of Kride. Kride was tall, fair, and blue-eyed, like her father, and at that time it was accepted as a matter of course in Yevgenia's circles that a woman should remain faithful to her husband, even after his death.

However, Yevgenia had turned up one day with a small dark-haired baby. Margarete must, of course, have had a father, but for many years I had no idea what he looked like. In those days Margarete was a small, short-legged, ugly little creature, with a broad, round face. She promised to turn out a second Yevgenia. There was nothing of a German Gretchen about her; she was much too dark-skinned.

Margarete was the Cinderella of the family, but without being able to profit by it. Kride treated her as if she didn't exist. Josefine, who sometimes had to look after her, treated her with the spitefulness with which only one small female can treat another. Yevgenia, with her head full of dress designs, world politics, and exciting novels, didn't have time to be continually looking after her daughter. After all, when Kride and Josefine had been Margarete's age they had had a nurse, a governess, and a maid to look after them. But now there was nothing but a kitchen, a living room, and a tiny bedroom in which the three girls slept, packed like sardines, while their mother lay on the big divan in the living room, smoking and reading novels half the night. She began going to pieces a little at that time.

So Margarete was neglected. Not that her mother didn't love her. To have loved her less than the others would have been entirely inconsistent with her *shirokaya natura*. But unfortunately Margarete, greatly to the disgust of her sisters, was not yet entirely watertight, which meant that she was condemned to spend several hours of the day sitting on a pot, a big dark blue pot decorated with red stripes and flowers and provided with an enormous handle. In the course of time she developed the ability to grip the handle with her strong little fingers and to go riding round the flat on her pot like a cowboy on his horse. She could make her mount take curves as well as go straight ahead, and when she reached a closed door she was unable to negotiate she would start whining, just like a puppy. At this her sisters' faces would assume an expression of agonized disapproval; and eventually one or the other of them would sneak out and drive the unfortunate rider and horse back into the kitchen, where the more intimate scenes of family life took place. When this happened Margarete naturally protested emphatically, and then visitors would hear the sound of slaps, followed by Margarete's howling. Thereupon Yevgenia, her mouth full of pins, would storm into the kitchen, and there would be two minutes of violent uproar until the parties were separated and everything returned to normal.

Margarete accepted all this with the greatest possible composure. She survived all ordeals unperturbed. She was capable of climbing ten times from the coalbox next to the oven onto a chair, and from there onto the window sill, and ten times falling down, bumping her thick head into the bargain, but she didn't seem to mind the bumps very much. Once she nearly cut off her finger with her mother's big tailoring scissors. She burned her little hands on the oven, and was scratched by the cat when she tried to take the kittens away, but she didn't mind that either. The girl must have been indestructible. Any other child would have died of tuberculosis, enteritis, boils, or blood poisoning, or would have broken its neck or have bled or been burned to death. Not so Margarete.

She adored me, probably because I was the only child who didn't pinch or strike or scold her. I found her fondness for me slightly embarrassing. She beamed when she saw me, called out "Da!" held out her strong little arms with dimples on the elbows and the backs of the hands, and immediately crawled onto my knees.

"You're a good boy, a very good boy!" Yevgenia would say, and nod at me encouragingly. Kride did not look up from her homework—she was at the town secondary school and had a lot of homework—and Josefine sniffed contemptuously and grinned. I sat there and contemplated the ugly black-haired little female, who always roamed about the place in a long, torn shirt, without much affection. But the imperturbability and self-control that my father preached bore fruit. I kept Margarete on my knees, caught her when she was about to fall, and looked after her as carefully as a mountain guide looks after his charge on the rope. I did all this not gladly, but dutifully. Yevgenia was perfectly well aware of my attitude. She showed appreciation of the fact by her encouraging smile and by saying I was a good boy. By showing her appreciation she could get people into all sorts of scrapes.

The family next door constituted a whole world in itself. After I had left and closed the door behind me I always sighed with relief. But after a while I found myself drawn back there again as if by a magnet.

They were a musical family, musical by nature. Yevgenia had a hired piano in her living room. It would never have occurred to anyone except a Russian, living in those conditions, to hire an expensive instrument like that. Whenever Yevgenia had a quarter of an hour to spare she sat down at the piano, improvised, played preludes, and sang in that deep, husky voice of hers, which must once have been very beautiful. As the daughter of a well-to-do Russian she had had a thorough musical training. In Russia, when she was growing up, studying music had been as natural as learning to read and write. When she had more time she would take out her music and really play, instead of just improvising.

On summer evenings I would sit with my father in the garden, and sometimes Yevgenia would play by the open window. I remember one evening in particular. Twilight fell—it was one of those gentle, protracted German summer evenings—and Yevgenia, entirely absorbed, played a Rachmaninoff prelude—ta-tamta-tamm-tamm-tamm—then Chopin, the prelude in E flat, followed by nocturnes and waltzes. Then, with a sudden transition to Vienna, she played Beethoven, the second movement of the Seventh Symphony.

Her playing that night wasn't just technically proficient, she was inspired. She was completely absorbed in her music. She played things I didn't know—but my father did. When I looked at him inquiringly he told me what they were. "Handel," he said, "from a Concerto Grosso," or "Philip Emanuel Bach," or "the partita in B flat." Yevgenia played for two hours.

Suddenly she stopped, and a moment later the Yevgenia family chorus was in full voice—Josefine's high-pitched, irritated treble, Kride's deeper organ notes, Yevgenia's own machine-gun rattle, all to the occasional accompaniment of Margarete's shrill alto. My father slowly shook his head. He had a bottle of wine beside him, and he took a sip from his glass.

After a while Yevgenia appeared in her garden, illuminated by the light of a distant street lamp. She was a big, stout woman in those years, and the dressing-gown that she generally wore emphasized her stoutness.

"You played beautifully, Yevgenia," my father called out quietly. She came over to the fence, looking as if she hadn't heard. Her face was serious, she was smoking a cigarette in a long holder, and she didn't smile.

"Margarete has been sitting on the new dress that's to be delivered first thing in the morning and completely wetted it," she said in her deep voice. Then she suddenly shrugged her shoulders, like one who has had many masterpieces wantonly destroyed.

"Did you like the music?" she said.

"It was wonderful," my father said. She accepted the compliment with a grave curtsy and trudged back into her house. We saw the pink light of the standard lamp appear in her room and heard her humming the "Red Sarafan," doubtless while she set about repairing the damaged dress with the deft fingers that for two hours had been playing Beethoven, Chopin, and Bach.

"Yevgenia's an extraordinary woman," my father said later when we said good night indoors. "She has two souls in her breast where we have only one." He gently tapped the top button of his jacket with his finger, laughing a little as he did so.

VI

So life went on between the two houses. It could have been more boring. School took a good deal of my attention.

At that time schools were brick buildings dating from the turn of the century. Many of the masters also dated from the turn of the century. They resolutely turned their backs on the contemporary world and took themselves very seriously, even if no one else did. There were masters of two generations—the old gentlemen, who still liked calling themselves professors, and the young, skeptical, embittered men belonging to the war and postwar generations. The old ones were German nationalists, and the younger ones, whether of the right or the left, were all extremists—that is to say, what were called extremists in those days. Even Social Democrats were called extremists then.

When I first went to school the old schoolbooks were still in use, and the staff took care to maintain a united front in the face of the pupils. But in the course of time the school turned out to be more and more an empty shell—a stately, impressive building from which the life had fled.

Politics cannot be introduced into the study of Latin grammar or Pythagoras's theorem, but it can be introduced into other subjects. I learned the history of Charlemagne four times, and each time it was different. The story of Charlemagne dogged me throughout my nine years at school. When I first heard his name mentioned by an old white-bearded history master, he was a good

German who had founded schools and the Holy Roman Empire. He was also something like the first chairman of the board of directors of the Main-Danube canal. We went on a school excursion to Weissenburg in Franconia and inspected not only the *fossa Carolina*, but the Roman *limes* as well. Charlemagne was in high repute. We learned a poem which said that position should depend on capacity and not on favor and that rank should depend on intelligence. That was the light in which Charlemagne was viewed when I was ten.

Two years later we had a new history master. He was young, atheistic, and not at all fond of the Popes. He still regarded Charlemagne on the whole with favor, but said he was a romanizer who had put the priests in the saddle in Germany. Also he doubted whether Charlemagne had really been able to write.

Three years later we were taught history by a French exchange teacher. According to him, Charlemagne was not German at all, but French, and Germany only really began beyond the Elbe. This got talked about in the town and caused something of a scandal. The result was that the Frenchman was forbidden to teach history; henceforward he was allowed to teach only French.

The last master to teach me the history of Charlemagne was a young, cheerful man, devoted to games and sport. He was in a rather difficult position because he was a member of the Nazi party. He prepared us for matriculation and took us through the story of Charlemagne all over again. For him Charlemagne was not a great man at all but "the slaughterer of the Saxons." The real national hero was not Charlemagne but the Saxon Duke Widukind.

In later years I have often wondered what the truth about Charlemagne is. I personally tend to think he was a great man, but that is probably based on sentiment, because my first history master was the one I liked best.

I once asked my father, and he gave me a whole lecture about Charlemagne. But he didn't really clear the matter up for me and all I gathered was that his own ideas on the subject weren't too clear either.

The school took itself seriously, but we didn't take it seriously.

Many ideas changed during my school years, and the school steered a zigzag course in their wake. The bottle was badly corked. The spirit, the essence, of the old humanism had evaporated, and nothing but water was left behind. For us school was just a symbol for the absurd seriousness with which grown-ups took themselves.

Sometimes reality intruded into the revered institution. There was the affair of the wreaths on Heroes' Day, for instance. The masters were divided into two groups, who treated each other with mutual respect. When it was the turn of the older generation to provide the organizer for our Heroes' Day celebrations, a wreath adorned with a black, white, and red ribbon lay under the porphyry tablet on which the names of the dead were inscribed. When it was the younger generation's turn the ribbon was black, red, and gold.

The headmaster's group said that the dead had died fighting under the black, white, and red flag, and the young ex-servicemen replied that it had been for a black, red, and gold Germany that they had fought. The two groups treated each other with mutual respect and without a trace of hostility, because it was necessary to maintain the outward appearance of a united front.

But one year there was a surprise. On Heroes' Day the usual wreath lay under the memorial tablet, but the ribbon was black, white, and red, though by rights that year it should have been black, red, and gold. The ribbon itself was red, with a white streak inside, and in the middle of the white streak there was a swastika.

There were sympathizers with the Nazi party in both groups of teachers, though officially there were no Nazis at our school. But the school was now confronted with the question of who had made the offensive ribbon and exchanged it for the proper one.

The culprit was never discovered. I don't know whether they couldn't find out who it was or whether they didn't want to. I could have helped in the inquiries. Kride had a definite talent for designing things, and her mother was an excellent seamstress. Also Kride had a very pretty mezzo-soprano voice and often sang solo in the school choir; and she had a key to the school hall so that she could practice there in the evening; and I knew that Yevgenia

had been the first person in our Social Democratic neighborhood
to become a Nazi. But I kept my mouth shut, because I admired
Kride.

It was one of those harmless, amusing events that serve as a
symptom of the times. For a long time I had liked Kride the best
of Yevgenia's three daughters, and not only because she was the
prettiest. There was no doubt that she was pretty, but also she
paid attention in school, had excellent reports, her handwriting
was big and easy to read, she always kept the lines quite straight,
and left an absolutely perpendicular margin. I don't think any
teacher could have resisted the temptation to write "very good"
under her work. Also she was older than I, and enjoyed enormous
prestige and authority in my eyes. Josefine was also pretty in her
way, but I didn't get on with her nearly so well. Josefine was the
same age as I was, wasn't very intelligent, and liked showing her
claws. I used to keep out of her way. Margarete was by this time
a funny little girl of eight, still a *femme fatale*, as her mother used
to call her, a young female to whom all sorts of things kept happening, even on her way to the nearest primary school only five
hundred yards away.

Things happened to her that didn't happen to anyone else.
Only Margarete could have encountered, on her way to school, a
stranger who enticed her into the entrance of a courtyard with a
handful of cream caramels. I don't know what happened there. A
strange, mysterious silence was maintained about it, and everything possible was done to hush it up. My father was consulted
and took certain steps. Eventually the same man, again with a
handful of cream caramels, was caught at the entrance of the same
courtyard after waylaying another child, and the courts section of
the newspaper spoke darkly of a sinister individual's being sen-
tenced to two years' imprisonment. Then the whole business was
gradually forgotten. But everyone shook his head over Margarete.

Nothing like that, of course, could possibly have happened to
Kride. I went for a walk with her one afternoon a few months
later. We walked from our suburb out into the open country and
eventually came to a little hill, where we sat down. We talked
about school, about the town, and about our two houses. She sat
next to me and leaned against my right side.

"What are you going to do when you leave school, Kride?" I asked.

"I'm going to study," she said.

"What do you want to be?"

Kride's answer was less elevated than it might have been. "I want to have a house," she said, "a house of my own. A big house, with flowers and a lot of big rooms and bright furniture, everything quite modern. I want to have a garden, with trees and roses, and a car and a sailboat and lots of visitors. I want to have visitors every day, all intelligent, well-educated people, and all well dressed; and I want . . ."

Her answer depressed me greatly. She was three years older than I, but was only one class above me in school, having lost several years because of her mother's unsettled, homeless life. I had been secretly hoping to marry her in the not-too-distant future. I was sixteen, and it didn't seem beyond the bounds of possibility. But these ambitions of hers now seemed to make my chances very problematical.

"My father has been earning less recently," I started cautiously.

Kride looked up. "Uncle Max is an ass! He sits there writing till his fingers get crooked, and is glad and grateful when some ridiculous paper prints an article of his and pays him a few marks for it. It's all the fault of the Jews, Rodie, it's all the fault of the Jews. They control the whole newspaper industry and—"

"What can be done about it?"

"Turn them out," Kride said. "They all ought to be sent to Palestine. Your father could earn thousands. After all, he's not so old!"

"He's seven years older than your mother."

Kride made an unintelligible exclamation. Then she went on, rather irrelevantly, "I shall be glad when I'm out of this hole. Josefine's a cat—"

"God knows she is!" I said zealously.

"And that little baggage Margarete," Kride went on in her singsong Baltic accent. "She's a bastard, too, into the bargain!"

I was somewhat taken aback and showed it. Kride only laughed.

"You're a good chap, Roderich," she said, "but you're still very young."

She suddenly turned to me, put one arm on my shoulder, and kissed me. It wasn't a quick, meaningless, friendly kiss, but a real one, rather wild, but heartfelt; she closed her eyes as she did it. I was so surprised that I nearly shut my eyes myself.

Then she jumped up, took me by the hand, and pulled me to my feet.

"That was only a joke," she said in her haughtiest manner. "You're to forget about it, you understand?"

Instead of forgetting about it, I went on thinking about it for a long time, but the occasion was never repeated.

VII

Kride matriculated in 1932 and went to the university. I missed her very much. At school I went up to the top form. I was the kind of boy who plays football passionately and is slightly above the average at lessons. I had no particular difficulty in keeping my place, and no particular ambition to do any better. Yevgenia's business was very bad at that time, when nobody had any money. People naturally got to know she was a Nazi. She was, of course, incapable of keeping her mouth shut. It lost her many of her best customers.

I don't know how Kride managed to stay at the university. That summer she had to hitch-hike home from Berlin, because Yevgenia wasn't able to send her the fare. I expected to hear wonderful stories and descriptions of Berlin student life, but she was silent and reserved, and had grown thinner.

When my summer holidays started I flung my books in the corner and went bathing with her. I was still a little in love with her. Perhaps she noticed it, but she always treated me in the same friendly, sisterly, rather tolerant way. At home she wasn't very happy. Yevgenia's poverty, Josefine's impenetrable silences, that child of misfortune Margarete—the whole atmosphere got on her nerves. In Berlin there had been something she had seen and hadn't been able to get. She wouldn't say what it was. But she was excited, politically excited. She had become an extremist, but not in the way our teachers were extremists. She was young and determined and didn't care what the outcome might be. She was ruthless.

Then there was all the excitement about the Beuthen murders. Today I couldn't say from memory what it was all about, but at the time it caused at least as much excitement as the sinking of the *Niobe*. My father was very much worked up about the business, which he condemned out of hand. He said it was murder and not to be forgiven by any party loyalty. But Kride was of a different opinion.

"Listen, Rodie," she said while we lay in the sun after our swim. "Those who still don't understand what is happening among us are beyond human aid. What is all this talk of murder? We're in the midst of a civil war, even if the government denies it; and in war you have to kill your enemy, don't you? That's the position today. You can't stand up in the middle of a war and say, 'I'm not going to shoot, please don't shoot me!' That won't stop the enemy from shooting. What restrains those Communist scum?"

I went home and shamefacedly read the newspapers. I read twenty of them, but they all said something different. The only definite fact I found out was that some Nazis had killed some Communists at Beuthen, and that the Nazi party and its leaders were supporting the murderers.

That evening, feeling ready to discuss the matter again, I took Kride to the movies. But she didn't mention the subject, and I might just as well not have read the newspapers at all.

"Come home with me after the film," I said to her. "Father said he'd open a bottle of wine."

It was a very good film. Very good films were still made then. It was about a young secretary who accompanied an old gentleman on a journey. In the end he turned out to be not so old, and in any case he had a great deal of money. There was a superb wedding breakfast, with very fine speeches; they were waited on by flunkeys in magnificent uniforms; they went to the Mediterranean for their honeymoon, had a lovely home to live in, and, in short, everything turned out marvelously for the young woman. True, you couldn't help guessing at the very beginning how it was going to turn out, but it was exciting all the same. The girl was played by a Hungarian actress with a well-known aristocratic name.

When we came out it was getting dark. I thought Kride must have enjoyed it. It was so pleasant for once to see other people getting what they wanted and being happy.

"Did you like the film?" I asked eventually, as she didn't say anything. She said, "Mmm!" and I put my arm under hers. I should have liked to kiss her, but she took my wrist between two of her fingers, dangled it for a few moments, and then dropped it. We walked on, past the privet and oleander hedges that surrounded the houses in our suburb.

"The film was a pure fraud, Rodie," she said. "I've seen what life's like in Berlin. I know the gentlemen who marry their secretaries! The films lie, and people look at them and believe what they see. Life isn't a bit like that. It's much meaner. It's mean!"

She had been to Berlin, and I hadn't; and she must know. I was sorry that she hadn't enjoyed the film. I had.

When I think about it today, it seems to me that Kride was just a little over-melodramatic that evening, like the film. But at the time I was full of admiration for her because of her experience of life, and I didn't know what to say. She was so much cleverer and more experienced than I.

When we got home my father was working in his room with his sleeves rolled up, and he had forgotten that he had ever invited us. I took Kride into his study. He didn't look up, but went on writing.

"What's the matter?" he asked over his shoulder.

"Good evening, Uncle Max!" Kride said. He turned around and jumped to his feet.

"Go out into the garden, children," he said. "I'll bring the wine out straight away."

I saw a light in his bedroom. After a while he came out. He had changed, and he had a bottle in one hand and three glasses in the other. The glasses clinked as he walked. He sat down, switched on the lamp, opened the bottle, and poured out the wine. He had such a charming way of doing all this that you only needed to watch him; there was no need to talk.

He raised his glass and said, "Your health, children!" In a second he had got Kride out of her gloomy mood. She actually started laughing and telling stories. We finished the bottle and had another. I felt tired and eventually rose to my feet. They didn't notice. They had started talking about politics and the Beuthen murders, and I was surprised at how tolerant my father was and how intelligently Kride talked.

I stood uncertainly behind my chair and looked round the garden. It had never looked so strange to me before. The bushes were black, and the leaves of the trees were drooping in the heat. The light of our lamp formed a ghostly circle in the middle of the darkness, and the whole place looked quite different. Big fat moths came shooting out of the darkness, struck the paper lampshade, and crawled across the table. But Kride and my father were too immersed in their politics to take any notice. There was no chance of breaking into the conversation and changing the subject. My father didn't like being interrupted by young people. I held my hand in front of my mouth and started yawning so much that tears came into my eyes. Kride sat there, calm and upright, taking a tiny sip from her glass every now and then, but I wasn't in love with her any more. My father drank as he always did, in long draughts that half emptied the glass. I knew his way of drinking and had begun by trying to imitate him, but I soon gave it up. I didn't like the wine; it only made me tired.

Eventually I said good night and went up to bed. I felt it wasn't a very graceful exit, but the two didn't seem to mind. My father said, "I'll take Fräulein von Haringen home." I had to rack my brains to think who Fräulein von Haringen might be, until at last it dawned on me that Kride's surname, like Yevgenia's, was von Haringen. Perhaps on another occasion I shouldn't have been so surprised. Perhaps that evening I was just a little drunk.

In any case I didn't do very much more thinking that evening, but fell straight into my cool bed. The voices went on murmuring outside, but I only heard them for a moment and then sank into a deep sleep.

A week later I went to the movies again. This time I was alone, and I took a cheaper seat. There was a very attractive blond actress in the film, who sang in a thin voice about how happy she was and how marvelous life was. I was just as fascinated as I had been by the film the week before, and when I got home, humming a new tune I had just picked up, Kride and my father were sitting in the garden.

"Are you home already?" my father said when I went and sat with them. This time they were talking about transcendental philosophy. After a while I remembered that Kride was studying philology in Berlin. So this was the result of studying philology! I hadn't known that lawyers knew so much about philosophy either. For a time I moved restlessly about in my chair, and then I went up to my room. This time I heard them talking for a long time—my father's dark, friendly voice and Kride's bright laughter. It worried me a little to hear them talking to each other without my being there.

Kride came to our house more and more often, but when she was there I went down less and less. I was seventeen years old, and everything struck me as being rather odd.

2 - Sicilian Intermezzo

The golden haze had evaporated. I stood on the deck of a big ship at Bremerhaven, looking down at my father and Kride on the quay below. Like everyone else, they were waving and calling out. The rail was black with people, waving to those below. Hundreds of colored paper streamers stretched from ship to shore. The band played "Oh, why must I leave my dear little town?"

Polite and assiduous stewards, absurdly assiduous with their little cellophane bags of confetti and streamers, moved about the deck, offering them for sale. Every now and then someone bought some confetti, and a little explosion of colored paper sailed over the rail. I watched it all very carefully because I had never been to sea before. I kept my hands in my overcoat pockets, because it was February and I felt the cold. I was going to Sicily on doctors' orders. They had told my father that the sea voyage, followed by the mild, dry Sicilian spring, would do me good. They said that that was the best thing after an attack of T.B.

My father and Kride had married, and they were standing arm in arm. I smiled until my cheeks ached. I wondered whether they could see that I was smiling. Very slowly the ship started to move; tugs were towing her away from the pier. Three yards of water appeared between the ship and the shore, then five. The paper streamers were torn and fell into the water. I showed my teeth and smiled. Kride smiled back and said something to my father. I thought I understood what she said. It was, "Let's go, it's cold here!"

My father put his arm around her and steered her through the throng. I watched them. Small groups were breaking off from the crowd and going away. My father, with his arm still around Kride's shoulders, suddenly turned and waved to me with his free left hand. I saw him smile, and then I felt sorry at being no longer able to shake his hand. I raised my arm and waved. I kept on smiling and waving until he and Kride disappeared. He was a good comrade, he had turned and waved to me.

Half an hour later cabin boys, directed by a sailor, started clearing the remnants of the paper streamers from the rail. We were now on the open sea, and the ship began rolling gently. The motion was not unpleasant. The wind whistled along the deck. I had a first-class cabin. My luggage was in it, but I had no desire to join the crowd that was blocking the gangways below. The ship's band had packed up and disappeared, and sailors were running about with tarpaulins to cover the cars that were ranged astern.

After a while I was alone on the upper deck, watching the land receding and getting grayer. Big clouds came up from the west and fine rain began sweeping the deck, so I moved a few paces, into the shelter of the superstructure. Another passenger was there, a thin little man with melancholy eyes. His overcoat was dark and rather worn, and his eyes were riveted on the outline of the shore. He had a big, round, slightly uneven nose, and he seemed to be trying to sniff the very last faint odors from the shore. He seemed nothing but eyes and nose—almond-shaped brown eyes and a big snuffling nose. Suddenly a mist came down, and the land was finally obliterated. The man emerged from his trance, took a deep breath, and said, "It's over!"

"What's over?" I asked.

He looked at me, turned away as if he were afraid of me, and walked off with quick, furtive steps. The moment he looked at me I saw he was afraid. Afraid? What was there to be afraid of? Me? Ridiculous!

Everything was as confused and bewildering as the sad February haze, half cloud, half mist, which hung woolly curtains round the ship and made the sea look brown. I had thought that the sea was always blue or green, but I had been mistaken; the sea was brown, a dirty, cheerless brown. Gulls sailed along in the lee of the funnel, floated along in the up-current behind the superstructure, gliding without moving their wings, only abandoning their vantage point when they saw a sailor coming along the deck with a pail. When he emptied it overboard they dived and started shrieking, quarreling and tumbling in a confused mass over the spot where they thought there might be something worth pouncing on. Then they climbed effortlessly aloft, to suspend themselves again in the eddies of air behind the superstructure. They had exercised their calling on steamships for generations and were far more at home than the passengers.

After our farewell lunch at the hotel, with half a bottle of champagne each, I had no appetite for another meal. I was alone, and no one took any notice of me. It was a strange feeling, slightly uncomfortable and alarming. I sought in my memory for something firm to which to cling. But everything was rather confused and indistinct.

The coughing had started just when I had been going to take my matriculation. I had had a continual slight temperature, attacks of perspiration and languor. That had been the beginning. The doctor had prescribed chest medicine and embrocation. Nobody worried very much about me, myself least of all. But whatever I did I felt languid and indifferent, and I needed more time than usual for everything. My father was too busy to worry about me very much. He had a great deal on his hands, because he had suddenly become politically active.

I remembered extracts from Kride's conversations with my father in the garden. At first they had talked about philosophy and the theater, music and books. But they had gradually grown closer and closer to each other, and then they talked only about the things that really interested them. The all-absorbing topic for everybody at that time was politics.

I remembered evenings at home, when it had become too cold and unfriendly to sit out of doors; evenings in our Spartan living room, over cups of weak tea. I sat in the corner, reading or working for my matriculation. I wondered why all over the world a student's summer vacation lasted for three months. Kride was there, as she had been the first evening. She preferred our house to her mother's. She didn't often mention the subject, but I knew perfectly well that the kind of life Yevgenia lived got on her nerves. Kride was all for tidiness, cleanliness, and having everything in its place. That couldn't be said for Yevgenia, who liked a kind of creative chaos round herself. Nothing about her was ever clear-cut, and her house was not especially clean either, particularly as she was never able to keep a maid for long nowadays.

So I spent my evenings over a cup of weak tea, sitting on one of our uncomfortable chairs with a book on infinitesimal calculus, or the German poets of the Romantic period, or modern history. But the words and sentences used to get rather jumbled, and I failed by a long chalk to understand all I read. Occasionally I'd start coughing, and then my father would interrupt the conversation and ask me whether I'd taken my medicine.

I would nod, suppress the cough, and bury my nose in my book again. Sometimes I didn't read, but listened to their conversation. Unemployment figures, the growing extremism, Communist processions, the League of Nations, the Danube conference, the Young plan, the Hoover moratorium, the Danat bank crisis, Hitler, Ludendorff, the Stahlhelm, and the League of Red Front Fighters.

Kride belonged to the student movement in Berlin and tried to rouse my father's interest in the new people who were active in Germany. Evening after evening they had earnest low-voiced conversations. They contained the whole uncertainty of our age. There was something intangible and threatening in the air. It had all started with the world crisis and the huge unemployment figures, and then the Nazis had come, and then the Communists. Or had the Communists preceded the Nazis? I didn't know. Both wanted violence and revolution. I had long since given up football and was excused from gymnasium and singing. I led a shadow life of my own and was entirely taken up with myself.

Eventually Kride left. My father began working again, but something of Kride's visits remained behind. I went to Yevgenia's less often than before. I had temperatures and often found that my shirt was wet. I had picked up from Kride the names of some books which it was essential to read. I got them from a lending library and sat up half the night reading them, but they gave me no comfort. Next day I'd have a heavy head, a salty taste in my mouth, and a feeling as if I had cotton wool in my ears. Sometimes I'd hear my father going out and coming back late. He'd explain that he'd been to a political meeting. That was another thing that happened after Kride's departure; he became politically active. I didn't know exactly what that meant. I found out one evening when he took me with him.

He took me to a big, badly lit hall, full of people. There was a platform decorated with flags, and a rostrum for the speaker. I sat very near the front. Behind the speaker's rostrum there was a long table, at which a row of men were sitting, each with a glass of water in front of him. They were in the party uniform, and the ushers in the hall were in uniform too. A short, stocky man stood up, raised his hand, and announced that the meeting was open. He introduced my father as the speaker that evening, and described him as a *doctor juri* (instead of *juris*). Then my father, wearing an ordinary lounge suit, but not such a smart suit as he wore when he went to see his editors and publishers, started speaking. He spoke in a simple, almost proletarian style. It was amazing how earnestly and effortlessly he spoke. He spoke for two hours, and there was no trace of self-consciousness about him. He talked about the international legal background of the Treaty of Versailles, about German rearmament, about Geneva and Locarno, about German relations with Russia, the world crisis, and unemployment. He spoke clearly, distinctly, and logically. I hardly recognized him; he had suddenly turned into a different man. Or was it because I was ill? I sat there in astonishment, and every now and then I took my handkerchief and coughed into it, sheltering behind the broad shoulders of the man in front of me.

When my father had finished there was a discussion. A young man in the seventh row got up and asked permission to put some questions. The uniformed ushers looked at him in an unfriendly fashion. My father answered the questions; his manner as he explained the questioner's mistakes was friendly and slightly condescending. The young man sat down, demolished. Then an older man in blue overalls, a Communist cell leader, got up. There was a slight movement among the uniformed ushers, but my father raised his hand, and they looked at the man threateningly but without doing anything.

"We served four years at the front, in the infantry," he said, "and we don't want to go to the front again. What you people want is war!"

The crowd suddenly grew tense. The word had been spoken. War!

"We don't want war," my father answered. "We don't want war any more than you do."

"Yes, but we were four years at the front and know what it's like," the man said. "What guarantee is there that you won't go to war?"

One of the uniformed ushers, a huge fellow with shoulders like a lumberjack, moved toward him, followed by twenty of his comrades. My father raised his hand again.

"I don't want war any more than you do," he said, looking sharply at the ushers, who moved back again toward the wall.

"That's an easy thing to say if you haven't seen what war's like," the man in blue overalls said.

"I have seen what war's like," my father said.

"Yes, but where?" a voice called out from the back of the hall. "In the Army pay corps?"

Part of the audience started to laugh. The dialogue had ceased to be objective, and everybody had forgotten all about the Treaty of Versailles. The meeting had turned into a quarrel between two men. No one doubted the Communist's word when he said he had served in the trenches. With his coarse face, his heavy hands, his round shoulders, he looked like a man who had spent four years in the trenches. My father gritted his teeth.

"I spent four years at the front just as you did, my friend," he said. "For the last year I was an infantry cooperation pilot, if you want to know, and I was twice shot down."

I sat up sharply. He had never told me he had been an airman. I didn't know what an infantry cooperation pilot was, but it sounded good.

The Communist was rather nonplused. "I didn't mean to say anything against you personally," he said. The audience's sympathy had now swung over entirely to my father's side. I couldn't believe my ears. I would have believed anything rather than that my father would stand up in public and start talking about his war experiences.

Later, when the meeting was over and the usual brawl was in

progress outside in the street, my father called me up to the platform. The men at the long table all looked very pleased with
themselves. Most of them had coarse faces; there was nothing to
choose between them and the Communist cell leader; they were
as alike as two pins. The chairman was rubbing his hands when
my father introduced me. I had the natural dislike of young people
for being introduced. The chairman slapped me on the shoulder,
and I didn't like that either.

"Young man," he said, "your father's a magnificent chap. What
a speaker! How he hands it out to them! When he speaks there's
never a row! He does things in the elegant style!"

My father doing things in the elegant style! I glanced at him.
He caught my eye and saw what I was thinking. We walked home
through the dark streets with a guard of honor of two men, to
protect my father's valuable life.

When he was alone with me he was slightly embarrassed. He
hesitated before he spoke.

"They're simple fellows, but as sound as a bell," he said.
"They're the fellows I spent four years at the front with. They'd
go through fire for me. Today they're the salvation of Germany.
Of course, the group leader is a little crude in his speech, but he's
as sound as a bell!"

Perhaps it was the illness that was in me, but I thought he
sounded as if he was apologizing to me. Later, when he started going out to meetings every night, I remembered something that
struck me that evening, something that I afterward forgot. Why
had he lived all these years like a monk in his cell, without taking
the slightest interest in the men with whom he had served at the
front? He had never told me that he had been an infantry cooperation pilot and had been twice shot down. Was I jealous? For
years he had hated being reminded of the war, and now all of a
sudden he got up in public and told a hall full of complete stran-
gers about his exploits. I may very well have felt like that because
I was ill. The doctors say that T.B. makes you irritable, and I
found myself often getting irritated with my father. He started
using expressions that he had never used before, and they came
out in his speeches. One of them was "four years' front service,"

and another was "sound as a bell." I stuck my nose in my books and tried to absorb knowledge for my matriculation—"the hardest test of one's life," as our headmaster called it.

One morning just before Christmas 1932 I woke up and found my pillow covered with blood. The cleaning woman came in and hurriedly woke my father, and the doctor came. I was too weak to be moved, so I lay in my room, staring at the ceiling. Two workmen spent half a day fixing a stove in the next room, and then my bed was moved in there. My father wrote to Kride, and she came and nursed me. I stayed in my room till January, and then I was sent to a sanatorium; and so I missed all the great things that happened in Germany in 1933—the accession of my father's party to power and his being summoned to Berlin, where he was received with honor for having won a vital constituency for the party at a moment when everything hung in the balance. Since then I've often wondered whether world history would have been any different if I hadn't spent my pocket money that evening on taking Kride to the movies against her will, and if she hadn't come home with me afterward and found my father sitting in his shirt sleeves, busy writing an article. The article was on "The Principles of Maritime Law since the Consolato del Mare of Barcelona, 1370." A long time afterward he found the article and showed it to Kride and me. We were convinced at the time that it had had a decisive influence on the struggle and that it had been a true blessing for Germany.

My father was given a job in the Foreign Ministry, and I was allowed to take my exam in writing in the sanatorium. In May 1933 my father and Kride got married, as was to be expected. They visited me during their honeymoon, and my father looked younger and livelier than I had ever seen him look before.

"It's the beginning of a new age, my lad," he said. "A great time lies before us. Germany has found herself again. She has come to herself. The Führer . . ."

He patted me on the shoulder, which was another thing he had never done before. He had used to be a man whom success made shy. If an article of his appeared in an important newspaper, he would show it to me casually, almost as if he were embarrassed, and then take me out for a good dinner; but he had always

taken pains to show no signs whatever in front of me of the
pleasure that success gave him. Now he had changed.

How irritable T.B. makes one! When my father and Kride left
the sanatorium I actually felt glad. Kride looked well and happy
and very beautiful, and she had lost the skeptical wrinkles on her
forehead. What had done him harm had done her good. From
one point of view, of course, it was the most natural thing in the
world for people who had been on the same side in a successful
revolution to marry. A revolution has a rejuvenating effect on
people.

"Now we'll see that you get well again quickly, and then we'll
send you off on a long journey," my father said when he left. It
sounded cheerful and consoling. All the same, I was glad to be
alone again.

II

I soon got over my seasickness. The ship sailed down the
Channel, and at night you saw the lights of the lighthouses and
lightships, and occasionally the lights of fishing boats and other
vessels. I found a sailor who explained to me how to tell the difference between passenger and cargo ships. It was exciting and
stimulating to stand at the rail at night, watching the lights appear and disappear. Every light indicated the presence of human
beings. At first when I went aboard I had thought I would feel
afraid, afraid of the great expanses and loneliness of the sea, but I
felt nothing of the kind. I enjoyed lying in my cabin, listening to
the mysterious throbbing of the engines deep below. The whole
ship was alive, vibrating with life. Occasionally she rolled slowly
over to one side, stayed there a moment, righted herself, and
then slowly rolled over to the other side. It helped you to go to
sleep. When you woke it was always dark because the porthole
was closed; a pull at it let in the gray, gloomy light of day, and I'd
quickly dress and go up on deck.

I didn't yet know it, but we were at the beginning of the period
of loneliness into which we were then declining. A new age had
begun, the age of loneliness. Was I homesick? Yes, I was homesick
for our little suburban house, which my father had now given up.

Yevgenia had new neighbors now. Life had been so simple and straightforward in that little house. It had been a static world.

In those days I had of course been well. The doctors said I was well again now, but in between there had been my illness and the experiences that had gone with it. The golden haze had suddenly evaporated.

I had overheard my father and Kride talking in the garden.

"The young man doesn't look at all well, Uncle Max."

"He's worrying about his matriculation, and overworking."

"You ought to send him to a specialist."

"If you think so, Kride."

I said I felt quite well and didn't go to the specialist. I felt I was like a dog unable to gnaw its bones properly; I was oversensitive.

I remembered another occasion, weeks after Kride left, when my father was sitting in the dining room with his new friends. The talk seemed to last all night. I could hear the voices through the thin partition. I couldn't make head or tail of the things they talked about.

"Things are looking bad, Herr Doktor; we've been losing votes ever since Strasser left. People thought a great deal of Strasser. I did myself!"

"Come, come, Herr Ortsgruppenleiter, you're not weakening, are you? An old soldier . . ."

I couldn't make head or tail of it. What had Strasser to do with old soldiers? How was it that my father came to be talking in such a firm, friendly fashion to men he didn't know? There was a hardness in his voice that I'd never heard before. My ears were sensitive. I was jealous.

Also remarks were made at school—admiring remarks and spiteful remarks. "Your father has suddenly become a great speaker, hasn't he?" or "I was at the meeting yesterday. My father says men like your father are what we need." My agreeable anonymity had suddenly been abolished. For years we had lived quietly and happily, and now suddenly the masters began looking at me in a special way, with friendly, frightened, or hate-filled eyes. I was proud of my father, but I wished he'd give up making speeches.

I remembered all these things, lying in a deck chair on the empty sun deck, wrapped in a rug brought me by a friendly steward. He also used to bring me hot soup with an egg in it, and he generally stayed for a few minutes' chat. I had cigarettes in my pocket, and we arranged that he'd smoke one but that I'd take it as soon as the first officer appeared, because stewards are, of course, not allowed to smoke on duty. When I left the ship I found he hadn't charged me for the soup. It was his way of showing gratitude.

Nothing encourages reminiscence so much as a ship's slow, steady, imperceptible progress along a coast, which can generally be seen only as a faint, distant shadow. Sitting still and dreaming was a good beginning to my journey.

When I unpacked my things I found a letter from Yevgenia hidden among the socks.

"My dear Rurik," she wrote—she always used the Russian form of my name. "I'm glad you're well again and are off on a lovely journey. Josefine is in Paris at a fashion school, training to be a mannequin. Kride is very happy, *mais ça va sans dire*. We were all very worried about you, and Margarete keeps asking after Uncle Rurik. You ought to see my new business, and the people that come to it. I've got two girls in my showroom now, and if it goes on like this there'll soon be four. I've been offered some premises at Düsseldorf. Isn't it wonderful how everything is on the up-and-up in our country? Naturally there are a few dark sides as well, but I always say that you can't have fur without having fleas. I enclose Josefine's address in Paris; perhaps you'll write to her sometime. Love from Yevgenia."

Underneath Margarete had written in her somewhat smudgy schoolgirl's hand. "Yevgenia's cat has had kittens again with a yellow spot over their eyes and they make a mess everywhere love from Margarete."

The letter made me a little homesick for Yevgenia. I could never think of home without thinking of the house next door. So Josefine was in Paris, training to be a mannequin. The last time I had seen her, when she had come with her mother to see me at the sanatorium, she had certainly looked very pretty. She was slender and graceful, with very thin wrists and a good figure. She used a little lipstick, and her eyes were fawn-colored and almond-shaped. She'd certainly make a good mannequin.

I don't remember all the other things I thought about as I lay in my deck chair. It was a remarkable time in Germany. Everyone was tremendously busy. There were processions and speeches, and everywhere work was being done and buildings were going up. Sometimes I had the feeling that, what with all the hustle, and all those tremendous speeches coming over the air about intellectuals and enemies of the state and reconstruction and equality of rights, there was no chance any more for anybody to sit back and think. As I was ill I had leisure to sit back and think a bit about how everything had changed. My father's face, for instance. I thought of him as he had been at our champagne lunch at Bremerhaven. He had always been a lean, slim man, but now he had begun putting on weight. He had small rings under his eyes, his cheeks were fuller, his brow was no longer so sunken at the temples. He looked younger, but I had liked him better as he was before.

How old was he? I worked it out. He had been born in 1886; that made him forty-eight. Kride was three years older than I, so she was twenty-two. Not half his age, in fact.

The ship called at Cherbourg and later at Plymouth. The steward came and pointed out the Gros du Raz lighthouse on the Cap de la Hague. I had a vague memory that a famous sea battle had been fought here, but the steward naturally didn't know anything about it.

III

During a sea voyage you can't help making acquaintances. When it got warmer people began coming up to the sun deck, and my loneliness was at an end. The Bay of Biscay was calm for the time of year. A number of Germans had disembarked at Cherbourg, including the little man who had said "it was over" after we left Bremerhaven. He was met by three depressed, shabby-looking individuals who were waiting for him on the quay when the ship tied up. I watched it all from the lower deck, and then, when we sailed down the warm Spanish coast, I forgot all about him.

The passenger who interested me most was a young actor from Berlin. I imagined he must play Hamlet or the young Piccolomini. One morning, when I saw him alone, I went up to him and asked him. He smiled and said no, he liked modern plays. Had I heard of *A Wreath of Roses on the Esplanade?* No? It was a wonderful play, he had played the lead in it. It was terribly amusing and was sold out every night.

"Excuse me, but are you a critic?" he suddenly asked.

I felt rather flattered, but said I wasn't.

"An art historian, then?"

I liked the sound of that. Hitherto I hadn't known what I was. I hadn't even thought about the matter. But "art historian" sounded fine. The combination of art and history appealed to me; it combined the agreeable with the serious. I nodded and said I was on my way to Sicily because I was going to become an art historian.

"There's a whole lot of old stuff in Sicily," my new friend said. "Come and have a drink!"

"Now?" I asked. It was Sunday morning, shortly before twelve o'clock.

"Of course!" he said. "It's just the time for a drink. Everybody has one now! It's what's known as the church cocktail, because you have it coming out of church."

"But we haven't been to church!"

"What has that got to do with it?"

I went with him. I was no longer alone.

A group of people were standing at the first-class bar. He introduced me to them. "There's a man you simply must meet," he said to me. "You're bound to like him. He's a musician. Hullo, Freddie!"

Freddie was a sulky-looking individual with long, untidy hair standing out from the sides of his head; it made him look slovenly. He had sharp, angry lines on his forehead, and generally he kept his eyes half closed. When he opened them properly, which was seldom, they were opaque and there was an almost dreamy look about them. Also he had sharp lines on both sides of his mouth. On the whole he looked rather an unpleasant customer. We forced our way through the throng with our cocktail glasses.

I didn't catch his name, but I was relieved when he suddenly became friendly.

"So you want to be an art historian?" he said. I said I didn't know for certain. I had no prospects. He fell silent and looked into his glass.

"I've no prospects either," he said in a husky voice. "Victor keeps wanting me to write another musical comedy for him, but I don't feel like it. How old are you?"

"Almost twenty," I said, somewhat ashamed. He didn't seem to hear, but kept staring into his glass, which he suddenly emptied. Then he handed it to the barman and had it filled again.

I tried to make up my mind how old he was. He looked older than the actor, but later I found out that he was only three years older than I. But he'd had much more experience. The others suddenly swarmed round him. The girls in particular seemed to be completely crazy about him.

"Freddie, play us something!" they said.

He emptied his glass and looked at them sulkily.

"Come on, Freddie, please play us something!" they clamored.

He looked at them even more sulkily. "What do you want me to play?"

"You know quite well!"

"Something from Victor's new musical comedy? Or from *The Merry Widow*? Why should I? It isn't the Führer's birthday!"

"No, you know quite well what to play!"

I couldn't make head or tail of this little scene, which they performed as if they had rehearsed it a dozen times. Freddie scratched his head and looked sulkier than ever.

"This is a German ship," he said, "and if anyone lets out that I play Weill and Spoliansky I'll land straight in a concentration camp when I get home!"

I didn't understand a word. Freddie looked round the bar, and his eyes settled on the barman, who was shaking more cocktails.

"He looks just as if he were from the Gestapo," he muttered. The barman smiled. He didn't seem to think it necessary to refute the allegation.

"Oh, well, it's all the same!" said Freddie. He had his glass refilled and walked over to the piano with it. The barman took the key from under the bar and threw it to him. Freddie caught it, unlocked the piano, and opened the lid. He started playing before he had even sat down properly. I had never heard music of that kind before. I had been several times to operas and concerts of chamber music with my father, and we had listened to Yevgenia playing her hired piano, but we had never heard anything like this. I couldn't make up my mind whether my father would have liked it or not. Probably he would have shaken his head, or, as his recent habit had been, have said something ideological.

We stood round the piano till lunchtime. There were some English and French people in the group, and one Spaniard, but most of them were Germans. When we broke up I wanted to go back to my seat at my usual boring table, with a Dutch family with a swarm of children, but Freddie wouldn't hear of it. He was a bit tipsy and insisted that, as an art historian, I must sit with him. So I went and sat at his table, with half a dozen girls and about the same number of men. Most of them came from Hamburg or Bremen, and they were nothing special to look at when you were close to them, but they were a pleasant, cheerful lot.

After lunch it started raining, so instead of going on deck we went to the cabin of the actor who had been so successful in *A Wreath of Roses on the Esplanade*. We sat on the bed and the luggage and drank spirits from a bottle. All this was quite new to me. Suddenly I didn't feel homesick any more and found I was enjoying myself immensely. I wanted nothing better than to stay with these people.

Every now and then somebody rang and ordered another bottle of brandy or another round of coffee. I took a cushion from the sofa, sat on it, and looked around at the circle. There was one girl from Hamburg whose name was Elsie, and she was very gay indeed. She wound up the gramophone and insisted on dancing. I danced with her, and she came and sat next to me. She had only just passed her matriculation, and her father had sent her on the voyage as a present. Did one take one's matriculation so late in Hamburg? No, she had failed in her last year at secondary school and had had to go to a private school to try again. She was the same age as I was. I told her I had been ill with T.B. and so had had to take my matriculation a year late too.

We talked and drank so much that I had difficulty in finding my cabin that evening. I woke up next morning with a headache, but I got up, dressed, and went up to my deck chair. It was cloudy and windy, and there wasn't a soul on the sun deck. After a while the steward arrived with my soup. He was smoking a cigarette and was keeping a weather eye open in case the first officer appeared.

"Weren't you with the young people from two-seventeen yesterday?" he asked.

I nodded and wondered how he knew. His face had suddenly grown serious and somewhat sour. ·

"That's no company for you, Herr Stamm," he said in a half-whisper. "Do you know what those people are? They're drones! They only travel to be able to do all the things they can't do at home. They ought to be locked up, they and their music and their talk!"

I felt somewhat shaken. "I thought they were very nice," I said.

He pulled at his cigarette and looked carefully all round again. "I've been in the party since nineteen twenty-eight, and what am I today? A steward! And they're not in the party and travel first-class and fling their money about!"

He looked quite serious as he said this, and I felt that—from his point of view, of course—he was quite right.

"But they're so cheerful," I said. "I particularly like the pianist —what's his name?—Freddie Karawan."

He pursed his lips, and his face remained gloomy. "He's no better than the rest," he said. "They spend half the night drinking and playing the piano and flinging their money about. Nothing but drones!"

He took my empty cup, threw his cigarette end overboard, and went away. I felt rather upset. My point of view, of course, wasn't the same as his. Perhaps it wasn't right that they should fling so much money about, but I'd found them very gay and cheerful. It made me feel uneasy.

At lunch I met Elsie from Hamburg and asked her whether she'd slept well. She half closed one eye and shook her head slightly. I found her most attractive and flung the steward's objections to the winds. He had no right to cast any slur on Elsie. I walked up and down the deck with her. She wore a Basque beret and a tartan skirt, which the wind blew about. I was suddenly very much in love with her, and she didn't seem to mind. I was shy, of course, but it didn't worry me. I spent the whole time with her all the way to Catania, where I had to leave the ship. We spent all our time with the other young people, who circled admiringly round the sulky-looking Freddie with the tousled hair and lined face. He certainly interested me, though perhaps I was less enthusiastic about him than the others, because my attention was distracted by Elsie.

He would never play the piano till he was drunk, but he played wonderfully, and in the course of time I got to know a few of his pieces quite well. By the time we got to Sicily I wasn't so shy any more. It was my first sea voyage, and I was sorry it was over. I wrote down Elsie's address, and Freddie's. The whole gang hired a car to drive to Taormina, and I should have liked to go with them.

My steward helped me to the gangway with my suitcases. He shook hands with me and wished me a good recovery.

IV

I had an uncle living in Sicily. I knew nothing about him except that his name was Martin and that he was my father's brother. The two barely kept in touch with each other. My father wrote to him at the time of my illness, and he answered, inviting me to stay with him, because Sicily was good for certain T.B. cases. I discovered on this occasion that my Uncle Martin had been a doctor but had given up practicing long before the First World War to become a painter. After running through all his money, he had met an Englishwoman in Naples and married her. Later they had bought a house near Girgenti in Sicily, and that was where he still lived, spending his time either painting or practicing as a doctor, as he felt inclined. He was certainly no ordinary person.

I had seen a picture of him, taken in 1900, when he was twenty-three. It showed a pale young man with lots of whiskers and wearing a stiff collar. To judge from the picture, he might have been a murderer, or a member of a South American revolutionary government. I stood on the quay at Catania and looked about me, but I could see no sign of a murderer or a South American minister. All around me people were shouting for a *facchino*. I had no idea what a *facchino* might be. Everything was new and unfamiliar. The *porto vecchio* was full of little boats with red sails, the sun beat down on the quay, and a crowd of incredibly dirty and ragged itinerant vendors were shouting their wares and jabbering all around me.

When I had got on board at Bremerhaven there had also been a crowd of people on the quay. The surroundings had been unfriendly and dirty, but the people had been clean and neatly dressed. Here it was the reverse. The landscape, so far as I could see, was warm and dry, but the people were all in rags.

I stood and waited. My steward was looking down from the deck of the ship. He raised his hand and called out something, but I couldn't catch it. I put my hand to my ear and shook my head. He called out again, but the itinerant vendors and other Sicilians were making such a noise that I couldn't hear. The steward pointed into the middle of the crowd, and I stretched my neck and looked in that direction.

A man in white linen trousers and a faded shirt was standing twenty yards away from me, obviously looking for someone too. He was clean-shaven, brown-faced, with a festoon of white hair hanging around his shoulders. His open shirt showed a few gray hairs on his chest. He was over the average in height, heavily built, but not stout. Suddenly he saw me and started. He smiled, and I smiled slightly in return. I thought that perhaps he was my uncle's servant.

He made his way slowly toward me through the throng, elbowing innumerable Sicilians out of the way. It was a wonderful sight to see him plowing through the mob of peddlers without once taking his eyes off me or stopping smiling. Eventually he reached me, took a sunburned hand from his pocket, and held it out to me. He had a gold ring on one finger.

"Roderich?" he said.

I nodded.

"I'm your Uncle Martin."

I heard someone shouting from the deck of the steamer and looked up. It was my steward, nodding and grinning and shaking his hands with pleasure. That was the last I saw of him.

"Come along!" my uncle said. "I've left the car behind the *dogana*." He picked up one of my suitcases but dropped it again and called out, "*Facchino!*" He had a voice like a foghorn, and when he shouted everyone on the quay looked around. A *facchino* came running toward us—a whole gang of *facchini*. They fell on my suitcases, and a battle royal began.

"*Due lire!*" my uncle said seriously, raising two fingers.

"*Per tutti?*" asked the man who had won the battle and had grabbed the suitcases. "*Mamma mia!*" he exclaimed, and dropped them. My uncle gazed at him silently. I noticed for the first time that he had gentian-blue eyes. The porter held up three fingers in front of his face and writhed like a snake, but eventually he picked up both suitcases and trudged behind us to my uncle's car.

"What on earth did you do?" I asked.

My uncle laughed. "He was frightened of my *mal' occhio*, my evil eye," he explained.

"Is holding up three fingers a protection against it?"

"So he believes."

We drove to Gela and had lunch at a *trattoria*. Everything was new and strange—the strange white bread, the wine and water, and the baked fruit swimming in oil in an earthenware dish.

"It's called *melanzana*," my uncle said. "And you can drop the 'uncle' and just call me Martin. But you'd better call my wife Aunt Mary."

I was so confused and bewildered by all this that I missed a question my uncle asked. When he repeated it I nearly collapsed.

"What did you say?" I asked again.

"I asked you how that old humbug, my brother Johann, was."

He laughed good-humoredly to show that he was only joking,

but the word "humbug" stuck in my mind. I tried to find out in what way my father was an old humbug.

"He's got married," I said.

"So he wrote and told me. Blue-blooded, isn't she?"

He laughed again. He had gold fillings in two of his teeth; they suited his sunburned face, just as the gold ring looked well on his sunburned finger. I had to think for a moment before seeing what he meant. I had the feeling that my uncle didn't think me very bright.

"Blue-blooded? Oh, I see!"

I burst out laughing. My uncle looked at me, interested.

When I'd recovered sufficiently from my fit of laughter I said, "I've never thought of Yevgenia as blue-blooded. Nor would you if you knew her!"

"But," said my uncle, beginning to suspect some frightful tragedy, "your father wrote and said that his wife came from an old, aristocratic family—von Haringen, or something."

I nodded but went on laughing.

"Is her name Yevgenia?" my uncle asked curiously.

"No, Yevgenia's her mother. She's got—she's a— Listen. . . ."

I told him all about Yevgenia, her dressmaking business, her cats, and her daughters. My uncle listened, sometimes laughing a little too. When I'd finished he no longer thought me a semi-idiot.

Late that afternoon, after driving for miles, we came to the Sicilian coast at Girgenti, which the Fascists had rechristened Agrigento. We turned sharp left and drove on for a while, and then came to a wood of orange and lemon trees that surrounded the house which had been my uncle's home for more than twenty years.

The house was run by an old Sicilian woman named Luisa. She summed me up in one severe look and then dismissed me. Nothing escapes the penetrating eye of an old family retainer. Luisa saw at a glance that I was a poor relation being received into the big house out of charity.

I didn't see my aunt that evening. Luisa said she had retired to her room. So my uncle and I dined alone in the candlelit dining room, and afterward we went into the music room. My uncle went over to the piano, opened it, played a couple of chords, and was just about to sit down and play when Luisa came in, holding her finger severely to her mouth. My uncle promptly withdrew the leg he had half thrown over the stool, closed the piano, and sat down at the round table.

"Bring some bottles of beer, but see that they're cold," he said to Luisa.

"You can drink beer?" he then said to me. "I mean, because of your illness?"

We went on talking for a long time that evening. I didn't find out whether he was a doctor or a painter; but I admired him, and he was aware of it. After we had drunk a few bottles I looked around and took in my surroundings.

"D'you know what this reminds me of?" I said. "Our house on the Rhine. Father sold it after mother died."

"That's the best thing he could have done."

I looked at him in astonishment.

"I was only in it once, soon after your parents married," my uncle explained. "Your mother was a delightful woman, a really nice German woman. But the house was simply appalling!"

"But—" I said, and stopped. That was what was always happening to me. For nearly twenty years I had believed that my father's house on the Rhine was very beautiful, and now it turned out to have been a mistake.

By this time my uncle had quite a respectable row of empty bottles by the side of his chair. The beer was good, and so cold that when you took a long draught it hurt your teeth. My uncle always drank in long draughts. His teeth, except for the two gold ones, were white and firm.

"That's what I might have been blessed with myself, if I'd stayed in Germany," he said thoughtfully. "A house on the Rhine or the Elbe, or at Solln near Munich. A broken-down house with a lot of broken-down guests. Your father was quite right to sell it. If you've got to live in Germany you can't live in a villa. You must either live in an old haunted castle or a block of modern flats. Tell me what things are like in Germany now. You can talk quite freely, there's no Gestapo here!"

"You can talk quite freely in Germany too," I said, offended,

but I had no luck that evening. My uncle just laughed at me, and
soon afterward we went to bed.

V

It was a big old house that my uncle and aunt lived in. Part
of it had been renovated, and marble slabs, woodwork, electric
light, a tiled bathroom, a radio and record player had been put
in. This part of the house was "tastefully furnished," as my aunt
described it.

In the evening you could turn on the radio and listen to music
from London or Beromünster, or to the crazy music of Radio
Rabat.

"Won't you put a record on, Martin?" my aunt generally said
when she came and sat with us after dinner.

"What record would you like, Mary dear?" Martin answered.

On the first occasion she said that the guest ought to choose.
I didn't know what to say. Aunt Mary was very cool and reserved, and you never knew what she was thinking. If I gave the
wrong answer, perhaps she'd look down on me. But suddenly I
remembered the evening my father and I had spent listening to
Yevgenia.

"The partita in B flat," I said.

"I think it's number seven," my aunt said, and my uncle
looked at me as if to congratulate me, and we listened in silence
to the music I had suggested.

That was right at the beginning, but it confirmed my position
in the household. My aunt was a Scotswoman and a Roman Catholic, and I was a Protestant and a German. In the course of time
I discovered that she enjoyed frigid conversations about religion.
Religion was her favorite topic. When Martin invited me to stay
with them, she was at first rather suspicious. I was a German, and
Germany, except for Oberammergau, was full of heathens and
devils. Occasionally she mentioned the children's hands that we
were said to have hacked off in the war. On these occasions my
uncle cleared his throat and looked up at the ceiling.

She took a certain pleasure in the prospect of trying to make a
new man of me. When she saw that I was able to manage a knife

and fork and actually knew the partita in B flat, I was no longer entirely beyond the pale.

At first I found the *ménage* a puzzle. After their marriage they had lived very happily together for two years while the house near Girgenti was being got ready. Then the war had come, and my uncle had gone back to Germany to fight against England. This was something for which she had never forgiven him. Being a Catholic, she did not divorce him. She simply withheld herself from him. She had inherited a lot of money in the shipping business; it was this that paid for the house in Sicily. Many English people, both rich and poor, take refuge in Italy. Aunt Mary was rich, not only by Sicilian standards.

Both were delightfully crazy, each in a different way. They were as crazy as children who have too much money to spend. My uncle was in love with his painting—and also, occasionally, with his models—and my aunt with her mixture of religion, Christian Science, and Sir Walter Scott. She adored contemplating Scotland, its mountains, rivers, moors, and lochs, from her home in Sicily.

To improve my English I had to have tea with her every day and read aloud to her. This was at her suggestion, but an invitation from Aunt Mary was equivalent to a command. It would never have occurred to anyone in the house to ignore a suggestion of Aunt Mary's. She was the lady, and everyone was her squire, as in Walter Scott. She had a picture of Scott in her room, and when I read to her I had his wig and pointed nose right in front of me. I found it very agreeable. I had the rest of the day to myself.

Aunt Mary was an excellent teacher, and it was a pleasure to learn English from her. The best French is said to be spoken at Geneva, and the best English in Edinburgh. My father had hoped I'd take the opportunity of learning languages while I was abroad, and I learned faultless English and fluent but vile Italian.

After the first few weeks I began to understand my uncle better. I began to feel like a visitor only in the civilized front part of the house. When mealtimes and the attendant conversation were over Martin used to retire to his own quarters. He had a studio, and next to it a little work-den with a rough desk, some bookshelves, and a big window overlooking the sea. When he wasn't driving his car around the countryside or going for long walks, he used to spend hours there. He had a fantastic style, but he could also paint very well in the old-fashioned, conventional way. He had portfolios full of studies of the monuments of the Greek period in Sicily, and eventually I found out that he was working on a book about the island. I saw only fragments of it, but later, when the house was burned down and everything was destroyed, I thought his manuscript was perhaps a greater loss than the pictures.

During the first few weeks I was bored sometimes, and felt glad when the gong sounded for meals. But very soon I stopped being bored. I discovered Sicily in the back rooms of my uncle's house, and the discovery was worth while.

VI

Behind the kitchen there was a wild garden, with pieces of hewn stone scattered about it. It was surrounded by big hedges of a kind of reed, in which the wind played and whispered all day long. Through the big, open, half-rounded kitchen door you could see Luisa and her assistants busy around the great brick oven. The kitchen was dark, because it had only one small window, and when Luisa raked the fire the glow was reflected on the corncobs that hung in rows from the ceiling.

The Sicilians excel both at talking and at keeping silent. At first I didn't understand a word of what Luisa and her girls were talking about, but I kept my ears open, and in the end I could follow what they said. Luisa nearly always had visitors in the kitchen, generally from San Giorgio, the neighboring fishing village, where her niece was married to a fisherman named Battista. She was a pretty girl, expecting her first child. She often came to see Luisa and always brought a baby with her, a friend's or a neighbor's or a relative's. The baby was left lying naked on a blanket in the sun and seemed to thrive marvelously under this treatment. Sometimes it would be completely black with the flies that crawled all over it and besieged its nostrils. When it found them disturbing it would patiently whisk them away with its hands, without showing any signs of complaint. I don't believe there was anything exceptional about this. Life is very natural in Sicily, and it's all taken for granted.

Luisa was a gloomy creature with a mop of black hair, which she covered with a brown handkerchief. She had a big, solid nose and a strong chin. Later on, when we got to know each other better, she told me there were a lot of lunatics in her family. One of these was Marcello; he threw stones at my uncle's car on one occasion.

The longer I watched it all and the better I understood the language, the more extraordinary I found it. I don't pretend I understood Sicily. You can no more understand Sicily than you can understand China. It's too complicated, or too simple. The Sicilians love their babies but leave them to roast in the sun and allow flies to swarm all over them. Luisa would never have laid hands on a lizard, but she butchered animals for the table with the greatest possible indifference to their sufferings, and apparently with zest.

She had a mangy old cat, which generally lay in the half-shade beside the doorstep, licking itself. It was hideous, but Luisa would have defended it with her life. But she allowed chickens, sucking-pigs, and lambs to come from market, tied together by their fore or hindlegs, and she would hang them up on a hook in the sun if they were not ready for butchering immediately. When slaughtering time came, a gleam of blood-lust came into her black eyes; she tested the knife with her finger, laid the little pig on a stone outside the kitchen door, and cut its throat. This was naturally accompanied by loud screeching, but Luisa was entirely deaf to it; she once gave an unruly young nannygoat a thorough talking-to, telling it that it had no business to screech so much while it was being killed. The stone outside the kitchen door was a sacrificial stone, and Luisa a Moorish priestess, if there is such a thing. She was a wholesale dealer-out of death to chickens, ducks, turkeys, and other such animals. Once when she caught a rat running across the kitchen she slit it in two with her big knife, before my eyes. This was as much as I could stand, and it was a long time before I went into the garden behind the kitchen again. But slowly I found out that southerners are like that. You must either accept them as they are or stay away from them. I sometimes wondered what my aunt, with her fine nerves and her sensitiveness about cutting off children's hands, made of these atrocities. Perhaps she was able to bear them because she lived in the marbled front part of the house, which chickens, sucking-pigs, and ducks never entered, except when they had been roasted or boiled.

My uncle reacted to his surroundings like a northerner. Sicilians are kind to their donkeys, but some of them prod their mules all the time and use their whips continually to get the last ounce out of them. They didn't do it when my uncle was about. He would overwhelm the tormentors with his rich vocabulary and his blazing blue eyes. There was something crazy about those eyes of his. Everyone knew that he had the *iettatura,* the evil eye, so when he was about the animals were left in peace.

At first I tried writing home about Sicily. But the more I saw the shorter my letters became. Besides, I lost the sense of time.

In Germany you can't lose your sense of time. Your attention is continually being drawn to the time and the date. In Sicily one day was like another, everyone did what he felt like doing, and time lost its meaning. Even the lemon trees ignored the seasons and bloomed continually, and there were always oranges and lemons.

Sicily isn't rich, but it has a rich history. In that respect it's rather like Germany, which isn't a rich country either, but has a long history too. But the Germans are an industrious people, like the Americans, and the Sicilians are not. The Germans are continually trying to make something of their country; the Sicilians take it as it is. Their substitute for ambition is a simple pride, which disappears if one's whole life is spent thinking about success. The German character is, of course, far more go-ahead and meritorious, but the Sicilians seem to me to be remarkable just because they don't attach the slightest importance to the things that are supremely important to us, and manage to live all the same. Words like industriousness and devotion to duty are unknown to them, and if one wants a rest from these things Sicily seems to me to be the place to go to. It is astonishing how matter-of-fact life is there. It is self-regulating in both its good and bad aspects.

The Sicilians freeze in winter and parch in summer. In the little villages in the interior they still grind their corn by methods described in the Bible. They expend vast amounts of energy and skill on the entirely unprofitable practice of painting their two-wheeled carts in gay colors; and they wouldn't give up such trifles for anything, not even for a modern threshing machine or a rolling mill. Occasionally Sicilians go to America or Italy and earn a lot of money by doubtful methods of various kinds, but when they come home again they are still just Sicilians, and their parents probably still live in one of those ancient square stone houses which have stood in the glowing, brilliant sunshine for hundreds if not thousands of years, surrounded by Indian fig trees, with a broken marble figure of unknown age and origin lying a few yards away.

All this didn't strike me as being so very remarkable at the time. I took it all in through my eyes, ears, and skin. The country seeped into me, and the T.B. seeped out. I would spend half the day sitting on the shore, watching Battista mending his nets, and sometimes he took me out fishing. Sometimes my uncle took me for drives through the island, and all that we saw and all that he said fused in my mind into a kind of Sicilian symphony. I saw nothing in Sicily that couldn't be done in a thousand times better and more practical fashion at home with us, but in the course of time I lost the feeling that there was any need to help these people. They had managed for so long without my help that perhaps they'd manage to get along without it for another few years. Very likely more children die and more people go mad in Sicily than is absolutely necessary. Very likely a great deal of afforestation ought to be done, and no doubt far more corn could be grown. But the Sicilians are quite satisfied with things as they are, and that is a good doctrine. They simply don't want to be any better off.

"Why did you come to Sicily?" I once asked my uncle while we were out driving. It was a question that one couldn't have asked him after a quarter of an hour, but that one could ask him after three months.

"It attracted me when I came here for the first time, in nineteen hundred," he said. "Not Taormina and Messina, but the west —Trapani, Marsala, Girgenti."

"Did you decide to live here right away?"

"No," he answered. "I went away again, but I had the island in my blood. I simply had to come back. These extraordinary Sicilians, and the country, and its history! The cradle of Europe!" He quoted a phrase from Goethe's *Italian Journey*. " 'Here is the key to everything.' "

"Did you have any other reason?"

"Come, let's go to Ortygia."

He turned the car, and we drove to Syracuse and went out to the peninsula of Ortygia, where the tyrant Dionysius built his citadel. We spent hours clambering over the rocks and up the glowing cliffs. Finally, somewhat exhausted, we sat in the shade of a wall and looked down at the green water of the harbor, in which marine snails were weaving their ghostly coils. My uncle populated the dirty, stagnant water with the Roman ships and rafts that had blockaded Ortygia to capture Syracuse for the Roman general Marcellus.

"One day I'll read you all about it from Plutarch," he said in his enthusiasm. "It was here that Archimedes set up the great engines with which he flung stones weighing ten talents down upon the rafts and destroyed them. Over there he erected the concave mirrors with which he set fire to the wooden ships."

He clambered about the bastions, rowed with his arms, pointed to right and left, conjuring up before my eyes the picture of a sinister, terrible Theomachy, the struggles with the Superhuman war machines. He vividly described the grappling devices which Archimedes' engineers let down like cranes from the walls, seizing the Roman ships, lifting them, battering them against the walls and then letting them crash into the water, where their crews perished.

"Can you imagine what a shock it must have been to the Romans to see their ships—ships as big as houses—being suddenly lifted clear into the air as if they were playthings and then dropped into the water!"

It was a horrid thought. It gripped him, and it seemed to me that he toyed with it not without relish. He told me the same day that during the First World War he had been medical officer to a well-known bomber formation, and had made numerous flights, particularly night flights. His experiences of sixteen years before mingled in his head with the picture he summed up of Archimedes' war machines in action. Suddenly he wiped his brow with the hand on which he wore a gold ring.

"I only wanted to show you the fortress of Ortygia," he muttered. "It's worth seeing, isn't it?" For the next couple of hours he was silent. He hadn't answered my question as to why he had come to live in Sicily.

VII

Luisa's niece's husband, Battista, was a big, gentle fisherman with dark blond hair. He came from San Giorgio, where there were others like him—men of slender build and of more than average height, with skin lighter than the usual Sicilian shade. The relics of some West Gothic or Vandal tribe must have mingled with Phoenicians, Dorians, or Illyrians to form a new people, the final result of which was a group rather less dark-skinned than the general run of Sicilians.

Battista was the same age as I was, and I grew friendly with him. At first I didn't dare ask him to take me out fishing. But one day he asked me in that gentle voice of his whether I should like to go with him, and I felt the invitation was an honor. Perhaps it was also an honor for Battista to be accompanied by the nephew of the crazy *dottore* with the evil eye. I went out with him practically every morning all through the summer and the long autumn.

His wife, whose name I can't remember, was expecting her first child. I found this rather embarrassing, though I didn't show it. She went about in a thin dress, and everyone carefully appraised the progressive alteration of her figure. I found the jokes that the other fishermen directed at Battista embarrassing too. In my country people offered their seats in the tram to women who were in that condition, but otherwise took no notice. It would never have occurred to anyone to talk about such a thing, or to shout at the top of his voice halfway across the harbor that Battista had better get ready for twins. But that's what they did here, and nobody turned a hair. In the end I got used to this frankness.

Also I liked the quiet dignity with which Battista accepted all the jokes at his expense as a kind of tribute that was his due. We referred to the subject only once.

"My wife's rather old, she's eighteen already," he remarked one day.

"Good heavens!" I exclaimed. "Do you call that old?"

"We wanted to get married two years ago, but I had to do my military service, so we thought it would be better to wait till I came back," Battista explained.

We hardly ever mentioned personal things, but talked about our work. I had always suspected that the question of Charlemagne's real nationality was unimportant, and that summer my suspicions were confirmed. In all practical matters Battista was admirably well informed. He knew all about the currents, and when the wind was going to blow onshore or offshore. He could tell whether the sirocco was going to be wet or dry; he knew the names of all the fish and the seabirds, and the season to shoot or catch them, and he knew all the reefs and shallows and the places where no fishermen ever went because they were the haunts of the sea monster, which was so huge that it could knock a man out of a boat. Two or three generations ago that had happened to one of Battista's relatives.

"The monster never dies," Battista explained. "It keeps on growing forever, unless it gets killed accidentally or tears itself to pieces in one of its rages."

"Can it do that?"

"Of course! When it's in a rage it's murderous," Battista said seriously.

He often used to catch little sea monsters. I envied him his skill at this, which I could not imitate. One of them would cling to his left arm while he took out his knife and stabbed it in the only fatally vulnerable place in its rubber body. It always seemed to me to be a miracle. One moment the animal would be hanging to Battista's shoulder, and a moment later the tentacles lost their grip, and it fell, a wobbling bundle of grayish-black, warty flesh. The most horrible thing seemed to me to be the way it changed color. After it had been taken out of its element it would do this a dozen times, passing from a fleshy pink to a purple brown. As soon as it was dead it turned an ugly gray. Battista was so used to it that he took it for granted.

When I went out with him I got up before dawn and dressed hurriedly. Outside there was a gray twilight. I put on some light shoes, ran down the steps past my aunt's and uncle's rooms, through the big garden, and then down the worn stone steps, which had been built in some legendary past and led straight down to the village of San Giorgio. On either side there grew vines, bamboos, and maize, or there lay bare rocks with dark green cacti growing over them. As I made my way down the steps it grew lighter, and when I reached the mole I saw Battista busy with the oil cask in his boat. He'd wave to me, I'd loosen the painter, push the boat off with my foot, and out we'd glide through the little harbor entrance and past the mole which the inhabitants of the village had long ago built out of the remains of a Greek temple. In earlier years my uncle had spent a lot of time at San Giorgio, looking for plinths and traces of Doric master-pieces. But the people of San Giorgio were completely opposed to the idea of letting their mole be sent to a museum. They took no interest in what might have happened twenty-five hundred years ago, having enough to do in the present.

At this time of day the sea out beyond the mole was smooth, waveless, almost without a trace of swell. We'd put on our straw hats and hoist the rust-brown sail. For a time we'd row with-out a trace of wind to help us, and then drop our oars, lean back, and watch the sun climbing out of the water. First a tiny red island would appear, then a crescent; then it would turn into an evil red eye, shooting out angry rays and stretching a trail of gold and yellow across the water. The land lay far away, and we were quite alone, except for one or two other square sails like our own, which dotted the water. In the course of time this loneli-ness seemed to me to be the best thing about Sicily. We had a bottle of water with us, a loaf of bread, and a handful of olives. We made very little use of the bottle, because the water quickly got warm. We'd put the net out, bait the line, or join with a few other boats to trawl with the big net, according to what we were after. Toward midday, when the wind dropped again, we'd lie on our backs in the boat, put our hats over our faces, and conduct serious, men's conversations.

"Are you married?" he once asked me.

I said I wasn't. With us men didn't marry so early.

"I don't understand," Battista exclaimed. "Children are the greatest blessing. Imagine my parents without children! They have seven—that's not such a lot, but five others died. If they had no children, they'd be poor. As it is they can manage."

"How?"

"*Dio mio*, I'm the eldest, and I'm a fisherman. My oldest brother is in the Army, so he doesn't need anything, though he doesn't earn anything either. My second brother works in the sulphur mines and makes quite a lot of money, and the one after that's a sailor, and he sends money home too sometimes; and the youngest earns money from time to time too, either at stone-breaking or on the roads. Also he helps father with his vines."

"That makes five."

"Yes, and then there are the two girls. One helps mother at home and the other works in your house."

"You mean the girl with the crooked nose?"

"Yes, she was kicked by a horse when she was a little girl, but it doesn't matter; she's engaged, and she'll be getting married soon. Then her sister will go and work in the house."

It was clear that a whole network of Battistas extended over land and sea, but that the most respected was Battista himself, because he maintained the family tradition of fishing.

"What do you do?" he asked next. I told him I was going to study.

"To be a *dottore*?"

I said perhaps, but I didn't know.

"You'd make a good fisherman," he said. "You like it, don't you?"

Yes, I liked it very much, but in my family there were no fishermen. In my family one had to study in order to be able to earn at least two thousand lire a month.

"Then you must be very rich in your family?" he said.

No, I explained, we were not rich, because we had to spend as much as we earned. We needed stone houses to live in, and heating and furniture.

"That one can make for oneself," he interrupted.

No, I explained. We had to buy it; and we had to buy all our food too. Also we had to have a radio, and at least two suits and two overcoats, as well as carpets, pictures on the walls, fountain pens, silver (or at any rate what looked like silver), dogs, horses, and cars. Otherwise life simply wasn't worth living.

"*Dio mio*, you certainly need a lot of money, then! Don't your children work?"

No, they went to school until they were thirteen or sixteen or even eighteen years old.

At this Battista was silent. He was no longer surprised at my uncle's being *mal i'testa*, rather queer in the head. How could he help it, living a life like that?

Battista had only the vaguest ideas about the history of Sicily. I tried to explain to him that the island's poverty dated back to the time of the Roman Verres, who had systematically plundered it.

"Verro?" he asked.

"*Si*," I answered, thinking one might just as well say Verro as Verres.

"Verro!" he repeated, wrinkling his brow. I explained that this was the man about whom Cicero had written five books.

"Cicero?" he asked.

I gave it up. Next day, when we were again lying in the shadow of the sail at midday, with Battista moving the oar from time to time to keep us in the shade, he brought the subject up again. He made one of his longest speeches.

"I asked the priest about it last night," he said, "and the priest said it wasn't Verro's fault that Sicily is so poor."

"Oh?" I said. "Whose fault did he say it was?"

"Verro," Battista explained, "was said to have murdered his wife and his mother-in-law, and he was arrested and kept in prison for two years, but they couldn't prove it. Then he died, and he still maintained his innocence on his deathbed. No, it can't have been Verro. The priest says you shouldn't believe everything the *cicerone* of Girgenti says."

"Who is the *cicerone* of Girgenti?"

"He's the crazy guide with the red peaked cap who takes the *inglesi* about in the summer. You shouldn't let yourself be taken in by him! Verro was quite a decent chap!"

"What Verro do you mean?"

"Giuseppe Verro of Trapani," Battista explained. "The one with the scar under his right eye. It's not his fault at all that Sicily's so poor!"

After that we didn't talk about the history of Sicily again. I told my uncle about this conversation, but afterward I regretted it. It was letting Battista down. My uncle laughed loud and long.

"There you are!" he said. "You see what ignorant fools these people are! Not even the priest has heard of Verres or Cicero's speeches! Not even the priest! What does that man know?"

VIII

I had known for a long time that there was a feud between my uncle and the priest of San Giorgio. It was a feud of very long standing. The priest went about the countryside denouncing my uncle as a heretic, and my uncle retaliated by denouncing him as an ignorant fool. The priest preached sermons about heretics and those who set themselves up as being better than God's own servants, and my uncle replied by denouncing the idle priesthood which lived off the sweat of the poor fishermen and sulphur workers. The priest called my uncle a drunkard, and my uncle's retort was that the priest committed misconduct with the niece of poor, crazy Marcello, who was not very strong in the head herself. Very likely both of them were speaking the truth. In the long run my uncle was the loser, but I only found that out later. The priest was a quiet, self-satisfied individual, who perspired freely and preferred visiting his parish in the morning and in the evening. Then he would be seen slowly approaching from a distance, his little book with its black and red lettering in his hands, walking along, perspiring and moving his lips, but never hurrying.

My aunt was the conciliatory element in the feud, the covering of heavy water that prevented the detonation of the bombs. She belonged to the same denomination as the priest, whom she supported liberally. She furnished his chapel on the road to San Giorgio, and the priest moderated his zeal and did not attack my uncle's character more than was absolutely necessary.

During my stay with him my uncle delivered a smashing blow at the authority of the Church. This was on the occasion of the birth of Battista's child, which occurred late in the autumn, when the sun no longer filled the land like a bowl with heat. By that time I thought I had plumbed the mystery of the relations between my uncle and aunt. I was leading a very full life. In the morning I went fishing with Battista and re-established my health, and in the afternoon I read *Rob Roy* to my aunt. She took a particular interest in the foreword to *Rob Roy*, which gives a detailed account of conditions in Scotland in about the year 1750. Sometimes I listened to gramophone records with her or wandered about the garden or watched my uncle painting. He was marvelously successful at turning the pretty, naked, brown-skinned girls who turned up in his studio as models into triangles, semicircles, and parallelograms. Generally I went to bed early.

There was an invisible dividing line in the house which neither party ever crossed. My uncle never went into my aunt's room, and she never went into his studio or saw his models. He drove around the country in his car, and she walked about the garden. He had any number of men and women friends, and went to the movies, the theater, or the opera at Palermo, while she read Sir Walter Scott, did needlework, prayed, and occasionally looked out of her bedroom window when Luisa was maltreating one of her sacrifices. I don't know what she thought on these occasions. My uncle was full of red blood, but she seemed to have no blood in her veins. In earlier years my uncle had been very pugnacious, and he still boasted about it in his bighearted way. She was afraid of spiders, mice, fleas, germs, dogs, crickets, and beetles. Also she had a morbid fear of fire. She kept a rope ladder rolled up under the window sill in her bedroom because she had once read how people can be trapped in upstairs rooms in a fire. When she told me about the rope ladder I nearly burst out laughing at the thought of her shinning down it in her nightgown like a cabin boy. Actually the whole house, with the exception of the stairs, the doors, and the furniture, was built of stone, so the risk of fire was small. I pointed this out to her from time to time, and it seemed to relieve her anxiety, but she still kept the rope ladder under her window sill.

My uncle was certainly the more active, the more colorful, the more attractive of the two, but the way in which my aunt insisted on her rights and made him accept them as a matter of course could not fail to be surprising to an outsider. When my uncle, for instance, was already seated at the piano and was getting ready to play, and Luisa walked in with her finger to her mouth and as suddenly walked out again, my uncle, as obedient as a poodle or a Newfoundland, would get up and shut the piano. These things surprised me greatly at first, but in the course of time I learned to accept the existing state of affairs without inquiring how it had come about.

My uncle's resounding blow against the priest of San Giorgio was delivered on an exciting night which I shall remember all my life. My uncle had been drinking heavily, and we had to use a whole jug of hot coffee to convince him that Battista's wife was in labor and that the baby would not come. Eventually he pulled himself together and took his seat in the back of the car with his little black bag, while Battista sat next to me. Feeling rather proud, I drove down the winding road toward the village. When we reached the chapel my uncle woke up, told me to stop, and disappeared behind it. Certain noises were then heard, and my uncle reappeared, with red eyes and holding a handkerchief in front of his mouth. We continued our drive down to the village, stopped outside Battista's whitewashed cottage, and went in to where his wife was lying. About seventeen people were standing around the bed. Martin promptly turned them out, telling them that if they showed their faces inside the door again the penalty would be an irremediable look from his diabolical gentian-blue evil eye. Then he caused huge masses of water to be heated and started scrubbing his hands.

"Fetch the candles!" he suddenly said to me.

"What candles?"

"Didn't Luisa pack any candles?"

I went out to the car and looked for candles. I used up half a box of matches but couldn't find any. The only light in the fisherman's cottage was a dim oil lamp. I went back and told my uncle there were no candles. He swore and asked Battista whether he had any candles. No, Battista had no candles. My uncle swore again and scratched his head. Suddenly he had an idea. I had felt sure he would.

"Go to the chapel and fetch the candles from the altar," he said to Battista.

Battista shuffled his feet uneasily.

"Hurry!" my uncle said. "Go and fetch the candles! I saw them in the chapel when we stopped."

"The priest!" Battista said. "He wouldn't allow it!"

The midwife nodded agreement.

"If you don't come back with candles in half an hour your wife will die!" my uncle said. "The child is upside down. I must be able to see, so that I can turn it around. If I can't turn it around I shall have to operate. But I can't do that without candles. Hurry!"

Battista still hesitated. "I'll fetch the candles, Doctor," he said finally.

"Roderigo will drive you to the chapel."

I started the car, and we drove back to where we had stopped before. Battista made the sign of the cross and looked around anxiously. Then he vanished into the chapel. A few moments later he reappeared, carrying two thick wax candles.

"They're consecrated candles," he said to me, shrugging his shoulders.

Meanwhile I had turned the car, and we drove back to the village.

My uncle was still standing in the room next to his half-empty black bag. He had rolled up his sleeves and was scrubbing his hands in a tubful of hot water. A big fire was burning in the kitchen, and a big kettle full of water was standing on the tripod.

"Cut the candles into pieces and stick them into bottles to make more light," my uncle said to me. I took out my pocket knife and began cutting the candles. An anxious murmur started outside.

"Battista, go out and tell them to shut up," my uncle said. "And I've finished with you. Don't let me see you in here again! But first hang a blanket over the window."

Outside the door the angry murmur turned into an argument. I could hear Battista's voice.

"The Virgin Mary and San Giorgio won't mind their candles being used for such a purpose," he said. "They won't even mind their candles being cut up for such a purpose. The doctor needs light. He says the child is upside down!"

"How can he know that?"

"He's a doctor!"

"He's a heretic, an unbelieving heretic, who has consecrated candles cut to pieces!"

"Be quiet, Giuliana, I'll replace them!"

"But first they must be consecrated!"

"The priest will consecrate them!"

"The priest will turn you out, because you took the candles and helped the two heretics to cut them in pieces!"

My uncle, busy with his work at the washtub, heard all this. He took a towel from his bag and dried his hands, after sprinkling them with disinfectant. Then, with the towel still in his hand, he walked to the door. Silence fell when he appeared.

"I see you all," he said. "I see you, Giuliana, with your slanderous tongue; I see Tonio, whose boil I cut last year; and I see Maria, who had the toothache. If you don't keep quiet immediately I'll see that your illnesses come back—and how they'll come back! They'll be twice as bad as they were before!"

He came back into the room and put the towel in his bag. Outside all was quiet. Nothing was to be heard but the flickering of the fire and the woman's groaning. I had to hold her knees while he felt her and tried to turn the child. Her face was red with pain and effort while he worked. It wasn't a pretty face. She was a pretty girl, but she didn't look pretty now.

Suddenly he stood up, hurriedly washed his hands, and took a syringe from his bag. "This will hurry the labor a little," he said. He put away the syringe, felt the girl's pulse, and looked at his wristwatch. After ten minutes the girl's groans grew louder. They came at shorter and shorter intervals, and a quarter of an hour later the child was born.

As we drove out of the village a stone struck the door of the car. My uncle put his foot down on the accelerator, and we flew past the chapel we had robbed earlier in the evening. "That was crazy Marcello," he said, not dissatisfied. A little while later he said with a chuckle, "Wasn't that a magnificent thing, stealing the Virgin Mary's candles? I could have had them fetched from home. It would have been just as quick, but it was far too good an opportunity to miss!"

IX

At Christmas my father wrote to say that he intended to come to Italy with Kride to fetch me. But difficulties cropped up, and at the end of March he wrote and said he wouldn't be coming himself, but that I was to meet Kride in Naples. He had sent her off on a holiday alone.

I packed my suitcases, not altogether gladly and not altogether sorrowfully. My uncle and aunt were both, in their ways, sorry I was going. Aunt Mary said she'd miss me at teatime, and my uncle was sorry he wouldn't have anyone to talk to about the passionate isle of Sicily. I promised to come back and I really intended to do so, but many years passed before I was able to keep my promise, and then everything had changed.

When I reached Naples Kride was not there. Instead there was a telegram waiting for me, saying she was staying with friends of Yevgenia's near Rome. I had three days ahead of me in which to look around Naples—enough to develop a dislike for the place such as I have never felt for anywhere else in the world. Such dislikes are generally mutual, and I had the feeling that the Neapolitans didn't like me either, and they were in the majority. I think that the people who discovered that one should see Naples and die did the place an ill service. It's possible that one might find Naples very beautiful if one couldn't speak Italian and hadn't spent a year in Sicily immediately beforehand.

On the second day, when I was sitting solitary and forlorn at

Zi' Teresa's, eating *minestra*, I noticed a couple at a neighboring table who seemed familiar. They were the pianist Freddie and the girl from Hamburg. I remembered that her name was Elsie.

"What are you doing here?" I asked.

"We missed the steamer," Elsie said.

"What steamer?"

"The one we came in!"

They explained that they had stayed at Taormina, and that the ship had sailed from Catania without them. They had sent a telegram to the ship at Genoa, asking for their luggage to be sent back to Naples, and they had stayed in Naples ever since. Freddie had had several jobs as a pianist, and now he had his own little jazz band.

I looked at Elsie's hands. She wore a number of rings, most of them cheap ones with imitation jewels, but there was nothing that resembled a wedding ring, either on her right hand, where German women wear their wedding rings, or on her left hand, where Italian women wear them. I began to suspect something but was careful not to say anything. Elsie looked at her watch and grew restless.

"It's time you went to your band, Fred," she said.

He grinned, stood up, laid a note on the table, bowed, said, "Don't let her talk your head off," and left. I found him still as attractive as he had been on the ship.

Naturally I spent the afternoon with Elsie. At first she didn't talk my head off. She was full of praise for Naples, for the Torre del Greco, Pompeii, and Vesuvius, just as if she were a guide. She spoke fluent Italian. She did some shopping, and I had to pay because she had left her money at the hotel, or so she said.

"Fred is a terrible fellow," she said suddenly, with an undertone of hatred. "You can't imagine how many good friends I've made here and had to give up, all because of him. It's his fault that I look like what I look like now!"

"That you look like what?" I asked.

"Oh, stop it, I can see in your face what you think of me!"

"What did your family say when you didn't come back?"

She shrugged her shoulders and didn't answer. Obviously she hadn't parted from her family on friendly terms.

"I adore Naples," she said. "It's such a wonderfully natural place. Don't you adore it too?"

"I think it's dreadful!"

"Oh!" she said.

Our relationship had altered. A year before she had had the advantage over me, but now the situation was reversed. When I disagreed with her, she said "Oh!" and was silent. But she wasn't silent for long. She soon became communicative again, and I learned some details about her life.

"He's not easy to live with," she said. "He's as temperamental as a prima donna. He can be charming, but you never know when he's going to be. He's got such a way of showing that he cares nothing for you that I could murder him! Sometimes I've thought I would murder him, but the women's prisons here are terrible. Have you ever been in a woman's prison?"

"No!"

She didn't elaborate on the subject. It slowly grew dark, and we went to the bar where Freddie played. There he was, on a dais, in a white jacket, conducting his four-man band, mostly with his feet and head, because his hands were busy at the piano. When he saw us he grinned and showed his teeth. In the interval he came over to our table.

"You can entertain our guest at home for a while," he said to Elsie. "I expect I'll be rather late."

He was still playing when we left. I had a room at a *pension* at Santa Lucia, but Elsie lived near the station, which was in the opposite direction. We strolled along together. She looked prettier now by electric light than she had looked in the bright sunlight on the shore. I had drunk several glasses of Barbera and was glad not to be alone.

Her hotel was a remarkable building. The entrance was not from the street, but from a courtyard. You didn't go up a staircase, but up a whole series of iron steps that led to separate balconies. I had never been in a house like that before, and found it curious and exciting. The balconies were iron too, and most of them were completely covered with washing. The light that came out of the rooms was sometimes concealed and sometimes as harsh as if a carbide lamp were burning inside.

We climbed four or five flights of iron steps, and at every story we had to walk back a few yards to get to the beginning of the next flight. The windows were open, it was oppressively hot, and one could get a complete view of Neapolitan life. I remember one room in which a fat naked man with black hair on his chest was lying asleep and snoring, with two children and a small dog beside him on the bed, resting their heads on his stomach. In the other corner of the room a woman was sitting, giving her baby the breast.

"Not very respectable, is it?" said Elsie. "But very picturesque!"

I should have liked to turn back, but she went ahead in such a confident and matter-of-fact fashion, and I could see her long, slim legs, so I followed her. Every now and then a powerful whiff of garlic and hot olive oil came through an open window, or someone could be heard strumming a mandolin and singing to it.

On the top story but one an old woman with graying hair and hollow cheeks was standing. She looked like the archetype of poverty, drawn by Käthe Kollwitz. She had staring black eyes, which she raised when we approached. She had some washing hanging over her arm, and her left hand rested on a torn red shirt. She looked at us out of her crazed, staring eyes. I said *"Buona sera"* as we passed, but her face didn't move; I might have been talking to a statue. I looked around when we reached the next flight of steps, and she was still standing there motionless, with her big eyes fixed on us like the empty craters of an extinct volcano.

"Did you know that woman?" I asked Elsie when we were in her room.

"What woman?"

"The one that stared at us."

Elsie shook her head. She hadn't noticed her. She turned on the radio, fetched some glasses, and put them on a stool. Then she opened a bottle of Marsala.

"Phew!" she said. "It's hot! I'll take my blouse off!"

She sat down beside the radio, twiddled the knobs till she found some dance music, and then turned it full on. Then she got up, disappeared into the next room, and came back wearing a bathrobe.

"Come on!" she said. "Take your shirt off—it's stifling!"

She flung herself onto what was either a bed or a settee—you couldn't tell for certain which it was because it was so untidy—and then switched off the light. Light from the street, from the flats opposite, and from a neon sign on the Vomero came in through the open door and window—white, green, and red light. The dial on the little radio gleamed yellow.

"You have to have a radio here, otherwise you couldn't stand it, with all the noises in the house," she said. "They're always either quarreling or making love. No, sometimes they sing!"

I had taken my shirt off, and I took a sip of the Marsala. Elsie stretched for her glass, and in doing so touched me with her shoulder. I put my hand on her shoulder, and she leaned against me and started purring like a cat and saying the most disconnected things. "I'm glad that you came back with me," she said. "He'll be sitting up till the early hours in the bar with some countess or *altezza*. They've all got their eyes on him, and then he goes home with them to play the piano for them, at two o'clock in the morning. Ha! Ha! But of course, as we're not married, he's free to do what he likes. I wouldn't like to be married to him either. I'm glad I wasn't so stupid as that!"

She went on talking like that all night. Occasionally she stopped and grew tender, or laughed at me, or shut her eyes and pressed her head against my arm.

"What muscles you've got!" she said admiringly. "A year ago on the ship you looked so delicate, and now you're tanned! Do you love me? Why have you stopped drinking? I like drinking, it goes with Naples. In Naples you must always drink and sing and either quarrel or make love. That's all there is to do here. Would you like to stay in Naples always? I would! I don't know anywhere else I'd rather be. Nobody does any work here. In Hamburg everybody works, or acts as if he does. Here, even if somebody does work, he doesn't act as if he did. Everybody lives off the foreigners, everybody!"

"Do you too?"

She shrugged her shoulders and was upset for a moment—but only for a moment. The light from the street and from the Vomero painted spots on her skin.

"You think I'm wicked, don't you?"

"Why don't you go home?"

"Home? I wouldn't go home for a million! At home they do nothing but work and march and sing songs and make speeches. I don't want to hear any speeches—from you either—and I don't want to be told that I'm wicked or that I ought to go home. They frighten you to death with their speeches. Don't you think so too?"

I explained that I hadn't been home for a year, and that before that I had been in a sanatorium.

"*Che povero*," she said, "*in ospitale!*"

"Stop talking Italian," I said. "I can't stand it!"

"What muscles you've got!" she said, feeling my arm. I had never considered whether I had muscles or not. I tensed my arm, and she laughed and threw back her head. I felt ashamed and filled the glasses again.

"I'm glad you're here," she said. "Would you protect me if anyone came? Sometimes I'm afraid someone might come and do something to me. They're cunning and mean. They don't come so long as he's with me. He's strong. He doesn't look it, but he's really strong. I love him for being so strong. Believe it or not, he can knock a nail through a tabletop with his fist. I know he puts a lira piece in his hand first, but all the same it needs a great deal of strength, doesn't it? They all respect him, and so nobody comes near me, even when he leaves me alone for a fortnight. Once he threw a fellow who wanted to do something to me down the iron staircase. He'd have thrown him over the railing down into the courtyard if I hadn't screamed. Since then they leave me in peace. They're crazy about blondes here in Naples. . . ."

She told me a lot more about "him" and about other things, all of which I didn't understand. Finally she asked whether she could keep the things she had bought that afternoon, and I said of course she could. As I made my way back toward my *pension* I found it all very amazing. It was quite different from Sicily. I should have liked to go back to Battista.

X

Next day I met Kride at the Termini Station. She was even more beautiful than I remembered. She was well dressed and as confident of herself as only a North European blonde can be who knows that every minute two dozen Neapolitans will look round after her, and that at least three of them will whistle through their teeth or call out, "*Che bella!*"

"Let's stay here for a few days," Kride said after the first greetings were over. She told me, but in a more cultivated manner, exactly what Elsie had told me the night before; that I had grown, looked older, had grown muscular, and was sunburned.

"We must go to Pompeii and Santa Lucia, and then there's that place on the bay called Aunt-something-or-other, where we must go and have a meal."

She was full of enterprise and enthusiasm. Sometimes she reminded me of a filly that had been kept in the stables for a week and now wanted to roll in the grass out of sheer joy of living.

At the hotel she disappeared into her room and came back wearing a yellow silk dress. She was slightly tanned and looked so pretty that she attracted the attention of the hall porter. He cast me an appreciative glance. I understood what he meant and looked at him coldly. He winked and whistled through his teeth.

I asked Kride how things were getting on at home.

"Oh! We've got a real surprise for you," she said. "Max has bought some land in the Heerstrasse and he's building a house on it. It's going to be a wonderful house, two stories, with central heating and grounds all around it!"

"Is Father as well off as that?" I asked.

"Oh! The land was cheap. It belonged to a Jew who wanted to sell quickly, and we got it for a song!"

"So you'll be able to have a sailboat and do lots of entertaining."

She looked at me radiantly. She really was a remarkably beautiful young woman, and I was proud of being with her.

"The house is nearly ready. That's why Max couldn't come. I've ordered the curtains and the carpets and the furniture, so

everything's in hand. Max said that when we come home at Easter
the house'll be ready to live in. So it's good-by to Lichterfelde
Ost, and about time too! I've been saying for a long time that in
the position he's in now Max ought to have a house of his own."

"What position is he in now? He never says anything about
himself in his letters."

"Doesn't he? He's a commercial counselor in the Foreign Ministry. He works in the Balkans department, in cooperation with
the Economics Ministry. He often sees the Minister, and the Finance Minister too."

"Then of course he can afford to build a house!"

Of course he could, said Kride, particularly at a time so favor-
able for building, when everything possible was being done to
create employment. Max was building a house, and other people
would be moving into the flat he was moving out of, thus freeing
a place for other people in turn. The conclusion was that my father's building a house in the Heerstrasse gave thousands of families all over Germany the accommodation they required.

"What is your mother doing?" I asked.

"Mother's still as strange as ever," she said with a sigh. "She
could have had a wonderful business in Düsseldorf now, if only
she'd been sensible. Max found it for her—he knows so many influential people. All she would have had to do would be to set
herself up as Von Haringen, Furs and Fashions, but she only
stayed there a week and took a dislike to the idea and came back,
and she still lives in the old house with Margarete. They want to
extend the front of the house and make a shopfront, but it'll
never be what it could have been at Düsseldorf!"

She sighed a little over Yevgenia's lack of common sense.
I couldn't understand either what had made Yevgenia behave
like that.

"And what about Margarete?"

"She's—let me think—she's twelve now, and goes to our old
school."

"But how is she?"

Kride seemed to find the question rather remarkable. She had
already given what she considered to be sufficient information
about Margarete.

"She's doing quite well at school. How do you expect her to be?"

She said no more, and I refrained from asking for the third time.

"And Josefine?"

Kride beamed. "Josefine's doing extraordinarily well for herself, you take it from me! I believe I should be quite jealous of her, if she weren't my sister! She's a beauty. Max raves about her. She was in Paris for a year, and she's had three proposals since she's been back. And then there's our name, you know. The old names have got their value back again. At school I often used to say my name was just Haringen, because of those wretched Socialists, who always started making vulgar remarks if anyone had a 'von' before his name. But all that's quite different now!"

We walked for a while in silence. The sun was hot, and it was stifling. Kride took a street plan of Naples from her bag. An urchin crossed the road and planted himself beside us. He stood with his head down, contemplating Kride with his dark eyes, full of ancient cunning. He had a hole in the front of his trousers, through which he occasionally put his finger to scratch where it itched. Many Neapolitan trousers have this practical arrangement.

"*Cosa vuoi?*" I asked him. "What do you want?"

He directed his eyes at me, without changing his position. "*Italiano?*" he asked.

I said I wasn't Italian.

"*Napolitano?*"

"*Siciliano,*" I answered.

He shook his head in surprise. I didn't look to him like a Sicilian, but he accepted my statement.

"*Una bionda,*" he said, looking Kride over from head to foot, as if appraising her market value. "*Una bellezza. Questa signora è una tedesca?*"

I nodded. "How did you know she was a German?" I asked.

He said only three words in reply, but they contained all the inherited wisdom of the born international guide.

"Very big feet," he said.

Involuntarily I looked down. Kride had normal-sized feet, in ordinary, solid, German shoes. She wasn't wearing the ridiculous high heels that Italian women like tripping about in, but that was nothing against her, in my opinion.

"Give me a lira or I'll tell her," the boy said.

"Questa signora non parla italiano."

"Io parlo doitsch!"

It was a trap. He had psychoanalyzed us and seen that it was important to me to keep the lady in a good humor. He knew that ladies do not like being told, even by ragged Neapolitan urchins, that they have big feet. He now proceeded to speak a few words of German, to show there was substance in his threat, and demanded his price to allow me to go in peace.

"Vai via, cattivo!" I shouted at him angrily.

"I speak good German," he answered in Italian, without changing his position, "and I know something else that the lady won't want to hear. I'll tell her she's a *deutsche Kartoffel*, a German potato. She very angry. You tonight not—" He made the international gesture with his thumb and two first fingers.

Kride looked up from her map. "The place where we want to eat must be somewhere over there," she said, pointing in the direction of Castellammare.

I had known for a long time where it was she wanted to go, but I had no desire to go to Zi' Teresa's again, because I didn't want Kride to meet my acquaintances there.

"It's two hours from here by car," I said.

"Oh!" said Kride and buried herself in her map again.

"Give me a lira," the boy insisted. I was growing very warm. We were standing in the bright sunshine outside one of those buildings that all look like banks, genuine banks of the classic period.

"Come along," I said to Kride. "I'll find somewhere nice to eat!"

But she was obstinate. "What does that young scalawag want?" she asked, for the first time noticing the boy.

"He's a beggar," I said.

"He looks sweet! Ask him whether there's a place near here called Aunt something-or-other. What's 'aunt' in Italian?"

"I don't know!" I said.

" 'Aunt' is *zia*," the boy chimed in.

"He talks German! Listen, how much do you want for finding me a restaurant beginning with *zia?*"

"Zi' Teresa's," the boy answered.

"That's it!" Kride exclaimed with delight. "How much do you want?"

"Five lire!"

"Give it to him, Roderich!"

"I wouldn't dream of it!" I said furiously.

"Then I will!" said Kride, starting to search in her bag. She produced a five-lire note and showed it to the boy.

"Where is the place?"

He thrust his head between his shoulders and marched ahead of us on his bare feet. Zi' Teresa's was only a few hundred yards away. We came to the tongue of land leading out to the Castel dell' Ovo. Zi' Teresa's was immediately to the left of it. The boy pointed it out.

"Five lire!" he said proudly.

Kride handed it to him.

"Two lire," the boy said to me in Italian, "or I'll tell the lady that all the same. Also I'll say she's a—"

At that moment somebody called. I turned and saw Freddie and Elsie coming along the beach. By daylight Elsie again looked worn, tawdry, cheap. Freddie's shirt was dirty, his chestnut hair was tousled, and his shoes hadn't been cleaned for at least a week.

My blackmailer promptly started yelling at the top of his voice, "German lady very big feet! German lady very big feet!"

He planted his hands on his hips and roared with laughter; it was the laughter of an operatic *buffo.* All the time he kept his eyes on me, intending to make good his escape if I showed signs of going for him.

"What is he saying?" asked Kride, looking down at her feet in bewilderment.

"Yes, yes, big feet, very big feet!" the boy yelled, again roaring with laughter. "German lady every year baby, no breasts, big belly! Ha! Ha! Ha! Ha! Heil Hitler! Big feet!"

"The shameless little rascal!" Kride exclaimed, turning as red as a beetroot. The color suited her, but I had no time to admire it, because I was searching in my pockets for a lira to give to the young blackmailer. Meanwhile he stopped laughing and began bringing up his heavy artillery.

"German lady no good in bed!" his new act started, but it was suddenly transformed into a howl of pain. He had kept his eyes fixed on me the whole time, in case I went for him; I hadn't done so because I knew that these boys were as slippery as eels and could run like hares. But he had not noticed another danger, advancing silently upon him from another direction, in shoes that were as dusty as his own bare feet—namely, Freddie. Freddie took him by the scruff of the neck, lifted him bodily with one hand, and shook him. A German boy's neck would have broken under such treatment. For a moment the little blackmailer tried to scratch, bite, and kick, but Freddie held him in his grip and shook him unmercifully, so he dropped his arms and legs and shrieked as if he were being impaled. Freddie possessed an admirable Italian vocabulary, of which he let the boy have the full benefit.

"Porco mattino, cattivo, figlio di una—"

"For heaven's sake let him go, Freddie, you'll kill him!" Elsie said, shaking Freddie's arm. Freddie looked up. His face was black with a completely unassumed rage. He hated this boy whom he was holding in the air, and he really would have gone on shaking him till he had broken his neck. I now believed the stories about Freddie's strength. Elsie said he could knock a lira—no, a nail—through a tabletop with his bare fist.

Suddenly he dropped the boy, who collapsed onto the pavement in a heap. Elsie knelt beside him and felt him. "Come! come, *piccolo!*" she said consolingly. The boy opened his eyes and looked at us.

"Come along, Elsie, he's still alive!" said Freddie. "Don't dirty your fingers!" Elsie went on kneeling beside the boy, who acted as if he were on the point of death.

"Stand up or I'll give you another shaking!" said Freddie.

In a flash the boy was on his feet, making off in the direction of the Castel dell' Ovo as fast as his legs would carry him.

"If you dare say another word—" Freddie shouted after him, but the boy took the hint and said no more. Freddie turned to us.

"Won't you introduce us, Roderich?" he said. I did so. We went to Zi' Teresa's. Freddie walked ahead with Kride, and I followed with Elsie.

"Did you sleep well?" she asked. "Is that your stepmother? What a pretty stepmother!"

"Oh, be quiet!" I said angrily. The very thing that I had wanted to avoid was now about to happen.

Sure enough, it did happen. Kride had a good look at Elsie and summed her up. Vesuvius might erupt and Naples be burned down, but there would be no altering the view she formed of Elsie. Kride's next look was directed at me. What extraordinary friends you have! it said. Elsie had only to lay her hand on my arm and take a fold of my skin between her fingers once or twice, and to keep on alternating between calling me *du* and *Sie* in that curious way she had, and Kride knew everything she wanted to know. She didn't say anything, but I could see how distasteful she found it.

Fortunately the sulky Freddie wasn't sulky that day. He could see which way the wind was blowing, and he took it upon himself to distract Kride's attention from social problems.

"My cousin and I often come and eat here," he said. "We went out with the fishermen this morning; that's why we look so untidy, ha! ha! Have you ever been to Naples before? No? A wonderful city! Nothing else in Europe to compare with it! Only Rio de Janeiro can sustain the comparison. . . ."

He went on talking effortlessly all through the meal, taking us all under his wing. Kride was impressed.

"You must have tremendous strength in your fingers," she said. "I can't tell you how angry I was with that shameless little rascal. I couldn't even understand what he meant!"

I gave a cautious explanation. Elsie and Fred laughed loudly at the way he had tried to blackmail me.

"They're cheeky, but sweet," Elsie said.

"They're born bandits," said Freddie.

"I don't understand," said Kride. She had flushed deeply again, and it suited her admirably. We stood up, paid, and left. Kride had promised Freddie to come with me to his bar that evening. I made up my mind not to go to the bar. I took Kride to the Maritime Museum, to the harbor, and up to the hill of Santa Lucia, where the painters lived, the German, Russian, English, and American painters. I had found this out on my first evening, when I had happened to find myself dining with a member of this colony. But Kride didn't want to see any painters.

"Who is that girl?" she asked after a time.

"She was on the ship, the ship I went to Sicily in."

"Oh? And what is she?"

"I think she comes from Hamburg, but she has quarreled with her family. She didn't go back. She has been in Naples ever since. She likes it here."

"Oh!"

We started talking about other things and went back to the hotel. I knew a restaurant in the neighborhood; it was simple, but the wine was good. I had got used to drinking wine with my meals in Sicily.

Kride found the place dirty and drew my attention to the stains on the tablecloth.

"But there are no foreigners here," I said.

"I've got nothing against foreigners. Who is that pianist? Was he on the ship too?"

"Yes, we were all on the ship together. He plays wonderfully."

"He must be frightfully strong!"

"He can knock a nail into a tabletop with his bare fist."

"How do you know?"

"I've seen him do it." When people keep asking you questions it's frightfully difficult always to stick to the truth.

"Have you decided what you want to do when you get back home?"

"I was thinking I'd like to be an art historian."

The truth was that I hadn't been thinking about the matter at all. Actually I had been wanting for some time to be a doctor like my uncle, but I had no desire to spend years studying.

"I think Max hopes you'll study law and enter the foreign service," Kride said. "He worries a lot about your future."

"Oh!" I said, picking at my plate of *carciofi*. But this was a subject I found it uncomfortable to discuss with Kride. Of course my father worried about my future, he always had.

"Come, let's go to the bar," said Kride.

"Do you really—?" I began, but didn't finish the sentence, because when Kride really wanted to do something you had to fall in with it.

xi

We stayed in Naples for a week. All sorts of things happened during that week, though I didn't understand some of them till later. I was still very young and not nearly so experienced as people supposed me to be, just because I had suddenly learned two foreign languages. I spoke English without a trace of accent, and my Italian was fluent, though not exactly diplomatic. But that's not a substitute for experience.

On the first evening we sat in the bar and danced occasionally. Alfred Karawan showed all his virtuosity at the piano, and he had a great deal of it. The guests clapped and applauded, and even Kride admitted that he was very gifted. When he had finished, the four of us went out to Santa Lucia. The amusement park was still open, and Alfred suddenly wanted to go on the scenic railway. I didn't want to. I wanted to go to bed and think a bit. I felt uncomfortable with Elsie. I didn't like her, but she seemed to have a definite liking for me and she showed it. We went to the amusement park and went on the scenic railway, and then Kride and Alfred had a ride on the boat swings, the kind that turn full circle if you work them hard enough. I didn't go on them, but Alfred was marvelous; he managed to turn twenty or thirty complete circles in succession. It was an extraordinary performance, and people stopped to look at him. When the pair of them had finished Kride was flushed again, and we wandered on. If the Negro who offered a hundred lire to anyone who could stand up to him had been boxing that evening, nothing would have stopped Alfred from going into the ring with him. What is more, he would have kept his end up, and the crowd would have gone wild, because he would obviously have knocked the Negro out. But it was the Negro's night off, and his booth was shut.

We lunched at Zi' Teresa's again next day. This time Alfred was well dressed, and he had actually brushed his hair, but Elsie was more made up than ever, and she was wearing an impossible dress.

She stroked my arm, called Alfred "darling," and generally made
herself unpopular. Kride was a lady and didn't notice. Later on,
in a taxi on the way to the Torre del Greco, Elsie took me by the
arm.

"You'd better keep an eye on your stepmother," she said.

"Keep an eye on your own stepmother," I answered rudely.

"You're sweet when you get angry, and besides you really have
got muscles," Elsie said.

We spent the week going on excursions, and in the evening we
went dancing. Alfred borrowed four hundred lire from me till the
banks opened, but there seemed to be a lot of bank holidays in
Naples, and I never got the money back.

On the last evening we were accidentally separated. We went
to the movies, and on the way out Elsie and I suddenly noticed
that we were alone. I spent some time looking for Alfred and
Kride, but they had disappeared.

"He'll look after her," Elsie said. "Let's go and have an ice!"

I blamed myself bitterly for not having looked after Kride more
carefully. Suppose the same thing happened to her that had happened to us, and she suddenly found herself separated from Alfred? But then I decided that she had money with her and could
take a taxi back to the hotel. We had had a slight quarrel that
afternoon, and she had told me I was an intolerable snob, perpetually trying to show how well educated I was. She said Alfred
was a most cultivated individual. He had taken her into a church
and played the organ to her. He could play Bach by heart, and I
had no right whatever to set myself up as any better than he.

I asked Elsie whether she thought I had been showing off in
front of Freddie.

"What?" she said, looking up from her ice in astonishment.

"I only wanted to know," I said.

"I saw no sign of it!" said Elsie.

I went to the telephone and looked up the number of our
hotel. I asked the porter whether the lady in number four had
come home. No, he said, the key was still on the board.

I rang off and went back to Elsie.

"You could come back with me for a bit and tell me your sorrows," she said. "Besides, tomorrow you're leaving *la bella Napoli* forever!"

Once more I climbed all the iron steps with her, past all the people sleeping in the stone caverns of the house. This time the old lady with the crazy eyes wasn't there.

"What kind of a chap is Alfred?" I asked. "You know him, after all."

"I don't really," she said. "He ran away from home with a concert pianist when he was fifteen, and he's been bumming around ever since. For a time he was with a circus, and he's also been an actor, but mostly he's played the piano. Everything he has ever done has been entirely by his own efforts. If he wants to play the piano, he learns it, even if it means starting from scratch. He says he spent years working to become a proper musician, but he never had a proper training. He's very talented."

I felt somewhat relieved. I remarked that if Alfred was such an able fellow he'd certainly be capable of taking Kride back to her hotel.

"Of course!" said Elsie, taking off her dressing-gown.

She was nice and affectionate, and not at all sad when I said good-by, only rather sleepy.

When I got back to the hotel the porter was asleep and Kride's key had disappeared. I chalked the time when we were to be woken on the porter's blackboard and went up to my room.

Next day we traveled straight through to Roveretto, where we changed to a sleeper. Kride was rather quiet, as if she was still angry with me. Or had she found out where I'd spent the night? I didn't ask many questions but looked for a book in my suitcase. I found one with a colored cover. It was about the theater in Shakespeare's time. As soon as I settled down to it I remembered when I had bought it and started reading it. I had got only half-way. The piece of paper I had used as a bookmark, to mark the place when the actor on the ship had asked me whether I was a critic, was still in it. I was astonished at how young I had been then.

Sometime during the day Kride asked me what I was reading.

I told her. I also told her that it had been through that book that I had met Alfred.

A little while later she said, "Naples really is a marvelous place, isn't it? A bit wild and adventurous, but marvelous all the same, don't you think?"

She didn't expect an answer. It sounded like something she had to get off her chest.

My own opinion was that Naples was dirty rather than adventurous, but everyone is entitled to his opinion. I thought it a good thing that most Neapolitans stayed in Naples and didn't travel. You didn't have to see them except when you went there.

3 - Berlin

Yevgenia and Margarete were coming to spend the Christmas of 1938 with us, and a few days beforehand I drove my father's car to the Anhalter Station to meet them. It was a new car and had a low number, which was considered smart. My father was now an important man and had a house in the Heerstrasse, not far from the Havel.

It was a fine, modern house, but it was really Kride's. It was she who busied herself about it all day long. In the summer she devoted herself principally to the garden. It contained trees, bushes, flowerbeds, lawns with flagged walks, and a pergola covered with vines and wistaria. Every year it grew more beautiful under her care.

In the autumn, when the trees and shrubs had shed their last red and yellow leaves, she turned her attention to the conservatory, which was protected on three sides by double glass walls and had a roof of thick green plate glass. An enormous aquarium was built into the fourth wall. Electric heating, thermostatically controlled, ensured that plants and fishes were kept at the right temperature.

Kride had to be surrounded by living things. From her East-European peasant ancestors she inherited the deft fingers which she covered with buckskin gloves when she worked in the garden. As a diplomat's wife she naturally had many social duties, and these required her hands to be well cared for. Many visitors came to the house. They all sang Kride's praises and always wanted to come again. She had no children.

It was a real Berlin winter day, dirty, gray, and misty, with fine snow continually falling. When I got out and locked the car it was beginning to grow dark. It hadn't been really light all day. The streets were full of slush.

Weather like that used to make me long for the south. Uncle Martin wrote to me from time to time, and I had had one or two letters from Aunt Mary, written in English as impeccable as her handwriting. But I didn't go.

Instead I stayed in Berlin, studying philosophy and the history of art. I had joined the National Socialist Students' League and spent a good part of my vacations in camp. It was amazing how clever they were at getting you to go to camp. I had also been to several military training camps. The Army camps were very like the student camps, but better organized. I had last been to an Army camp in the autumn, at the time of our recovery of the Sudetenland. I had been training with a Flak troop at Aachen. For practice we had had to dash thirty times a day from the shelter to the gun and back again. Then the conversations between Hitler and Chamberlain took place at Godesberg and Munich, the newspapers came out with special editions, and I went back to Berlin. We had been told that we would receive a decoration.

Aunt Mary and Uncle Martin wouldn't have understood what it meant when the special editions came out in the evening and suddenly the threat that had been hanging over our heads was over, and the whole of our troop sang and shouted and danced for joy because there wasn't going to be a war. They simply wouldn't have understood, and that's why I didn't go back to Sicily, though I often longed to go. I intended to take my degree next autumn, and then perhaps I'd go abroad for a holiday, perhaps to Sicily.

Yevgenia's train was late. I hung about the platform for a bit, and then a man came and got busy at a blackboard with a pot and a piece of chalk. On the blackboard were the words: "Train No. —— from —— due at —— is —— minutes late."

The man wiped the blackboard with a wet rag before he started writing on it. Some time after he had finished, the words he had written came out thick and clear. Yevgenia's train was going to be eighty-five minutes late, so I telephoned Kride because I knew she had a meal waiting for us.

"How annoying!" she said when I got through. "Will you wait?"

"Yes, if Father doesn't want the car. If he does I'll come home and fetch them later in a taxi. Ask him."

Kride went to ask him, while I held the receiver between my ear and my shoulder, trying to light a cigarette. After a while I heard a buzzing on the line and then a click. I heard Kride's steps on the staircase, and then her voice when she picked up the receiver.

"Hullo!" she said.

"Hullo!" said a man's voice before I had a chance to answer, because I was puffing at my cigarette.

"Who's that? Is that you?" said Kride.

"Yes!" said the voice. "Good evening!"

"Konrad!" Kride exclaimed. "How did you manage to get on the line?"

"I put a coin in the slot and dialed," the voice said. "I wanted to ask whether you were free this evening."

"But someone was on the line! I was talking to Roderich!"

"Is that your stepson?"

"Yes!"

"Perhaps he's rung off!"

"Hullo, Roderich, are you there?"

I didn't answer.

"He has rung off!"

"It looks like it!"

"Are you free this evening?"

"I'm expecting my mother. Please get off the line, Konrad, and ring again in ten minutes!"

"I can't, I'm on the way to Lichterfeld. Are you free or not?"

"My mother's coming," Kride said, but this time she didn't sound so decided.

"I'll pick you up at the corner at half-past eight."

"Make it ten o'clock. By that time I'll have got her to bed."

"All right, ten o'clock then!"

Kride didn't answer. I heard the man grumbling, and then there was another click. I rang off too and went on smoking my cigarette. When I'd finished it I put another coin in the slot and dialed again.

Kride picked up the receiver as soon as the ringing started. "Hullo!" she said.

"Well, what about the car?"

"Oh, it's you! Did you ring off?"

"I was trying to light a cigarette and cut myself off by accident."

"Oh, I thought—"

"Well, what about the car?"

"Are you sure you were cut off?"

"Yes!"

I heard a sigh of relief and I suddenly felt sorry for her. She was young and attractive and was always beautifully groomed when she was busy about the house.

"I'm sorry I kept you waiting," I said. "I rang you again at once but got the busy signal because you hadn't put back the receiver."

"No, I didn't put back the receiver. I thought—I thought you'd be coming on again!" She was quite calm now.

"How stupid! Well, what about the car?"

"Max says you can keep the car as long as you like, if you don't mind waiting."

I rang off and went back to the car. It was still fairly warm inside it, and I sat by the wheel and thought for a while about the conversation I had overheard. I didn't understand exactly what it meant, and in any case it was really no business of mine.

After a while it grew cold, and I got out of the car and locked it. There was still an hour to wait before the train came in. I joined the crowd streaming toward the Potsdamerplatz. Sleet drove slowly past the street lamps, and the faces of all the people were blank and expressionless. They kept their hands in their pockets and trudged along silently, with bent heads. They looked empty, as they always do after a hard day's work. They were longing to get home, to get to a café or a cinema or a restaurant, or to meet a friend or a girl. Their faces were all alike. They resisted the snow and the cold and the damp by withdrawing entirely into themselves.

II

I had gradually discovered that there was also something else behind their emptiness. Berlin was the capital of the Reich, of the new Reich that had now been in existence for several years, and of the future Reich, which was destined to last for a thousand years. All these people were burdened and weighed down by the whole responsibility for the next thousand years, which lay on them like the pressure of many atmospheres.

I had been a student in Berlin for three years and there was a good deal I could have said about this. Anybody could have said it, but nobody did.

When I came back from Sicily I plunged enthusiastically into the new, millenary Berlin. I didn't feel a trace of that curious irritation with things that I had felt when I was ill. I was fit again, and worked and played games and was ready for any call that might be made on me. Nobody likes being a spoilsport. We had a new Reich, and we knew that it demanded sacrifices—great sacrifices, so we were told. We were ready to make great sacrifices. But what did our sacrifices consist of?

We were not called on to make any sacrifices at all. Instead we were called on to take part in a kind of organized agitation in the void. As students we were constantly being called on to march, go to camp, and sing, and we belonged to a uniformed organization. When we had got used to the minor inconveniences, there was nothing difficult about it. On the contrary, it was all far too easy.

All this business of marching, drilling, singing, marking off so many paces, torch-carrying, shouting, and marching again was an end in itself. Those with easygoing natures accepted it as naturally as a heathen accepts the rites by which he keeps evil spirits at bay. The evil spirits by which we were plagued were all on paper. They consisted of a thousand tricks by which we could be plagued from the beginning to the end of term, all of which made work more difficult. The only way to escape them was to submit to the rites expected of you as punctiliously as an Australian aborigine submits to the ordeal of rolling about on red-hot stones. You knew in advance that the results wouldn't be fatal, and to that extent it was tolerable. But the burden clung to you; it was like having leaden soles on your feet. It made all independent work more difficult. It led ultimately to one's being able to do one's prescribed task and no more. All free speculation, all independent intellectual inquiry, became impossible.

At first we thought that it was just chance, just a result of the wrong people happening to be in positions of authority. But in the course of time it became clear that it wasn't the result of chance but of deliberate policy. Philosophers, thinkers, idle speculators were not wanted. A few slogans were repeated at every meeting and at every camp. Down with intellectuals and idle speculators, they said. What was wanted was men of action, men ready to believe first and think afterward. It was a wonderful time for the practitioners of applied science, for chemists, physicists, architects, doctors, lawyers, and efficiency experts. But it was a very bad time for those whose field was pure science or pure knowledge. They were practically done for. For several years now they had been regimented, turned into a kind of civil service.

It was all so simple. You still had to pass exams, but they were said to be easier than the exams in the old days, in the crisis period before the new Reich came into being. All that the organizers of the new regime cared about was the masses. The old professors, observing with dismay the deterioration in the standards of their students, said that the new generation was entirely lacking in quality. The students were regarded with suspicion by both sides. In addition, our faculty was exposed to the sharpest criticism. The spirit of pure science had reigned undisputed in German universities for more than a century. What was a chemist or a physicist or even a doctor who took no interest in theory? A contemptible specialist. But now everything was reversed. A specialist was now a good man, and those who devoted themselves to the pursuit of pure knowledge were low and contemptible intellectuals.

It is possible to study medicine and incidentally roll about on hot stones in one's spare time; it does not prevent one later on from being able to cut out an appendix or paint a pharynx. But is it possible to be a pure scientist if one is forced at the same time to believe that the progress, the development, the whole future of mankind depend on a handful of primitive and unproved slogans? Therein lay the dilemma of the university to which I and thousands of others belonged. It was with this dilemma that we woke in the morning; it accompanied us when we ate and drank and engaged in our military sports, and it confronted us in forming our philosophy of life. When we worked we were not scholars, honorably devoted to the pursuit of pure

knowledge, but unworldly eccentrics who eliminated ourselves
from contemporary life. Oh, no, we were not martyrs. A few of us,
like the young Schindler, who drove to the Bodensee, leaving behind his Hölderlin fragments, shot ourselves, and others went
abroad. The rest of us capitulated in the face of the dilemma.

An unholy atmosphere hung over Berlin during those years.
People walked past one another with blank, empty faces, entirely
withdrawn into themselves. Nobody trusted anyone else. Those
willing to swim with the stream were sought out and given jobs
in the state machine. Once they were in it they attracted others
who were willing to swim with the stream, and the result was that
the whole country was covered with a network of people provid-
ing each other with mutual support, a network of terribly well-
intentioned people for whom the supreme commandment was to
avoid conflict and never get into anybody's bad books. Conflict
and tension no longer existed. Everyone crept into his own cubbyhole, shone in his own cubbyhole, excelled in his own cubbyhole. But something was missing. The whole thing was a tremendous agitation in the void. It was all too simple.

I sometimes suspected my father of having gone over to the
specialists' side. All Kride's dreams had come true. She had built
herself a beautiful house and had many guests. What kind of
guests? In the first few years, up to the Olympic Games, they included many friends from abroad. They talked, argued, let themselves be convinced, or tried to convince us. But gradually they
stopped coming. They gave up visiting Germany. But what did
that matter? Other guests came in their place, German guests, people whom we had not used to know. They behaved very well and
set greater store on formalities than the foreigners. The character
of the conversation altered too. It consisted largely of the exchange of assurances of extreme optimism. There was, of course,
whispered criticism of minor defects, but everyone was full of
confidence for the future. Army officers came, and people from
the ministries, and later people from the party machine. These
people's attitude was even more positive and less critical. Their
job was to see no difficulties. After all, what difficulties were there?

It was hard to say. Everything was going so wonderfully. Ever
since the march into the Rhineland things had been going better

and better. But the better things went with us, the more hostile foreign countries became, and the more cut off we were. You could buy a ticket at one of the big state or semistate tourist organizations and cruise off twenty coasts, or you could, if you wanted to, dash through a foreign country in a coach, with prearranged stops for coffee and rooms for the night booked in advance. But you were always in a group, and contact with the country through which you passed was lacking.

In the course of time foreign countries loomed collectively in our minds like an ominous, dark cloud, full of brooding, evil powers. It no longer occurred to anyone to travel to Paris or Rome or Moscow to see and talk things over with a friend. A decent German no longer had friends abroad. We cut ourselves off and no longer knew what lay beyond our frontiers. Things you don't know grow dangerous and sinister. Foreign countries hated and wanted to exterminate us. Aha! But we'd show them, and the sooner the better. Perhaps we'd exterminate them. More and more of the fine threads that linked men across the frontiers were broken, and the broken ends were used to weave the German carpet thicker. But it wasn't a substitute.

I often wondered whether my father did not see this, for he was a far-seeing man. He had a French friend, an international lawyer. They had corresponded for years, and after the new house was built he was invited to stay with us. He came twice, but when he was asked a third time the invitation was politely declined. What was the meaning of that?

"Certain differences of principle," my father answered when I asked him, "on policy toward minorities."

Was that the reason he didn't visit us any longer?

At that time we all lived not in the present, but under the spell of the future. This was hammered into us all the time. Everyone said that what mattered was not what was, but what was going to be. We were going through a short but inevitable transition period, calculated to turn the Germany of the thirties into the Germany of the forties, and to convert my father from the man he was when I was at school to the man he was when I was a student in Berlin.

His character was full of contradictions. He still had the gift of putting other people, particularly older people, at their ease and understanding and sympathizing with their difficulties. But he also had a number of blind spots. There were certain things that he had the gift of not seeing; he just acted as if they didn't exist; and this was a dangerous gift. Earlier he had always avoided people of the loud, successful, pushing type, but now he had too much to do with them to be able to afford such a luxury. At the same time he was quite capable of denying his own nature to the extent of failing to see their unpleasant characteristics. Sometimes this led to contradictions that were as comic as they were tragic.

III

One of his attractive weaknesses was for his black uniform. It suited him admirably because he still had his tall, slim, ex-cavalryman's figure. A retired cavalry captain is, of course, something quite different from a retired infantry captain. To Kride's great delight, he started wearing an octagonal monocle. She liked going out with him when he wore his uniform. They attracted attention at Horcher's or the Kaiserhof.

But all these things were externals. He ate and drank more, and his face had grown a shade fuller. On the other hand he worked tremendously hard. There was nobody who was better informed than he about the world's diplomatic and trade relations. His knowledge was immense, and he had it all at his fingertips. He was behind most of the foreign policy decisions that were made, and he was indispensable. He sometimes said the word "indispensable" with a touch of pride. One is something when one is indispensable to the great ones of this world.

All the same, I think I sometimes detected a trace of uncertainty in him, the flaring up of a terrible fear that slumbered deep within. He didn't show it openly. You had to have sharp ears and to know him well to be able to detect it. It only came out in rare conversations—sometimes on an evening when we had no visitors and Kride had gone to bed early. We talked as we had in earlier years, but as I listened I was astonished at the strange trend of his thoughts and at how often they seemed to move in circles.

"It's no use attempting to disguise the fact," he said. "We're steering toward a war. Everything depends on who's ready first. The side that's ready first will win. That's the situation nowadays. Wars are won by a country's economy. I'm glad we're starting with the four-year plan immediately after the Olympic Games."

"Are you certain we should win a war?"

"There'll be losses, of course, but we mustn't think of them," he said. "We need the Ukraine. HE says we need the Ukraine."

"And what do you say?"

"Well, you see, there are two lines at the office. I'll call them line A and line B. According to line A we need the Ukraine. According to line B it would be better to ally ourselves with the Russians against the English. I'm in favor of Line B."

It was a continual matter of argument whenever we had visitors. The soldiers and the aristocrats were in favor of line A. The big industrialists were partly in favor of line A. There were also some naval officers who came to our house—old gentlemen with white hair and severe faces, with a lot of gold braid on their sleeves. They were very reserved and spoke with pursed lips. Like my father, they were in favor of line B. After they had gone so far as actually to express their opinion, the other visitors always said that of course the Navy was for plan B because it would mean that they would get more battleships, and because of the old bone they had to pick with the British because of Scapa Flow. No wonder they were in favor of line B! That used to make everybody laugh, but the naval gentlemen then became more reserved than ever and said they were in favor of plan B because in a struggle for command of the sea there could be no compromise. This sounded mysterious, and nobody understood it. Those people were obsessed with the command of the sea.

Plan A and plan B were not really plans but symbols, symbols of our torn and divided world. My father, like a jeweler with his most prized possessions, was able to produce them from his showcase, polish them, compare their weight, their brightness, their cut, and then put them back again. In his showcase he had not one plan but two; he was doubly rich. If he was forced to say which was the plan of his choice, the one in which he really believed, he became uncertain, and a gleam of anxiety came into his eyes.

"That's not for me to decide," he would say. "The decision rests with HIM. The power and the responsibility are HIS. Perhaps one day both plans will be put into execution."

"That would mean another war on two fronts."

"The decision rests with HIM."

That was as far as we'd ever get. We had reached the barrier, the invisible glass wall, the HIM who kept everything in his own hands. All the administrators, generals, journalists who came to my father's house were exceedingly thoughtful, intelligent, conscientious men. But when it came to making the final decision they abdicated. For that only HE was competent.

No matter what we started with, we always arrived at the same point. The only alternative was to talk about harmless, trivial family matters.

One evening we were listening to the radio, to a broadcast from Sweden. My father understood Swedish and he followed with interest a report of the proceedings of the Council of State. He translated the most important points for me. When the broadcast was over he remarked casually, "The Swedes have the best system of government in Europe. They have a king, but it's a minister's duty to express his opinion even if it's contrary to the king's decision. If he fails to do so, he can be tried and punished."

"That sounds very sensible," I said. "Why don't we have the same system?"

My father started out of his daydream. "Oh, with us that would be quite impossible," he said. "A system like that can only work in Sweden."

That was the end of the matter. The fundamental dogma had been touched on.

Another time we were sitting and talking about Kokoschka. I had been to the Exhibition of Degenerate Art and had seen a Kokoschka there. It was a very fine painting, with Kokoschka's peculiar blending of brilliant color and movement.

"You once had a weakness for Kokoschka," I said.

"Yes, I certainly did," he said enthusiastically. "There was an exhibition of his work at Vienna when I went there that time, don't you remember? The German Goya—"

"Why was he included with the degenerates?" I interrupted.

"I haven't the slightest idea. I must remember to ask the head of the department at the Reichskulturkammer."

The head of the department concerned was quite possibly a former bricklayer, or had a diploma in agriculture or for teaching German shorthand. But now he was the head of a department in the Reich Chamber of Culture and made decisions in HIS name. They could, therefore, not be questioned.

In the end we avoided all conversations of this sort. But the invisible worm that gnawed at us, the threatening dilemma, the unholy Berlin atmosphere, the split between one's private views and those publicly prescribed, were capable of insinuating themselves into the most harmless chatter.

"Sometimes I think I'd like to be your age," my father said. "D'you know what I'd do? I'd go to Africa and farm. I'd do honorable, back-breaking work; get up at five o'clock every morning, work hard all day, and tumble into bed exhausted every evening. Wouldn't it be wonderful?"

"With your injured back you wouldn't be able to do it," I said.

"That's perfectly true," he said. "It was only an idea. Damn that war!"

"Are you dissatisfied?" I asked.

"Dissatisfied?" he said, sitting up. "Not in the least! After all, I've got somewhere, I'm indispensable. I couldn't leave my post even if I wanted to. The Navy people rely on me entirely. How could I clear out and leave the field clear to all the upstarts and yes-men who are now streaming into the office? What are needed are men who know their business!"

There we were, back at the same point again. He sipped at his drink, relaxed and contented after his day's work. The telephone rang, and we heard Kride answer. She talked for five minutes, ten minutes. Then she came in and blew us a kiss.

"Can I take the car?" she said. "I want to run over to the Steuwens', they've got a new Bokhara carpet."

Off she went, smiling at us. My father sat back again.

"A new Bokhara carpet!" he said. "That's something we never dreamed of when we lived in the Nissels' little house next door to Yevgenia's! But that's what women are like, you know. There's always something they simply must have, a poodle or a Persian

rug. But what a change since the old days, by the grace of God!"
There was no telling whether he was joking or talking seriously.
Suddenly he looked at me and laughed in a slightly embarrassed
way.

"I liked living in that old house," I said. "It wasn't a bad time.
It was so quiet!"

"Yes, I liked it too. They were the happiest years of my life.
But this place is something, after all, isn't it? Do you like your
work?"

"I don't know. Sometimes it all seems so pointless."

"That's because of the times we live in," he said. "They're completely pointless. Everybody spends his time blowing smoke into
his neighbor's window. That's what the party machine does to the
state machine, and vice versa; and then there's the Army in between."

He fell silent and filled his glass. He had a wonderful capacity
for drink. He held the bottle with a perfectly steady hand.
Though relaxed and at ease, he sat perfectly upright, holding his
head slightly to one side, watching the golden-yellow liquid pouring into his glass. He had his own way of looking at things. Sometimes I thought that he looked at the whole world through
cognac-colored spectacles.

IV

All this could be read in the faces of Berliners going home from
work on a winter evening; or rather it could not be read; it could
only be felt. They withdrew into themselves because the outside
world was full of contradictions. During the day they were cheerful, busy, energetic, patient, confident, optimistic, childishly gay,
and entirely without fear. When they were working or enjoying
themselves or making love, while they were gathered round the
kitchen table or sitting in cafés or restaurants or watching the
Avus races, they were the liveliest, cleverest, the most quick-witted
people that it was possible to imagine.

But at night, in the streets, in places where people gathered
without knowing one another, their faces altered. Berlin's catas-
rophe threw its shadow ahead. In the streets at night people's

faces were blank, empty, dead, with the signs of the future upon them. Perhaps the inhabitants of Pompeii and St. Pierre and other towns destined to be overwhelmed showed the same signs in advance of the calamity. Perhaps they too began walking like phantoms through the gullies of their streets, listless, apathetic, and with bowed heads, filled with awareness of the inevitable.

I remember only the deep excitement that one sometimes felt when one or another of the tremendous ceremonies took place in the city. Some of them, like the air-raid precautions exercises carried out with plaster bombs in the city center, were distinctly, almost comically, sober. Others were impressive, like the torch-light processions or the thanksgiving service in the Lustgarten. Others again were wild, unbridled, orgiastic, like the celebrations for the Austrian Anschluss. I remember standing jammed in the middle of the crowd, shouting till I was hoarse, completely carried away by the ear-splitting roar that we kept up, which rose and fell like the swelling of an organ. It was just like being carried away by the swelling of the organ in church, but we were not in church but standing in the street, and instead of organ music we were surrounded by the roar of human voices and shrill hysterical "Heils!" interrupted by the nervous staccato of the radio announcer coming through the big loudspeakers. I found myself clinging to a second-floor window in the Ministry of Civil Aviation. I don't know how I got there. It must have been by way of the lightning conductor.

I should like to know whether the little man who stood next to me in the Wilhelmplatz is still alive. He was so small that he scarcely came up to other people's shoulders. But he had a stick with two small mirrors attached to either end of it, arranged like a periscope, and he used it to obtain a view of the historic balcony. At such moments everything was historic. The marksmen strained their eyes from their hiding places behind the chimneys of the Reich Chancellery, and from time to time one of the men for whom we were waiting would appear. One of them, with his hat pulled down over his eyes, was HE. Another, carrying a white staff in his hand, was his champion. Everyone yelled as if possessed, and I looked sideways and saw the little man beside me, standing with his back to the balcony and staring into his mirror, in which he could see it all, and shrilly yelling "Heil! Heil!" into it.

After these celebrations you were left exhausted, pumped dry, with the roar of the crowd still ringing in your ears like the sound of the sea retained by a shell. You felt you were taking part in the present, that nothing whatever mattered in comparison with this unique, tremendous, overpowering present.

One night when I had returned to my room in the Wörthstrasse after one of these occasions, which had lasted half the day, I had an extraordinary dream, or rather nightmare. I saw a huge bird, a crane, standing over Berlin, continually stretching its long beak down over the city. The bird was so huge that its legs towered above the buildings. It kept lowering its beak and snatching up whatever it could reach—houses, monuments, banks, buildings, people. The people stuck in its beak, struggling. Some fell out again, but others disappeared down its huge gray throat. The bird was tremendously energetic; it was an ostrich, a pelican, a crane. It kept on eating indefatigably. The city gradually grew quiet and the shouting died away, and suddenly I was alone in the middle of a huge empty square, such as at that time there had never yet been in all Berlin. I stood quite still, to avoid attracting the bird's attention. So long as it kept on eating I didn't feel afraid, but when everything grew quiet I felt afraid. I knew that this was wrong, because so long as one wasn't afraid the bird would do one no harm. But, as I was afraid, it turned its head and looked at me out of its age-old, Archimedean eyes, and it seemed to be interested in me. Its eyes were circular and lidless, like the mouths of guns. Slowly, very slowly, it approached. There was a reddish glare, I knew its eyes were on me, and, knowing its hungry beak was about to descend, I screamed.

A doctor named Friedrich Feldmann lived in the room next to mine. He came in and found me sitting up in bed. My heart was thumping, but after a while it stopped. I got out of bed and looked for my cigarettes.

"What was the matter?" Feldmann asked.

I told him my dream.

"My God!" he exclaimed. "What suggested all that to you?"

I told him I had been reading Plutarch a few days before, and perhaps because of some short circuit . . .

"What makes you want to study philosophy and the history of art?" he asked. I told him I didn't know. But the question fascinated me.

"Oh, well!" he said. "No wonder you have such dreams! Why don't you take up something practical?"

"Why did you take up medicine?" I asked, somewhat nettled.

"Because I want to be something," he said. "My father wasn't a great man like yours is, you know. He used to play the fiddle in a café. We never had any money. I want to have something of my own, you understand—a practice, a house, a car." He puffed thoughtfully at his cigarette. "What a dream to have!" he went on. "You ought to go to a psychologist sometime! He might be able to tell you something."

"Are you a psychologist?"

"Good lord, no," he said. "I'm something practical, I'm a surgeon. I'll be needed sometime."

"Yes," I said, "when the crane comes."

"Don't talk nonsense!" he answered. "I don't want anything to do with any crane."

All this provided food for thought when one walked the streets of Berlin at night and looked at the faces of the people.

v

I crossed the Potsdamerplatz, and at the corner I knocked into somebody. We both apologized and were just going on when the man looked at me sharply. A street lamp was behind him, so I couldn't make him out clearly against the light. All I could see was that he wasn't wearing a hat or overcoat, and had a mop of untidy hair. I took a step backward and recognized him. He was Alfred Karawan, the pianist from Naples.

"Good heavens!" we both exclaimed, and I asked him how long he had been back in Germany.

"Three weeks," he said.

"And how are you?"

"All right, thanks. And you?"

"Oh, I'm fine, thanks!"

"Shocking weather today, so damp and foggy."

"Yes, it's much nicer in Naples now! What's Posilippo doing?"

"It's still there!"

I thought we'd go on chatting for another five minutes in this stimulating manner and then say good-by. I was glad to see him; he looked exactly as he had always looked—untidy, but perfectly self-possessed and as explosive as a loaded revolver.

"Where are you going?" he suddenly asked. I told him. I'd left my car outside the Askanischer Hof and was meeting Yevgenia and Margarete in about twenty minutes.

"I'll come a little way with you," he said. We strolled toward the Anhalter Station. Instead of an overcoat he had a shabby scarf around his neck.

"What are you doing now?" I asked.

He shrugged his shoulders and muttered something unintelligible. Then he pulled himself together and said, "I've spent the last two nights in a dosshouse."

"No work?"

He shrugged his shoulders again. "Nothing that suits me."

"What suits you?"

"Not unskilled labor in a factory."

I waited for him to go on, without asking any more questions, and he went on. It was a staccato, sulky monologue. He was obviously in a bad way.

"I've been away for five years, and you can't imagine how things have altered," he said. "Abroad I could get work as a pianist in a bar or somewhere whenever I liked. But here you have to have papers, and I haven't any papers. Before you're allowed to play the piano you have to be a member of the Reichskulturkammer. Just imagine that! God knows what papers you have to have before you're allowed to sit down and play a few dance tunes. What a bloody country!"

I had heard complaints of this kind so often that they got on my nerves. "Why didn't you stay abroad, then?" I asked.

He shrugged his shoulders. "I don't know myself. It must have been homesickness or something. You heard and read so much about Germany that I thought I'd come and see it for myself. The last place I was in was Lisbon, where I played at a Jewish club."

"You'd better not talk so loud," I said. "People don't like hearing that sort of thing."

"I'm not talking to them, I'm talking to you. They all spoke German at that club, and suddenly it made me feel homesick."

We reached the station, but he showed no sign of saying good-by. I went around the car, kicking the tires, trying the handles, and tapping the windows. Everything was in order.

"Your car?" he asked.

"It belongs to my old man."

"Don't talk so arrogantly!" he said.

It was absurd. There he was, obviously down on his luck, and yet he could take offense at the way I said something.

"Have you had anything to eat today?" I asked.

"No."

"Come along, then, we'll go to the Bols-Stube. I've still got a quarter of an hour."

"You seem to have plenty of dough!"

I said nothing. I saw I was going to be lending him money again. It couldn't be helped. You can't travel with a man in a ship all the way from Bremerhaven to Catania, meet him again in Naples, and then leave him in the lurch in Berlin. Apart from that, I could afford it. He chose a cold dish that they had ready, and ate hungrily but with restraint. He was a very self-controlled human being. I felt my old liking for him returning.

"First of all I'll see about a room for you," I said. I searched in my wallet for a piece of paper and wrote down the address of my room, as well as the nearest underground station and tram stop. He carefully studied the address, the message I scribbled for my landlady, and my telephone number.

"But what about you?" he said.

"I'm staying at home for Christmas. Ring me up, and we'll go out together."

"You mean you're living at your father's, and that this is his telephone number?"

"Yes, why?"

"Oh, nothing in particular! Many thanks. At any rate, now I've got somewhere to spend the night."

"Do you need money?"

"One always needs money!"

"Will fifty marks be enough?"

"You're just like Father Christmas."

I gave him fifty marks and got up. Outside fine snow was still falling and the stream of people had grown thinner. That's what's so remarkable about Berlin. You walk along, thinking about nothing in particular, and then you bump into somebody from Naples. I paid the bill and took my overcoat.

"Haven't you got an overcoat?" I asked.

He shook his head. "I've got nothing except what you see me in," he said without the slightest embarrassment. I took the bunch of keys from my pocket—the key for the car, the latchkey of my father's house, and the key of the wardrobe in my room. I removed the wardrobe key from the ring. Perhaps it was a bit of a risk, but I thought I'd take it.

"In the wardrobe there's a coat that'll fit you," I said. "I don't need it; I've got this one. You can take anything else you need as well!"

"Have you got books there too?" he asked.

I nodded.

"Good!" he said. "I don't think you're Father Christmas. I think you're St. Martin; you know, the one with the coat!"

He seemed a little moved when he took the key and put it in his pocket, and when I walked away he looked after me. I hadn't done it for his sake, I'd done it out of gratitude. I'd walked so often through the streets of Berlin, hoping to run into somebody whom I could talk to, somebody with whom I had something in common. I had spent many evenings in Berlin and had talked to the most extraordinary people over a glass of beer. Sometimes I'd paid, but generally I'd been stood a beer in return, and we'd talk about the weather, or the new subway, or the Sudeten Germans, or Winston Churchill, or Max Schmeling, and part with no obligation on either side. I'd talked to taxi drivers, policemen, night watchmen, prostitutes, billiard players, but the talk had always been Berlin talk, an exchange of words leaving no echo behind. But here was someone who was glad because I had done him a service. This made me so grateful and happy that I whistled as I mounted the steps of the Anhalter Station. Berlin had suddenly become a slightly friendlier, a slightly less lonely place.

VI

Yevgenia and Margarete arrived as expected, exactly eighty-five minutes late. Yevgenia had grown stouter. She greeted me cordially but then lost her temper because Margarete's briefcase was missing. I climbed into the compartment and found it. A porter fastened Yevgenia's trunk on his shoulder with a strap, took her suitcase and another small case, and tramped ahead of us.

"There was an accident on the line!" Margarete burst out, happy and excited. "A freight train collided with a passenger train, and five people were killed!"

She was just at the age when girls are neither one thing nor the other, the age when they are most uninteresting to a young man. She was tall, had fat legs, and looked silly and affected, except when she was talking about the train accident. Then her face looked quite pretty and nice because she wasn't thinking about herself.

"Oh?" I said.

"Just think of it, five people were killed!"

"Margarete, don't trample through the dirt like that!" said Yevgenia. "Has Josefine arrived yet?"

"No," I answered. "Is she coming?"

"Hasn't she written to Kride?"

"Kride's said nothing about it to me!"

"Josefine's got herself into a fine mess, Rodie. Just think—" Margarete burst out, her face looking even more radiant than when she had told me about the accident.

"Margarete, you know you're to keep your mouth shut, and not say a word about it to anyone!" Yevgenia said.

"But we must tell Roderich!"

"Be quiet, Margarete!"

The girl's face grew uncertain and affected again. She stared at a Luftwaffe officer walking across the square. His chest was covered with decorations, which he must have won in Spain.

"Smart, isn't he?" Margarete said confidentially and quietly to me.

"Who's smart?"

"That officer!"

"He's in the Condor Legion."

"How do you know?"

"Margarete, for heaven's sake get out of the habit of staring at men like that! Anybody would think you were completely uneducated!" Yevgenia exclaimed.

I was glad when we reached the car.

"An Admiral!" Margarete shrieked.

"You mustn't stare at every officer you pass!"

"I mean the car, *Mamushka!*"

"What car?"

"Roderich's car!"

And so it went on. The girl was a perfect pest, and so she remained all through the holiday.

After dinner Yevgenia made a revelation. She said she hadn't made it sooner because she hadn't wanted to spoil our appetites. I think she put off telling us as long as she possibly could.

"Josefine's expecting a baby!" she said.

Kride flared up, and my father whistled through his teeth and smiled slightly. We were sitting in the conservatory, and the fish were moving about in their heated aquarium.

"Aren't you going to send Margarete to bed?" Kride asked, but Margarete answered first.

"There's no reason why I shouldn't stay," she announced. "Josefine told me first! The father's a married man with five children!"

She smiled agreeably and sat back in her chair. What she said was perfectly true. Josefine had come home and told her mother she was pregnant. She had also said that there was no point in fretting about the father, who was a happily married man.

"Ah! I knew it!" Yevgenia exclaimed.

"Knew what?" Kride asked. But Yevgenia didn't know what it was that she knew. She was worried to death, as she had a perfect right to be. She went on lamenting for a while, until Kride got up and said she had a headache and must go and get Josefine's room ready. Josefine had sent a telegram saying she was coming by the night train and was arriving at eight-thirty next morning.

Next morning I met her at the station. I half expected to see a broken woman getting out of the train, with the marks of destiny on her face, but instead she came tripping along, carrying a small leather case, very smartly dressed indeed and with no noticeable characteristics other than looking remarkably attractive. That's what everybody thought, particularly the visitors who came to see us over Christmas. Josefine was the center of attention, and heaven knows she deserved to be.

VII

Sometimes Yevgenia was plunged in gloom, but every now and then her old temperament broke through. Then she stormed around the house, making the welkin ring with her flat Russian vowels and rolled rrs. When she was sad she sat in an armchair in the conservatory, sighing melodramatically.

"Oh, Josefine, how could you?" she exclaimed.

Josefine would sit by her side, fondle her hand, purr, and pacify her.

Everyone cursed Yevgenia and her family, but everyone was glad they were there. They provided a welcome break in the monotonous routine of the house. Everyone was glad except Kride, the blond, proud, superior Kride, the childless housewife and gardener.

I sat in the sitting room, listening to Yevgenia play the piano. She didn't play as well as she had in the old days when we lived in the little house next door to her; or was it that my ear had been less pampered then? In the interval I had heard a lot of music, because plenty of good music was played in Berlin, where a lot of money was spent on Beethoven and Furtwängler but not on Hindemith. But who wanted to hear Hindemith? Who could understand him? At a cabaret an old half-blind entertainer recited comic couplets about Hindemith, and people laughed.

Yevgenia played Beethoven, the Moonlight Sonata. No, she didn't play well, but the love with which she played enabled one to forget her deficiencies in technique. She was in love with this music. Perhaps she was in love with Beethoven, or perhaps she was thinking of someone else, the dead von Haringen, perhaps, or Margarete's father. Nobody knew who Margarete's father was; perhaps he had five children too. Perhaps he wasn't a sixty-seven-year-old *tenente colonello*, but a young Don Giovanni, a young *capitano* with a black mustache and a shrewish wife at home. But whoever he was, if he had never existed Margarete would never have existed either. True, the child was a perfect pest; all the same, one wouldn't want to be without her. A slight irregularity had occurred, and the result had been Margarete. Slight irregularities of that kind were always occurring. Just think of Josefine, for instance. Only a moment or two ago she had been sitting on the floor at Yevgenia's feet, purring and wheedling and saying, "But *Mamushka*, Mummy darling, it's not so bad, after all, and just think, you'll be a grandmother!" And now Yevgenia, who had been groaning melodramatically, was sitting at the piano, playing the Moonlight Sonata, and Josefine, after prowling around the room, came and sat on the arm of my chair.

"Mummy plays well, doesn't she?" she said in my ear. I said she did and went on listening, though less attentively than before because Josefine was wearing a faint but delightful perfume. She was quite unconcerned. She leaned forward and laughed slightly. Her black hair was combed close to her head, her tiny ears looked tinier than ever, her head was shaped like Nefertiti's, and her dress was cut low.

Tum-tata, tum-tata, tum-tata, tum-tum, Yevgenia played, completely absorbed in the Moonlight Sonata.

"Are you angry with me?" Josefine asked.

"Why should I be angry with you?"

"You're not angry with me, then?"

"No, of course not!"

She leaned forward slightly again. She had a lovely firm bosom, with which, quite accidentally of course, she grazed my ear; then her hair tickled my ear. I looked up and saw her black eyes. She had remarkable eyes; they were untransparent, opaque. They reminded me slightly of Alfred Karawan's eyes. No, the resemblance didn't occur to me then, but later. As I made no further movement Josefine got up and went on prowling around the room and purring. That made one less person in the house who was angry with her.

I went to see Alfred Karawan and asked him to come and see us and play the piano. My father knew the head of a broadcasting station who might be able to give him work.

His face brightened. "That would be something to start with," he said. "Head of broadcasting station very good. Head of broadcasting station always good."

"Don't have any exaggerated hopes," I said. "It's only an idea of mine."

"May God grant you many such ideas!"

He turned up at our house in a new suit, which he had bought at Brummer's. He looked exactly as a young pianist is supposed to look. He kissed Kride's hand and thought she looked younger than she had in Naples. He kissed Yevgenia's hand and Josefine's hand, and was impressed by her. He then kissed Margarete's hand, thereby demonstrating great diplomatic adroitness.

He seemed to like talking to Josefine. In the presence of visitors Josefine was very reserved; perhaps she was afraid of Kride's eyes, but I had the feeling that she didn't dislike him.

One of the guests that afternoon was a keen young naval lieutenant, who had spent two years abroad. That was all I knew about him. He had good clean-cut features, and he was said to be in Intelligence. After coffee we went into Kride's drawing room, where the big piano was. I asked Alfred to play. He began with classical music. His expression was aloof and slightly haughty, as it always was when he played. Everyone put on an important expression to listen to the classical music and tried to conceal his yawns. Even Yevgenia, who preferred playing to listening, yawned when he played Schumann.

Unobtrusively he started playing lighter music. When he played something from *The Merry Widow* nobody felt tired any more. Yevgenia started humming the tune, and the gentlemen looked at each other significantly. Then he played more modern things, including some tunes from the old days, and I said to Kride, "Don't you remember that? That's the tune from the film we went to after you came back after your first term!"

"So it is!" said Kride. She walked across the room to where my father was sitting, sat on the arm of his chair, and said, "Good old Max!"

Then Alfred played still more modern music, music that wasn't known in Germany at all. The naval lieutenant was delighted, but the other guests began yawning again. He played some Weill and some Spoliansky, just as he had on the ship, but I saw my father didn't like it. Alfred also took a theme from Bach, played it through perfectly seriously, and then turned it into a fox trot. My father started but didn't say anything, and then Alfred played something from *The Gypsy Baron* and everyone was happy again.

Afterward I drove him home, and he explained that he always began with something boring. That made them so grateful when he started something else.

"What's your favorite music?" I asked him.

He laughed and answered, "What's yours? The classics, of course, I suppose!"

"I've got no favorite music," I said.

"You'll laugh," he said, "but I prefer playing Bach to anything else."

"And then you turn it into a fox trot! You startled my father. He goes to the St. Matthew Passion every year. I think he was the only one who noticed it."

"Then he doesn't understand Bach," Alfred said. "Bach wrote wonderful fox trots and tangos."

"You're crazy!"

"It's true," said Alfred.

After he had finished playing he had spent a long time talking to the young lieutenant from the Ministry of Marine. I thought they had been talking about the forbidden musicians, but Alfred explained that the lieutenant had taken a great interest in what foreign languages he spoke, and what dialects of what languages.

"Then you may find yourself working for the secret service for a change," I said. He shrugged his shoulders.

"Who knows?" he said. "Why not?"

In the meantime my father gave him an introduction to the head of the broadcasting station. First he had to promise to eliminate forbidden musicians from his repertoire and never to make

fox trots out of Johann Sebastian Bach. Soon afterward he began to provide the musical background for the little plays that
were produced on the women's hour. He didn't do at all badly out
of it.

VIII

That year we gave a big New Year's Eve party. It was a very
large party indeed, and among the guests you saw a lot of faces
that were generally to be seen only in the newsreels—generals, ad-
mirals, and such people. There were also friends of my father's
from his student days and from the war years, as well as his present colleagues. And there were some younger men with hard, cold
faces, who worked in the newly created offices and provided a kind
of competition for my father's generation. A minister actually
came that evening, a big, powerfully built man in a well-fitting
uniform with a sash. He had an aristocratic name, and Kride was
extraordinarily proud at his having turned up. On these occasions
Kride was just as she had been when she was a girl.

"Oh, Rodie!" she said, flinging herself into a chair beside me.
"Isn't this wonderful? This is what it used to be like at home, in
St. Petersburg."

"How old were you in St. Petersburg?"

She looked at me radiantly. "So high?" she said. "Well, perhaps
those days'll come again!"

"Do you think the Stamms will be given a title for your sake?"

"Don't be silly!" she said. "It isn't titles that matter, but all the
people and the excitement. I can live without a title, but I must
have things going on all around me!"

She jumped to her feet and walked quickly away. What I'd said
must have struck a chord in her, because I heard her talking to
the minister. Did he think there was going to be a war? The minister was reserved. There had been enough scandals because of
things that ministers had said in the hearing of the press which
had afterward had to be denied. But Kride was very attractive,
and he liked talking to her; it flattered him.

"It's possible that there may be a war," he said. "Perhaps only a
little one!"

Kride was gay and happy and fluttered away again. Soon afterward the minister paid my father a compliment about his charming wife. "You shouldn't keep her shut up in Berlin, Herr Doktor," he said. "With a temperament like that she ought to be in the country. On an estate!"

"If I were a younger man, I'd go to Africa and farm," my father said. "But with these relics of the war in my back it's out of the question."

Everyone was cheerful and full of good-fellowship. A very important man was sitting in the conservatory, a Reichsleiter with a pale, pasty face and a little mustache. He had brought his secretary with him because his wife couldn't come. She never could come. Every now and then the Reichsleiter took off his spectacles, polished them, and talked to one or another of the hard-faced young men about the danger in the East. His secretary listened breathlessly. She always listened breathlessly when he spoke. He took a knife from a cake dish and used it to show the way to the East.

"The first thrust," he announced, "is as far as the Urals. Then a pause for regrouping, followed by another thrust, into the heart of Siberia."

There was dancing and drinking, and I felt sorry Yevgenia wasn't at the party. She had retired to her room with Margarete. I went to see them. Margarete was lying on the bed in her dressing-gown, pretending not to hear the voices and the music. Yevgenia had drawn a small table up to her chair and was busy with her astrological cards. What she was doing was strictly forbidden. For several years astrology had been absolutely banned in Germany. Astrologers had been banned, just like Bible Leaguers.

"What are you?" Yevgenia asked after a time. "What was the time and date of your birth?"

Margarete got up from the bed and came and joined us. I gave Yevgenia the information she wanted and went downstairs and fetched a bottle of champagne. When I came back she had laid out her cards and consulted a table, and she was now rearranging the cards according to some system.

"Bad!" she said several times. "Bad, but not very bad! Could be worse! You'll survive!"

"What is he, Mummy?" Margarete asked.

"Born under Aquarius. What else could he be?" Yevgenia replied, as if she were stating a self-evident proposition.

"Oh, Aquarius," said Margarete in as matter-of-fact a way as if her mother had told her I was, say, a cabinet maker.

"Your health!" I said. But they were too busy with my horoscope to take any interest in champagne. They were like a couple of sibyls looking into the future.

"You'll be a good soldier, Rurik," Yevgenia announced after a while. "Very good soldier, Rurik!" This was new to me.

"Aha!" I said. "Here's your health, Yevgenia!"

"You'll see, you'll be a very good soldier."

"Very good private," I said. "Ha! Ha!"

"Why don't you want to be a good soldier?" said Margarete, starting to drink from her glass.

"What is Margarete?" I asked. Yevgenia sighed.

"Born under the sign of the Crab. Stupid animal! Always goes sideways instead of straight ahead," she said, putting her spectacles back in their case.

I left them and went downstairs again. It was nearly midnight, and all the guests had red faces and were talking noisily. My father was sitting in a corner, engaged in earnest conversation with a gentleman from the Ministry of the Interior, who looked like an enormous baby, with a small, receding chin and a big, dome-shaped forehead. Without his glasses and in a pink silk bonnet he would have looked exactly like a baby. He was very excited and was talking to my father about the fundamentals of German life.

"You realize, Herr Doktor," he was saying, "that if war comes the historic task of defending German living space will devolve upon the generations born between the years, let us say, nineteen ten and nineteen twenty. Earlier and later generations will naturally also be called upon—"

"Naturally," said my father.

"These generations, bitter though the thought may be, must be sacrificed so that Germany may live."

"Naturally," my father said politely, nodding to me at the same time.

"I don't think I shall be committing an indiscretion, Herr Dok-tor," the big baby went on, "if I tell you, naturally in the strictest confidence and for your ears alone, because it is Top Secret—"

"Naturally," said my father, handing me a glass of champagne.

"Well then," the gentleman from the Ministry of the Interior continued, "I believe that it would not be entirely unwelcome to HIM if the unreliable age groups born between nineteen hundred and nineteen twenty-five were eliminated. It is those age groups which are continually throwing up reactionary elements. Now in a war those age groups would be capable of great things, but they are entirely unsuitable for assuring the political succession. They are still far too much under the influence of their upbringing in the days before nineteen thirty-three. No," he said with em-phasis, raising his glass toward my father, "the Third Reich is the creation of men of your generation, Herr Doktor, and one day the young generation which is now growing up will take over from it. A war, Herr Doktor, would, from the standpoint of the Ministry of the Interior, eliminate the inconvenient intermediate genera-tion and relieve our police of the task—"

"Very interesting!" my father said.

I was rather irritated and said, "Here's to the unwanted interme-diate generation!"

The gentleman from the Ministry of the Interior was quite upset that he could be so misunderstood.

"My dear young friend," he said. "You mustn't underrate the task devolving upon your generation. Not once in a thousand years is a generation confronted with such a heroic destiny. There are generations whose task it is to fight wars, and other genera-tions whose task it is to consolidate what the sword has con-quered—"

"Your health," said my father.

"Your health," I said.

"Your health," said the gentleman from the Ministry of the In-terior. "This is excellent champagne!"

Soon afterward everyone began looking at the clock. I wan-dered around till I found Josefine, who had been in the center of a group of men the whole evening and really looked lovelier than ever. She was in a good humor and said, "Stay near me, and I'll give you a kiss when the lights go out. At midnight Kride's having the main switch turned off."

"No better choice?" I asked.

She shook her head. "Nothing but a lot of old bores. The others don't trust themselves away from their wives."

"Josefine, you're immoral," I said.

I stayed with her, and we had a drink together. I had been drinking quite a lot and was nearly on the point of falling slightly in love with Josefine's immoral ways.

Suddenly the bells began ringing on the radio, the housekeeper turned off the main switch in the basement, everyone shrieked and laughed, I felt Josefine's warm mouth on my cheek, and I put my arm around her. She was wearing a low-cut dress, and her shoulders were bare. I felt her throat with my hand and then felt her pressing her head against me. She was as light as a feather, but I couldn't concentrate properly because I was watching for the lights to go on again. But Josefine didn't seem to care whether the lights went on again or not, and in the end I didn't care either, and when they went on nobody was looking at us. Everyone was in an embrace, and outside the maroons were going off, and everyone wished each other a Happy New Year.

All the taxis in Berlin were engaged, so I had to drive some of the visitors home. When I got back I found my father sitting alone in the conservatory, drinking a glass of punch. I helped myself to something from the cold buffet and went and sat with him.

"A very nice party," I said, taking a bite of cold meat. My father seemed to be in one of his contemplative moods. He was smoking a small cigar and took no notice of what I said.

"It's strange," he said eventually. "We make a new Reich, and all we can think of when we want to enjoy ourselves a bit is to have a party exactly as in the good old days! This evening's party might just as well have taken place under Kaiser Wilhelm."

"Wasn't it supposed to be like that?" I asked. "I thought Kride's idea was to have everything as in the old days."

"Oh, yes," he said, his mood suddenly changing. "Perhaps it's the only way of doing it. And it's not so expensive, it's not so expensive at all!"

IX

Two days later they had all gone. Josefine went, and Yevgenia and Margarete went too. I stayed at the house for a few days longer, until Alfred Karawan had found himself a room at Halensee, near the broadcasting studio. Then I went back to my own room. The money was still in the moneybox in the wardrobe, and the landlady praised Alfred to the skies and said her husband had nearly died laughing at his stories. Alfred, in fact, had left an excellent impression. Every now and then he dropped in to see me, and the landlord and landlady carefully studied the radio program to find out when he was on the air. They listened to him religiously for about eight weeks, and then he suddenly vanished from the program. I rang up the studio, but they couldn't give me any information. Eventually I went there and found out that he had been taken away by the Gestapo. This made me very worried about him, and I decided to telephone the naval lieutenant with whom Alfred had had such a long conversation. I found his number in the telephone book and dialed.

"Konrad von Borsin speaking," a voice answered.

"I'm speaking from Dr. Stamm's house," I said. "Can I speak to Lieutenant von Borsin?"

"Speaking," said the voice.

I had heard that voice on the telephone before.

"This is Roderich Stamm," I said. "I wanted to ask— You met Alfred Karawan, the pianist, at our house."

"Oh, him!" he said, and his voice suddenly grew very friendly.

"I rang the broadcasting studio, and he's left. Do you know what has happened to him?"

He laughed, a dark, pleasing laugh. "Don't you worry about him!" he said. "He's better off than you are!"

"Oh? Really? At the broadcasting studio they said—"

"Yes, I can imagine what they said. Camouflage, don't you see?"

"No!—Oh, I see!—Yes, of course, camouflage, I see. So he was forbidden to say good-by to me?"

"That's right!"

"Many thanks."

Konrad von Borsin hesitated for a moment, as if he had something else to say, but then said no, that was all. I rang off. During the next few weeks I kept thinking about Alfred. His was such a determined character, so different from mine. He didn't study, but seized the world by the horns. I often wondered where he might be, but it was obviously impossible to find out. Knowing Alfred was rather like knowing a character out of a detective novel.

Two months after her departure Josefine wrote to us from Düsseldorf. She had accepted a very good offer to go to Brussels in ten days as the representative of a Franco-German fashion house in Düsseldorf. She mentioned quite incidentally that for three weeks she had been rather ill. She had slipped on some ice and had had a miscarriage. There was no need to worry, because she was quite well again. Because of all the things she had to do before she left, she wouldn't be able to come and see us. Love from Josefine.

Things had certainly turned out for the best. All the complications had been removed at a stroke. The family's good name was no longer endangered.

But Kride didn't seem to agree. She talked about it to me in the sitting room, while arranging some flowers in a vase.

"I told her I'd take the child," she said. "Max would have adopted it. The slut! As if we wouldn't have done everything—"

She suddenly sat down in an easy chair, rested her head on the arm, and burst into tears. She wasn't like her sister Margarete, who could weep with economy and almost noiselessly. Kride's sobs were uncouth, violent, and uncontrolled. I laid my arm on her shoulder. The sobbing gradually died away, and eventually she looked up.

"Lend me your handkerchief," she said. I gave it to her, and she blew her nose and wiped her eyes. Then she sat up, put her elbows on the table, rested her head in her hands, and stared in front of her. Her face reminded me of the Kride who had hitch-hiked home from Berlin at the end of her first term—a rather unsettled Kride.

I knew that she prided herself on being without weaknesses. I took my arm from her shoulder and waited.

"Do you know how old I am now, Roderich?" she said. "Nearly thirty! At thirty the best years of one's life are over. And I've got a house and car and a garden, and I'll still have them when I'm forty!"

I didn't know what she was driving at.

"Oh, hell!" she said suddenly in good Baltic. She wiped her nose again and went back to arranging her flowers.

I was alone again, and I told myself that I must really get down to hard work for my degree. But there were too many distractions, and I couldn't get down to it properly. I'd sit in the State Library, for instance, reading the history of Dionysius of Syracuse and thinking about my uncle.

In the spring I went on doctor's orders to Bavaria for a fortnight, to get rid of an obstinate cough. I stayed in a mountain hut that belonged to a friend of my father's. I enjoyed it, but I didn't entirely get rid of the cough. At the beginning of term I returned to Berlin without much appetite for work. I didn't really know what I was working for. Everything in Germany was so extraordinary. That spring it was Czechoslovakia's turn, and everybody began talking about war. I resumed my wanderings about the city, the weather grew warmer, you could hear people's radios through the open windows, and the worst of it was that nobody knew whether this time the situation was more serious than usual, or whether it was just the usual din.

It was all very uncertain.

4 - Grindadrap

There were many foreigners in Bavaria that April, and you kept running into them—foreigners traveling by themselves and others who arrived by one coachload and then drove on again. Germany is so cramped and densely populated and has so many roads and railways that you keep running into people all the time.

Feldmann had passed his exam and had been appointed an assistant at a Munich clinic. I went to see him on my way home, and he was very superior and slightly condescending.

"Are you still civilization-sick?" he asked.

"There were such a lot of people in the mountains."

"There always are at Easter. Going to the mountains is much healthier for them than to hang about the cafés. After all, you went to the mountains yourself!"

I said there was a difference. I had gone by myself, but the others were always at least in company strength. But Feldmann only laughed at me. He had been on military training and had been promoted.

"What does your old man say? Is there going to be a war?" he asked.

"I haven't discussed it with him lately. I expect so," I said casually.

"Then I'll order my uniform," he said. "Later on there won't be any of the right material left for us reservists."

This was the old Feldmann, practical and resolute.

"What will you do if there's a war?" he asked later on.

I didn't know what I would do if there was a war. At my last camp I'd been promoted to lance-corporal, but I hadn't yet received my decoration for the liberation of the Sudetenland. I had been told it was going to be a yellow one.

"I expect I'll be called up," I said.

"As what?"

"As a lance-corporal."

"I hope you enjoy it," he said. "Why don't you do some training? It's much better to be something. You've still got plenty of time!"

That was perfectly true. I still had plenty of time. The thesis I was writing for my degree was still lying in the drawer.

"I wish I were in your shoes," he said. "I had a perpetual struggle to get through at the university. Thank heaven it's over now. Oh, well, you were born with a silver spoon in your mouth!"

"Yes," I said, "that's true, but afterward they took it away again."

"But then they gave it back to you."

There was no denying it. They had given me back my silver spoon.

I asked if he could recommend a nursing home for a friend of Kride's who was expecting a child and had got it into her head that it must be born in Bavaria. Her name was Maria Freibe. She had been married to an airman who had crashed on a training flight, and she was convinced that more beautiful babies were born more easily in Bavaria than anywhere else. Feldmann, who had fallen in love with his new home, was rather inclined to agree.

He recommended Dr. Rauh's establishment at Schwabing. But he said she'd have to book a room soon, because it was always filled up. All the clinics were full. The birthrate was rising rapidly.

"In Austria—" he said and started laughing.

"What about Austria?"

"In Austria at Christmas all the hospitals and nursing homes were full of women having babies."

"Do they always have babies at Christmas in Austria?"

"No, but Christmas happened to be nine months after the Anschluss. The German Army sent up the Austrian birthrate with a rush. By the way, you may as well take me in your car. I'll get that material for my uniform straight away."

We drove to the Ludwigstrasse and bought some lovely gray-green material. It was firm and silky, absolutely first quality. Then I booked a room for Kride's friend at Dr. Rauh's nursing home at Schwabing. I still had a few days left before the beginning of term, so I drove to Yevgenia's.

One evening Feldmann had shown me over Munich. He took me to all the historic places and to the Platzl, and I understood why he was so fond of the place. "If I were you," he said to me when he said good-by, "I'd go to the North Pole. There at least you wouldn't have people to worry you!"

I thought of this as I drove along the Autobahn to Nuremberg and then turned left through Wurzburg to Yevgenia's. There was sense in what Feldmann said. But the North Pole was rather a long way away. Perhaps there was some nearer spot where nobody yodeled at dawn every morning, and litter wasn't left lying all over the place. But roads were being built everywhere nowadays, and that was something about which I, driving my car, had no right to complain.

I didn't get to Yevgenia's till late in the evening. She was lying under the pink lampshade on the sofa in her showroom, reading and smoking a cigarette through a long holder, as usual. I'd left the car in a garage and walked to the house. When I tapped on the window she started; obviously it frightened her. She was enormously relieved when I called out my name.

"Thank God!" she exclaimed. "Thank God!"

"Why thank God?"

She put on the kettle for some tea and cooked me a pancake on her electric stove. I sat in the kitchen and watched her. Yevgenia had always been a kind of mother to me, a muddle-headed, restless, bewildering mother, but I was very fond of her.

"Why did I give you such a fright just now?" I asked. She put the pancake on a plate and placed it in front of me on the table. Then she sat beside me on a stool.

"Eat!" she said. "Would you like another one?"

I shook my head. "Why did you say 'Thank God' like that?" I asked.

Her face darkened. She went into the sitting room and came back with her cigarette holder. Then she went back to the sitting room to fetch a cigarette. She sat down, put it in the holder, and then got up and went back again to fetch her lighter.

"Haven't you forgotten the ashtray?" I asked. "Why did you get such a fright just now?"

She looked dramatically around the kitchen, and then whispered, "Because of Margarete!"

"What's the matter with her?"

"Margarete's father wrote a letter, and they opened it. It was thoughtless of him, and now I don't know what to do to prevent him from writing again."

I had never been told who Margarete's father was. Naturally I was interested. I finished my pancake, and said, "Why shouldn't he write, Yevgenia? I never knew that Margarete had a father!"

"Don't be stupid!" Yevgenia said. "Of course she has a father!"

Now that Yevgenia had started, she told me the secret of Margarete's parenthood. She didn't tell me all the details, but she made it clear that Margarete's father was alive and that he had had to leave Germany for political reasons several years before. Margarete's birth had been the result of a brief episode, and Yevgenia had long since lost touch with him. But he wasn't dead, Yevgenia said. Not by any means.

"You remember the bad times, don't you?" she said. "Everybody speculated, and I speculated too. But I speculated badly, and lost all my money. Then a gentleman named Seidenbaum helped me, and I did well. Earned dollars. That's all!"

"Seidenbaum?" I said.

She nodded.

"So Margarete's name ought really to be Seidenbaum?"

She nodded again.

I burst out laughing. I couldn't help it.

"But, Yevgenia," I said, "you were the first member of the party in this district!"

She nodded again. The expression on her face said, You may find it amusing but it's true!

"And Seidenbaum writes letters? Where does he write them from?"

"He travels a great deal. He's a buyer for a Norwegian firm that deals in salt and coal. His last letter was from Bodö. This summer he's going to Reykjavik."

"And his letter was opened in the post. And now you're afraid."
She nodded. "Not because of myself, but because of Margarete.
The poor child's whole future will be ruined if it comes out."

"Does Kride know?"

Yevgenia nodded again. This threw a new light on certain
things. Kride had been Yevgenia's confidante since childhood. It
was obviously because she knew this story, which represented a
continual threat to the whole family, that she couldn't stand
Margarete.

"Who else knows? My father?"

She shook her head. "No one else knows but you."

I began to laugh again. The whole situation, and Yevgenia's
confessing like this in her flowery dressing-gown, was indescrib-
ably funny. Normally she spoke good German, with a slight Sla-
vonic accent, but when she was upset or excited her accent was
much stronger.

"You're laughing," she said. "All right!" and she cheered up a
bit. "You were a small boy, but you'll remember. I went to
Rome and stayed with friends but didn't like it. I went to Mar-
rakech, and to Paris, but didn't like it anywhere. My husband was
a German, a Balt, which is as good as German, isn't it? So I went
to Berlin. I had no money and lived in a little *pension* in the
Kochstrasse. Everybody speculated, and they asked me why I
didn't speculate too, because it was so easy. I speculated, but it
wasn't a bit easy. I speculated in dollars, pounds, Swiss francs,
but it was difficult, very difficult indeed!"

"Stop it!" I exclaimed. "For heaven's sake stop it!"

But Yevgenia didn't stop it. She liked it when people laughed.
"There I was, broke, two weeks, three weeks, absolutely broke, no
money left at all, only a little jewelry. I was ill with worry about
where the next penny was to come from."

"And then Herr Seidenbaum came along!"

"Sh! Don't talk so loud! He was a very friendly gentleman, as
clever as Rothschild. There I was, absolutely penniless, and with
everything very dear. There was Kride's and Josefine's boarding-
school bill to be paid. I was at my wits' end. Everything in Berlin
was crazy; some people had a lot of money, and others none at
all. I went to see some old friends of my husband's, but they had

no money. Everyone was doing badly. Then Herr Seidenbaum came along, as clever as Rothschild, and very polite. 'You are enchanting, madam, how much do you want for that ring?' he said."

"Did he do you out of it?"

Yevgenia energetically shook her dyed hair. "Certainly not! He took the ring, had it valued, and brought it back. It was worth a hundred and twenty English pounds. He asked whether he should speculate for me, and I said, 'Please.' He came back and had earned money for me. He gave me the money, and I kept the ring. He was a gentleman. . . ."

She told me all about this and other mysterious financial transactions. So far as I could find out, the Seidenbaum affair had come to an end because of Yevgenia's refusal to marry him. He had wanted to marry her; he was clever, capable, and a dozen years older than she. After she had refused him for the fifth or sixth time it had been the end. Yevgenia had gone to Paris and had come back with a daughter. Margarete was therefore a French citizen by birth, but in the mild, democratic sunshine of the early thirties she had assumed German nationality. As Yevgenia had not wished to state the father's name, Margarete's surname had been registered as Katushin, which was Yevgenia's maiden name.

"Now what am I to do?" Yevgenia said. "He wants to see her!"

"Then take her abroad to see him!"

Yevgenia thoughtfully screwed up her big nose. The idea of going abroad didn't appeal to her at all. It meant applying for a passport, visas, and foreign exchange. It would attract the attention of the police, and that wasn't advisable. They stuck their noses into everything.

"Isn't there something you could do?" she said.

"What could I do?" I asked.

"I don't want to write to him, it's too dangerous," she said. "But your father's in the Foreign Ministry. Couldn't you use the diplomatic pouch?"

"One of his letters was opened. What was in it?"

"I told you, he wants to see his daughter. The best would be if you went and talked to him. Would you do that?"

"What could I tell him?"

"About Margarete."

"He wouldn't be very interested in what I had to say. But I'll see if Father can do anything about having a letter sent through the diplomatic pouch. What did you write to him?"

Yevgenia assumed a crafty expression. "I typed a letter to him and posted it in another town. I told him to wait until he heard from you."

"From me?"

"Ah! You've always been a good boy! You always held Margarete on your knees when she was a little girl!"

This was a typical Yevgenia *coup*. She was completely unscrupulous in her lovable way.

I was just going to say something when the door opened and in walked Margarete. She was in a bathrobe, and her eyes were heavy with sleep. She was yawning and blinking, and she asked what all the noise was about. Then she opened her eyes and woke up.

"You're here!" she exclaimed. "Will you fetch me from school tomorrow in the car? Oh, Roderich!"

She sat on the table and helped herself to a sip from Yevgenia's cup and a puff through Yevgenia's long cigarette holder. She struck me as having grown prettier.

I stayed at Yevgenia's for two days and took Margarete out in the car.

II

I corresponded several times with Herr Seidenbaum in the course of the summer. His office was in Oslo, but he was thinking of moving to New York. He wasn't just in the salt and coal business, he was also a representative of Shell Oil, and he didn't seem to be doing at all badly, though he had lost twenty houses in Berlin in 1933. The letters went to Norway in the diplomatic pouch and were not opened. When I told my father I wanted to write to a gentleman named Seidenbaum in Oslo he didn't bat an eyelid, but gave me the number of a room in the Foreign Ministry. I didn't tell him why I wanted to write, but he must have mentioned it to Kride, because one day she asked me what it was all about.

"It's not my business," I answered.

"It looks like Yevgenia to me," she said bitterly, "and naturally you're the idiot that falls for her talk. You may make things terribly awkward for all of us!"

"It might be even more awkward if the Gestapo started taking an interest in Yevgenia and found out why it was that Herr Seidenbaum wanted to see one of her daughters."

Kride pursed her lips. "Do what you like!" she said. "The whole thing's ridiculous!"

Herr Seidenbaum was a man of the world and understood perfectly why it was necessary to use the diplomatic pouch for our correspondence. He suggested meeting Margarete in Denmark, or, better still, in Iceland. It was quite possible that in Norway or Denmark the meeting might come to the knowledge of the German political police. Eventually we agreed on a place called Thorshavn, "the harbor of Thor." I had to look it up in an atlas to find out where it was. After a search I discovered it was in the Faroes, between Scotland and Iceland. Meanwhile Yevgenia had twice come to Berlin to see how things were getting on.

"You're a good boy, you'll arrange everything," she said.

Eventually I wrote and told her that Margarete must leave Travemünde for Copenhagen on June 23, and that she must sail for Thorshavn in the *Dronning Alexandrine* from the Island-splads in Copenhagen on June 25. She would arrive on the twenty-seventh or twenty-eighth, and could return a fortnight later.

Yevgenia wrote back and said she couldn't let Margarete travel alone.

I went back to the State Library and grew absorbed in studying drachmae from Segesta and tetradrachmae from Acragas, with the celebrated crab under the goddess's head. Whenever I looked at the pictures I imagined myself back in my uncle's house. I heard his voice in my ears, talking about theomachy, and when I walked down Unter den Linden I only had to look up to see the aircraft circling over the city. People often stood in the street, watching them practicing theomachy in the sky. Since the completion of the Air Ministry in the Leipzigerplatz, the number of aircraft had been growing constantly. They didn't need money now to pay for the building, so they could afford to build aircraft.

Summer arrived, and on some days it was intolerably hot. In the Friedrichstrasse tar dripped onto the heads of people going into or coming out of the underground. A subway had been built in Moscow, which made Hitler so angry that he ordered a subway to be built in Munich too. The whole world's press united to sing the praises of the Moscow subway, and Hitler quite rightly decided that this was done purely to annoy him.

In the course of time one had grown used to the fact that things were continually happening. Political events had been crowding on each other's heels ever since Hacha had come from Czechoslovakia to offer us his country. Hacha had done this quite voluntarily, and, though the Russians had a subway now, they no longer had the Prague airfield, and they had lost the Skoda works too, which served them right. The Spanish civil war was over, and the good Spaniards had beaten the bad Spaniards, and I read several leading articles which compared General Franco to King Ferdinand. Both had defeated the Spanish separatists.

Then one day there was a telephone call from Yevgenia. She had a severe attack of rheumatism and couldn't go with Margarete to Thorshavn. Josefine couldn't leave her work in Brussels, and Kride had flatly refused to go. Yevgenia and she had quarreled so violently on the telephone that Kride had ended by hanging up. The result was that half an hour later Yevgenia got through to me and told me at once that I was her good boy. Anyway, I agreed to go, and packed my suitcase and went to meet Margarete at Travemünde. My father had arranged to come with us as far as Copenhagen, where there happened to be an economic conference in which he had to take part. At the last moment Kride decided to come too, and so all four of us sailed from Travemünde to the Danish Venice. Next morning Kride and my father came with us to the Islandsplads, from which the *Dronning Alexandrine* sailed shortly before midday. It was all rather as it had been five years before—but all the same it was quite different.

I watched my father standing on the quay, with Kride by his

side. Five years before he had struck me as astonishingly young, but this time he looked as old as ever, or perhaps a little older. This time he didn't put his arm around Kride's shoulder as they walked away, but he smiled at me long and cordially.

The evening before we had sat in the garden of the Hôtel d'Angleterre with some Danish friends of my father's. They were white-haired and well nourished and spoke excellent English with a slight Danish accent, which made their way of speaking all the more attractive. They were very much concerned about what Germany was going to do. Was it really going to war? Chamberlain wouldn't go to Godesberg and Munich again, not even with a new umbrella. If there was going to be a war, they said, they would buy Baltic shares, which were bound to go up.

Kride tried to convince them that Denmark's future lay with Germany. "Just think of the bombardment of Copenhagen by the British Navy in eighteen six, or was it eighteen eleven?" she said. "The British are Denmark's natural enemies."

The Danes, however, were of the opinion that the bombardment of Copenhagen had happened rather a long time ago, and since that time the British had become customers for the whole exportable surplus of Danish eggs and bacon, to say nothing of Esbjerg fresh fish. That enabled a little thing like a bombardment that happened a hundred and thirty years ago to be forgotten. In any case, neutrality was the best policy. But the great thing was to know in good time what shares to buy.

Before I went to sleep that night my father came to see me. A waiter brought us whisky and ice. My father sat on the edge of my bed and drank my health. We talked about one thing and another, and he wished me a good crossing.

"Perhaps Herr Seidenbaum might be quite useful to us," he casually remarked. "We need good friends, willing to act for us, all over the world. You might perhaps be able cautiously to raise the matter with him. Another thing I wanted to mention was that there's no need for you to hurry back. Take your time over it. Enjoy the northern landscape while you're about it. Perhaps you'll be able to go to Iceland."

He kept obstinately returning to this theme, which rather surprised me. I thought that perhaps he might have had a little more

to drink than usual, but he wasn't the type that drink makes talk-
ative.

When it came to saying good-by he took a very long time over
it and was very solemn.

"And don't forget!" he said. "Take plenty of time! I want you
to get thoroughly well again!"

Next day he was his normal self. Only when they started
throwing paper streamers and the band struck up did I notice
how old and bent he looked. Or was it the effect of looking at
him from above?

Margarete was entirely at home. She had picked up *tak* and
farwell and several other Danish expressions, and enjoyed herself immensely.

III

At about four o'clock a couple of mornings later I left my un-
quiet cabin and went up on deck. In these northern latitudes it
was already daylight. The air was sharp and damp and full of
sea-smell, just as it had been on my previous voyage; there were
even the same gulls.

After gazing out over the sea for some time on the port side, I
went over to the opposite side, and there I saw the Faroes. At first
I couldn't tell that they were islands. All I could see was five or
six round domes, which might have been made of soft molten
glass. They didn't seem to be made of earth at all; they looked
much more like water—but an extraordinary kind of water, because at this hour of the day the sea was a grayish blue, but the
domes were of all colors—light green, violet, pink, and yellow. I
stood and gazed at them, and gradually they altered, assumed
shapes reminiscent of hills, while the colors faded until finally the
only color left was a dull olive green. These were the Faroes. I
promptly forgot my grudge against Herr Seidenbaum, Yevgenia,
and Margarete. I stood gazing at the islands taking shape before
my eyes, and as soon as we entered the harbor I went downstairs,
packed my things, called Margarete, and went up on deck again.

The nearer we came to land, the grimmer and gloomier it
looked. There was little vegetation, and the dark-green meadows

were everywhere broken up by rocks. The border between land and sea was marked by a perpetual line of white foam. It was hard to imagine anything grimmer than the Faroes, particularly when one's first sight of them had been of a series of rainbow-colored domes in the distance.

On the shore to the left of the harbor were two enormous Shell Oil tanks. The bay was divided in two by a projecting tongue of land, and wooden houses stood in a semicircle all around it. We passed the end of the mole and tied up at the quay. It was still early morning. I looked around for a porter, but none was to be seen. I asked a small boy if he knew where I could find one. He shook his head, so I pointed to my suitcase. Without saying a word, he picked it up and walked ahead of me on his bare feet to the Faroes Hotel. When we got there I felt in my pocket for a krone and offered it to him, but he shook his head and walked away. It took me some time to find out that the Faroese refuse to accept money for doing one a service. Unlike the *ragazzi* and the *facchini*, they neither plunder nor besiege you, and, if they feel friendly toward you, they refuse to accept tips. They feel friendly toward you for nothing.

They gave us the two rooms that had been reserved for us. I washed, changed, and went across to Margarete. She was looking out of the window and brushing her hair.

"What an extraordinary view!" she said.

"Aren't you excited?" I asked.

"Why?"

"After all, he's your father!"

"Oh, I see!" she said. "No, I'm not a bit excited."

A maid came in with Herr Seidenbaum's visiting card. She said something, but we couldn't understand her. She was small and not young, and she looked at us very seriously. I thought for a moment that she disapproved of my being in Margarete's room, but afterward I found out that she always looked serious. We followed her down to the dining room.

Herr Seidenbaum may have been a forceful, keen, go-ahead type when he first met Margarete's mother—he hinted as much later on, when we got to know each other better—but that morning he was only a little man with unsymmetrical dark-brown eyes.

His whole face was unsymmetrical. A year before he had had a motor accident near Narvik and had fractured his skull. The whole left side of his face hung downward slightly. This gave him a sardonic expression, but actually he was very agreeable and concerned that we should have a good breakfast. I was afraid that there might be an emotional scene, but there was nothing of the sort. Herr Seidenbaum was very nice. Margarete alternately called him *Sie* and *du*, but later called him *du* only. He called her *du* from the start.

He was anxious that we should have a good time in the Faroes. He didn't think the Faroes were a place one would choose for a holiday, and he was sorry that another steamer wasn't leaving for Iceland for several days. Wouldn't we like to go to Reykjavik? Reykjavik was the Paris of the north, with bars, dance bands, and really modern hotels, and all the women wore silk stockings. He had set up a silk-stocking agency there himself some time ago, and it was doing well. Besides, Iceland, with its geysers and its volcano, was far more interesting, and one could go everywhere by car; it was so cheap.

A suspicious gleam came into Margarete's eyes, but I wasn't in favor of going to Iceland. I pointed out that we had had a good reason for choosing the Faroes, and Herr Seidenbaum agreed. He realized that I had fulfilled my part of the contract and had no particular wish to be seen with him in Iceland.

"Would you like to stay here too?" he asked Margarete.

"I don't know," she said, hesitating over the plate of strawberries and cream with which she finished her breakfast. "I haven't thought about it!"

There was, of course, no objection to the two of them going to Iceland without me. There would be nothing to attract attention if Herr Seidenbaum appeared in Iceland with his daughter. He was known there, and nobody would take any notice of Margarete.

"We can talk it over again later," Herr Seidenbaum said and then turned his attention to me. He thanked me repeatedly for having brought Margarete to Thorshavn. Yevgenia had written and told him that I was a kind of brother to Margarete, and he found that very charming. Had I yet managed to see anything of the

Faroes? Had I seen the Thingstead? No? It lay on the tongue of land in the harbor. It was a real, ancient Teutonic Thingstead.

I told him that so far I'd seen nothing but my hotel bedroom and the quay.

"Then you must certainly go and see it," he said. "There's something that you as a German will be very interested to see— a real swastika, dating from the year one thousand. It's scratched into the stone, but you can make it out distinctly."

I told him I hadn't come halfway across the North Atlantic to see a swastika, of which we had plenty at home.

"But it's very interesting all the same," he said.

After breakfast I left the two of them together, arranged to meet them at dinnertime, and went off on my own. Thorshavn is not a big place, and you can see practically everything there is to be seen there in two hours, from the curing stations to the dance hall and the old harbor where the fishermen build their boats, which are pointed at both ends, with their own hands. I looked for a place where I could have a meal, but couldn't find one. Instead I found a fisherman who could speak English.

"Are you the German who arrived this morning?" he asked.

I said I was.

"I expect you came to see a *grindadrap*."

I didn't know what he meant. He looked out to sea and said the weather was right. It was the weather in which the *grind* came. I believed him. He looked as if he knew what he was talking about.

I walked a little way out of Thorshavn and reached a place where the road led over a pass. I sat on a rock. It was absolutely still, with not a breath of wind. The sun shone brightly on the gray stones, and everything was strange and a little different from home. I had been too long in Germany and had forgotten what it was like to be in another country, in another world. Every stone had something special about it. I looked at the stones like a collector looking at butterflies. When I got back, I'd say all sorts of things, but I wouldn't be able to explain what it was really like here. That was something impossible to explain.

A young man came up the road from Thorshavn and talked to me in broken German.

"Are you the German who arrived this morning in the *Dronning*

Alexandrine?" he asked. I nodded and stood up. He offered me
a cigarette from an English packet of Players. Had I seen the swastika at the Thingstead? No? As a German I certainly ought to go
and have a look at it. He looked around, sniffed at the wind, and
said that it seemed to be good weather for a *grindadrap.* I should
certainly see one. Then he went on his way.

The air was sharp, in spite of the sunshine. As soon as clouds
obscured the sun it grew too cold to be comfortable. I got up,
put on my coat, and wandered on. It was extraordinary how the
scenery altered. I reached a small *bye* and asked the peasant
woman if she could give me something to eat. She brought me a
glass of milk, bread, and sheep's-milk cheese. Conversation was
rather difficult, as she knew neither English nor German, but with
considerable trouble and a great deal of laughter we managed to
make ourselves understood. She asked whether I was the *Tysker*
who had arrived that morning. I nodded. Everyone seemed to
know about me. She said, "Hitler," and made a grimace. Then
she said, "Denmark," and made another grimace. I waited for her
to say something that wouldn't make her grimace. Then she said
something that sounded like *"Sjolvstyri,"* and looked very
pleased. I concluded that *Sjolvstyri* must be a good thing in the
Faroes. I got up and took money from my pocket, but she made
another grimace and wouldn't let me pay. I shook the woman's
hand, made a grimace, and said, "Hitler." She nodded meaning-
fully. Then I said *"Sjolvstyri"* and smiled pleasantly, and she
burst out laughing at my pronunciation. Then I went on my way.
The woman hadn't said anything about a *grindadrap.* Perhaps
our exciting political discussion had made her forget about it.

I did a great deal of walking in the next few days. It was a magic
world. No matter in which direction you went you could always
see the sea.

On the evening of the second or third day Margarete unexpectedly came into my room. I was in bed, reading. She was in her
pajamas and dressing-gown. She was rather excited and upset.
She kept wandering around the room and noticed that I had written a letter.

"Have you been writing to Josefine?" she asked.

I nodded.

She said, "Fff!" with her lips and sat on a chair back to front. "What am I to do, Roderich?" she asked.

"I don't know," I said.

"Yevgenia thinks I ought to stay with him."

"Has he asked you to?"

"Yes. He says he's got two grown-up daughters by his second marriage, and they're married and living in New York and can look after themselves. He could get me Icelandic or American citizenship. I could stay with him."

"That's fine!" I said.

"But I don't know whether I ought to."

"What have you got against it?"

"I'm frightened. I can't even talk one language properly yet. Besides, I like living in Germany. I think I should be homesick. I think I'm homesick already!"

"Come, come," I said. "After all, he is your father! I think he's very nice."

"Yes, he is," she said. "He's promised to buy me new clothes in Reykjavik or Bergen."

"Oh, well then," I said. "Then everything's all right!"

"But I'm frightened. I don't know, but I don't think I'd feel happy about it inside. I think I'd always be frightened."

"Only at the beginning," I said.

She got up and wandered restlessly around the room again. It was extraordinary how she altered from month to month. She wasn't slender—not so slender as Josefine, for instance—but she was getting prettier and prettier.

"What did you write to Josefine?"

"That doesn't concern you," I said.

"Josefine's a bad lot!" she exclaimed. "Yevgenia said so!"

"The things you people say about Josefine!"

"She did something to get rid of her baby!"

This was going too far. I put down my book and raised myself on one elbow. Margarete was standing in front of the desk, fiddling with my fountain pen. Suddenly she picked up the letter, crumpled it, tore it into little pieces, and threw it into the wastepaper basket.

"You make me sick!" she exclaimed and flung out of the room.

I got out of bed, wrote another letter to Josefine, and addressed it to her via Bergen, air mail. It would leave for Bergen next morning, and Josefine would get it in three or four days. The ship would be coming back a week later, perhaps with an answer from Josefine.

The idea of writing to Josefine had come to me quite suddenly. I had thought about her in Berlin but hadn't been able to make up my mind to write, but here, in the loneliness of the Faroes, among all these strange people, I suddenly longed for her and wrote. I don't know exactly what I said, but I hoped that perhaps she'd understand and write a similar letter back. Perhaps she too sometimes thought about that kiss on New Year's Eve. I had held her in my arms, and she had been as light and soft as a feather, and she had a passionate mouth.

I wrote her a serious and quite colorful letter, all about the Faroes—"the Sheep Islands"—and the swastika at the Thingstead, and I told her I couldn't forget New Year's Eve. I was glad that Margarete had torn up the first letter, because when I read the second letter through it seemed so much warmer and more cordial. I put it in the envelope, sealed it, and went back to bed, intending to read a little more.

As I lay there, reading, the door suddenly opened and Margarete crept in. It was after midnight. Her eyes were red with tears. I closed the book over my first finger and looked at her in astonishment.

She sat down in the chair and gulped slightly.

"Why aren't you asleep yet?" I asked.

Suddenly she came and sat on the edge of my bed, put her arm round my neck, and started sobbing. Her hair tickled my ear. It was a little wet from the tears on her cheeks, and I wished she'd stop pressing her wet cheek against my face.

"I only wanted to tell you how sorry I am that I tore up that letter!" she said.

"You needn't have come and told me that! I'd forgotten about it long ago!"

"Really?"

"Of course!"

She sat up, said, "Pooh!" blew a wisp of hair from her brow, and looked happy again.

"Good night, Rodie!" she said.

"Good night!"

She stood up and walked over to the window, through which you could see the view in the dim twilight of the midsummer night. In those latitudes it never gets really dark in summer. Suddenly she stopped in front of the table. She'd seen the letter, and I thought she was going to tear it up again. But she only said, "Fff!" and stalked out of the room, tossing her head contemptuously.

IV

Next day a tourist steamer called at Thorshavn on its way to Iceland. Herr Seidenbaum asked Margarete whether she'd like to go to Iceland with it, and of course she said yes, she would. There wasn't enough doing in the Faroes for her.

He tried to persuade me to go too, but I didn't want to. When I said I wouldn't go Margarete muttered something about waiting for an air-mail letter from Brussels. It was after lunch; the steamer was due to sail at six o'clock, and it would be off Westmannö about two days later.

"Doesn't the old Norse island attract you?" he asked. "It's where those extinct birds lived—what are they called?—Dronte, isn't it? And then there's Hekla and the hot springs."

It did rather attract me, as a matter of fact, but all the same I decided to stay in the Faroes. According to Herr Seidenbaum's description, Iceland was a kind of Kurfürstendamm of the North Atlantic, and I hadn't come all this way from Berlin to see another Kurfürstendamm. Every day I stayed in the Faroes I found them more interesting.

"So I shan't be seeing you and Margarete again?" I asked when I was alone with him.

A thoughtful expression came over his face. "That depends on her," he said. "I don't know whether she wants to stay with me."

"But she likes you very much. She told me so herself."

"Thank you," he said dryly. He suggested that we should go for a walk, the two of us alone—a conversation between men, in fact.

We walked down to the Thingstead and sat in the sun. When the wind wasn't blowing it was always warm, almost hot. But the wind was always liable to start blowing, bringing up brownish-gray rain clouds from the northwest, which covered the islands with a thick mist in ten minutes.

"I don't know whether you'll take amiss what I'm going to say," Herr Seidenbaum began, after lighting a cigar. "I'm an old man. At the moment I'm not doing at all badly. If war breaks out, I shall do even better. I've got a lot of money in shipping and steel and oil, for which there's a huge demand in wartime."

I said that was very gratifying. Did he believe there was going to be a war?

He smiled. "There's no doubt about it," he said. "In August it'll have started."

"Then it's time for me to be going home."

"Perhaps," he said. "Or perhaps not."

I looked at him in astonishment. He was being mysterious and enjoying it.

"Do you set such great store by war?" he asked.

I shook my head.

"Of course not, you're a sensible young man. What will you do if there's a war?"

"Go home," I said.

He thought for a while and changed the subject. "Margarete's nearly sixteen, and she's my third child. A pretty girl, isn't she? "Have you ever wondered why it was that I've never troubled about her before?"

The question had passed through my mind, I said, but it was his business, not mine.

"Of course," he replied. But he couldn't be silent that afternoon. "It was Yevgenia's fault," he went on. "She is a muddle-head and, besides, she's a snob."

I said I didn't agree.

"What reason had she for not marrying me?" he asked suddenly, with anger in his voice.

"I don't know. I've never discussed it with her."

"But you do know! You know perfectly well. You know that my name is Seidenbaum. One's name must be von Haringen, not Seidenbaum! That's why she didn't marry me!"

I racked my brains, but didn't know what to say. My saying nothing irritated him.

"You know perfectly well that it's the truth. And you say nothing. Perhaps out of politeness. Perhaps out of pride!"

"What am I to say?"

"All right, all right," he said contemptuously. "But you're the same as the others. I'll tell you something. The reason why I didn't trouble about Yevgenia for so long was that I knew nothing about the child. She never wrote to me about it. I found out by chance. I met her at Bad Oeynhausen. She was wearing the party emblem. That was in nineteen thirty-two. She said her eldest daughter was in the party too. She said it was out of the question. With me, you understand?"

There was another pause.

"I wanted to have the child. I'm fond of children. She said she was fond of children too. A year later I had to leave Germany. I tried not to think about it any more. But then I had my car accident. I lay in the hospital at Narvik and thought about the child. I wrote to Yevgenia, and she answered. Perhaps she had changed her mind, but now it was too late. Her daughter had married your father. Nobody in Germany, even if he wanted to, could—"

As he didn't go on, I said, "That's all very well, but what can I do about it?"

"Keep quiet!" he said. "Keep quiet!"

I said no more. He extinguished his cigar and lit another one. I felt sorry for him, but there was nothing I could do to help him.

"Yevgenia sent me a typewritten answer," he said. "She said I was to wait till I heard from you. She was cautious, quite rightly. It was very friendly of you to write. But I want the child."

"You've got her," I said.

"Yes," he said. "But have I?"

"I don't understand."

"All right, you don't understand. She's my daughter, but until three months ago she had never heard of me. Then she was told who her father was. He couldn't come to Germany. Just like a criminal. Am I a criminal?"

I didn't answer.

"Am I a criminal?" he repeated.

I didn't answer.

"You don't answer. That means no—or yes. It all depends on which way you look at it, doesn't it? You are polite. Your father is a diplomatist. I'm not a criminal. But the child thinks I am!"

"She doesn't!"

"She doesn't say so," Herr Seidenbaum said. "Perhaps she doesn't even know that she thinks so. But at bottom she believes what the world she was brought up in believes, that we're criminals. What am I to do?"

I didn't know what he was to do. I felt sorry for him. But perhaps what he said was true, and Margarete couldn't look at him without prejudice. This was something I'd never thought about.

He abruptly changed the subject again. "I'm under a great obligation to you."

"Oh, don't mention it."

"No, I'm really under a great obligation to you. I said to myself, Here's a young man with brains. He's changing sides in good time. He has helped you, why not help him? One hand washes the other, doesn't it? I'm willing to give you a big chance. I'm willing to send you, if necessary by air, to a friend in Panama. Such cases are known there. You'll be granted Panama citizenship; my friend can get it for you in a fortnight. I'll see that you get a job. You'll be given a sum of money, let us say five thousand dollars, and recommendations to business people. You can take up a career, or, if you prefer it, you can study. You'll be free to do as you like!"

He extinguished his cigar again, though he had smoked only half of it. For a time I was speechless. The thing struck me as utterly fantastic.

"Why should I do that?" I said eventually. "I've all I need in Germany."

"And after the war?"

I was at a loss what to answer. Who thinks about what might

happen after a war that hasn't started yet? I shrugged my shoulders.

"You're going to make war and you're going to lose it," he said. "You may win at first, perhaps, but then the Americans will come, and then you'll lose!"

He was so positive that I couldn't help laughing. "Good heavens, Herr Seidenbaum!" I said. "You've no idea how many aircraft we have! The sky is full of them. And then our tanks! I'm certainly not a good soldier, but there's one thing I can tell you, and that is that whoever starts a war with Germany today will lose it!"

"That's quite possible," he said. "Today, yes, but tomorrow? Tomorrow Germany will lose! What is your steel production and what is the American?"

I didn't know. My father would certainly have known, but I had never troubled about the matter.

"Our soldiers are the best in the world," I said.

He only shrugged his shoulders. "I've read that before," he said sarcastically. "But what counts today isn't soldiers. What counts is economics. And that is against you."

I started arguing with him, but he listened only with half an ear. Now that I had declined his proposal he no longer seemed interested in me. Eventually we both fell silent. The silence was like a declaration of war. I had the feeling that he hated me, though he hadn't said a word against me. Suddenly he stood up.

"If you change your mind, you can send me a telegram to Iceland," he said. "I'll leave you my hotel address. But I don't think you will change your mind. You'll go back to Germany and think you're safe. Perhaps there will be a war, you think, but supposing there is? You'll be called up, and that means a risk, certainly, but there are always more who come back than are killed. Besides, there's your duty to your country, isn't there? You're a romantic, like all Germans. You believe that patriotism is still important today. You believe you're doing a fine thing in going back to your country, and that heaven will reward you."

He lit himself another cigar and looked at me out of his sad, uneven eyes. He smiled, but I felt he was neither friendly nor hostile to me now. He was merely completely indifferent. He walked a few paces and turned to me.

"I'll tell you something," he went on. "You'll laugh at what I'm going to say, because you've no need to take anything from me. But I'll tell you all the same. Never do anything good because you believe it ought to be done. Never do anything because others do it. Be selfish. If you do good, do it because you want to. If you do evil, do it because you want to. Don't do good because you think heaven expects it of you. To heaven it's a matter of complete indifference what you do. Heaven pays no dividends!"

That evening the two of them sailed for Reykjavik.

v

After that I was alone in the Faroes. For the first few days I thought a great deal about this extraordinary man and didn't know what to make of him, but then I forgot about him because of all the other impressions.

I made friends with a young Scottish businessman, who had big plans. He always had a little notebook with him and a couple of sharp pencils in his outside pocket. He bought dried cod for the Spanish and Portuguese market. During the day he was to be seen clambering, with flying coattails, over the cliffs behind the basalt quarry, and making contracts. In the evening he came back to the hotel, changed his suit, and sat down to table in a good humor. After dinner we'd sit by the radio, drink aquavit and grape tonic, and listen to the Iceland or Oslo radio, or to one of the B.B.C. stations. He knew every inch of the Faroes and told me where to go.

I didn't miss Margarete. She was very dependent and sometimes she was a pest. When I ran into the Scotsman at work in the daytime he used to wink and look at the pretty fishergirls. They earned by their work more than the men, who spent half the year fishing off West Greenland. The result was that they wore silk stockings on Sundays and bought lipstick in the shops. Not knowing the language, I couldn't talk to these girls. One day I said "*Syolvstyri*" to one of them, but instead of smiling she just tapped her forehead. So I kept on going for walks about the island. In the end I picked up a little of the language and found out that that difficult word was the name of one of the island's four political parties.

One Sunday I went with my Scotsman to a lake that was full of gulls and salmon. We spent half the day fishing and came back with a dozen fish. We didn't once mention politics.

The reason we got on so well was that we both liked the people of the Faroes. He liked them because he earned money in the islands, and the landscape reminded him of home. I liked them because I hadn't been away from Germany for such a long time, and because nobody except me knew them. They were more comfortable than the North Pole. They actually had taxis, but if you wanted to avoid seeing taxis you only had to walk for half an hour along the paths leading to the *fjälls*, where it was lonely and full of stones and coarse grass, and only the *tjaldur* tirelessly followed you. The *tjaldur* is a bird about the size of a chicken, which is plagued by insatiable curiosity. It has a long red beak, through which it can whistle like a cabby. When anybody, particularly a German, approaches, it is overcome with astonishment and watches him carefully from behind a rock. As soon as he passes it whistles, whereupon it becomes invisible—and a hundred yards later there it is, sitting behind another rock, sticking its head and red beak out and whistling again.

I found the *tjaldur's* habits very agreeable. On my walks through the *fjälls* I never had the feeling of being alone. It was possible to walk for several hours in sunshine, or through one of the sudden mists that came down, without seeing a single house. Every house lay at the water's edge and had a little jetty, a small boathouse, and one or two of those long boats, pointed at both ends.

One afternoon I arrived at one of these houses just when the boat was being put out. I asked if I could go with it, and room was made for me. We traveled for two hours through a fantastic landscape of rocks, fjords, and inlets. I couldn't talk to the people in the boat, but they offered me bread and spirits and a piece of mutton which had been dried in the open air and tasted like sweetish sole leather. They told me they were going to the *grindadrap*.

I had found out by this time that *grind* meant whale and that a *grindadrap* was a kind of whale hunt, but that was all I knew for certain, because the descriptions varied so much. Some said that the *grind* committed suicide, and others that men drove them mad and tortured them till they dashed ashore.

Eventually we entered a gentle fjord, where several boats already lay. I went ashore, thanked the people in the boat for my trip, and climbed onto a rock. The whole shore was black with people. It was Sunday afternoon, and they were all in town clothes or wearing their beautiful Faroese kneebreeches with ribbons and colored stockings.

Finally the fjord became rather crowded. From my cliff I could see the whales, which were restless and excited, raising their heads a little way out of the water, perpetually stirring up foam. They scented danger. A phalanx of rowing boats crept silently behind them, driving them into the *cul de sac* of the fjord. The battle had been going on for hours. Again and again the whales tried to break out, and again and again the fishermen threw stones at them and drove them back. It would have been easy for the whales to break out, but what a disgrace it would have been for the fishermen! Their boats were full of stones, and when the supply ran out they went ashore for more.

Whales come to the fjords only in certain weather and at a certain season. The Faroese know all about it. They also know that the whales must be driven inshore at high tide, so that they will be stranded by the ebb.

When I climbed up to my rock it was just before high water. The people already there made room for me. They knew I was a stranger and were proud to have me see their *grindadrap*. Among them was a pretty girl from Thorshavn, one of the fishergirls whom I had noticed several times at work behind the quarry. Today she was smartly dressed; she was actually wearing a fur coat. She could speak a little English and had a smiling face.

"Is a *grindadrap* so interesting?" I asked her.

"It's the most wonderful thing there is," she answered. "Look at what's happening now!"

The whales were still restlessly plunging about, blowing and snorting. The rowing boats suddenly started advancing stern foremost upon them. For another moment their snorting could still be heard on the shore. The crowd on the bank held its breath and then said, "Ah!" The girl next to me said "Ah!" too and clenched her fists. Normally she was pale and looked a little anemic, but now her face was pink and there was blood in her cheeks.

I looked at her only for a second. When I looked at the fjord again the first ten or a dozen boats had reached the whales. The men had shipped their oars and were attacking with lances. Some had long harpoons, others nothing but short fishknives. Others had horrible hooks fastened to chains fixed to the boats' thwarts. Every man had his own way of torturing the whales and set about it with great deliberation and gusto.

Meanwhile they shouted, and the people on the shore responded, as in a great liturgy, and the shouting echoed against the cliffs and blended into a single roar.

"Hey! Ho! Ha!" the fishermen in the boats shouted.

"Hey! Ho! Ha!" the people on the shore shouted too.

Wherever the lances struck or the slate-gray backs were slit blood spouted high, and, where the lances struck deep enough, blood ran into the water.

"Splendid!" the girl from Thorshavn said. "Splendid! Now they won't get away!"

The whale is a stupid, gregarious beast, and when he has once lost blood in a fjord he never leaves it alive. No *grind* that sees a bleeding comrade by its side ever breaks out. That is what the fishermen of the Faroes believe.

It was a horrible butchery, but it was impossible to look away, because so much was happening, just as in a battle. Here a fisherman who had not withdrawn his harpoon quickly enough was flung into the water by the whale's movement. There a whale, bleeding from a dozen wounds, leaped high out of the water, looking for a moment as if it were standing on its tail before it fell back across the bow of a boat. Men were continually falling into the water and being dragged aboard again. One whale leaped up and fell right across a boat and sank it, but the men clambered on board again, bailed out the boat, and then plunged back into the fray. They laughed and shouted the whole time, and the laughter and shouting spread right across the inlet and was echoed by the people on the shore.

There were children in arms among them, and old men supporting themselves with sticks. They were unanimously agreed that the whales must be killed. They were also unanimously agreed that they must make a great noise, laugh and shout, to cheer on the men in the boats to greater efforts, and make fun of the stupid or clumsy ones. Everyone had seen at least a half a dozen *grindadraps* and understood all the finer points of the ritual. The old men shouted advice to the men in the boats.

"Don't get your trousers wet!" . . . "Careful, it bites!" . . . "Look out, it's bigger than you!" . . . "The head's at the other end, you're sticking it in the tail!"

The fishergirl from Thorshavn translated for me and shook with laughter at all this humor. But then she grew serious again. The first whales had started breaking away from the herd and dashing, half under and half over the water, toward the shore. The men on the shore drew their fishknives and waded into the water. They slaughtered the whales like pigs. They seized each whale by the spout and cut through the covering of fat on the neck until they came to the muscle. Then a few more short cuts, and the whale's head, deprived of its strength, sank forward, the animal's neck broke, and it was left lying among the rocks, a grayish-black, piglike sausage.

What excitement about every single whale! A man stood on his prey, his legs apart. It curled up like a caterpillar. The man rode five or ten yards on the animal's back, and then both man and whale sank. After a while the man waded ashore. For two minutes the whale swam in crazy circles and then dashed onto the rocks again.

Some young men showed off by going for the whales in their Sunday best. But the dangerous ones were the grown-up men, who showed no excitement but watched a whale wallowing on the shore in its pain and stupidity, approached it cautiously, and then cut its throat with a couple of skillful movements. They went about their business with the skill of the experienced butcher. But here we were in the open, in the midst of nature, with a whole inlet of the sea as the theater, the forum, with death taking place publicly in the presence of several thousand people who had hurried from near and far to watch the whales die. The whales were all killed that afternoon, and not a single one escaped. When the tide receded, one hundred and twenty motionless torpedoes of flesh, bone, and fat were lying there, and in the middle of the inlet, where the boats of the fishermen had been, a broad red stain lay in the turquoise-blue water.

VI

Later that evening I went with the fishergirl from Thorshavn to the home of her relatives and had supper with them. There were several sorts of bread and cheese, and fish sausage and freshly cooked *grind* steaks. Some small children were playing in the corner, where a large piece of *grind* lay. With their knives they cut off little slices of the bacon and ate it with relish. I was invited to do the same, but I couldn't manage it.

We went for a walk along the shore and greeted the people we met. Sometimes we stopped and chatted for a moment.

"That was a lovely *grindadrap* this afternoon, wasn't it?"

"Yes," I replied, as was expected of me. "You ought to be grateful, it was a very fine *grindadrap!*"

"Ha! Ha!" they said. "You don't have anything like that in Germany, do you?"

"No," I answered. "I came from Germany specially to see one. A *grindadrap* is a very fine thing!"

They were delighted that I had enjoyed it. They were very friendly toward me and full of innocent pleasure. They had shown their guest the best that the Faroes had to offer, a brilliant gladiatorial combat, presented by the most experienced performers. It had been wild, bloodthirsty, and pitiless, full of manly humor but with a faint odor of sweat and blood. They were fully at one with themselves and the world. The *grind* was a stupid beast, but at the same time it was a devil because it could swim under water. If it weren't stupid it would just swim away. How exciting, how dangerous, how disgraceful it would have been if the whales had really been allowed to escape! Even mothers

wouldn't have spoken to their sons any more! True, in return for
all the effort, for all the anxiety, trouble, and work the whales
caused, they had to suffer a little, but only enough to let everyone
have his fun.

Dancing went on all night in a big barn behind the village
above the fjord. While the sun dipped beneath the horizon for a
few short hours a pale, sickly moon made its way across the sky.
I went to the barn with the girl. They were dancing a round
dance. Men and women were holding hands in an endless chain,
and an old man was standing and singing in the middle. He was
singing a song called the "Kvaede." After it had lasted for some
time he started singing the "Omkvaede," in which everybody
joined. They had already danced the Viking dance and the Norman dance. They moved to the right, then to the left, stopped,
flung themselves this way and that way, swung their partners
backward and forward, leaped high in the air, formed figures, ro-
settes, crosses, stars. The extraordinary thing was that everybody
knew his place in the figures.

They had tins of smuggled liquor from Aberdeen, Copenhagen,
and Bergen. A man would take a tin, knock a nail in it to make a
hole, then raise it and pour a thin stream of liquor down his
throat. I drank too, and the liquor tickled and burned my throat.
I took my place among the dancers, and after I had drunk a little
I didn't bother any more about the rules but just did what the
others did. I stamped my feet, swung my partner about, ran and
leaped in the air; and in the big barn, which was dimly lit by a
few petrol lamps, the people looked like hobgoblins, the shadows
of hobgoblins. The old man went on with his hoarse, monotonous
chant. The tune consisted of only five notes, but it was that that
made it so exciting. It quavered and missed a little, and then came
the refrain, the "Omkvaede," and everybody joined in.

It was only a hoarse shout, the words had long since vanished,
and it was all to do with the *grindadrap*. "*Grindadrap* hi!"—and
we all leaped in the air. "*Grindadrap* hi!"—and we all dashed
round to the left. "*Grindadrap* hi!"—and we stepped past each
other.

After a while I was wet through with perspiration. My heart
was pounding, and all I could see was a jumble—the singer, the

dancers, and the lamps, which had faces like the suns in Van Gogh's pictures. I went outside with the fishergirl, and she clung to my arm. By this time I was smeared with blood, like the other dancers, whom I had kept brushing past, but I no longer cared. Outside it was somewhat lighter, the wind was whistling across the fjord, and the mountains all around seemed to be somewhat farther away, but the village was asleep. Two other dancers, a man and a girl, were walking ahead of us. They were staggering slightly and every now and then they stopped and kissed. We stopped and kissed too, and then walked along behind them again. Eventually we came to another barn, which was half full of hay. At the door we found the couple who had been walking ahead of us, talking to another couple who were just coming out, and we joined them. One of the young fishermen had a flask full of liquor, which he offered me. We all drank, and then we went into the barn, while the others, who had already been inside, went back to the other barn where the dancing was going on. It wasn't daylight yet; the sun was still below the horizon.

A few days later I went out with the fishergirl again, this time in Thorshavn. We went to the cinema and saw a well-known British film. It was about a girl whom her father beat with a riding whip. She was in love with a Chinese who kept poisonous snakes. The father set fire to the snake charmer's house, but the Chinese had put a poisonous snake in the Englishman's bed, and it bit him, so both of them died. It was a very well-known film and had won several prizes. The girl was delighted with it. Afterward we went to the Thorshavn dance hall. A lot of young men and girls were there. The music was provided by a gramophone with a loudspeaker. We paid one krone admission and danced tangoes and fox trots.

VII

The day before my departure a motor yacht arrived from Reykjavik with Margarete and her father on board. They were delighted to find me still there. The yacht belonged to a friend of Herr Seidenbaum's who was going on to Bergen, and they were going with him.

Margarete said Reykjavik had been wonderful. She had seen

everything and gone everywhere in a motor car. She had been to the high mountains, Askja and Hekla, she had danced, and she had met lots of nice people. She hadn't been a bit seasick and had had a room with a tiled bathroom. Smart, what?

"Are you staying with me or going on?" I asked. She looked at me with that uncertain look in her eyes again.

"He told me he offered you a job."

"Something like that, at any rate," I said.

"And you don't want it?"

"No. Why should I? I've no reason to. He's not my father!"

"*Jaso!*" she said, like a real Icelander, and I teased her about it a bit. After that we didn't discuss the matter again.

"Has Josefine written to you?" she asked.

I shook my head.

"Poor chap!" she said. "She hasn't written to you! I told you she was a bad lot!"

"Mind your own business!" I said.

I saw her again for a short time on board the yacht, to which I was invited. Herr Seidenbaum had a conversation with me in the saloon.

"Have you thought it over?" he asked.

I told him I had. I'd go to Panama if I wanted to, I said, but I didn't want to.

"So you think yourself a hero," he said.

"Why?"

"If you want to go back to Germany now, you must think yourself a hero. You won't go on thinking that for long. You'll think of the offer I made you, but then it will be too late. The big mousetrap will have shut, and no one will be able to get out!"

"I think you're mistaken," I said.

"As you wish. We'll see! My beautiful houses in Berlin will have gone too. Besides, if you won't listen to me, perhaps you'll be willing to listen to your father."

"What do you know about my father?"

"I know that he wouldn't be at all displeased if I found you a position in another country. Margarete heard him saying so to her mother."

"Margarete says all sorts of things," I said. "My father has never mentioned it to me!"

"As you wish," he said.

They went on to Bergen, and next day I sailed for Copenhagen. I spent half the night beforehand drinking with the Scotsman and the fishergirl. He said he had often noticed her, and he liked her very much. We drank a great deal, and they were both sorry that I was going. I promised to come back next year, when we'd all three go to a *grindadrap* together.

VIII

During the crossing from Copenhagen to Travemünde destroyers were engaged in a night exercise in the Baltic. It was conducted under realistic, warlike conditions. The destroyers were blacked out, and occasionally used their searchlights. This maneuvering in the dark was rather sinister. Aircraft flew over our heads and dropped flares. The Danes and Swedes on board walked about with grave, anxious faces, and before I went ashore I used my last foreign money to buy half a pound of plug slice tobacco from a Swedish steward.

A policeman at the customs shed examined my passport very carefully, held it against the light, and seemed to be rather suspicious; but I had a good conscience and he let me through. At the customs all the women had the butter they had bought in Sweden taken away. Nearly all the women had brought butter and coffee with them, but they had to give it up. I had hidden the tobacco among my dirty shirts, but my luggage was scarcely looked at. The customs officials were interested only in the women.

At Lübeck station I was given a single piece of sugar with my coffee, and a very thin pat of butter. Only then did I realize how well I had been living all this time. The meals had been so good that I had hardly thought about them. Then I went on to Berlin. In Berlin things were humming; it was like a beehive. Yevgenia was staying with us, and at first she was delighted when I told her that Margarete was staying with her father. Kride was delighted too.

Later Yevgenia cried, although she had been so delighted. I tried to console her. I told her that Margarete would be coming to see her soon, or she would be going to see Margarete. But she refused to be consoled.

Huge air maneuvers took place over northwest Germany, huge warlike maneuvers. The British were not idle either, and their air maneuvers took them deep into France. The British made derogatory remarks about our maneuvers, and we made derogatory remarks about theirs. Everything was as it had been before.

And then one morning I woke up in my room in the Wörthstrasse, and my father was standing by my bed. He had a yellow envelope in his hand, and I knew that this meant that we should be earning another decoration for another Sudetenland. This time it was Danzig.

While I shaved, my father was very solemn and said several times, "My dear boy, the Second World War has broken out."

"Oh, hell!" I said. "In eight weeks' time I'll be home again!"

I went away, but in eight weeks' time I wasn't home again. I was still running backward and forward between my plankbed and the gun to which I was married. What I had told Seidenbaum turned out to be quite right; it didn't take long to finish off the Poles. But in the meantime other countries had declared war on us, and there could be no more thought of going home. All the same, if someone had told us we should lay down our arms, as Johanna Selzer later on told me we should have done, we would only have laughed. Lay down our arms after finishing off the Poles in eighteen days? We would have been crazy!

A letter came from home with news about Yevgenia's family. Josefine had gone to Paris just before war broke out, and Margarete had turned up one day in Hamburg on the express from Fridericia. She had brought a trunk full of new clothes with her and had gone back to her mother's. My father made no comment on all this, but one could read between the lines that he and everyone else thought that Margarete was crazy. I didn't find out what happened to Herr Seidenbaum.

5 - The Good Years of Victory

We spent the whole first winter of the war in a concrete shelter beyond Aachen. We were a troop of four guns and the corresponding number of men. Our unit was part of a battery which was part of a regiment responsible for the defence of a part of Aachen against enemy air attack.

If the winter hadn't been so severe it might have been quite comfortable. Nothing at all happened during all those months, except that it was dreadfully cold and our quarters were primitive. Eighteen of us were billeted in a small concrete shelter, containing eighteen bunks, eighteen cupboards and eighteen stools, a stove, and two tables. It was cramped and stuffy. Either the shelter had been built too quickly or the earth had sunk; in any case a crack appeared halfway up the wall. There must have been an underground spring not far away, from which water flowed through that crack. The result was that the floor was swimming in water, which had to be swept away every morning with a squeegee to provide us with ground to walk on. The matter was, of course, reported by the troop to the battery adjutant, by him to regimental headquarters, and by them to heaven knows whom. The result was that several gentlemen in uniform came with rulers and theodolites. They measured everything very carefully and confirmed that the shelter really had sunk. They spent half the day over this and then went away again, but the water went on pouring through the crack. We borrowed some planks from the neighboring village and used them as duck-boards, and then it was more comfortable. But the winter was long and cold, and every morning there were icicles on our beds. I slept on the top deck and had more icicles than most. When one of the men underneath me reported sick—I heard about it in the troop office—I

offered him two packs of cork-tipped cigarettes to change bunks
with me. He agreed, and we changed bunks immediately, to prevent anyone else from grabbing his bed while I wasn't there. But
next morning the M.O. examined him and declared him fit to stay
with the troop. He wanted his bunk back, but by that time he'd
smoked all the cigarettes and couldn't give them back, so after
that he had the icicles instead of me. That was by far the most
important event of the whole winter. At Christmas we were sent
presents. We weren't too far from the Rhineland, and a well-
known firm of wine merchants sent us some cases of champagne
and wine. The champagne got lost on the way, or ended up in an
officers' mess, but we got three bottles of wine each.

That winter we took a great deal of pride in our simple pleasures. I hadn't known before what a pleasure it could be to wash
in an open wooden shed, at twenty degrees below freezing, in a
pail of hot water that one had heated oneself in a scullery. Afterward I'd run two hundred yards through the east wind back to
the billet, wearing only P.T. kit, and sit in front of the hot stove.
It didn't do me any harm, and I remained perfectly fit.

We were a group of men thrown together by chance. Our battery captain was a reservist and our troop sergeant major a regular.
We should have preferred things to be the other way about. The
sergeant major took pleasure in making life as unpleasant for us
as it had been made for him when he was a recruit. I don't know
what he hoped to gain by this, but it is characteristic of that sort
of person always to do to others exactly what was done to him.

The captain was an elderly man with a lined face. He was always smartly turned out, and he spoke very little. There were
some older men among us who looked as if, with a little luck, they
might have been captains too. But they were ordinary gunners
and had to sleep in the cracked shelter with the rest of us. It
wasn't our captain's fault, he never bullied or browbeat anyone.
It wasn't his fault that we weren't all officers yet. But the older
men grew very indignant from time to time. They said they had
imagined war to be quite different from this.

They spent all their time after duty writing letters, and always
hurried over their meals to get back to the shelter and spread out
their writing things. They wrote to their families and their busi-

ness friends. Most of their letters were aimed at getting themselves released. Sometimes they applied for release through the official channels—that is to say, their letters were handed in at the troop office—but everybody knew that applications through official channels were quite useless. Their other applications went through unofficial channels—that is to say, they were sent home by the Army post office. In these cases everything depended on how well the writer stood with the addressee and how much influence the addressee had. This procedure was strictly forbidden, but it at least produced results.

In the evening, when the petrol lamp was lit, they sat writing their letters and seriously discussing what else they could do. They all wanted to go home. They weren't against the war, assuming that it was absolutely necessary, but they didn't want to lose business because of it.

In the face of all that industry the rest of us seemed rather superfluous and useless. We too, of course, hadn't imagined that war would be like this. Our sergeant major was a black-haired, broad-shouldered man, with a high-pitched squeaking voice. Everyone expected fire and brimstone to issue forth when he opened his mouth, but instead his high-pitched voice spoiled the whole effect. We very soon found out, however, that it isn't the voice that makes the man. He told us that he used to have a deep, booming voice, but that he had lost it in the Spanish war. You could always put him in a good mood by getting him to talk about Spain. He had several decorations, including a very complicated one that the Spaniards had given him, but our captain had the Turkish Crescent.

"Pah!" said the sergeant major. "My father was in Turkey in the last war. He says you could pave the streets with Turkish Crescents!"

Whenever I was on duty in the troop office I used to ask him how he had got to Spain. Then he'd describe in full how they had crossed the Bay of Biscay in a merchant ship, dressed as civilians. After reaching the north Spanish coast they had followed it all the way around to the south. They had been forbidden to go on deck, and had all been seasick. He told us all about the Spanish war, which had been quite different from the war we were now engaged in, because in Spain there had been real fighting. He had the advantage over us, because he knew what war was like. While he talked nobody did any work.

I had hoped to rejoin the battery I had been with at Aachen during the Sudetenland crisis, but something must have gone wrong because I had ended up in a completely different unit, where it was not even known that I was a lance-corporal. In the records I appeared as not having passed matriculation, and the clerk had entered my civilian occupation as artisan. I thought the war would soon be over, so I didn't bother about having the entry corrected. I'd become rather indifferent about everything. I had the feeling that a jinx lay over me. I was a misfit in civilian life, and I felt I wouldn't be able to influence the course of the war either. No matter where you went in the world, it was full of ambitious people who managed to get on. They always saluted correctly, and their movements had the smartness and precision laid down in military regulations.

In the course of time I grew friendly with a young man of about my own age who was an architect by profession. He explained to me how houses were built, and in the evening we sat together in the corner and smoked and talked about housing developments. One day he was called to the troop office. He came back excitedly and packed his things. He had been released—he of all people! He was crazy with delight, kept making jokes, and had quite forgotten his normal self-control. He gave us good advice about how to win the war and then left the troop and returned to civilian life.

The older men took this very much amiss, and for a time I did so too. I tried to think of reasons why I might apply for release, but I couldn't think of any good ones. I might have said I wanted to take my degree, but that seemed absurd. What was the use of a degree in art history?

So I didn't apply for release, but smoked and sometimes thought about Josefine, of whom nobody had any news. I felt sorry for her because I thought she must have been interned in Paris as an enemy alien. But she couldn't have been much worse off than I was. Yevgenia wrote and sent me socks, and once she sent me a civilian silk shirt. It was a very nice shirt, but I could

wear it only when I went out, and we seldom went out, because it
was so cold. It was an infernal winter.

II

That April, when the invasion of Norway took place, I was at
home. I had wanted to be at home for my birthday, February 14,
but shortly beforehand the sergeant major discovered that I was
no artisan, merely a wretched art historian. He threw the clerk
out of the troop office and got a new one. This caused a lot of
trouble and cost money, as my records had to be altered. As a
punishment I was given three extra rounds of guard duty, and my
leave was postponed. But the good side to it was that it led to my
having my first war experience.

Shortly before I went on leave we had the first casualty in our
troop—a lance-corporal who was very adventurous by nature and
despised us all because we never went around "the left side of the
hill." There was a place on the left side of the hill from which
you could see a French machine-gun emplacement. The Frenchmen could, of course, see you too. All through the winter we had
a kind of gentleman's agreement with them; we didn't shoot at
them without good reason, and they didn't shoot at us. On one
occasion some officers from Supreme Headquarters came to see us,
accompanied by a civilian. They spent a long time examining the
lay of the land and had themselves shown the enemy's positions
by the sergeant major. They were very cautious, and we hoped
that the French would open fire on them, but they only did so
half an hour later, after the staff officers and the mousy gray little
civilian had left. Apparently it had taken all that time for the
news to get to them, or perhaps the man who gave the fire orders
happened to be at coffee. When the Frenchmen opened up, another of their positions started firing at us. Then the troop next
to us started firing at them, and this went on until everyone had
fired three rounds each. After that we stopped.

"Just you watch," the adventurous lance-corporal said one
sunny March afternoon, and walked toward the point on the left
side of the hill, where he placed himself boldly and defiantly in

the sun. He'd show them, he said. A senior officer must have happened to be in the French machine-gun emplacement, because very soon a rat-tat-tat started. We heard it at troop headquarters and dashed toward the place, but the man had been shot in the stomach; he was lying on the ground, shrieking. We all lay under cover and wondered what to do. The Frenchmen sprayed the whole area with machine-gun bullets, and then the guns started firing, our own and the French, all because of a lance-corporal. Our sergeant major appeared on the scene, walked straight up the left side of the hill, picked the man up like a child, carried him back, and laid him in our gun emplacement. We fetched a stretcher, the M.O. was sent for, and then we and the other guns of our battery opened fire. This time we fired more than three rounds and aimed by indirect fire at the machine-gun emplacement. We hit it two or three times. All that was left of it was a heap of rubble, and then we stopped firing.

Everyone went and stood around the wounded man, who had shut his eyes and had blood at the corner of his mouth. It gave one an uncanny feeling to see him lying there like that. He had had his midday meal with us a few hours before, and now he lay there, with only his eyelids fluttering a little. The M.O. wasn't there, so another one came from headquarters. He turned out to be Friedrich Feldmann, wearing a smart uniform. He went and knelt beside the man and didn't see me. But he was too late. The man had died. Underneath the stretcher there was a pool of blood. Feldmann went to the office with the sergeant major, wrote something, telephoned, and then came out again. I wanted to talk to him, as it was pleasant to see an old acquaintance, so I stepped forward when he walked toward his car.

"Good afternoon!" I said.

He looked up. At first his face was absent, but suddenly he started laughing, not very loud. He looked at my sleeve and said, "Bombardier Stamm! Who would have believed it? How are you?"

"Very well, thank you. And how are you, Feldmann?"

"I'm addressed as 'sir,'" he answered stiffly.

"Very good, sir. I'm sorry, sir," I said.

"Don't mention it," he answered. "Good-by, Stamm. Heil Hitler!"

"Heil Hitler, sir," I said.

I tried to convince myself that I didn't mind this little incident, but I did mind it. For a whole week I minded it very much indeed. I imagined all the things I'd say to Feldmann after the war when I met him in company. Oh yes, I'd get my own back on Feldmann all right! But then my leave came, and I forgot about it and went home. I was so delighted to get home and be able to wear civilian clothes and have a hot bath and sleep in a soft bed.

On the way from Frankfurt to Berlin I met a girl who was traveling to Berlin too. She was a governess with a family in Frankfurt. She was slender and rather pale, and said the war was as good as lost. I asked her how she knew, and she said that the people she worked for, who were a very respected family in Frankfurt, said so, and they knew. They were now moving to Bavaria, where they had bought a small country house, because the war was as good as lost. She was going to Berlin, and when they had moved into the house in Bavaria she would be going there to join them.

I laughed at her, but she stuck to her point. She was a pretty girl, with fair hair and an energetic face, and she didn't look like the kind of person who says a war is lost before it has started. I gave her my field post-office number, and she told me her name. It was Johanna Selzer, and she came from somewhere in the Rhön. She was going to stay in Berlin with her sister-in-law, who was living alone there with a small child. Her husband had been killed in Poland. He was Johanna's brother.

"He was lucky to be killed so soon," Johanna said. I couldn't get her to change her mind. Because her brother had been killed in Poland she was seriously convinced that the war was lost. She gave me her telephone number in Berlin, and I meant to ring her up but I forgot and didn't.

When I got home Yevgenia and Margarete were there. Margarete was now in the top class but one at school. They were all very excited about Josefine, who had written them a letter by way of Switzerland. It had been forwarded by an acquaintance of my father's, who was in the legation there. Josefine was well and was happily married to a Vicomte de Maergruive, who had a magnificent flat in Paris. She had exchanged her German nationality for

French in good time and had not been interned. No doubt she had said she was Russian. She was quite capable of it.

My father had aged considerably and had worries at the office. He was greatly concerned at the policy of the Russians, who had disgraced themselves in Finland and were now demanding the Bosporus. There was no intention of giving them the Bosporus, but they seemed to be demanding it as their price for keeping the peace. The whole office was indignant with the Russians, first because they had made such a deplorable exhibition of themselves in Finland, and secondly because they were now behaving as if they were a great power.

"It's not only that," my father said to me after the family had scattered a little. "All this has very disagreeable repercussions on me. Everyone knows that I advocate a policy of cooperation with the Russians in Europe and Asia. The Russians should busy themselves with the East and leave the West to us. There's room for both of us to live. Let the Russians have India and the Philippines and the Dutch East Indies, and leave Western Europe and Africa to us. All that is made much more difficult by the crazy attitude of the Russians. They act as if they had lost something in the Mediterranean."

"What's going to happen next?" I asked.

He shrugged his shoulders. "Things will happen in the West," he said. "I hope we'll have finished off the French within a year. The soldiers are very optimistic. But they were optimistic in nineteen fourteen too, and then there was the Battle of the Marne. Perhaps the British will capitulate when they see we're masters of the Continent. That would be the sensible thing to do. But everything depends on what sort of policy we have."

"And what sort of a policy have we?"

"An obscure one," he answered. He didn't sound very optimistic.

Two days later the Norwegian operation started, and it was still in progress when I returned to my troop. I had ten days' leave, and for a week of it Norway was the only subject of conversation, from morning to night. My father knew Norway, and Margarete now suddenly became an authority because she had been there the previous autumn with her father, Herr Seidenbaum. To listen to her, you'd have thought she had spent not two months there, but two years. But there were some places that she really knew.

Each time I saw her she looked a little prettier. She was full of plans for the future. She wanted to be in the movies, or work in an X-ray clinic, or pilot an advertising aircraft. With her mother it was just the opposite. Each time I saw her she was a little stouter and looked gloomier and more depressed.

"How's the astrology, Yevgenia?" I asked.

"Oh! the stars are very bad," she said. "Things'll be good for a year, perhaps two years, but then bad times are coming, very bad times, I say!"

"Mother!" Kride exclaimed and turned to me. "They're terribly down on astrology here, Rodie! I simply can't understand how Mother can believe in such rubbish! It's not only stupid, it's dangerous!"

"Nonsense! I don't talk to anybody about it. I only do it for myself. I'm not a baby!" Yevgenia said.

"So I hope," said Kride.

To change the subject I told her what the girl I had met in the train had said.

"Disgraceful!" Kride exclaimed. "A person like that ought to be locked up! Going about telling people the war's lost!"

"Oh, leave her alone," my father said. "I expect she's got her own troubles. Good heavens, Kride, we can't lock everybody up!"

"Do we lock so many people up?" I asked.

"Nothing worth mentioning," said Kride. "Only a few traitors and defeatists."

"And the Jews," my father said. "The whole Olivaerplatz will soon be empty. They take whole families away, night after night."

"Families?"

"Women, children, everybody."

"And what do they do with them?"

"They resettle them in Poland, where they belong," said Kride. "After all, they're not citizens, Max! You used to say yourself that the Jews were our misfortune. We can't be weak now!"

"No, no," my father said.

Kride sighed and shook her head. She was rather indignant.

I had a talk with Yevgenia the first evening. I felt sorry for her

"You think so?"

"I know it! How did von Haringen die? He was in a village, in command of his company. There were Germans to the right and Germans to the left. 'Lads, let us attack these accursed Germans,' he said. They didn't want to. He lit a cigarette, took his riding whip, and whipped them. He advanced, and they followed him. He ordered them to fix bayonets, and they followed him. The Germans had a machine gun. Rat-tat-tat-tat-tat! and it was over. Von Haringen fell. He had a cigarette in the corner of his mouth and his riding whip in his hand. The Germans gave him a good burial. He got a grave with a cross all to himself. All the others were put in a mass grave. A mass grave is good enough for me and good enough for you. But von Haringen gets a grave and cross all to himself. That's the difference!"

It was the first time I had heard this part of Yevgenia's philosophy. It wasn't a bad philosophy. All we were fit for was a mass grave, but we deserved no better because we marched loyally behind the aspirants to individual graves.

"Josefine is something different again," said Yevgenia, continuing her observations. "She's like my mother. When my mother was a girl she danced like—like Anna Karenina! Lightheartedness, happiness, love, adventure! Not proud, but obsessed. Obsessed with good living, beautiful living, laughter and love. Oh, I know it all! I've experienced it all! I was a bad mother!"

Yevgenia went on talking, and I sat with her for a long time. She was skeptical about Josefine's success in Paris. What would she do when the Germans came? How had she managed to acquire French nationality so easily? There was something Yevgenia didn't trust about all this. She knew her Josefine. "She's frivolous, Rurik, frivolous." She wasn't a bad girl, she'd give her shirt away to anyone who needed it, but she'd take ten thousand marks and blow it away like that! Pouf!

"Why didn't I go to Switzerland?" she said. "In Switzerland they do everything right. They're clever. They sow a little bit here and a little bit there. They don't commit themselves. If Hitler comes, they're on good terms with him. If another comes, they're on good terms with him too! They're always on good terms. But

I was a bad mother. Switzerland? Pah! Too boring! No nice men, no life, nothing but good food! So I came to Germany. Kride marries Max. How stupid of Max!"

I moved slightly in my chair. "They're both very happy."

"Happy?" she said. "Pah! You forget that Max is seven years older than I am! He ought to have married me!"

"Are you jealous?" I asked and laughed.

She made a contemptuous movement with her hand. "Jealous? I wouldn't have had him as a gift! He could have done with me when we were both young. I'm not a good mother, but he's an excellent father. I tell my girls everything that comes into my head —about my husband, about the Revolution, when I'm happy and when I'm sad. I tell them everything. I'm a bad mother. But I've got ideas. I've got more brains in my little finger than Max has in his whole head!"

She snapped the fingers in which she had such a lot of brains.

"And what about Margarete?" I asked.

Her face grew old and troubled again. It was as if she had a bad tooth, which she had forgotten about but had suddenly touched with her tongue. It started aching.

"Why did she come back?" I asked and looked around to make sure that Margarete wasn't listening. But she had started a telephone conversation with another schoolgirl of her own age who had also come to Berlin, and at that age, when they once start, they block the line for hours.

Yevgenia didn't believe that Margarete had told her the real reason why she had come back. She said she hadn't got on well with her father. That was stupid, Yevgenia said. How can you not get on well with a man who buys you a real gold necklace?

"You must see it," she said. "It's a wonderful necklace."

"And now it's all over?"

"I don't know," said Yevgenia. "She won't say."

We talked for a time about Margarete's prospects. At school a questionnaire had been sent around, inquiring which girls would be interested in serving as Army auxiliaries. Margarete had filled it in and said she would be very interested.

"I expect she thinks she'll be used as a fighter pilot, or to ride torpedoes," I said.

"She doesn't think at all," Yevgenia answered. "She's like someone with ants in her pants. That's why she came back to Germany. If you came back, she thought, she ought to come back too!"

"So it's my fault?"

"No," said Yevgenia. "It's not your fault. She's the kind of person who thinks she must always choose the hard way."

"Where does she get that from?" I asked and laughed. Yevgenia laughed too. But after a time she grew serious again.

"I'm very worried about Margarete," she said. "She's such a child. But she's a good child. You must never forget that Margarete's a good child, Rurik. She's sometimes silly and often thoughtless, but she's good. Will you remember that?"

"Why do you ask, Yevgenia?" I said. "Of course I'll remember it. I like Margarete. I always have liked her."

"Yes, yes, I know, you were always a good boy! Who knows what will happen in Germany? They won't like losing the war!"

"But they're going to win, Yevgenia. You can depend on it, they're going to win!"

"Oh, well, perhaps they may! But you won't win, Rurik, and I won't, and Margarete won't either!"

III

On the day after my return to the battery we left the cracked shelter forever and moved north. We set up our guns opposite a peasant's whitewashed cottage. Through our field glasses we could see the window that had been painted on the whitewash. If you looked more carefully you could see the slits for the machine guns inside. I used to lie on the parapet for hours, looking at the little slits, until in the end I could have found them in the dark.

On the morning of the day I was Number One on the gun I sat in the little seat, my hands on the elevating and traversing gear, and adjusted the sights until the cross-threads lay dead on the slits in the peasant's house. At the prearranged time we fired. The first round fell a little short. In my excitement I nearly lowered the muzzle instead of raising it, but I did raise it, and the second round fell closer. After that I forgot to be excited.

Guns roared to right and left of us, the shells flew westward, and I watched the cottage disintegrating bit by bit, exposing the pillbox underneath. We went on firing, and a crack appeared in the pillbox. We had shot ourselves in beautifully. The crack grew bigger and bigger, and each shell fell more accurately than the one before it. The pillbox split apart and eventually broke in two.

We went on firing at the bigger of the two portions of it, and after that it didn't last very long. The material of which it was made grew brittle under the shelling, and it increasingly disintegrated. We had fulfilled our task, but we went on firing until all that was to be seen through the sights was a heap of rubble from which dust rose and flew in all directions.

Meanwhile the other guns all around us had been doing an equally good job. A whistle blew, and the tanks and infantry behind us started moving forward. The infantry moved in small groups behind the tanks. We were hot with excitement and drank our breakfast coffee, which was brought us from the cookhouse, watching the tanks advancing toward and disappearing over the horizon, with the infantry moving in small groups behind them.

Aircraft flew overhead all day long. At first we counted them, and every time we counted up to a hundred we were delighted, but then we got bored with counting, and in the end we didn't even look up when they flew overhead. They were all our aircraft. No others seemed to exist.

Later on we limbered up and moved to an airfield, from which only seven ambulance machines went up the whole time. Only once did an enemy aircraft appear by night and drop a few bombs, which whined and whistled before exploding somewhere in the night. No one was hit. The weather grew warmer every day, summer began, and then the French capitulated.

Everybody thought the war was over. We had beaten the Poles, and now we had beaten the French, who had declared war on us. Our troops had reached the Atlantic, and the British had experienced Dunkirk. It was all very simple.

We were moved again, this time a long way, all the way to a suburb outside Paris. Paris was out of bounds, particularly for other ranks. So we stayed in our suburb and ate our field rations and gazed longingly at the Eiffel Tower stretching its spidery legs in the air in the distance. Somewhere in the neighborhood of the Eiffel Tower was Josefine.

I stood high in the regard of the troop sergeant major because of the way I had shot up the pillbox. We had received a commendation for having provided such excellent support for the advance of the infantry and the tanks. Everybody received a commendation. But that was of no use to me, because there we were, stuck in the outskirts of Paris, and Paris was out of bounds. The French with whom we had dealings were very polite. They brought us ham and eggs and red wine, and were paid in francs. That was all very fine, but Paris was still out of bounds.

Then, after the first cases of illness had occurred, notices were put up, warning us that it was our duty as soldiers to look after ourselves and announcing that it was permissible to resort only to the authorized establishments. I once went to one of these establishments because they were so well advertised. But we found them all too hygienic. In the end I went to the sergeant major and told him I had a sister-in-law in Paris. At first he wouldn't believe me, but I told him the name and address, and he scratched his head and looked very thoughtful.

"Do you speak French?" he asked.

I told him I did.

"Will you come along with me this evening and interpret a little for me and my girl? Then we'll see what can be done."

I interpreted for him, and he gave me a pass to go to an Army office in Paris. Going to Paris without a pass was strictly forbidden, but everyone had a pass. Paris was full of uniforms, and I wasn't in the least conspicuous. I duly obtained a requisition form for an electric light bulb, put it in my trousers pocket, and went to see Josefine. I was rather excited, but I had known Josefine for such a long time, and besides, all I wanted was to pay her a friendly visit. I owed it to my family.

IV

That summer I worked up a colossal racket. I didn't spend my time trying to organize my release; I hadn't the slightest desire to be released. I had no complaints about the war; war, in fact, seemed to me to be a very fine thing. You knocked out a pillbox, and a whole country was conquered. Nobody worried about the dead and wounded. I had one or two acquaintances who were wounded, and they wrote to me from hospital, where they seemed to be very well off. They said the nurses were delightful, and the food excellent. There seemed to be about one nurse to very wounded man, and a doctor for every two wounded men.

Our battery's task was the protection of the Paris garrison supply depot against air attack. The enemy air force cannot have realized what a vital target it was, because they never attacked it. If it had been destroyed the Paris garrison would have had nothing to eat, so the administration of Paris would have suffered severely; and if Paris had not been properly administered, our glorious victory over the French would have been a hollow one. For Paris, according to the ancient saying, is France. But we protected the depot, and Paris was well administered.

One of the many branches of the colossal racket I worked up that summer was Josefine, who had a delightful *salon*. You were equally welcome there, whether you were a private or a general. Josefine had a visitor's book, in which the most distinguished names began appearing after a time. Her guests included district commanders, adjutants, bomber pilots, U-boat commanders, leaders of the civil administration, directors of the Todt organization, and all of them wrote something in her book. It was surprising how well some of them could draw. They wrote little verses, drew little hearts, or bunches of flowers, or frivolous figures that said thank you for the charming hospitality they had received or for a delightful *tête-à-tête*, and one young lieutenant had actually been bold enough to confide to the visitors' book a few lines in incorrect French about an *heure bleue*. Josefine enjoyed the universal favor of her friends, and some of them occasionally enjoyed her favor too, but I only found that out later. The Vicomte de Maergruive did not trouble much about his guests. He was a shriveled little old man who came from Flanders. He spent most of his time in bed on the top floor, and seldom appeared. He was as rich as he was old. He used to say he was delighted that Josefine was having a good time, and then he rubbed his hands and blinked.

"*Voilà Paris!*" Josefine's guests said, returning through the dark streets to their offices, bedrooms, barracks, or hotels. "Voilà Paris!" All this would of course have been unthinkable at home. But the delightful thing was that one was not at home, and there was no need to be excessively worried by the customs of a foreign country. After all, one hadn't chosen to be sent to Paris, one had been sent there on duty; and one couldn't alter Paris. The thing to do was to take it as you found it.

When I saw Josefine again she spoke German with a slight guttural accent, though she had spent ten years at a German school. She spoke German like a Frenchwoman who had lived for a long time in Germany. She skillfully walked a kind of linguistic tightrope. To many people this is very attractive. She was neither one thing nor the other.

When I went there she was obviously delighted to see me and to hear news from home.

She told me to come in and make myself at home. How manly I looked in my uniform! Would I like a cognac, or would I prefer a Cointreau? Men always said they wanted cognac, but then they drank Cointreau or benedictine or chartreuse. Wait a minute, she'd make me some coffee. "You like it strong, don't you? Well, you've got a whole campaign behind you. Was it dangerous? Isn't this war dreadful? Oh well, it'll soon be over!" Or— "I adore being in Paris, I think it's really my native town. Why did Yevgenia go and live in boring Germany? She could have come to Paris, but she insisted on going to Germany. No, I'll certainly never leave Paris again. What does Uncle Max write? Is he still involved in high politics? You must tell me all about everything. How is Kride?"

I told her they were all well. She poured water into the coffee machine, fixed the electric plug in the wall, and went on chattering.

"Come and sit nearer me," I said. "You're as elusive as a piece of quicksilver!"

She came and balanced herself precariously on the arm of the couch. She was wearing a black silk housecoat fastened on one side with a bow. She looked as if she were going to lose her balance at any moment, but instead she went on talking and looking at me out of her dark, opaque eyes. Her ears looked smaller and her hair blacker, silkier, and smoother, but otherwise she was the same Josefine who had spent Christmas with us eighteen months before.

"I thought you'd at least greet me with a family kiss," I said.

"Oh!" she said and leaned forward. For a second her lips were cold and reserved and indifferent, but then she lost her balance and slid down onto the couch. I caught her in my arms. She made no attempt to free herself but looked at me, her face close to mine, and then she shut her dark eyes, and her mouth was no longer indifferent but as passionate as it had been at the New Year's Eve party. The only difference was that this time there was no need to worry about the lights being turned on.

When she opened her eyes again the water in the coffee machine had all boiled away, and she had to pour more into it. We had coffee and talked like ordinary people, but she began to get very restless. She kept jumping up, rearranging the flowers, tidying her hair, using her lipstick, powdering her face, and then coming and sitting on the edge of the couch again, whereupon I made it my business to undo all her good work.

"Now you must behave yourself!" she said, her eyes only an inch or so from mine. "You must be good now! My friend Paule is coming in twenty minutes' time, and I invited her to coffee, not you! Behave yourself!"

Then she lost her balance for the seventh time and collapsed onto the couch again. It was exciting and very funny, and we laughed, and for a few minutes she forgot to be restless. Eventually the bell rang, and the maid showed in Josefine's friend Paule. Paule was attractive and very lively, but not nearly so attractive as Josefine. There was something imperious about her. She and Josefine chatted in quick, chirping French, and I couldn't understand all they said. But Josefine told her all about me and my family and my father. Eventually Paule smiled at me in a way that was not imperious but charming, terribly charming, and her charming manner seemed almost more dangerous than her imperious manner. Josefine wagged her finger at me and said something, and Paule also wagged her finger at me and said, "*Il est très dangereux,*" and then they both roared with laughter. This was their way of paying compliments. At first it made you feel like a Spanish or

Rhode Island Red chicken. Then you got used to it and ceased
to be shocked. You can't alter Paris. We hadn't come to Paris to
alter it.

For six or eight weeks I went to Josefine's whenever I could. I
never found out whether she was in love with me. Actually I don't
think she was; I think it was something else. I'm inclined to think
she was afraid of me. She was one of those women with whom
love and fear go hand in hand. I used to meet Paule at her house,
as well as a lot of other people, some in uniform and others not.
Some wore civilian jackets over their uniform trousers. When she
had visitors there were generally a lot of girls there too—not dom-
inating women, like Paule, but harmless little girls, with names like
Fifi, Louison, Charlotte, Toto, Marion, Elaine, and so on. Josefine
had a whole racket of guests and girls, or so it seemed to me, and
they all used to like calling on her; and the Vicomte de Maergruive paid for all the Cointreau and the coffee that they drank.

I couldn't go to Paris without a pass, and to be able to get a
pass I had to build up my own racket, to keep the men who signed
the passes sweet. There was no difficulty about this. I was only a
lance-corporal, but my father used to send me money through an
office in the garrison administration, and I'd buy them something
and get my pass. A military policeman who stopped me three
days running, and noticed that each time I was under orders to
pick up electric light bulbs from the quartermaster's stores, grum-
bled a bit the third time. He seemed to think I had picked up
enough electric light bulbs, so after that something different was
written on my pass.

I also had another racket. I read Baudelaire and Verlaine and
kept up a correspondence with Johanna Selzer in Bavaria. Writing
to her and getting letters from her was very soothing. She looked
at everything so differently from me. There she was in Bavaria, living in a newly built country house in the neighborhood of the
Tegernsee, looking after her employers' children and entirely surrounded by nature; and here was I, living in a horrible suburb of
Paris, in an old school building that had been requisitioned for
us, and I never saw anything but soldiers and Josefine's *salon*, and
saw no nature at all. I had also taken part in a victorious war and
was convinced my point of view was right. I teased her a little for

having said that the war was lost. Did she see now how stupid of her it had been to think that? A week later the answer came from Bavaria. She told me to wait and see. I might be on my high horse now, but it was stupid to suggest I had won the war because I had shot up one pillbox. I didn't think it fair of her to say that. I had certainly told her I had knocked out a pillbox, but it was the truth, after all. I had never suggested having fought the war single-handed; all I claimed was that I had played my modest part. At first I intended not to answer her, but there were a lot of other things in her letter, so in the end I wrote again. I had translated some poems of Mallarmé, and I sent them to her. A week later another letter arrived; she thought the poems simply hateful. Well, well, she wasn't in Paris. Later on I took a dislike to Mallarmé myself, but at that time I was very fond of him; he seemed to fit in with the whole atmosphere. Johanna Selzer was all part of my racket too; she provided the foil for my visits to Josefine.

It must have been in October or November that the air offensive against England was called off after we'd lost thirty-six Stukas in a single day over the port of London. It was said that there was going to be another quiet winter and that we were going to cross the Channel in the spring. A great deal of talk about the war and the prospects ahead went on in Josefine's house. I received a confidential letter from my father. He said that a new department had been established at his ministry, and he had been assigned to it as a Russian specialist. He had been dealing with Russian affairs for many years now, and his new job was to help the military in working out a Russian plan of campaign. I told Josefine about this. We were in her bedroom. She had discreetly turned various pictures of Luftwaffe pilots, army lieutenants, and a naval ensign to the wall, and it was warm in her house, though in most Paris houses it was cold. We talked about one thing and another, and I was surprised at the interest she took in politics nowadays. I told her about the new Russian plan. She asked what sort of a plan it was. I said I didn't know exactly. Presumably it was a plan of campaign against Russia. Did I mean we were going to war with Russia? I had no idea.

"Good heavens," she said, "but it's important!"

"Important? Why?"

"Good heavens, if you're going to war with Russia, just think!"

I said it was no affair of mine. That's all we said on the subject that day.

But next day I was unexpectedly able to get away from the troop, and I went to see Josefine again. Paule was with her, but left soon after I arrived. Josefine was charming to me this time. Sometimes, when I had called on her unexpectedly she had had no time for me, or had been in a hurry, but this time she was obviously overjoyed to see me, and there was no question of her not having enough time for me.

"I've been longing for you so much," she said. "I was beside myself all night because you weren't here!"

It was very pleasant to hear this. "Why?" I said. "Is anything the matter?"

She said she was just in love with me and had been longing for me. "You frightened me so much with what you said last night about war with Russia!" she said.

"I didn't say anything about war with Russia."

"You did!"

"I only said my father was working with some military staff officers on a Russian plan."

"But that's the same thing!"

"No, it's quite different," I explained. "Father wrote to me through an acquaintance at Vichy. It wasn't the sort of letter you could send through the Army post office. What he said was that it looked as if plan B may now be collapsing, and that they may be taking up plan A again. But all the same he's glad he's being used. It confirms his position, don't you see?"

Josefine didn't seem to see. "I don't understand at all," she said. "But I don't mind. Do you love me? I'm crazy about you! I wanted to telephone you. What were you doing last night? Did you have to stay by your gun? Did you think about me at all? Yes? That's good! Tell me, am I beautiful? Do you like me? I think you're frightfully nice! Shouldn't we say what we think? Tell me, what is this plan B on which Uncle Max is working? I want to be able to understand the things you tell me! I want to understand everything you tell me!"

I told her all about plan A and plan B. I explained that my

father favored a policy of cooperation with Russia, with Germany and Russia standing back to back, so to speak, Russia facing the Pacific and Germany the Atlantic. This plan had scored an unexpected success at the beginning of the war, when the Minister had gone to Moscow to sign a pact with the Russians. But now the policy seemed to be endangered. The good side to it was that in spite of that my father was being used as an expert to work on the new plan.

"That's fine," she said. "I'm very fond of Uncle Max, and I like him to be successful. But what is he working on now?"

I explained that he was preparing a report on Russian material resources and the key points in the Russian economy. That was what the strategists wanted nowadays. Since the time of Moltke wars had been fought not against armies, but increasingly against industries.

"Ah!" she said. "Come, take me in your arms! I'm cold! It's horrible outside today. In November I always want to go away, but Maergruive won't go. He insists on spending the season in Paris. . . ."

I woke up and saw that she wasn't in the room. It was very warm and dry. I got up and drank a glass of water. Then I heard her voice murmuring. She was in the drawing room. I went to the door and heard her voice and Paule's voice, and after a few sentences I understood.

I got up and started dressing. I half dressed and then sat on the bed. I was suddenly completely sober. The whole time previously I had been in a kind of continual intoxication. I was a victor in a foreign land, a land full of drink, coffee, and beautiful women. I had been undermined and poisoned by these things. One thing had led to another. It had been marvelous after the boredom and privations of a soldier's life to enjoy the pleasures of another world, the world of clean, white linen, chartreuse, Chanel, and coffee machines. But now I was awake and sober. After a time Josefine came back and sat beside me. She was tender and affectionate and tried to make a fuss over me. I had often wondered whether she was pretending or was really fond of me, but strangely enough I had always had the feeling that at bottom she was fond of me. I had it even now. This depressed me so much that I could scarcely bring myself to speak to her.

She tried to argue with me and talk me around, but I had heard her telling Paule what I had told her about my father, and I had heard Paule's answer. I tried to be angry, but I was only just angry enough to be able to finish dressing and go away.

"It's all a mistake, a terrible mistake," she called down the steps after me.

v

That night I walked three times past Notre Dame, and I nearly went in, though it was a Roman Catholic cathedral which had nothing to do with me. I walked along the *quais*, then to the Gare St. Lazare, then up to Montmartre and along the Rue des Martyrs, where there are few martyrs but a great many prostitutes. They joked and called after me when I passed, but I wasn't interested. Everything was sober and clear and gray, and I no longer found Paris exciting as before. When I had walked through the streets and looked at the girls and they turned and looked after me, I had felt like a king, a Norman or Viking or Teuton conqueror. But now I had lost interest.

Sometimes I still wonder what made me turn down a little side street off the Boulevard Rochechouart and go into a little bar, the entrance of which was nearly invisible. I sat at a table and ordered a Suze. I didn't drink much of it; I ordered it only because I had to order something. There was a Suze advertisement on the wall near the piano, and underneath it a man was sitting and playing. I stared at his back and thought over everything. I thought of the racket I had built up since I'd been in France. I was surrounded by a huge racket—currency transactions, passes, girls, drink, coffee, music, girls, drink, coffee. Everybody had helped to build up the racket, some in a big way, some in a small way. Some were continually sending off parcels and employed a whole army of black marketeers to fill them. Others spent their time running after French girls and thinking up a thousand dodges and stratagems to be able to continue to do so undisturbed. We had come

as conquerors, as the founders of a millenary Reich, to establish
the New Order in Europe, and no sooner had we settled in than
we sat in a corner and gaped at what we had conquered and forgot
the reason why we had come.

Nothing was taken seriously any more. I could hear the voice of
our sergeant major, reading out standing orders on parade. "Beware of enemy agents. . . . Army socks will be washed only in
tepid water and with Army issue soap. . . . Beware of infectious
diseases. . . . The practice of dropping cigarette ends in the gun
emplacement will cease forthwith. . . . Members of the armed
forces will not make purchases in French shops except with the
currency with which they are issued. . . . The regulations con-
cerning saluting will be rigidly observed, and no laxity will be tol-
erated in any circumstances." A whole chain of standing orders,
warnings, threats, which nobody took seriously. The officer who
drafted them kept a mistress in a flat. The warrant officer who
read them out sent coffee home and had a girl friend too. The
men listened, yawned, and thought about their girl friends, or the
little parcels they packed after duty in the evening.

Of course Josefine had led me down the garden path. Perhaps
she was so deeply involved that she couldn't help it. Perhaps her
husband, the *vicomte*, was no *vicomte* at all, and perhaps his
name wasn't de Maergruive but Jean Pellier, and perhaps he belonged to some movement that was fighting against us. We had
been told about such movements but hadn't taken them seriously.

I could go to a military headquarters and make a report. No, I
could do nothing of the sort. It would lead to arrests and inter-
rogations. The truth about Josefine's *salon* would come out.
Names would be dragged in, well-known names. Our name would
be dragged in; and I would expose myself. All I could do was not
to go to Josefine again.

Perhaps she was not really so guilty. Perhaps she believed in
what she was doing. Who knew what she might have experienced,
or with what grudge against Germany she might have left the
country? So much the worse for us.

The pianist was playing "*Auprès de ma blonde*," and I stared
at his back. He had a broad back and he played excellently. The
Suze advertisement above his head was slightly crooked. He

stopped playing, turned, our eyes met, and we recognized each other. He was Alfred Karawan. He turned away and started playing "*Je chante pendant le jour et la nuit.*" He had recognized me and had turned away. He didn't want to have anything to do with me.

I sank back into my abyss. The Frenchmen at the other tables sang or hummed the tune. Lucky French, they hadn't won a war. I started ordering double cognacs. The little saucers started piling up. But I didn't feel any more cheerful.

The place began to empty, the waiter began to count the takings, Karawan closed the lid of his piano, made himself a cigarette, lit it, and walked slowly past me. He winked at the waiter, said good night to the proprietor, walked slowly past me again and made a movement with his thumb. I went on sitting there a little longer and then got up. I felt I was walking on a cloud. I said good night, the waiter opened the door, I pressed something into his hand—presumably the change—and went out. The street was empty.

I walked away at random. I didn't know what to do. I didn't want to go back to the battery. I wanted— I wanted . . .

Suddenly I noticed that someone was walking beside me. It was Alfred. There was nobody I felt the need of more, but I felt angry with him. He put his hand on my arm and said, "You've had a little too much, haven't you? Come along!"

"Go to hell!" I said and walked on. He stopped for a moment, but then I heard his footsteps behind me again. I was very tired from walking and would gladly have sat down, but in this street there were no seats; there was nothing but street lamps and houses, houses that seemed as high as the sky. Both the houses and the street lamps were swaying slightly. When he took me by the arm again I said nothing. He steered me a few hundred yards along the street and then down some steps into a little all-night café. We sat at a table in the back room. After the third cup of coffee I woke up. I was sitting on a plush sofa, and Karawan's face towered about half a mile above me. The bar revolved slowly from left to right, and then from right to left. Then I was sick. The men behind the bar grinned, because I was in uniform, and Karawan laughed.

"Pity to waste the good coffee," he said.

"Leave me alone!" I said.

Then I was sick again. I no longer cared about anything.

Suddenly I felt better. I had another cup of coffee, a waiter came with a cloth, and I cleaned myself up. The people behind the bar stopped staring at me and went on with their own conversation. I told Karawan everything. There was nobody to whom I would rather have talked. I didn't ask him how he came to be playing the piano in a basement café in occupied Paris. I told him everything, and he said I'd strung a fine noose round my neck. I said I didn't care, but he said sarcastically that when I'd recovered from my hangover I'd find myself very interested indeed in whether this business was going to cost me my neck or not. I didn't agree with him, but I didn't argue because he was so positive and superior and I was far too weak. He rolled himself another cigarette and rested his head in his hands, with the cigarette dangling in the corner of his mouth. He looked exactly like all the other people in the bar. Suddenly he got up, told me to wait, and went outside. I waited and had another cup of coffee. This time I managed to keep it down.

A big man from behind the bar came and asked me whether I had a cigarette to spare. I searched my pockets and gave him a pack. He sat with me and asked me whether I had had too much to drink. I said no, I had had too little. Everybody laughed, and he laughed most of all. He opened the pack of cigarettes and passed it around. They smoked, said, "Tabac blond," and we talked. They asked how much longer we were going to stay here. I said, "Sais pas," and they asked me whether I liked it here. I said I'd rather be here as a civilian. They liked that too. They said the German Luftwaffe was kaputt. I asked why. Kaputt against England, they said. I ordered a bottle of cognac and told them that next year they'd see that England would be kaputt. They raised their glasses, said, "Salut," but looked skeptical and said England was very tough. We should have made England kaputt instead of them; then everything would have been all right. As it was, we had made France kaputt, and now the English came with bombs. Why in all the world had we waged war so brilliantly against France and then failed to cross the Channel? I tried to think what "more haste, less speed" was in French, and told them to wait till next year; they should wait and see. At that they drank a glass of cognac and looked skeptical again, but not quite so skeptical as before.

It was just like one of those moments after an illness. You suddenly see everything very clearly. I saw, for instance, that if we made England kaputt all these people in the bar would shrug their shoulders and admit we were right. But if we failed they'd be angry with us, and the longer we stayed here the angrier they'd become. They were still willing to drink cognac with me because I was a human being who had been sick in spite of his uniform and said he had drunk too little when he had drunk too much. Very little was needed to gain people's confidence, but it was a matter on which everything depended. We only needed to be human beings, and we'd win them. But we weren't human beings; we were in uniform. In other words, we were symbols, and no pleasant symbols either. We were reminders of Dunkirk and Paris and Vichy, of all the things they hated. We were divided from them, not because we were different, but because we were in uniform; and because we were divided from them, we ended by living an absurd, phantom life, either obsessed or greedy or stupid. It might be all right for a year, or perhaps two. But then they'd start hating us because we stood for all the things they had to do without because of us. Now they said, "Quel grand malheur que la guerre!" and meant it. But soon they'd be saying, "Quels diables, ces allemands-là!" and they'd hate us. They'd allow us no good points whatever, and they'd put on uniform themselves, an inner uniform. They'd hate us too much to be able to see our virtues, and they'd ridicule our vices. Just look at those giants, those heroes, the conquerors of the Maginot Line, the heroes of the tank battles of northern France! See how they go drinking and whoring, black marketeering and smuggling! See how they torture and sweat people! Trick them, laugh at them, give them no quarter, stab them in the back, pour sulphuric acid over them, shove them in the canal when they're drunk!

I looked round, and saw nothing but friendly, harmless, good-humored faces. My stomach felt weak, and my morale was weak too. I was sorry for everything. "Come," I said, "let's have another bottle. Don't let's talk about the war. A bas la guerre! A bas ces idiots-là qui font la guerre! Vive le cognac!" They sat and laughed slightly incredulously. They still had in their minds a vision of the steel squadrons that had come clanking down their roads, roaring through their air. Perhaps we really would make the English kaputt. Who could tell? In any case it was an honor to sit and drink with one of these giants, particularly if he was a little weak in the head and paid the bill. What did he say? A bas la guerre! Perhaps he'd be sitting here and drinking our cognac even if there were no war. But he's a friendly giant. Let us drink with him.

"Compère," one of them said, helping himself from the bottle. "What have you done so far in the war?"

I might have answered that I was the man who had shot up the first pillbox on the Maginot Line, but I didn't. I said I hadn't done very much. I had fired at a few British aircraft.

I saw at once that I'd made a mistake. I had diminished myself in their eyes. What? Hadn't I done anything? No, I had no decorations. Perhaps I wasn't a real giant after all.

I poured myself a glass of cognac and said my unit had blown up the first pillbox in the Maginot Line. We had crept up to it at night and blown it up.

"What?" they said. "Is that true? Blown up a pillbox?"

"Merde!" another said. The pillboxes hadn't been difficult to blow up; they were made of cardboard. Their generals and politicians had had them built of cardboard and pocketed the money. Ha! Ha! Ha!

My reputation was again threatened, but I had no need to intervene again because they started squabbling among themselves. Some said the pillboxes had been as good as they possibly could be, and others said they had been useless. They made an unearthly row and emptied the bottle. There was nothing wrong with their humanity. It was all very human indeed.

At last Karawan came back. He had managed to get a car. He said we were going to Josefine's. He said he wanted to see that numéro.

I told him the address. Outside in the street it was still pitch dark, and the open bar door let out a flood of light. Good night, monsieur, sleep well, monsieur, thank you for your entertainment, monsieur. Oh, they're very polite in Paris, there's nothing boor- ish about them!

Karawan realized with astonishment what I'd been doing in his absence. "You seem to be insisting on getting yourself court- martialed for high treason," he said. "You've only got to go on the way you're going! True, the German Intelligence Service is gen- erally asleep, but sometimes it wakes up!"

I felt weak and indifferent. I asked him what he was doing in Paris. He laughed and answered darkly, "Keeping an eye on peo- ple like you; preventing them from doing any harm!"

Twenty minutes later we were in the side street off the Boule- vard Sébastopol where Josefine lived. She opened the door and was delighted to see me. Had she thought the security police were at the door? Karawan kissed her hand, explained that he'd fished me out of a bistro dead drunk, and that I'd given him her address. Nothing was said about Paule or my father's letter. Josefine was dressed, but there was nobody in the house. I was so tired that I collapsed into a chair and went to sleep. For a time I heard the two talking, but then it became nothing but an unintelligible mur- nur. . . .

VI

A fortnight later I plucked up courage, got myself a pass, and went back to see Josefine. The flat was empty. The concierge laughed at me and said I was the twentieth gentleman who had inquired. No, the police hadn't been. *Monsieur le vicomte* and *madame* had gone to their place in the country, in Normandy. I asked her for the address, but she either didn't know it or wouldn't tell me.

I saw Karawan again once or twice. All I had to do was to go along any evening to the underground café near the Boulevard Rochechouart where he played. But just about the time I went to see what had happened to Josefine he vanished too. The propri- etor didn't know where he was and was most annoyed at his dis- appearance. He was such a good pianist, and so cheap too. Things were very bad with him, and he was willing to take less than any

other musician; and he played so well. Another pianist no
played under the crooked Suze advertisement.

All my efforts to find them were vain. I was fed up, and for
few weeks I made up my mind to be a good soldier and do my dut
and nothing else. I remembered to wash my Army socks in tepi
water with Army issue soap, to salute in an exemplary manner, t
drop no cigarette ends in the gun emplacement and to avoi
catching any infectious disease.

But it didn't last long. I made myself conspicuous, and ever
one thought I was suffering from overstrain or was after prom
tion. I got myself laughed at for my pains, and I ended by givin
it up, after I'd made myself so unpopular that one night the
threatened to beat me up. It was no use trying to swim against th
stream. Saints are not wanted in any army in the world.

So I started going out again and talking to the girls who waite
in the little cafés of our suburb as soon as it got dark every ev
ning, and everything returned to normal, and it didn't occur t
anybody to want to beat me up.

All the same, I'd learned something. Johanna Selzer wrote an
said there was a new note in my letters, and that I no long
sounded so dogmatic. I answered that I hadn't been dogmatic a
all, and that quite possibly it might be a long war—it might dra
on till 1942. She wrote back that she was sorry about this, for m
sake. The Bavarians were much more optimistic than the Rhin
landers. She said that where she was they believed that Hitler ha
a bomb no bigger than a handbag that could kill a million peop
at once. Perhaps it would be used against the British if the
didn't see reason soon. It was quite incredible what perfect
serious people said about this new weapon. She herself wasn't y
convinced that it existed, but all the same it was quite poss
ble. I sent her no more poems by Mallarmé, but instead an o
volume of Hölderlin I'd picked up at a Paris bouquiniste. It w
quite a valuable edition. The bouquinistes now had more an
more German books for sale, because the Parisians didn't wa
them any more, and German soldiers were only too glad to bi
them. I also bought myself an old copy of Robinson Crusoe and
book called History as a System, by a Spaniard. Reading was
good thing. It killed a lot of time and didn't give you a hangov

wrote and told her that too. She asked what gave me a hangover,
and I explained that Paris was one big hangover.

We got more and more into the habit of writing to each other.
The post took four days from the Tegernsee to Paris, but only
two from Paris to the Tegernsee. I never found out why the
Army post office played havoc with the laws of probability like
that. Perhaps they had so many other things to do that the letters were left lying about. Or perhaps they were suffering from
hangover too.

She sent me her picture, and I hung it next to my shaving mirror, and I got into the habit of seeing our faces side by side when
I shaved. She had a long, narrow face, an energetic mouth, and a
thin, straight nose on which there was a small birthmark. I saw my
own face in the mirror every day and had got used to it, but I got
to like the look of her face better and better. I liked everything
about her. She was so honest and reliable, she never glossed over
anything or beat about the bush, and she never paid me compliments. She never paid any compliments. Perhaps that was a mistake. The girls who got on best in wartime were those who knew
how to pay compliments. She was a little stiff and prim and dry,
but I think they're all like that in the Rhön. But during the weeks
when I was really down, when I couldn't sleep for nights on end
because of the Josefine business, her letters were the only thing
I could depend on.

Eventually I wrote and told her that I would be getting leave in
June, and asked her whether she would like to meet me. First she
thought she couldn't manage it, but then she wrote she had taken
two rooms at a *pension* on the Ammersee. This was in May 1941.
In June I went on leave.

I saw and heard no more of Alfred Karawan. Sometimes I
thought of ringing up Counter-Intelligence headquarters in Paris
and inquiring after him, but those people were too fond of asking
questions, and I decided it wasn't a good idea. So I did nothing
about it, and in the course of time he faded from my mind again.
The extraordinary thing was the way he kept appearing and then
disappearing from my life; and he was always the superior, the
more experienced, the more confident. Whatever happened, he
always knew what to do. He never worried about anything except

the immediate object in hand. You go farther if you're made like Alfred Karawan. Above all, you never have a hangover or a guilty conscience.

VII

I hadn't seen her for more than a year, and I was rather surprised at how vivacious she looked. I had imagined her rather like our literary nun, Hroswitha. I told her so at Munich station where she met me. We didn't kiss, or embrace tenderly; there was only a prolonged handshake, which suddenly ended by itself.

"How now, Hroswitha?" I asked. This question puzzled her and I tried to explain it, but it didn't work, so I dropped it. We had a meal in the town and later took the train for Ammersee. She wore a tartan skirt and green shoes with red borders and brass buckles. We talked seriously about these shoes for a quarter of an hour—about how terribly difficult they were to get nowadays. Then there was a pause. Then we talked about the war, but that didn't last long, because we were both sick of it, and then we looked out of the window at the mountains. She spent some time telling me the names of the various peaks, but it was hot and misty, and all I could see was a light blue outline across the whole horizon, and I couldn't make out any of the individual mountains that she mentioned. I had long since given up taking an interest in the names of mountains. I had tried in Bavaria once before and always muddled them. But she knew them all and never made a mistake.

At Ammersee we got out and went to our *pension*. An enormously fat woman, who looked as if she were all the world's mother, was sitting behind the desk. All her single rooms were engaged, she said; she had only a double room left. Were we married? No? But the gentleman was a soldier, and we were certainly as good as married. I said I'd better see about the luggage, which our porter had dropped outside the door, and when I came back after a decent interval Johanna had straightened everything out. She had signed the register and even knew the date of my birthday, which I must have told her sometime. She never forgot anything.

By now it was midday. We handed over our luggage, took our bathing things, and went down to the lake; it was a hot day, and the shore was full of people bathing. There were a surprising number of attractive-looking women in modern bathing costumes. I had been out of Germany for more than a year, and I'd always thought that at home they went about in sacking and lived on dry bread and coffee and chicory. But the girls here didn't look in the least like that. We went to the bathing cabins, changed, and swam out into the lake. We hardly talked, but kept on swimming until Johanna said she had had enough and asked whether I was strong enough to be able to help her the last part of the way back to the shore. It was a kind of trial of strength. There was no need to help her when the time came, of course, but afterward we were tired and sat silently side by side in the sun and rubbed ourselves with oil.

We lay there the whole afternoon and hardly spoke ten words. It was so restful being with somebody to whom you didn't have to talk. In the troop, and, indeed, everywhere else, talking had become a kind of bad habit. Everybody talked about his troubles and his ideas, and in the end no one listened any longer. The only words that amounted to anything were those you exchanged with the girls who waited in the evening around the school where we were billeted. These words always meant more than they said, and to a certain extent were a kind of established ritual. You knew what you meant, and waited for the appropriate answer. No matter what the conversation led to, you were on firm ground; you were dealing with something definite, which had to be discussed in appropriate terms.

But with Johanna it was entirely different. It was also entirely different from being with Josefine, who was never at a loss for words. Johanna and I lay there in silence until it slowly got dark. Then we got up, went back to our bathing cabins, changed, and found somewhere to eat. I had no marks, but Johanna had plenty, so we ate all there was on the menu.

"I'd so love to have had a bottle of wine," Johanna said suddenly. This took me by surprise because I hadn't suspected her of being guilty of the degenerate French habit of wine-drinking. After a search around the town we eventually found a waiter who told us he had no wine himself but knew the address of an old gentleman who sold it. The old gentleman did it only to oblige, and because the wine had cost him such a lot. I believe he was the waiter's father. He had a lot of bottles, some with and some without labels. I bought a bottle of champagne and three bottles of wine. They cost as much as the finest wine at the finest restaurant in Berlin. We walked away with a bottle in each hand, and then Johanna said she'd like to see the moon. Had I a corkscrew? You could see the moon so beautifully from the Lände.

We sat for an hour on the Lände and emptied the first bottle. Just when we were going to get up and go back to the *pension* we found ourselves involved in a serious conversation, so we went on sitting there and opened the second bottle, which we emptied too. I had got used to drinking wine in France. We had acquired a technique for consuming large quantities in a decent manner. We got drunk, but we knew from experience that our drinking companions would be just as drunk, so we managed to last out. How Johanna had learned to hold her drink I don't know.

Toward midnight another couple arrived on the Lände, and we opened the third bottle and invited them to join us. They were a bit suspicious at first—perhaps they thought we were offering them poison or a sleeping draught—but then we convinced them that it was all right, and they joined us. The third bottle passed from hand to hand and from mouth to mouth, and we emptied it so quickly that I opened the champagne bottle. It popped. The cork jumped into the water and made silver circles on the dark surface. We all agreed that this was the right way to drink champagne. Most of this bottle was drunk by the men. The women said the champagne went up their noses and made them sneeze, or went down the wrong way. But the other man and I drank it quite easily, and weren't worried by the fizziness. We threw the empty bottles into the Ammersee, and then the four of us walked back to the *pension* arm in arm through the streets of the little town.

The door was open, the key of our room hung all by itself on the board, and the porter was fast asleep. I took the key, we went up to our room, locked the door, and didn't turn on the light. I went over to the window and looked out at the lake. It was black,

with a silver trail of moonlight in the middle. The outlines of the
houses were black, and all was at peace. I was at peace too.

I tried to think. I tried to think that this was a great day in my
life, but it was only a day among others, among many future days.
I didn't think about the war, or all the things that had moved me
in the last fourteen months. I thought of quite simple things.
This is a good hotel, I thought to myself. You can tell at once
from the smell of the rooms; and how is it, I wondered, that everything doesn't get stolen when the porter's fast asleep? This was a
peaceful neighborhood, I thought to myself, and I thought of a lot
of other simple things besides. Then I turned and saw Johanna
lying in bed, with the blankets drawn up to her chin, gazing at
me with eyes that looked black in the dim light.

"What are you thinking about?" she asked.

"I don't know," I said. "Just simple things."

"Come and sit here and tell me something," she said.

VIII

It is very possible that one only dreams such things. Only in
dreams do things go so smoothly, so obviously, so unproblem-
atically. Perhaps most of the things we think we remember are
only dreams that objectively never happen at all. Perhaps they are
only lurking inside us, and our treacherous imagination says, It
might have been!

She said, "Tell me something about yourself."

"What shall I tell you? About when I was a little boy?"

"Yes, tell me about when you were a little boy!"

"Well, I sat underneath a table, with a lot of legs all around me,
and a friendly hand came down under the table and gave me
something, a praline or a piece of cake."

"Is that true? You're not making it up?"

"No, it's true."

"Tell me something else!"

"I was in Sicily, and Luisa used to cut chickens' heads off and
whirl them about and hang little sucking pigs on a nail in the sun.
And my aunt used to look out of the window."

"How disgusting!"

"Aren't you going to ask whether it's true?"

"Is it true?"

"Yes, it's true."

"Tell me something else."

"I don't know anything else. I was a student in Berlin. I don't know what my subject was; I've forgotten all about it. It doesn't matter. They don't need people with degrees."

"Tell me some more."

"Yes, about the Faroes. They massacre the whales, and then they dance all night and drink liquor out of square tins. They dance solidly for seven hours without stopping, and without a band. They sweat and drink liquor and dance. And then they go into the hay barn."

"That sounds good!"

"It is good! They don't think about it at all. They just go on dancing till they've danced all thought away."

"I'd like to dance like that sometime!"

"It's difficult. But, when you come to think of it, everything's a dance."

"Everything?"

I had three weeks' leave. I stayed at Ammersee for a fortnight, until Johanna's holiday was over. I went with her as far as Munich, where we parted. We had changed roles. Now she was optimistic, and I didn't believe peace would ever return.

"It's going to turn out all right," she said. "Everything's going to turn out all right, you'll see. You're stationed in Paris, and the worst that can happen to you is that you may get drunk and break your leg. Then you'll get the war service medal in bronze without swords, and a fortnight's sick leave!"

"At Ammersee?"

"Of course! Where else?"

"You think the whole German Army revolves around Ammersee?"

She leaned out of the window and gave me a kiss. I wanted to pull her out of the window for the sake of another half-hour with her. But I didn't do it. After all, we are reasonable people, aren't we? The train pulled out of the Holzkirchner station, leaving a thick trail of smoke in the air. The smoke descended and obscured the train from view. Then it had gone. I went to Platform 14—Munich, Hof, Berlin. My suitcase was already lying in a second-class compartment, and I gave the porter his tip. A suspicious sergeant came in and wanted to know what a lance-corporal was doing in a second-class compartment.

I told him I was on special duty. Lance-corporals of my kind always traveled second class.

He asked to see my papers. I said I'd show them to him if he could show me what authority he had to ask for them.

He went off and started looking for a military policeman. I sat and waited impatiently for the damned train to go. At last the whistle blew. I looked out of the window and saw the sergeant approaching with a railway transport officer. The train started to move, the R.T.O. was left on the platform, and the sergeant jumped in. Nothing happened. But all that excitement! And what for? For nothing at all. Just to annoy people.

IX

My father was waiting for me on the platform in Berlin. It must have been the twentieth or twenty-first of June. He was bent, and his hair had gown quite white. He was in civilian clothes and was smoking a cigarette. I stopped for a moment and looked at him before he saw me. There was something about him that differentiated him from all the other people. It wasn't only that he had aged so much; there was just something about him that marked him off from them. During all the years I'd lived with him I hadn't observed him as closely as I did at that moment.

He was standing on a girder, staring at a point in the crowd. He wasn't looking about for me; his gaze was completely concentrated on that point. I would have given something to know what he was staring at and what he saw in it.

Eventually I went up to him and called him. He raised his eyes, smiled, and threw away his cigarette. "My dear boy," he said. "My dear boy." He had never been an emotional man, and he wasn't now. But there was something in his voice that nearly brought tears to my eyes.

"What's the matter? Is anything wrong?" I asked him as we walked through the station. Nothing, he said, nothing, only rather a lot of work. We couldn't talk properly, because I had to keep saluting. We drove into the Tiergarten. He said no more, and I looked at his round shoulders. Kride had written and told me that he was at the office early and late. He suddenly turned into one of the side roads of the Tiergarten, stopped the car, took out the ignition key, offered me a cigarette, and leaned back.

"Listen," he said. "I've got a position in the Foreign Ministry in view for you. They need a young man to deal with a specific question connected with England, for which a good knowledge of languages is required. I can get you away from your troop any time you like. What do you think of the idea?"

I said it didn't sound at all bad. The thought of joining the foreign service had never entered my head, but I'd be willing to do anything to get away from the boring task of defending the supply camp of the Paris command.

"Incidentally, I'm leaving the foreign service next week myself and joining up," my father said casually, looking out of the window.

"What?" I said in astonishment. "You're leaving the foreign service? And you expect me to join it? For heaven's sake! What for? To take your place?"

He drew at his cigarette before answering. "Listen," he said. "I don't need to tell you the policy I stand for. It's the Rapallo policy. Well, it's a state secret, but tomorrow morning you'll hear what's happening on the radio."

"What shall I hear on the radio?"

"That we're at war with Russia. We're marching into Russia early tomorrow morning. Before winter the Army hopes to be in Moscow, Rostov, and Leningrad."

I said nothing. I was too astonished to speak. If he had told me that Kride was dead or had hanged herself it wouldn't have sounded more incredible.

"But we've been on quite good terms with them," I said. "Didn't we say that they could carry on with their bolshevism, and so on, while we— Then why on earth—?"

"It's HE," said my father. He lowered the window a little, threw his cigarette away, but promptly lit another and again began staring at fixed points in the distance.

"Well," I said eventually. "If we're going to be in Moscow by Christmas, why not? Everything has gone all right so far!"

"Everything?" said my father.

I said yes, everything.

"What about England?" my father said.

I said I'd thought it was going to be England's turn next.

"So did everybody else," said my father, suddenly starting to talk again. "It's we who are in a cleft stick, and not the Russians. We're in more of a cleft stick than the British. HE miscalculated twice, first in the Polish business and then about the British. The whole world is arming. In two years' time we'll have been left hopelessly behind. Our only chance of doing anything is now. We've still got a shot in our locker. If we waste it, we'll be done for."

"Come, come!" I said. "Why should we waste it? Is that why you're leaving the office?"

He nodded. "I can't undertake the responsibility any longer. The whole thing shrieks to high heaven. It has all been worked out. You know what a coefficient of safety is? It's something that every businessman uses. He says to himself, Such-and-such a deal may bring in so-and-so much, but it may bring in so much less. He takes the smaller figure. Then he says, it'll cost so-and-so much, but it may cost much more, and he takes the higher figure. HE does exactly the reverse. I was at two conferences with HIM when the date was fixed. HIS calculations are based on the smallest foreseeable risk combined with the biggest foreseeable gain."

My father's way of calculating struck me as being rather absurd. "Oh, well," I said, "if we're not there by Christmas, we'll be there by Easter. Don't you think we'll manage it?"

"By then the surprise will be over," my father said. "By then they'll have had time to mobilize their masses. Their age-groups are double the strength of ours."

"Yes, Russian age-groups," I said.

He smiled suddenly. "I'm glad that's the way you take it," he said. "By heaven, perhaps we'll really bring it off after all! Listening to you gives one some hope again."

"Surely it's rather mean to fall on them like this out of a clear sky?" I said.

"Yes," he said. "If we don't bring it off, then heaven have mercy on us!"

He sounded very solemn and began staring ahead of him again. Then he put in the ignition key, started the car, and drove me home.

"I wanted to tell you that I've got myself engaged," I said to him on the way.

He said he had expected something like that.

I told him about Johanna, and when we were held up by the traffic lights I showed him Johanna's picture. He seemed to like her; he smiled again, and when the cars behind us started hooting he put our car into gear and we drove home.

That evening we sat in the conservatory and drank a bottle of champagne. We talked it over for a long time, but I refused to join the Foreign Ministry if my father was going to enlist. My father hadn't yet told Kride he was going to enlist, but I blurted it out, and she gaped in astonishment. She said it was completely and utterly crazy on his part to be thinking of throwing up his work at the ministry. It was an act of fantastic frivolity, because he could be far more useful to his country where he was. If he joined up, at best he'd become garrison commander in Rome. But he had made up his mind. It was the first time for a long time that I had seen him so adamant. At first I was too taken aback to say anything, but then I became adamant too. I said I couldn't possibly work at the Foreign Ministry if he enlisted. I should feel like a cripple.

"But you said yourself that you're not happy in your troop in Paris," my father said.

"That may change," I said and winked.

He grew violent. "You can be far more useful to your country using your special knowledge than sitting in Paris gazing at holes in the air."

"That may change," I said.

Kride looked at us, goggle-eyed. She understood only half of what we were talking about, because she didn't yet know about next morning's special announcement on the radio.

In the end she said she thought we must both be drunk. "Here am I, preaching my head off at Max, telling him not to make a fool of himself playing soldier but to use his special knowledge in the Foreign Ministry, and here's Max preaching the same to Rodie. Tell me, what is all this about?"

We didn't tell her. My father dropped the subject and told Kride I was engaged. She asked to see Johanna's photograph, and I showed it to her, and she was full of her praises. This was obvious, but I was flattered all the same and I talked to them about Johanna.

"She must come and stay with us sometime," said Kride. "I'll tell her what sort of chap you really are!"

The mood changed, and we sat and talked and laughed and forgot the question of which member of the family should represent the Stamms in the Foreign Ministry.

"She made a bad mistake in falling for you," Kride said. "Just you wait till she comes here!"

It was all very friendly and jolly. We emptied several bottles, and I was glad to be home again. We went on talking and laughing till long after midnight. Just before twelve o'clock my father tuned in to Beromünster, and we listened to the news. There was nothing in it about the invasion of Russia. We both listened excitedly, and when there was nothing about it I said, "Oh! What luck that no man's eyes can pierce the veil of Puck's disguise," and my father and I both laughed heartily. Kride said we were both drunk. She couldn't see anything funny in the Beromünster news.

I went to bed and thought about the invasion of Russia. I thought of the gunners standing by their guns, training their sights on the Russian pillboxes, and of the tanks standing ready, and the infantry, and I felt sorry I wasn't with them. I'd already been through a whole series of wars. I'd been at Aachen during the Sudeten affair, I'd been at Aachen again during the Polish affair, and during the French affair I'd shot up a pillbox. During the Balkan, Greek, and Cretan affairs I'd been in Paris. Before I went to sleep I said to myself that I hoped they wouldn't polish off the Russians before I got a chance at them.

X

On one of the following mornings I woke up and found Kride sitting at my bedside.

"Rodie," she said. "Max went to the office for the last time this morning. Tell me, has he told you the real reason why he resigned? I tried to get him to change his mind, but he wouldn't. Tell me, do you think it's my fault?"

I rubbed my eyes and said, "Of course not!"

"But why is he doing it? Why?" She was beside herself, and her hair was hanging over her face.

"He sees something in the Russian campaign," I said. "He doesn't agree with it. He thinks he can't be associated with that policy. I don't fully understand it myself."

She sighed deeply and said that if that was so, it was all right.

"Why should it have anything to do with you?"

She didn't say but walked once or twice up and down the room.

"You haven't told me anything about Josefine," she said suddenly. "Didn't you see her in Paris? Or had she already left?"

I tried cautiously to tell her the truth, but I was never a good diplomat. The truth must have come out pretty baldly. But Kride didn't seem to be much shaken by it.

"Josefine was always a bad lot," she said. "That business with the child . . ."

"I hope she's clever enough not to get caught," she went on. "Just imagine what a scandal there would be, Rodie! It would be terrible. But I'm not surprised. What was there between you two?"

I told her. She listened seriously and didn't smile. She wasn't angry either.

"Poor Rodie, how she led you on!" she said eventually. "And now you're engaged. On the rebound, I suppose!"

This took me aback, and I protested indignantly, but Kride didn't seem to be listening. She suddenly sat on my bed and tucked the blankets around my shoulders.

"Poor Rodie!" she said. "Just think of all the things that happen to you! I shouldn't have married your father, should I? You two would have led such quiet, happy lives! You know, Rodie, life sometimes doesn't keep its promises. It's useless to try and force it. But now it's too late."

She left the room before I could say anything. What with the war against Russia and my father's joining up, she was rather upset. My father was given the rank of major, got his uniform, and became commandant of a transport airfield in Russia. He had hoped to be able to fly himself, of course, but the Luftwaffe didn't want fifty-five-year-old majors for flying duties.

I broke my journey back to Paris to visit Yevgenia. She was alone in her house. Margarete had joined the women's auxiliary service, either as a switchboard operator or in the fire brigade, Yevgenia wasn't sure which. All Yevgenia's girls had long since left to work in a uniform factory, and she was alone in her house. At night she slept in the cellar, so as not to have to get up when the sirens went. She said that in the long run she thought this better for her rheumatism than perpetually running up and down stairs. The sirens went every night now, but she no longer heard them. No bombs would be dropped in that neighborhood. One incendiary had fallen in the Nissels' garden next door and destroyed two apricot trees. Herr Nissel was heartbroken, because he was so devoted to his trees. Ott-Heinrich, the Nissels' son, had become a lieutenant. This was the first time in eight years that I had heard his name.

"What do you live on, Yevgenia?" I asked.

"Live?" she said, with more accent than usual. "Live? We don't live any more. Oh, Rurik, everything's very bad. For we shall soon be cut down like the grass and wither as the green herb!"

She had the Biblical quotation at the tip of her tongue. She hadn't been able to quote the Bible so readily in the old days. I looked around and saw a Bible lying on the table, next to her glasses.

"What I mean is, how do you manage to pay for everything?" I said.

She stuck out her underlip and snorted through her big nose.

"Pay? What do I have to pay for? I have no expenses any more. I'm a lonely woman, Rurik. They've all gone. Now Margarete has gone too. Josefine's in Lisbon."

"Where is she?" I exclaimed.

Yevgenia told me she had had a letter from Josefine from Lisbon. She had mentioned that she had seen me in Paris. I didn't comment on this. So Josefine was a long way away and safe and sound. Yevgenia went on talking to me for twenty minutes about how lonely she was. She talked like a minor prophet. Anyone who did not know her might have thought she was religious. In the end I asked her where all this wisdom came from. Had she joined the Bible League? She nodded. For some time she had been reading nothing but the Bible. She said there was a great deal in it about the end of the world, the beast that shall ascend from the bottomless pit, the slain lamb, the seven seals, and the dragon that must be loosed after the expiration of a thousand years. She said the thousand years were nearly up.

"But I thought you were an astrologer," I said. This was grist to her mill. She fried me some potatoes, broke eggs over them, and opened me a bottle of beer while expounding the results of her astrological studies. Hitherto she had put her faith in astrology alone, she explained, but that had been a mistake. But if the Revelation of St. John were taken into account in conjunction with it, everything was clear—the great whore of Babylon, Gog and Magog, the age of Aquarius and Armageddon. A huge catastrophe lay ahead, she said, sprinkling salt over the eggs, but it was useless preaching to mankind because they would not understand. I said she had better not try preaching; her preaching would not be appreciated by the party. There was only one kind of sermon that was permissible, and the text had to be: "Keep the wheels rolling for victory," or "The Rome-Berlin-Tokyo axis," or "The German soldier is the best in the world."

"Oh, stop it!" she said. "I'm not a child."

"I'm only warning you to be careful. They don't like it," I said.

Yevgenia contemptuously screwed up her big nose and filled my glass. She was, perhaps, a little crazy. But her craziness had the advantage of moving with the times. No, it was always a little ahead of the times. She was always a little crazier than the times. By the time Yevgenia's craziness became the fashion she had moved on to something else.

Later she talked to me very proudly about Margarete. Margarete had being doing a lot of athletics during the last year, and she had become a first-class discus and javelin thrower. She had actually had hopes of possibly being selected for an Olympic team. For a quarter of an hour Yevgenia was quite normal while telling me all this. She was very proud of Margarete. "She's such a pretty girl, Rurik. You can't imagine what a pretty girl she is!"

I felt sorry for her when I left her alone in the house and walked through the night toward the station. All her children had left home and were scattered about the world. She was an old woman who read the Bible and made astrological calculations. I didn't feel sorry for her because she read the Bible, but because she was so old and lonely.

6 - Under Fire

And now things had come to this pass. Previously all that had happened had been playing, experimenting, gesturing. Certainly there had been losses, but peacetime has its fatalities too—its railway smashes, its road accidents, its tragedies in the mines. You deplored them and forgot them; there was nothing so very extraordinary about them, after all, because people were always dying. We all knew that one day—not today or tomorrow, but one day—we should have to die. All the same, there had normally been something distinctive and solemn about death. But now it became commonplace and universal. Men were shoveled wholesale into the huge ovens of the bombed towns and the huge crematoria of battle.

It was a terrific performance. So tremendous, impressive, and moving was it that it was scarcely possible to think about it, let alone discuss it. Fortunate was he who secured a place in the audience—in the balcony, the dress circle, or the orchestra—because on the stage things were happening in earnest; it was real action, with real passions and swords that were not made of wood. Often the players were so weary that they would have liked to slip away. But no matter, there was a quick change of scene, and the police drove them back before the footlights.

We had a whole life behind us, and everything had been too simple. We merely had to turn a switch where our ancestors had laboriously to make a fire of pine cones. We had swum and played tennis and gone to the movies and drunk and made love and enjoyed ourselves. But it had all been too simple, and it had grown simpler and simpler. It had grown to be scarcely any trouble at all. We had begun to dream, and the easier life had grown the graver our dreams had become, and now the dreams had become reality.

We had conquered a whole series of countries. They didn't like it, but they waited. They didn't know what we were going to do. They wanted to see what would happen next. We ourselves hadn't known. We had only one brain to do the thinking for us, and its owner hadn't said where he was taking us. But now he had told us. The conquered, occupied countries went on waiting, but we waited no longer.

First the usual news came in: a thousand tanks captured or destroyed, another thousand tanks, two thousand guns, a hundred thousand prisoners, three hundred, six hundred thousand prisoners. The program seemed to be going according to plan. The curtain seemed to have risen on a new act—an act on a vaster scale, true, but one not fundamentally different from those that had preceded it. In fact the act was said to be already really over, and it was believed that the curtain was about to fall—the curtain of the year, of the campaign.

But then there must have been a hitch, and the curtain didn't fall. The play went on, and new actors were wanted on the stage. What need had the commander of the Paris garrison for a special Flak battery to protect his supply depot? He must manage without. So the guns and signaling equipment were dismantled and packed on flat trucks. The men didn't have to be dismantled. They were given movement orders and set out on a long journey, from the pleasant winter weather of France to the unpleasant winter weather of Russia. They were given two extra pairs of pants and an extra supply of socks to be washed in tepid water. The quartermaster's department thought this sufficient to defy the Russian winter. Anything else that might be necessary, we were told, would be issued to us by the competent authorities in Russia.

It was a long journey and very cold, and everything was covered with snow. The holes in which the men had to live, the gun positions, everything had to be dug out of the snow. The men's task was to provide air protection for an operational airfield used by fighters and reconnaissance and transport aircraft. An arterial road led to the airfield, but it was often so thickly covered with snow that the trucks got stuck. Later a field railway was to be built, but in the meantime we were short of food, of fuel, and of everything else. The competent authorities were a long way away. You heard from them but never saw them.

Things had grown serious. Every day was serious, and every hour of the day, and every minute of the hour. In France things had been fine. The French were a polite people and produced a lot of wine, and at night you hadn't been disturbed, even if you sometimes slept away from barracks. Sleeping here in this cold was a different matter. You never knew for certain how you managed it; presumably it was the result of sheer exhaustion. When you woke in the morning the sky was gray, the country was gray, and life was gray. As soon as it grew light the aircraft got to work. Sometimes it was so cold that the aircraft wouldn't start, but the airmen, in their fur kit, were indefatigable, and they came from their huts and worked on the engines until they started, and then they took off and flew to where they were needed. And then the Russians came with their aircraft, and shots were exchanged with them. It seemed as if things were going to go on like this to all eternity. Eventually the snow would give way to mud, and mud would give way to hard-baked ground and heat, but then the mud would return and it would get cold again, and the land would turn white. It ate up men, living and dead. It ate up souls. This was Russia.

In the autumn a reconnaissance aircraft had flown over the wide steppe and taken a photograph of a crossroads—a photograph of two square kilometers of steppe, with the crossroads lying in the middle. Perhaps it had been intended, in one of those gigantic plans that the Russians had, to build up these roads properly, but in the meantime only the crossing had been properly finished. The roads led from nowhere to nowhere. Later it occurred to somebody to transform the crossroads into a landing T for aircraft. Trees were cut down, sawn into boards, and stacked. This was a very wise precaution, because a time came when the crossing was at the front. Here was a place where fighters, reconnaissance and transport aircraft could establish themselves and take part in the winter battles. The Russians, however, did not like having them so near, so they raided the airfield, and that was why the Flak was sent for to protect it.

Somewhere, eight miles the other side of the front, was a pocket of German troops that had been cut off, and from time to time supplies were sent to them by air. Transport aircraft flew low over the forest where they were and dropped what they needed in order to live—primarily ammunition and spare parts, and secondarily food and drink. Even their mail was occasionally dropped to them from the air. Two aircraft had been shot down because the Russians had set up machine guns in the woods. Now, when the transport aircraft carried out a drop, the Flak shot into the forest to harass the machine guns. So there was plenty to do.

You had to adapt yourself. If you didn't know how to beforehand you had to find out now. Previously you had been able to a certain extent to keep out of the way. Now you were thrown back upon yourself and your companions. Standards of value had altered. Previously a man had been able to hide his scorn, his fear, his envy, his greed. He had been able to create a small zone of privacy around himself. But here that was no longer possible. Here he had to fit in or make life hell for himself and others.

The old gentlemen engaged in the application-for-release racket had long since been sent home, and nobody missed them. Other old gentlemen remained. They had had plenty of time to make their applications, and heaven knows why they hadn't sent them in before. Some of them started sending them in now, but it was too late. But there were some who actually turned out to be willing to experience war a second time. And then there were the young men, with their parcels rackets and their girl friends. Had they gone in for these things seriously or just to pass the time? You found out now. And the art historians, with their useless occupation, would they always remain useless? You found out now. Everything was found out. We had been sent here to be revealed in our true colors. There was time, plenty of time. Everybody's turn came. Some got home, others got a hole in the ground. There were the lucky ones who came down with jaundice or angina pectoris. They were driven away somewhere in an ambulance, into some Promised Land. Others got their hands or feet frostbitten. At first they were driven away too, but later on they were punished instead. At first frostbite was regarded as a result of carelessness, but later on it came to be regarded as equivalent to a self-inflicted wound.

We had started a war, a tremendous war. To a certain extent we had even improvised it. Who was it who had started it? Nobody really knew for certain. You? I? He? No, it hadn't been any of us three; it had been HE. HE had decided it was necessary. But we were all involved, because all of us had capitulated before HIM during all these years. We had all given HIM permission to start a war at HIS discretion, when HE decided it was necessary.

Once I had been a spectator at the trapping of big whales, and had seen how none of them escaped because one of them lost blood. Here you could see trapped men behaving exactly like the whales. Because one of them lost blood they all stayed where they were. When the whales did that it was called stupidity, and they were given the name of *grind*, which means folly. When men behave like that it's called something else.

Men, looked at from our present point of observation, took on a new look. There was our sergeant major, for instance, who was so fond of talking about the war in Spain. When he talked about Spain everyone stopped work and listened. Once he had picked up a lance-corporal and carried him out of the fire of a French machine gun, and we respected him for it. And now in Russia? He still had the same yellowish look. He grew yellower and yellower and lost weight. He grew skinny, sulky, dangerous, but he stayed with the troop. Perhaps he thought it couldn't carry on without him. Perhaps—but what does one know about other people? One day the M.O. came and examined him, made him strip, and pointed to an extraordinary vein, growing like a strange sign across his stomach. He had cirrhosis of the liver, and the vein was a *caput Medusae*. He went off in an ambulance, and we thought how lucky he was. A fortnight later we heard he had died on the way. He did his duty to the end. Perhaps he thought that if he reported sick everyone else would report sick too. How extraordinary of him! Why should he have cared? He hadn't started the war, after all, and he'd still draw his pay in hospital.

One day our smart good-natured captain flew in a transport aircraft to the place where the pocket of surrounded men was, to observe the effect of our harassing fire on the Russian machine guns. He didn't live to report on what he saw because the aircraft caught in a tree, crashed, and burst into flames. Replacements were sent both for the transport aircraft and for the captain.

His successor was younger and far more energetic. He remained in command of the battery for nine months, and nobody liked him. He kept us on the move from morning to night, and it was he who introduced the system of punishing the corporal of the guard when a man got frostbite, on the ground that he hadn't relieved his sentries often enough. The system worked, and we had no more cases of frostbite. In the end the partisans got Captain Jenkuweit, and his remains were buried. After his death everyone said he was a fine chap. He left a good reputation behind him.

Everything is different from what one imagines it to be, different from the descriptions that one writes home—completely different. We belonged to the Flak, and our guns were officially called 88 mm. At home we were scorned. Men said, "I've got three sons; two are soldiers, and the third is in the Flak!" But the 88 mm. was no ordinary gun, but a thing of glamour and reputation. It was the only weapon that, year after year, could knock out any tank by direct fire. Its successes against aircraft were problematical, but its successes against tanks were a matter of fame and glory. It didn't run after tanks, and it didn't run away from them either. It just stayed where it was and accepted battle. Year after year enemy tanks gave the 88-mm. gun a wide berth. Year after year the 88 mm. was sent to spots threatened with tank attack. That's what Mannstein and Lindemann did, as well as Rommel in Africa. All the same, the men who served the 88 mm. enjoyed no high reputation at home. One of the guns in our battery had thirteen rings around the barrel. Eleven were for tanks and two for aircraft. There was no doubt about the tanks, but the aircraft were a different matter. They simply crashed, and no one knew for certain who had brought them down, so they were attributed to that gun.

After the sixth tank the gun commander received the Iron Cross, first class. After the twelfth success the troop commander, being an N.C.O., received the Knight's Cross of the Iron Cross. Seniority must be observed, after all.

The N.C.O.'s ambition, however, was not set on getting the Knight's Cross but on getting a nice comfortable wound, just serious enough to get him sent home. But he lived under a kind of spell and never got a scratch. Russia might have been made for him. He hadn't done his two years' military service before the war, or he would have got much further by now. The reason was that he had once had T.B. So first he sat grimly and confidently in the gun-layer's seat and later stood beside the gun, looking through his field glasses and giving orders. He was something he had never been in his life before. He put every ounce of himself into what he was doing. He grew a little proud and indifferent. To the right and left of him were men, most of whom were there for only a short time and then disappeared. His life could have been different. But by the time he started wanting it to be different it had become impossible to change it, because everyone else would have liked a change too, and they saw to it that he stayed where he was. So he had to put up with it. After a year or eighteen months he had got over the worst. He knew Russia, or thought he did, and, within the limits of his experiences, he was right. For the time being he was satisfied with his life and didn't want a change.

There was a good deal of pride and self-satisfaction in his attitude. He was one of the old members of the battery. He was, so to speak, a founder-member of that remarkable body of men. There were only seven or eight men left who dated from the early days, and of nearly all of them it could be said that it was surprising to find them still there. They hadn't seemed predestined for heroism. But they wondered what would happen if they were sent away. They knew this life and had got used to it. They knew exactly the price they had paid for getting used to it. To a certain extent it was laziness on their part. They didn't want to have to start paying the price all over again. Pride entered into their attitude too. They didn't want to give up the little privileges they had acquired, and they saw to it that nobody took them away. A slight aura surrounded them, and was inside them too, and they saw to it that it was kept alive.

II

The rest of the battery traveled from Paris through to Warsaw in an ordinary troop train, but we old hands were given special orders to carry out, as well as leave passes and railroad warrants to enable us to rejoin the unit in Warsaw. On our way through Berlin I saw Johanna Selzer.

I went to Wiesbaden, duly handed over the parcel of butter and coffee I had been entrusted with, and then sent a telegram to Johanna. I had half a day to spare, which allowed me time to go and see Yevgenia. Margarete was staying with her mother, and Yevgenia was perfectly right, Margarete had grown remarkably pretty. It was astonishing how quickly it had happened. Only yesterday, it seemed, she had been a fidgety and excitable schoolgirl, with all her bulges in the wrong places. But now she was a quiet, confident, reserved, and attractive young woman, and all her bulges were in the right places. It must have something to do with hormones. It was one of the last cheerful evenings in Germany. I had always had a horror of Russia. Even the illustrated Intourist advertisements I used to see in Berlin had given me the creeps. I had never traveled to Russia via Intourist and seen Leningrad, Gachina, and Oranienbaum. Now, however, I was going to Russia under different auspices. But we didn't talk about it. We sat in Yevgenia's kitchen and talked of the old days. I had brought some coffee and liquor and tobacco, and spent half the evening making cigarettes for them and talking about the time when I had gone to school with Ott-Heinrich Nissel. Ott-Heinrich Nissel had been home on leave a few days before. He was now a lieutenant in a reconnaissance battalion, and Margarete had gone out dancing with him. I teased her a bit about the reconnaissance battalion, but she remained completely unruffled, and my teasing didn't have any effect. She was very composed indeed.

I had told Johanna in my telegram that my train would be coming into the Schlesischer Station by way of Spandau and the zoo, and when I looked out of the window at Spandau there she was. She had traveled overnight from Tegernsee to meet me. I had expected it, but all the same it was good to see her. She was so dependable. She got into the train and stood with me in the corridor. A railway transport captain came past and pointed out that this was a military train, on which civilians were not permitted. Johanna explained that she was getting out at the Schlesischer station. He said she must get out at the Friedrichstrasse. He was small, round, and red-faced. I can hardly remember now what Johanna looked like that day, but I shan't forget what that captain looked like to my dying day.

At the Friedrichstrasse station he was busy, but after the train left he came by again, and this time he grew very angry indeed. He was so angry that I thought he was going to throw Johanna out of the moving train. Instead he said she must get out at the Alexanderplatz without fail. When he found her still there after we had passed the Alexanderplatz I thought he was going to pull the emergency cord. Johanna argued with him and said she was my wife. I wanted to say something too, but he kept me standing to attention, and he looked me up and down to make sure my heels were together and my feet at the prescribed angle of nearly ninety degrees. He made a long speech about my being sent to a punishment company for refusing to carry out orders, and all this took up the greater part of my reunion with Johanna.

We stood for about twenty minutes in the east wind at the Schlesischer Station, because I wasn't allowed to leave the platform. Johanna was freezing, and I put my greatcoat around her. I took her in my arms several times, but it wasn't the real thing; it wasn't like it used to be. When I thought about it afterward I felt sick with longing for her and I was sorry I wasn't a captain yet. I was only a lance-corporal, and anybody could do what he liked with me. That was because there were more lance-corporals than captains. When the guard blew his whistle she started crying. She was so severe with herself and with the world that I hadn't expected her to cry, but perhaps it was just the east wind. She took my face in her hands, but I couldn't feel it because my cheeks were quite frozen. After I got in and the train moved off I saw her for a few moments longer, standing at the edge of the platform and waving. Every time a lighted compartment passed her I saw her face, and in the end I only imagined I saw it. I went on seeing her face, with the tears running down her cheeks, for a long time.

I wrote to her about all this, and she answered. She asked whether it was cold where I was, and whether there was anything she could send me. The cold was simply infernal. We laughed when we thought of how cold we had felt in the shelter near Aachen during the first winter of the war. It hadn't been cold then at all, though it had seemed cold enough at the time. Now, before going to the latrines, we would consider at length whether or not to unbutton our trousers beforehand, and whether to take greatcoats with us or not. The pros and cons provided the subject for endless discussions in the evening. I didn't mention this in my letters to Johanna, but asked her to send me liquor. She sent me some in a kind of little ink bottle. It wasn't at all an agreeable time.

My father was in Russia too, and he wrote and asked whether I should like to be transferred to the Flak at his airfield. He had influence and could arrange it. I thought it over for a few days and then wrote and told him I'd prefer to stay with my troop. My father and I were fond of each other, but he was a major, and it would have created all sorts of difficulties. He answered that he understood perfectly. He always did, and I was very grateful to him for it.

Then spring came, and we started moving about all over Russia. I had thought we'd be in Moscow by Easter, but we weren't. We were transferred to the southern sector, and for a long time we were stationed near an airfield on the Don. The Russians attacked our flank, and we shot up some tanks. I was awarded the Iron Cross, second class, for shooting up two tanks, and my decoration for the Sudetenland affair arrived on the same day. So I got two decorations at once. I believe about a hundred men had been kept busy in Germany finding out the present whereabouts of the man who hadn't yet received his Sudetenland decoration. I was now a big man in my troop.

So far as one could tell, the Russians didn't seem to want to lose the war. They kept on attacking with tanks, and by this time the legend about "the last Russian aircraft" had worn a little thin, and nobody believed it, except at home in Germany. But we were advancing in the Caucasus and had reached Stalingrad, and day and night supplies kept moving eastward by road and rail.

Kride wrote to me in her firm, straight handwriting. She was rather lonely, she said; the house seemed so empty since Max had left. She had been wondering whether she ought to join the Red Cross. I remembered Yevgenia's having once mentioned years ago that it would have done Kride good to have had children. She could have done with them now. But I couldn't write to her and say that.

It was extraordinary how different the world looked. We were in it now; we were in it up to our necks. The Russians didn't want to lose the war, but we had attacked them, so we had no choice, we had to go on, we had to win. There was no point in that accursed country where we could stop and say, We'll draw our new boundary here. We had to subdue it all. It often seemed to me impossible that we should ever succeed. It was so big, so tremendously big. Perhaps it was true that all that was necessary was to cut a few main arteries, and that that was what we were doing now. But whenever I made up my mind to believe this, Ils, Yaks, Stormoviks, and Katushkas came swarming and buzzing overhead, or a few huge tanks came lumbering across the steppe, and my heart was in my boots. Then I had to start building up my confidence all over again. Who were we, with our little country, to try to subdue the whole of Russia? They had a political credo different from ours—or perhaps it wasn't really so very different. And they had such a tremendous number of men.

I never became religious in Russia. Occasionally a chaplain turned up and arranged a service. We'd go and listen to the singing. Sometimes they sang hymns that I remembered, and I joined in and felt I was back at school. Most of them also made us sing patriotic songs, which were less enjoyable, but the chaplains thought that this was expected of them. But one day one of them came and made us sing "The olden sun, whose blissful rays," and that we all enjoyed singing. But the sermons used to leave me cold. They used to remind me of my old sergeant major, who died of liver trouble. He always rattled off orders in just the same way.

No, the chaplains didn't help us. We had to start building up our own beliefs again from scratch.

I used to think about many things at that time. It took me a long time to find out that when you're stationed between Stalingrad and the Don there are certain things you have to avoid thinking about; otherwise you go mad. I should have given a great deal to have had Alfred Karawan there, with his piano, but thinking about it made my heart grow heavy, and then I'd be useless for days on end. The only thing to do was to crack jokes and laugh— about the whores in Paris, about the easy life we'd led, about everything in the West. The thing to do was to scorn it all. You didn't scorn it, of course; you longed for it. But you had to avoid letting it occur to you and letting your mind dwell on it. That sounds very simple. I allowed my homesickness for the West to occur to me only twice a week, and it always lasted for two or three days. The rest of the time I was invulnerable.

Then in September there was a whole week without a single attack of homesickness, but a great many Russian tanks. Things always happened in spasms. Fighting was still going on in Stalingrad. At home they had coined a new slogan—"the hell with Stalingrad"—and they talked of nothing but "our brave soldiers at Stalingrad." Sometimes, when the wind was in the right direction, we could hear the growling and thundering of the guns at Stalingrad. Once a railway coach full of severely wounded men was shunted onto a siding to allow the munition trains to go through. The coach was left there for thirty-six hours. Eventually somebody went over to have a look at it and found that all the occupants were dead. That was the kind of thing one didn't write home about. The dead were buried, the coach sent back to Stalingrad, and Captain Jenkuweit wrote a report about the matter, but that was the last we ever heard about it.

After the tanks had withdrawn, leaving a few charred heaps of metal opposite our battery, my father wrote to me, saying he was coming to see me. He said he had enough petrol to be able to fly over and pay me a visit. He arrived on a day when promotions and decorations were being handed out. He had been promoted to lieutenant-colonel and looked tremendously smart. An official war reporter also turned up, and we had to paint rings around the muzzles of our guns for his benefit and stand beside them. While the decorations were being handed out he did nothing but take photographs. He explained that some would be published and that the remainder were for the records. If they intended keeping photographs of everybody who received a decoration they must have had gigantic office buildings in Berlin to hold all the files. He also took a photograph of my father and me. It appeared on the front page of an illustrated weekly and showed my father shaking me by the hand. The caption was: "Two generations—a white-haired lieutenant-colonel congratulates his son (the corporal, right) on being awarded the Iron Cross. Lieutenant-Colonel Stamm was a redoubtable airman (infantry cooperation) in the First World War." The result was that I got letters from Johanna, Margarete, and two young women unknown to me, who sent me their photographs in bathing dress.

In the afternoon I went with my father for a walk. We took a water bottle full of liquor with us. He had to go back in his Storch the same evening. It was all rather irregular and therefore all the more delightful and agreeable.

"Tell me," he said, "I don't want to interfere with your plans, but don't you think it would be a good idea to apply to be trained for a commission?"

I had been afraid that this question was coming. People couldn't leave you alone; they were always wanting to make something of you. I spent a long time thinking over what to answer. It was so difficult to know what to say that I nearly said yes to avoid having to talk about the matter. But if I'd done so he'd have moved heaven and earth to have me sent on a training course, so I said no.

"I've thought about it a great deal, but I don't want the responsibility," I explained. "As it is, if I get fed up one day I can report sick, or get a few fingers frostbitten, or have a breakdown. Nobody would think anything of it. I don't have to set an example. But as an officer you have to set an example the whole time; it's expected of you. I'm not an example. I know many officers who are not examples either, and I've no ambition to be like them. I don't want to be like the others either. Sooner or later they all get killed. I've never known a good officer who wasn't either killed or crippled after a few months. I want to be able to do what I feel like doing and avoid doing what I don't feel like doing, and that I can do as an N.C.O. I'm not ambitious!"

My father said that that was a point of view, of course, but a great deal could be said against it. Even as an officer I should be able occasionally to take time off to blow my nose.

"Yes," I said, "but not with a good conscience."

I still often think about that conversation. It was one of the moments when I saw things clearly. I don't believe my father understood me. But perhaps he felt I was in less danger as an N.C.O. Anyway, I said I'd think it over again and let him know, and then we started talking of other things.

"What do you think of the situation?" I asked.

"If this present business doesn't come off, we're in the soup," he said.

I liked the way he put it. "That's exactly what I think," I said. "And what happens next?"

"I don't know."

"They won't stop at the German frontier."

My father shook his head. "Perhaps the Americans will help us."

"Do you really think so?" I asked.

"No," he answered.

We didn't mention HIM once. But there was one thing my father knew, and that was that some of the generals had opposed this double campaign but had fallen into line when HE had called them a lot of idiots. They didn't like being called idiots.

"Do you know that Margarete's getting married next week?" my father said.

I was very surprised.

"To Ott-Heinrich Nissel!"

We both laughed. Ott-Heinrich had been awarded the Knight's Cross in the Crimea. Yevgenia had mentioned it in a letter, but she hadn't mentioned Margarete's engagement. Perhaps she hadn't known about it herself when she wrote. At that time everything happened very fast.

My father flew back to his airfield that evening, but first we both dined with the commanding officer. I was told this was a great honor. We talked about Crimean wine, Moselle wine, Rhine wine, and Burgundy, and everybody stuck up for his own favorite. Only when I said I liked Italian wines because of the iron tang and the flavor of fine spirits in them, both the old gentlemen smiled. They both said it was barbarous.

On my way back from the airfield, after my father had left, I saw an elderly man standing by the roadside. He had been driving a truck toward Stalingrad. He was a tall, worn, elderly man, and he had taken off his cap and was wiping the sweat from his brow. He was in Army uniform and appeared to be at his wits' end. Two other elderly men were sitting in the ditch, eating Army bread and sausage. They looked rather less at their wits' end, because they had left all the responsibility to him.

When he saw me coming he put his cap on and came up to me with a piece of paper in his hand.

"Excuse me," he said in his Saxon dialect, "but can you please tell me the way to Tiflis?"

I took his piece of paper and examined it. He had been sent all the way from Riga to open a forward transit office at Tiflis. His piece of paper was covered with rubber stamps. It had been stamped at Warsaw, at Lodz, and at a lot of other places I had never heard of.

"But Tiflis is near Persia," I said.

"Emil, did you hear? The gentleman says Tiflis is near Persia!" he called out to one of the sausage-eaters.

"So what?" one of them answered. "Does he know the way?"

I told him they were on the wrong track, that this wasn't the way at all, and I told them to go to the airfield and ask for the ground commander. He thanked me, and I went on my way. A few minutes later I looked around and saw that the three old men had got up and were preparing to make their way to the airfield— three old men, coming from heaven knows where, who wanted to go to Persia. I can still see in my mind's eye the driver's old, good-natured, rather bewildered-looking face, his light-gray mountaineer's eyes, the work-worn hands in which he held his piece of paper. They had ordered him to Tiflis, and he was going to Tiflis. At that time nothing was impossible. Why shouldn't a forward

ansit office be opened at Tiflis? The whole world was full of for-
ard transit offices. I felt sorry that my contact with the man had
een so brief, and I'd have liked to meet him again. At the time
was too occupied with myself. Today I realize how extraordinary
10se three old men were. They were the ghosts of this war. They
ere driving to places that had not yet been captured.

III

Soon we were on the move again, and during the later part of
1e summer and the autumn we were in a position from which we
3uld no longer hear the guns at Stalingrad. But the Junkers still
ew overhead day and night, and we kept on shooting and shoot-
1g to keep the Russians away from the airfields. Then, after it
egan to freeze, we were moved again. This time we moved back-
ard with our transports. We were moved seven times, and each
me it was farther back. Nobody took any interest any longer in
nding out exactly where we were. These constant changes of po-
tion were a good thing because they kept us busy and didn't
ave us so much time to think. Something new happened every
ay, and it was always something unpleasant. We weren't yet so
sed to unpleasant news as we afterward became. Eventually we
opped by a little river near a wood.

For a time I received no mail at all, and then a whole bundle
rived. It was a quiet afternoon, the men off duty had gone
)wn to the river to fish, and I settled down to read my bundle
f letters. First of all I opened all Johanna's letters and arranged
1em in order of date. This enabled me to get a consecutive pic-
1re of what she had been doing, what books she had been read-
1g, how the children had been behaving, and what films had
2en shown at the Tegernsee cinema. She also sent me a book,
hich I knew I should enjoy as soon as I opened it. It was an old
)ok, with beautiful engravings, and it was all about a man
1med Bob Singleton, who was a picaroon. At that time one's fa-
)rite reading was about other times and other places—the more
stant the better. I didn't know what a picaroon was, but I felt
ire I should be interested.

Then there was a letter from my father, who said he had got

back safely and that he perfectly understood my point of view about applying for a commission. In his time things had been different. A man who had been to a university either became an officer or was exempted or was put in the Army pay corps. But nowadays everything had changed. He asked me to give the commanding officer his kindest regards, but I didn't think this a very sensible request, and I decided not to give the commanding officer his kindest regards. It would have looked very peculiar.

Last of all I found a letter from Kride. She congratulated me on my decoration and said how delighted she had been to hear of it. For an N.C.O., the award was almost as good as a Knight's Cross. She went on very sensibly for two pages, all about the house and about an epidemic that had killed off all the fish in the aquarium, and she mentioned that Frau Steuwen and her husband often came to see her and that they talked about the old days. I looked through the remaining pages, of which there were seven altogether, and I had only read the first two. I lit a cigarette and settled down to finish the letter. Every now and then I looked out of the hut window at the river and the wood. It was slowly getting dark.

Between the river and the wood there was a big compound with a lot of little huts, surrounded by barbed wire. The barbed wire and the huts had been left behind by the Russians, and the huts were now inhabited by concentration camp inmates, who were employed on building up the highway. They had been brought in trucks from the area of Minsk and Pinsk for roadbuilding purposes. In the morning we used to hear the shouting when they were woken, and later on we saw them marching in groups down toward the highway, guarded by older men with rifles. They were wizened, shabby little men, and they often used to beg for bread. The N.C.O. in charge of the cookhouse used to leave stale bread and leftovers from his pots and pans outside the cookhouse door and go away. The prisoners knew about this and crept away from work one by one to help themselves. Sometimes the guards took no notice, and there was actually one who used to walk away at the end of our mealtime and only reappear half an hour later. But there were others who kept their eyes open and kicked and beat with their rifle butts any prisoners who a

empted to leave their work for a moment. On such days the rem-
ants of our food were thrown away in the evening.

I sat back and picked up Kride's letter again. She kept on for
quite a time with her descriptions of Berlin life. She also told
me that phosphorus bombs were now being dropped on Cologne,
which caused flames as high as a five-story house, and that at Gru-
au they had held a regatta for amputees, which had been a huge
success. Then I came across something that made me sit up.

I read on with great attention because Kride wrote: "Rodie, I
know that you like me as much as I like you, and you're a damned
fine chap, and that's why I'm writing to you. Konrad von Borsin is
now at Bernau, with Dönitz, and—you know, it's an old story
now, but, to put it in a nutshell, I want to get a divorce. I'm
thirty-one now, and I've no children yet, and I know we'll never
have any. But it's not my fault. And I want to have children so
much, Rodie; I believe you're old enough to understand that a
woman of thirty-one wants children, and that's why I want a divorce. I don't want to hurt Max. Do you think it will hurt him a lot?
I so much want to do the right thing, but I want to have children
too, and that's why I'm writing to you. I know you'll say that I
ought to have thought of all this sooner, but I was young then,
and he was younger than he is now. Oh, Rodie, I don't know if I
ought to write this to you, but you're the only person with whom
I can discuss it, the only one who knows the whole relationship. . . ."

And so on. I read to the bitter end and didn't know what to say.
I knew Kride, and I had sometimes thought this or that about her,
but I'd never thought she'd want to discuss such a thing with me.
I read through the last part of the letter again and found a sentence in which she said she wanted a quick divorce, and that made
everything clear. I wasn't angry. I was the last person who had any
right to be angry with her; I had once been fond of her myself.
But for my father this would be a terrible blow. I knew he had
always been very fond of her. It was extraordinary how things went
together. First he got married, and things got better and better,
and one day things started getting worse, and here he was going
to be divorced.

I went on sitting and thinking. Meanwhile it had got dark. Behind the barbed wire you could see a few fires gleaming, and the barbed wire fence was floodlit. Occasionally when a guard on one of the towers thought a prisoner was going to try to break through the barbed wire fence a shot rang out in the night, and you could hear the humming of the motor that provided the electric current.

Yes, it would be a heavy blow to my father. He was fond of her and he had done a great deal for her. Actually he had done everything for her. Well, perhaps he had done it for himself too. It would be a heavy blow for him all the same.

I wondered whether I should write to him, but I had never been good at writing letters. Everything came out so dryly, even if you didn't mean it to. So I decided not to write. Should I write to Kride and tell her to write to him? If she wrote to him, I feared it would be a cruel blow. She'd spend a long time beating about the bush and then suddenly blurt it out. No, it would be better if she didn't write. It suddenly occurred to me that the best thing to do would be to go and see him.

I went to the office and asked to see Captain Jenkuweit. I told him I wanted to go and see my father, who was at an airfield a hundred and twenty miles away. I wanted to talk to him urgently. Captain Jenkuweit was a short, offhand little man, who attached great importance to cleanliness. He always had a little manicure set with him. He was capable of suddenly ordering us on parade and inspecting our fingernails. It was a peculiarity of his which you had to get used to. He manicured his nails while listening to me now.

"What's the matter?" he asked. "Have you got something on your mind?"

I said it was a private matter.

"Have you caught something?"

"No, sir."

"Hm! Do you want to be an officer?"

"No, sir."

He looked at me in surprise. He was obviously wondering what on earth it could be that made me want to go and see my father.

"It's not about me, sir, it's about my father. I've had a letter from his wife."

"His wife? You mean your mother!"

I explained that she was my stepmother. He looked thoughtful for a moment.

"Is she having a baby?" he asked.

I said she was.

"But not by him?"

"Not by him, sir," I said.

"Is it yours?"

This Strindbergian possibility seemed to appeal to him, and he was obviously disappointed when I said it wasn't.

"Very well then," he said, obviously pleased at having found out something. "Go to the sergeant major and get yourself a pass written out. You'd better telephone your father to let him know you're coming. Perhaps there's an aircraft going that way. The pass is to say that you're to return immediately on completion of your orders. Orderly, fetch me the papers!"

He was fond of talking like officers in the time of Frederick the Great.

I went to the orderly room and had the papers written out. While they were being got ready I got through to my father's airfield. I had rung him twice before and knew the ropes. Hullo, Pinewood, give me Lion." Lion was the Luftwaffe exchange. "Hullo, Lion, give me Wooden Shoe." Wooden Shoe was the exchange at my father's airfield. Wooden Shoe answered. "Zebra speaking, give me Dorothea." I waited for a moment, and then heard my father's voice. I told him I'd been given a pass to go and see him. Did he by any chance know of an air connection? He told me to hold the line. He must have had things very well organized at his airfield, because in less than three minutes he was back and told me to be at my airfield at eight o'clock. He happened to have a courier machine in the air with which he was in wireless communication. Could I be at the airfield at eight o'clock? I said yes, I'd manage it. I rang off, took my papers, and went back to Captain Jenkuweit. He was now at work on another finger. I gave him the papers, he signed them, made sure they had been properly stamped, and gave me a Top Secret envelope. It was a quarter past seven, and the airfield was at least an hour away. I'd have to risk it. I asked him whether by any chance he knew of a vehicle that was going to the airfield. That was the way to broach the subject. He said he had no chance vehicles. Why? I explained that a courier aircraft of my father's would be waiting for me at the airfield at eight o'clock.

"Very well, then," he said. "Take my car!"

I'd managed it. He telephoned the orderly room and said his car was to be ready in ten minutes' time. Then he put his nail file back in the box and told me to sit down.

"Tell me, Stamm, would you like to be an officer?" he asked.

I said no, I wouldn't like to be an officer. He asked me why. I said I had the feeling I wouldn't make a good one.

"Am I a good officer, in your opinion?" he asked.

I said yes, I thought he was a good officer.

"Is the C.O. a good officer?"

I said no, in my opinion the C.O. was not a good officer.

"Do you say that because you know we can't stand each other?"

"No, sir," I said. "The reason I say that is because I think I'm more like the commanding officer than I'm like you. I could be like the commanding officer, but not like you."

"No, you wouldn't make a good officer," he said. "Do you know what you lack?"

At this point I should have said no, but I didn't. I said yes, I knew what I lacked. He took no notice, but went on. "What you lack is a bit of bolshevism in your blood. You need a little more iron in your blood. We all need a bit more Russia in our blood. We're still far too German, sentimental, dreamy. What do you do in your spare time?"

I told him I was just going to read a book about Bob Singleton.

"Pah! Read!" he said, and took his nail file out again. "Just as I thought! Remain a gun commander, Stamm, and enjoy it."

I told him I'd certainly remain a gun commander. There was a knock at the door, and the driver came in. Captain Jenkuweit told him to wait outside in the car and then take me to the airfield. He took a bottle of red wine from the cupboard and filled two glasses.

"Your health, corporal," he said. "Be careful how you break the news to the old man! Are you engaged?"

I said I was.

"Is she a blonde?" he asked.

I said she was.

"Take my advice, and don't have anything to do with blondes," he said. "They're too expensive. Brunettes are the best. Sometimes they're a bit flighty, but then you must show them your fists. But they're good at frying potatoes."

He drank and filled the glasses again. He was very dogmatic, but all the same there was sense in what he said.

"Well," he said, "you'll be more successful with women than I've been, Stamm, if you remain an N.C.O. You've got such a soulful look. Actually you've been very lucky. When I took over the battery I said to myself, That man Stamm's a rotten egg, and I'll take it out of him. But then you turned out well, and now you're a hero. Would you like to go on leave soon and see your fiancée?"

I said yes.

"Well, we'll see! Perhaps things will soon be quieter."

He filled the glasses again. "Here's your health, Stamm, and break the news gently to the old man!"

I said I'd do my best. I looked at my watch, got up, and asked for permission to fall out.

"Off with you!" he said. "Don't keep the old man waiting! Smart fellow, flying in a courier machine! Keep that Top Secret envelope, it's for all eventualities. The Military Police are very keen nowadays. They've a nose for the slightest irregularity. Oh well, your old man will know how to keep you under his wing. Finish your glass!"

I said my piece and went to the door. He keep his eyes on me and when my hand was on the handle he called out "Corporal Stamm!" and I stopped.

"You'll become an officer yet," he said. "In the next war! Off with you!"

I went out, told the driver to hurry, and we hurtled down the track to the main road. The conversation struck me as having been rather funny. I quite liked being a soldier, but deep inside me there was a civilian who kicked against the pricks. When they'd been officers for a time they all talked as martially as if they were in Wallenstein's camp, but those who talked like that weren't the worst. It certainly couldn't be easy to be an officer all day long, and to act as if you always knew what to do and always to have the right explanation for everything ready at the tip of your tongue. Jenkuweit was a quite simple man. He had once told us that his father was a miner in the Ruhr and had had seven children. He must be the pride of his family when he went home in his captain's uniform, and no doubt he talked as if he were five officers.

When we reached the airfield we saw the courier machine approaching, showing its red and green navigation lights. Ten minutes later I was in it, and we took off. We were in the air for a good hour, and then I was with my father.

He came to meet me in his car. When we got into the car he said, "Franz, this is my son," and the driver turned and made something in the nature of a respectful movement. I thought it rather strange for my father to introduce me to his driver, and he explained later that he had introduced a new kind of socialism into his unit; he said the result was that his men would go through fire for him. When I spoke to the men later they told me he was a good-natured old stick, but they said that only as long as they didn't know I was his son.

He had a nice little house at the edge of the airfield, and that's where we went. It was very comfortably furnished; he was, after all, a lieutenant-colonel. He was delighted to see me—and I had come to give him a heavy blow. I decided to put it off for a bit. He didn't even ask why I'd come. He thought I'd just come to see him.

After a time a woman orderly came and brought in the fish. There was also pork, which was very nicely served too. There was also Rhine wine. We set to, and I ate zealously because as long as I was eating I didn't have to talk. After the meal we settled down comfortably in his room. It wasn't so luxurious as our conservatory, but the armchairs were comfortable, and there was plenty to drink and smoke.

"The chief air staff officer's a comrade of mine from the last war," he said. "We were in Flanders together. He's a colonel now, and he'll soon be a general. He's an able fellow."

"Tell me about the first war," I said.

He talked about it the whole evening. It was thrilling and tense and exciting. They had open aircraft, protected with armor, and they flew over the trenches, dropping small bombs and firing at the trenches with machine guns. Sometimes they were fired on, but generally they managed to get away. Once his observer, who served the rear machine gun, had been shot right behind my father's back, and once he himself was hit in the calf. He had crashed twice, but each time he had been rescued by the German infantry. He seemed to have been a kind of hero to the infantry, who were always delighted when the ground cooperation aircraft came and raked the trenches opposite. It was a more dangerous job than that of being a fighter pilot and didn't bring so many honors. You could come back and say you'd destroyed an enemy machine gun with a bomb or machine-gun fire, but you could never prove it. To prove it you'd have had to come back with the English company commander's cap, and you didn't fly low enough for that.

My father had the gift of being able to talk without ever giving you the feeling that he was boasting or shooting a line. In his day that was something they learned how to do. Nowadays they either keep their mouths shut entirely or talk about everything under the sun—about blondes and brunettes and so on—but as soon as they start talking about themselves it stinks. You can tell at once that they're shooting a line. We've lost the art of talking about ourselves. It needs a great deal of skill.

The whole evening I kept on making up my mind to tell him *in a minute*, but I put it off and put it off, and next morning I slept late, and then we started talking about the war and the political situation, and that was very interesting too, and I simply couldn't bring myself to tell him. I stayed with him for three days, and then he gave me a message to my unit and sent me back with it in a courier aircraft.

"My dear boy," he said, when I was getting ready to go. "I hope that one day things will be better for you. We've all made mistakes, but perhaps you'll profit by them. Remember me to your fiancée when you get home. I'm looking forward to meeting her. I think she's the right girl for you."

It was all so human and heartfelt that I felt glad I hadn't told him. I kissed him before I left the house, and he held my shoulders. "My dear boy," he said. I was unable to say anything.

I flew back to our airfield. For the first half-hour of the flight I was depressed, thinking about my father. Then I looked out of the window of the little Junker at the country down below, which was as flat as a pancake. I looked at the white streaks of the roads and the circles which indicated gun positions. So that's what we look like to the aircraft who attack us, I said to myself. I opened the little window and looked out, but the wind was terrible and I withdrew my head quickly. The cold was insupportable. Then I looked out of the window again and noticed that the wing-tips were vibrating. This gave me a terrible fright; I thought that something must have happened and that perhaps they were going to break off. I hadn't been given a parachute. Nobody had parachutes. After a time I looked out of the window again, and they were still vibrating. They went on vibrating throughout the flight. I think they always do.

It struck me that throughout the three days we hadn't mentioned Kride once. We had talked about Yevgenia and about Margarete, who had gone back to her work as an Army auxiliary in Rotterdam after her wedding, and about Josefine. I had told him about my affair with Josefine in Paris, and he had laughed heartily and said it was just like her. But neither of us had mentioned Kride. There might have been a tacit agreement between us on the subject.

From the airfield I went straight back to the battery and reported to the sergeant major. He said Captain Jenkuweit wanted to see me. I went in. Captain Jenkuweit was standing in front of his desk.

"Well, Stamm? How did the old man take it?"

"I don't know, sir," I said. "I didn't tell him."

He looked at me for a moment in astonishment. "What! You didn't— You went there specially and then you didn't tell him?"

"You see, sir," I said, "I simply couldn't do it."

He leaned back and laughed. Perhaps he was angry for a moment, but then he laughed.

"Stamm," he said, "you need another five years of Russia. At least five years. What are you by trade?"

"An art historian, sir."

"Oh, art," he said, and I went out. I wrote to Kride and said she must do what she thought best. What was done could not be undone. But she should write to my father frankly and without beating about the bush. Love from Roderich.

IV

Something horrible had happened during the three days I had been away. Opinion in the troop was split over it. I got the corporal who had been acting for me to tell me about it.

An order had arrived on the morning after my departure. The Russians had now encircled Stalingrad, and their forward columns were advancing into our area. The barbed wire compound near us had to be evacuated. It contained about three thousand men. But there was no rolling stock to spare to move three thousand men, so the S.D.[1] had been ordered to liquidate them. The inmates of the camp were White Russian Jews from the Polish border zone. They had been brought from their villages to build roads, and the problem of disposing of them had become acute.

The S.D. commander felt that the forces at his disposal were insufficient to carry out the liquidation efficiently, so he applied to the Army for assistance. But the Army replied that it had its hands full with Stalingrad and dealing with the partisans on the steppes, and the S.D. should do its own dirty work. A whole series of wireless messages was exchanged, and eventually the S.D. commander made a proposal that was regarded as a compromise. In view of the Army's refusal to assist him, and in view of the fact that the Army had a number of strong men at High Command who backed it in its refusal, let the huts with the prisoners inside be shot up by the Flak. The Flak were only half soldiers anyway. The S.D. would be stationed around the camp, ready to liquidate any who got away.

The order came, and Captain Jenkuweit refused to carry it out.

[1] The S.S. security service.

He tried to appeal to the commanding officer, but the commanding officer happened to be away, and so did the adjutant, who was engaged on an inspection, and nobody knew where he was. Captain Jenkuweit then sent a wireless message to regimental headquarters, but the officers were unfortunately in conference and could not be disturbed. The S.D. sent an officer over to inquire when the Flak was going to open up. Jenkuweit told him to go to the devil, and then an S.D. officer of field rank arrived. Jenkuweit was only a captain. The S.D. major brought the file with him. He showed it to Jenkuweit and proved to his satisfaction that headquarters had consented to the proposed method of liquidation. The major also pointed out that failure to carry out the order might have unfortunate consequences for the captain. But what really caused Jenkuweit to give in was the major's threat that if he persisted in his refusal the S.D. would soak the prisoners' huts in petrol and burn them alive. Jenkuweit thereupon told the major he could return to his unit. The operation would begin in half an hour.

The troop used a hundred and twenty-three rounds of high explosive with percussion fuses. Jenkuweit stood at the edge of the emplacement and gave the fire orders. The operation went off without a hitch. After the collapse of each hut the S.D. fired, and when everything was quiet the troop was dismissed and went to dinner. But that night Jenkuweit got blind drunk, went around the troop, bawling and belching, cursing the men and making speeches that might easily have led to his being sent to a concentration camp himself. The extraordinary thing was that, though nobody liked him, nobody denounced him. He was feared but not hated.

That evening the S.D. sent over a few cases of beer, with their thanks for the splendid support given them in Operation L. L. for liquidation. But Jenkuweit had already got beer and spirits to treat the troop with, so he sent the S.D. beer back. He sent a note with it, but nobody knew what he said in it.

We didn't have much time to think about all this, because the Russians, after encircling Stalingrad, had begun to put pressure on our flank. The Russian winter suddenly began; Christmas was approaching, and we were kept tremendously busy. We changed our position again, this time to a bridge across the little river. Germans, Italians, and Rumanians streamed across it night and day. They were streaming back from the crushed flank which had been intended to secure Stalingrad. It was a terrible sight. Sometimes there was half an hour's pause, but then another column started coming through. If a vehicle broke down the whole column was held up, because nobody could pass. The vehicles behind would hoot until their batteries ran dry, but it didn't help. It grew colder and colder, and we had to wear two pairs of gloves to hold the elevating and traversing gear of our guns, and in spite of that we had cases of frostbite. It was my second winter in Russia, and I had hoped to be able to go home for Christmas and see Johanna, but there wasn't a chance of it. We were needed to keep Russian aircraft away from the bridge. We had plenty to do at that time, and when we weren't firing we watched the huge army streaming past—trucks and cars, privates and generals, all driving across the little bridge, on which there was a notice saying: MAXIMUM WEIGHT FOUR TONS.

Things went on like this for three or four days, and then information came that partisans had appeared on both sides of the road and that the rearguard was being pursued by tanks. We thought it was time for us to be changing position too, but a wireless message came from headquarters saying that we and a battalion of infantry were to go on covering the bridge until the last troops had crossed.

Captain Jenkuweit kept sending for me. He was drinking even more heavily than usual, but he liked having somebody to talk to, he said, and the person he talked to was me.

"The last over the bridge, Stamm," he said. "The last shall be the first, and that means the Russians. We shall shoot up a few more tanks—aren't you looking forward to it? You only need a few more rings on your gun to get the Knight's Cross."

I said I'd prefer to do without the Knight's Cross and join the troops driving over the bridge.

"Yes, you would," he said.

We drank, and I must say that at that time I got to like drink better and better. There were two things in the war that really made sense, drinking and playing cards. When I wasn't drinking

with Jenkuweit and we weren't firing, we sat in our shelters and
played Skat. We played for a pfennig a point, and you had to keep
your eyes open if you didn't want to lose your shirt, because the
standard of play was really very high. Sometimes I nearly lost my
temper when a batman came in and said, "Stamm to go and see
the old man!"

"What's that, you stinker?"

"Sorry, corporal! Corporal Stamm to report to the troop commander!" The others blinked in astonishment, and off I went.

One of those nights partisans were reported. They were in a
wood behind the burned-out camp. The camp was now covered
with snow, and all you could see was the barbed wire and white
heaps where the huts had been. The partisans had only light
weapons. We fired a few salvos at them, and they withdrew. But
they came back next night, and Jenkuweit decided to take out a
patrol. When he got ready he didn't take his greatcoat but put his
belt over his tunic, took his pistol, machine pistol, and ammunition, and off he went. I spent about an hour with him that evening.

"It's all over, Stamm," he said. "It's all over. The big dream's
over. We're done for. Stalingrad was a fine stroke, but it didn't
come off. So much the worse for us!"

I suggested that perhaps we might be able to withdraw and
establish a firm line somewhere farther back. "Then perhaps we
might be able to stop them and keep them away from the German frontier," I said.

"Stop them? My arse!" he said. "A retreating army isn't an
army any more. Haven't you seen the faces of the men streaming
back? Haven't you seen the sheer fear in their eyes? They all
thought we'd always go on advancing, like in France, Poland,
Greece, and God knows where else. But now it's all up!"

"Do you think the troop will be able to get away?" I asked.
"We could blow the bridge and withdraw with the guns."

"Yes," he said slyly. "We could, but we shan't. This time we're
all going to heaven. Do you believe in heaven?"

Then the message about the partisans came in, and he loaded
himself up like an ammunition carrier and went off to the wood
with his patrol of sixteen men. For a time we heard nothing. Then

we heard firing and saw Very lights going up. I thought it was time to do something, but there was no one there with any authority. The lieutenant had gone on leave because his wife was having a baby, and the new sergeant major had no power of decision. So we stood staring out over the white fields of snow and listening to the whining and rattling of the vehicles on the road a hundred yards away. All we could see was the Very lights, and after a time these stopped too. We stood by our guns all night, looking out, but nobody came back from the patrol. When it began to get light we sent a messenger over to the infantry, and they sent out a lieutenant with a platoon. I asked permission to go with them, and the sergeant major gave me permission. We penetrated some way into the wood, and were fired on, but they stopped when we fired back. We came to a clearing, and there lay Jenkuweit and his sixteen men. They had taken the manicure instruments from his pocket and driven them through his eyes and nose, but when we reached him he was dead.

We reported by wireless to headquarters, which was somewhere in the rear, and this time the commanding officer wasn't away but ordered us to hold ourselves ready to move. We held ourselves ready to move all day, but vehicles kept on coming over the little bridge, and eventually night fell. We didn't sleep that night either. We kept our eyes riveted on the bridge, waiting for Russian tanks to appear. But individual vehicles and groups of men kept coming over. Once or twice somebody said, "I think that's a Russian coming," but every time it turned out to be a German tank or truck or armored car.

At last we decided that this night was going to be like other nights and that the Russians must still be a long way away, but suddenly they appeared, advancing across the fields of snow. It was uncanny to see them advancing, in close order, wave upon wave, shouting "Hurrah!" We turned our guns and fired at them, and the infantry opened fire too. And then their tanks appeared on the bridge. I took over command, because the sergeant major had disappeared and I was the senior N.C.O. left in the troop. I had two guns turned on the bridge, and they got a tank with every round. It was as easy as shooting rabbits. We sent up Very lights over the bridge, and every time a tank advanced into the circle of light we fired and hit it, and it burst into flames. We counted nine tanks before the bridge was so jammed with wreckage that it was impassable. That was what saved us. Meanwhile the infantry kept on firing with their rifles and machine guns at the Russian infantry advancing over the snow. There was nothing to do but go on firing. But in the end the infantry's ammunition ran out, and they withdrew. That was clever of them. We should have withdrawn too, but we went on firing our high explosive shells, and then there were the Russians suddenly in our midst, and hand-to-hand fighting started, man to man. . . .

v

I had plenty of time to think about all this. So far as I was concerned the war was over, because I was sent home. I've tried to piece together everything that happened. I was asked about it so often, and at first I was quite willing to tell the whole story, but I must have told it once too often, because in the end it all became much more confused and muddled in my mind than it was in the ambulance. All I can say is that we fought and kicked and shot, and then I felt something in my arm and leg, and then someone kicked me in the mouth. Then I lay quite still and heard the others growing still too, and I lay there for a long time, and all the warmth went out of me.

I had had a great deal of warmth in my body; during the fight I had had so much warmth in my body that my shirt stuck to my skin, but it all went away. I lay there, listening or dozing, and then fighting flared up again; there was a lot of shouting, and men jumped over me and fired, but when it grew quiet again I was surrounded by German voices. They were S.S. troops who had come back—or perhaps they hadn't come back but had come from farther forward, from the same direction as the tanks. I heard them talking and I could see them, and I thought that perhaps they'd think I was dead. I was terribly afraid they'd think I was dead. I managed to raise my arm and touch one of their boots.

The man looked down and saw me and said, "Good God! He's alive!"

He knelt beside me, opened my tunic, and felt my heart. "He's still alive!" he said. "Send for the M.O.!"

The M.O. came and examined me. He looked rather like Friedrich Feldmann, but then I thought that all young M.O.s looked like Feldmann. He gave me an injection and said something, and they fetched splints and bandaged my arm. Then they lifted me and laid me down again, but this time I was covered up, and they put something warm beside me. It was one of those belts that get warm when you pour water into them; they contain some form of chemical. We didn't have them because we were only Flak, but the S.S. had them. They put one belt on my heart and another around my body, and I heard one of them say, "Put one between his legs and see how he'll perk up!" But they were genuinely concerned about me. They always did everything, both killing and the opposite, very efficiently, and I was very grateful to them.

They had a wireless, with which they sent for an ambulance, and I was driven away, with three S.S. men who had been wounded in the battle. For a long time I didn't find out what had happened to my troop. The sergeant major was later picked up somewhere along the road and shot, but our commanding officer got the Knight's Cross because he and our troop had blocked the bridge and destroyed nine Russian tanks. So everybody got his deserts.

I was taken to a field hospital. I had always wanted a nice wound to get me sent home, but this was a rather serious one, because they amputated my arm at the elbow. Perhaps it might not have been absolutely necessary. At the first hospital I was sent to they did nothing, but at the next there was a keen young doctor who cut off half my arm straight away. I thought it strange that nobody should ask my opinion first, and that they should just operate right off. But there was no point in getting depressed about it; it was only my left arm anyway, and I'd had my bellyful of war; I'd even seen the whites of the enemy's eyes, to which so much importance is attached. Actually it had been too dark to see the whites of their eyes properly, but if it had been daylight I should certainly have seen them. I've always been a peaceable person, opposed to violence, but that night I truly laid about me.

But no more of it—they were the stronger. Anybody who had seen them, particularly coming on the way I saw them, advancing through the snow and shouting "Hurrah!" like that, would have done the same. They give no quarter when they attack. I kicked one of them in the stomach and emptied my whole magazine. Then one of them fired, and another kicked me in the mouth.

I lay in a hospital in Thuringia and was given some beautiful false teeth for the left side of my face, where they were needed. I was told that later I'd get an artificial arm, but for the time being there weren't any for amputations at the elbow. A fibula in my leg had also been broken, and had grown together crookedly, and they said it would have to be broken again so that it could be reset properly. But for the time being I didn't worry about that, because I spent nearly all my time lying down. When I walked I limped slightly, but all the walking I did was from my bed to a chair, so it didn't worry me. At first the fingers of my missing left hand itched, but that stopped eventually. With my false teeth I looked almost as beautiful as ever. If I'd had any desire to appear in the public eye, I could have taken part in the Grünau amputees' regatta.

This was in the summer of 1943. First I was in Thuringia, then in Franconia, and finally I was moved to the blessed land of Bavaria. I was sent to the finance school on the Ammersee—the Ammersee, as Johanna had foreseen. It was a handsome stone building, built by a man named Reinhard. It had been intended as a training center for the finance experts of the future, when world trade was to be conducted entirely in marks. But the war had unfortunately intervened, and the need for a training center for financial experts had disappeared, and so the building was used as a hospital for amputation cases.

I lay there and thought how nice it would be if Johanna Selzer were to come, so that things would be as they ought to be at the Ammersee. But she had become a nurse at a hospital in Berlin and she said she couldn't get leave. I wrote to her with my remaining hand, and the paper had an annoying habit of slipping away. Johanna answered but didn't come. I was very lonely at that time, and hungry for people, and needed her a great deal, but she had her duty in Berlin and didn't come. She was indispensable. A lot of people thought they were indispensable; it was a kind of pride. They would have been willing to creep into a hot oven to demonstrate their indispensability. I never saw an officer or man at the front who was indispensable. They were just there and didn't worry their heads about it; there were too many other things for them to do. After a time they were generally killed anyway, and then they were no longer indispensable, because they couldn't be. They knew it but stayed in the firing line all the same. All those fine young men, all those straight and confident young men whom I'd seen sitting at the edge of a trench, smoking cigarettes while they waited for the artillery preparation to finish, after which they attacked and died, were not indispensable. But the farther away from the front people were, the more indispensable they became, and at home in Germany everyone was indispensable.

Now I'd never had any ambition to be indispensable, and I'd never been called on to be, and it infuriated me to find that my future wife apparently had that ambition. She wanted to be better than I was. I wrote to her rather crossly on the subject and got into hot water accordingly. We squabbled for a time and then made it up. But she didn't come to see me.

Instead Kride turned up one day. She came in the spring, after the Stalingrad business was over, and the radio was full of talk about total war. Her figure was rounded slightly, and she looked younger and lovelier than ever. I was lying on the terrace outside the finance school and was reading about Sicily when she came up from Herrsching. I saw her coming from a distance and didn't recognize her, but said to myself, That's a damned good-looking young woman dressed all in black! How well it suits her fair complexion!

Then I heard voices, and a medical orderly brought her in. He fetched a chair, looked at her appreciatively, and went away. At close quarters she really looked lovelier than ever. But her face was worried and her hands restless. She had brought flowers and some English cigarettes. We smoked and looked out at the lake, over which two Dornier 17s were engaged in their daily test flights. They had rockets fixed under their wings. They flew straight for a time, suddenly you'd see a little flame shooting out forward, and at the same moment they'd turn away to right or left. Then there'd be a terrific explosion. They were said to be experimenting with a new weapon to be used against the bombers. I explained this to Kride. She said, "Oh," and didn't even start when the explosions came.

"Are you quite all right again?" she asked.

"Except for my hand," I said. "I still miss it a bit. And my leg's got to be broken again, but that's only a detail. They'll be able to do it in eight weeks' time."

"Oh," she said. "You didn't say anything about that in your letter."

"No," I explained. "They only found it out after the fracture had grown together again. They X-rayed it."

Suddenly she put out her cigarette and laid an arm on my shoulder. "I've bad news for you, Rodie," she said.

I knew at once that it was about my father. I'd been wondering why I hadn't heard from him, but the front was in a state of confusion, and perhaps his letters had gone astray. But Kride must have written to him.

"Is it about Father?"

"Yes."

"What is it?"

"He heard from your commanding officer that you were dead, that your whole troop had been wiped out. He telephoned to his chief and got permission to fly to Stalingrad to relieve somebody there. He was actually promoted to full colonel. He was there for two days, and after that no more aircraft came out of Stalingrad. He wrote me one more letter."

"Where is it?"

"Here," she said. I read it and handed it back to her. My father explained in the letter what he was doing and why he was doing it, and he said he'd made all arrangements with his lawyer in Berlin for the divorce. I was afraid Kride was going to burst into tears, but she didn't. She felt *she* had no business to weep.

"Listen, Rodie," she said eventually. "You mustn't judge me too harshly. I didn't want all this and couldn't foresee it. I've made terrible mistakes, and whatever you say to me I'll have to listen. But I couldn't foresee this—"

"What do I care about your mistakes?" I said and wondered why she told me all this. I didn't care about her, I cared about him.

She was hurt and fell silent, but I couldn't help it. After a time the two Dorniers came back and fired two more rockets. It went on all the morning and all the afternoon, with two hours off for lunch. They flew, turned away, and then there was a crash.

My mind was on my father, and if I'd been alone I should have broken down and wept. I disliked having Kride's arm on my shoulder, but I'd hurt her enough and didn't move. Eventually she took her arm away. Tears came into my eyes when I thought of my father, but I didn't want to break down, so I tried to think of something else.

"And how are things with you?"

"Thank you, all right," she said.

"Do you know what Josefine—what somebody once said? 'The first one for beauty, the second one for health.' You'll be lovelier than ever, Kride; you'll be irresistible."

"Oh, stop it," she said and laid her arm on my shoulder again. I forced myself not to think about my father, and we went on talking quite calmly.

"What's it going to be? A boy or a girl?"

Her gray eyes grew thoughtful. She looked as if she were peering into herself to see whether it was going to be a boy or a girl.

"A boy, of course," she said.

"Unless you're mistaken," I said. "Suppose it turns out to be a black-haired devil like Josefine?"

"It won't," she said, rather sharply.

"No, of course it won't," I said. "How could it? It'll turn out a little von Haringen, won't it? Born with a riding whip in its hand, and fair hair!"

"You've altered," she said. "You've got so hard!"

"Only on the surface."

She took me by the back of the neck, and I didn't dislike it. If you've once been fond of a woman, even if it didn't come to anything, something always remains. I remembered how she had sat next to me at school, and how she'd always been at the top of the class.

"You should have married me," I said. "I once thought of marrying you."

"You're crazy!"

"Then you'd have had several children by now and a husband with one arm!"

"If I'd married you, you wouldn't have remained an N.C.O. I'd have seen to it that you took an officers' training course."

"Of course you would. That's what you do with everybody. What are you going to do with Konrad von Borsin?"

"Marry him," she said. "In eight weeks."

"But are you divorced?"

"Max—arranged everything. He wrote to a lawyer in Berlin and said he agreed to everything, and he made a statutory declaration. We were divorced immediately. Five days ago. We had to do it, because of the child. It would have created untold difficulties if we had wanted to acknowledge the child subsequently."

"So everything's all right, then?"

"How you've altered!"

"You think so?"

"You used to be so soft and unsure of yourself; I sometimes thought it was a pity about you. You were always floundering about, taking things up and then dropping them again."

"You, for instance."

"Nonsense, you were only a child. It would have been like the massacre of the innocents. Did you really think you wanted to marry me?"

"It was just one of those crazy ideas that you have when you're seventeen."

"I'm three years older than you."

"You'd have had a good chance of surviving me for twenty years, if I hadn't been lucky enough to get away with my skin. And in the meantime we should have got on quite well."

"That's true," she said. "But nobody thought of war then."

"No," I said. "We didn't think of war then. But there were some who did."

"Sometimes you make me think you're embittered."

"I'm not embittered. But we've all grown a little wiser."

After that we stopped talking about ourselves and talked about practical matters, such as where Kride was going to live, where she was to have her baby, and what she and Konrad were going to do after the war. She seemed to be very happy, which rather irritated me, but fortunately she didn't notice my irritation. If she had, she'd have told me I was embittered again. Then we talked about Johanna.

"Don't you want to marry her?" she asked.

"Not so long as she's indispensable in Berlin."

"Are you angry with her?"

"No, not angry. But if they must go on with their bloody war they ought at least to leave my wife out of it. Why isn't she at Tegernsee, looking after her banker's cubs?"

Kride said she'd seen Johanna several times. She liked her extremely well. She was such a sweet, unsophisticated girl, but at the same time so practical, and she had a head on her shoulders and knew what she wanted.

"You'll make a good couple," she said.

"That's what I write and tell her twice a week, but do you think she comes and sees me?"

"I'll talk to her," Kride promised. "I'll talk to her and tell her how you're grousing. She's tremendously fond of you. When I'm with her she talks about you all the time."

All this was good and pleasant to hear. "Then why the devil doesn't she come and see me?"

"She says she doesn't want to be one of those frivolous nurses, always thinking about having a good time."

"But damn it all, we want to get married. Is that too frivolous for her?"

Kride said Johanna had certain ideas in her head. In such times, she thought, what mattered was morale. She believed it was necessary to set an example. She was convinced that the only thing that mattered now was winning the war. But it couldn't be won unless everybody put his last ounce into it. That was why she'd given up her job with the banker's family and gone to Berlin.

"Believe me, if you were in danger, or were in real need of her, Johanna would be the first to come to you," Kride said. "But she says you're safe and sound here at the Ammersee and can wait a bit. She wants to show you she can make sacrifices too."

"But I really do need her," I said angrily. "What do you suppose? Tell her I've made enough sacrifices for the pair of us, and that I don't care a damn about the war. Let her banker and other big shots who are exempt from war service go in for a little self-sacrifice. Tell her that the sacrifice of one arm, five teeth, and a broken fibula provide a sufficient foundation for our marriage. Tell her she can have a little bit of my arm, if she wants it. Tell her to chuck her damned Joan of Arc complex in the fire. Just you tell her that!"

"Poor Rodie!" Kride said. She put her arm around my neck again and laid her cheek against mine, but in an entirely sisterly fashion. "Poor Rodie, are you terribly bored?"

"Well, yes," I said.

"I can understand you, and I'll talk to Johanna about you. Perhaps she'll see that it'll really do you good if she comes and sees you."

It was nice to see Kride again, but all the same I was relieved when she left. I was sitting in my room, which I shared with a sergeant, when the surgeon came in. He was a solidly built man, with clever fingers, with which he was said to be able to perform miracles. I hadn't seen any miracles yet, but he had discovered my broken fibula.

"I've heard that your father was killed at Stalingrad," he said. "I want to express my deepest sympathy."

"Thank you, sir, that's very kind of you."

He said no more, but stood there for a moment and then went out. That's the only tolerable way of doing it. He must have brought bad news to many men, for the world was full of bad news at that time. But he did the only sensible thing. He said a single sentence, paused for a moment, and then went out. After he had gone I wept a little. I thought of my father as he had been in my boyhood, and how he had helped me with my homework, so skillfully that he always made me feel that it was really I who was solving the problem or whatever it might be. I remembered how he had sent me to holiday camps, where I sailed and fished and boxed, though he had had very little money then. I thought of his clever way of talking, of his handsome, slender figure, and of the many, many nights when he had sat up working, and all for nothing. He had flown into Stalingrad because of a mistake. I knew he must have made a good impression there. In matters of routine, perhaps, he sometimes made himself slightly ridiculous, particularly in his later years, after he had seen his mistake, like everybody else. Sometimes he tried things that seemed rather forced and strained. But that was only in externals. When it came to the last hour there had been no flaw in him. I had learned so much from him, and now he had shown me the way to die. I doubted whether I should learn to imitate the way he lived.

I sat there and went on weeping. When once you start weeping it's difficult to stop. I went to bed and turned out the light. Later the sergeant came in. He didn't speak, but walked about on stockinged feet and soon turned his light off too. He must have heard the news. I listened to his snoring for a long time, and then went off to sleep too and started dreaming about my father. He was walking down the long road on which we had last been stationed, and he kept on walking straight ahead. He kept on walking, but I stayed near him all the time, like in a film, in which you see columns of men marching and marching and always remaining the same size. An endless stream of trucks and vehicles of all kinds was streaming past him in the opposite direction. In them I saw generals and soldiers, all with faces distorted with fear, streaming away from the goal to which my father was walking. They had had enough and were thinking only of saving their skins. But my father kept walking on. His service dress jacket was properly buttoned up, the clasp of his Iron Cross, first class, was on his left breast, and he was smiling all the time.

VI

Yevgenia suddenly became of great importance to me. She spared herself no trouble or inconvenience, but came to Herrsching to cheer me in my loneliness. She found a room in a guest house and had an hour's walk to come and see me every day, and then an hour's walk back.

I had never been able to see anything significant or impressive about Yevgenia. She was an untidy, disorderly person in a tidy and orderly world. She muddled everything, mislaid everything, forgot everything. She was clever, but the things she undertook never came to anything because she always put obstacles in her own way. When the Nazis were in their early, struggling days, she became a Nazi and delivered tirades against the Jews, who were her best customers. But when the Nazis were in power she refused to take over a dressmaking business in Düsseldorf because it belonged to some people named Salomonski.

The good thing about her was that she never forgot the little things that people liked. She never forgot, for instance, that so-and-so liked prunes but couldn't stand mutton. She'd sit up all night to finish some work that somebody wanted urgently, and then wouldn't charge for it if the customer said he couldn't afford it. She was full to overflowing with kindness and sympathy and all the human qualities, but you could search her in vain for a trace of common prudence or intelligent thinking ahead.

When I saw her sailing up the road from Herrsching in her billowing black dress I was overjoyed. She came and sat with me on the terrace. She opened her handbag, from which she was inseparable. It was an old morocco bag, the silver buckle was worn, and in many places the morocco was as raw as deerskin. She produced two packets of tobacco and laid them by my side. This was a luxury she could have procured for me only by depriving herself. She also produced a hip flask full of brandy. In the twinkling of an eye she had created the atmosphere of comfort about her which only women can produce. On a subsequent visit she brought me a squashed piece of cake, wrapped in writing paper, and sometimes she'd arrive with a smoked herring. After she'd been there for three days she knew all the shopkeepers in Herrsching, and all the shopkeepers in Herrsching knew me through her descriptions of me, and kept me supplied with little things through her. She also knew all the medical orderlies and nurses, and it was noticeable that all the simple people greeted her with respect, while the matrons and doctors smiled slightly when she sailed past like an old Dutch fishing-smack. She also brought me a rice-paper edition of the Bible, the kind with a leather binding that overlaps all around, with loops, so that it could be carried like a bag. She told me to read it, and I did so and was surprised at the things I found in it. We had been taught that it was a Jewish book and should therefore be treated with caution, and that in any case it wasn't to be compared to the Edda or the Nibelungenlied, but all the same I read it with pleasure.

At first we talked only about trifles, and sometimes an argument started. I was impatient and violent because I was lonely and longed for Johanna. But Yevgenia put up with me, and after she had gone I felt rather ashamed of myself, and next time I tried to be less violent and impatient. She never complained about the long walk from Herrsching; on the contrary, she said it was good for her—she was having a kind of summer holiday.

Later on we talked about things one seldom talks about. We talked about my father, and I told her about the last time I had seen him.

"Oh, Rurik, he wasn't as unhappy as you think," she said. "Perhaps he was actually happy. He'd seen you, and he thought he was going to see you again."

One could talk to Yevgenia about certain things one had seen in Russia for the first time. I told her about Jenkuweit, for instance, and how he had stood in the gun position, calling out his fire orders, systematically wiping out the huts, and how he'd never got over it.

"You weren't there, were you?" she asked.

"No," I said, "but that doesn't affect it very much. If I'd been there I shouldn't have refused to carry out Jenkuweit's orders. When you're in it you can't say no. Somebody would have carried out the order anyway. If I'd refused, somebody else would have taken over my gun."

"Yes, but it worried you," she said.

"Yes, it worried me."

"Then it's all right," Yevgenia said. "If it worried you, then it's all right."

"It's not all right, Yevgenia. It's all very confused, and I don't know what to think."

She quoted something from the Bible. She seemed to know half the Bible by heart. But her quotations made sense, and afterward I sometimes read the Bible. The phrase that Yevgenia quoted was, "For now we see through a glass darkly; but then, face to face."

We talked about such things only once or twice, of course. Generally we talked only about the trifles that concerned us at the time—the bombing, the war prospects, the rations, and the campaign in Africa. I looked forward to her visits more and more, and when she left I was very sad.

It must have been in the summer, about the time the Italians made a revolution and got rid of their Duce. My arm had healed up well; the skin formed a kind of bag over the stump. All that was missing was a zipper. I was transferred from the Ammersee to Munich, where they were going to break the bone in my leg in order to reset it. I wrote to Johanna less and less often, but she wrote to me every week. She wrote to me regularly on Saturdays when she had time off, and her letters always arrived by the first post on Tuesday.

She described what went on in her hospital. I noticed that she took care to put down only things likely to have a cheering, heartening effect. But I could tell that she was working herself to death, putting her last ounce into it, and that I existed only on the periphery of her life. She was no longer the girl who had once confided to me in the train that the war was lost. Now, when the war really seemed to be lost, and all the wiseacres and talkers about Blitzkriegs and the greatest military genius of all time had stopped wagging their tongues and had anxious wrinkles on their brows, she sprang into the breach. That was Johanna. And there was I on the Ammersee, getting more and more irritable.

She wrote to me: "What would you have said if you'd come back from Russia and had lost both legs and both arms, and your nurse had no time for you because she was gadding about the country all the time? Be glad that you got off so lightly."

I answered that next time I'd take care to have a little more of myself shot off, and then perhaps I'd do better with her. She didn't answer that. Of course, in a way she was right, and we were all shockingly selfish. But in another way I was right, for she was only being exploited by other egoists. But she had her own ideas of her duty in a time of national emergency, and when she'd once made up her mind there was no getting her to change it.

I had plenty of time to think that summer. I got myself books and began making notes for a thesis for a degree. Our ideas at that time were very immature, but honorable, I think. We told ourselves that one day the war would end, and we had seen the results of allowing a few people to do the thinking for everybody. We must go on cooperating until the war was over, we said to ourselves, but after that things must be changed. We didn't know how they must be changed, but in the meantime it was essential to win the war, because, after all the things that had happened, if we lost now we should be exterminated. Enemy aircraft, which now started flying over Germany in daylight in huge numbers, dropped leaflets called the *Wolkiger Beobachter*,[1] which were full of plain threats. No, we had no choice. We must win the war. Johanna was right. Everyone was right who thought along those lines. When I'd thought as far as that I felt a certain pride in her and wrote her a friendly letter, but then I grew lonely again for someone to talk to, and wrote her an irritable letter.

I was released from the finance palace at about the time when they freed the Duce in Italy and stabilized the front again, without anyone's really knowing how it was done. The scar on my arm was dry and "very nice now," as the doctors put it. We had a tank corporal with us who had lost a leg. His only ambition in life was to return to his old tank battalion. He remorselessly practiced walking, in order to be able to go about without attracting attention, and he was the favorite of the whole hospital. His leg had been amputated above the knee, and he had been given an artificial leg with a patent knee. He could actually walk upstairs without his disablement being noticeable.

"What will you do when you get back to your unit?" we used to ask him, to give him pleasure.

He went outside and knocked at the door. We called out, "Come in!"

He came in, advanced three paces, halted, stood smartly to attention, saluted, and said, "Corporal Herbertsmüller reporting back from hospital, sir!"

He did it a little better every day. The man had iron nerves. One of us would say, "Well, Herbertsmüller, everything all right?"

"Yes, sir! Everything all right, sir!"

---

[1] "The Observer in the Skies." A pun on the name of the Nazi newspaper *Völkischer Beobachter*, "People's Observer."

Then he'd sit astride a chair, wipe his brow and ask, "D'you think it'll do?"

We assured him it would do, and that his unit would take him back.

"But as a gun-layer, not as a storeman or clerk," he'd say.

One day we were assembled for final inspection and release. I was to be sent to a school in Munich, where my leg was to be dealt with, and the tank corporal was going to his regimental depot. I didn't say very much; the medical sergeant filled in my papers and put them in a file for signature.

The senior medical officer, wanting to pull the tank corporal's leg a bit, said to him, "Well, Herbertsmüller, and what will you do if we put you down as fit for front-line service?"

"I'll go to the front, sir, get my head shot off, have a wooden one put on, and become a senior medical officer, sir!"

We were still laughing when we reached Munich in the bus.

I was given a room in the school, and I spent five days going for walks. I'd got my old uniform back, as well as my service pistol. I had a good deal of trouble with that pistol. It was a Polish Radom, with a safety grip, and I didn't like being separated from it, but medical orderlies steal like crows if you don't keep your eye on them. I had been clutching it when the S.S. men picked me up, and I didn't let go, and someone had put it back in the holster, and there it stayed. At Herrsching they said I didn't need a pistol, but I'd scratched my name on it and got it back. You feel different when you've got eight rounds in your magazine, and what did they need a pistol at Herrsching for?

On the fifth day I lay on a padded couch, a kind of helmet was put over my head, and when I woke up I felt rotten, and my leg was stretched out, thickly encased in plaster, and with a cord underneath it that led over two pulleys to a weight. It was uncomfortable, and my leg hurt as if it had been kicked at football, but not worse than that. The worst thing was waking up. I felt I was coming out of a deep cellar, a catacomb, and there were stairs and still more stairs, and it slowly grew lighter, and then I reached the top. But I couldn't move. My uniform and things were hanging next to me on a rail, and I was in blue and white hospital pajamas.

They were darned in several places and were hard from the mangle. After I had seen all there was to be seen I closed my eyes again. The pain in my leg wasn't too bad, but not being able to move worried me. If only Johanna were here, I said to myself. But nobody was there. I was alone in a room with four beds. Occasionally I heard someone walking down the corridor, and then I heard the clatter of knives and forks, but the thought of food made me feel sick.

I thought of my father talking about the war—or, better still, not talking about the war. I saw now why he had been so reticent about it. At Herrsching I had worked up another little racket, writing to Johanna and Yevgenia, and Margarete had sent me a pound of butter from Holland, and an old woman who was a painter—she had spent the last thirty years painting nothing but the lake—had come to see me and had brought me Abdulla cigarettes, which she got from Switzerland. What she did was to sell her pictures in Switzerland, where she had a customer who gave her a foreign exchange voucher which was honored by the Reich. No doubt we used the Swiss francs so earned to buy 2 cm. shells from the Oerlikon people. She took her change in little parcels of sugar, coffee, and cigarettes. True, she had to pay duty on them, but, as these things were simply not obtainable in Germany, it was worth it. The result was that she made quite a good living, because the peasants liked drinking coffee and cooking with sugar. I took part in her little racket by talking to her about Russia and giving her a chance to exercise a little sympathy.

But now it was over, and here I lay, with my leg tied to a weight, helpless and unable to move—completely helpless. After a while a nurse came with a bedpan. I gave her two cigarettes, and she promised to come back later and read to me. She went away, and it grew dark. There was a twelve-bed ward next door. I could hear the men's voices, and I'd have liked to be with them. They were joking and laughing, and I listened hard, but generally I missed the point because they lowered their voices when they came to it, and all I could hear was the laughter. I rather envied them for being able to laugh so much.

I remembered what my father had said. "It was dreadfully boring—only sometimes in hospital it was fine." I now understood everything he used to say. Every now and then I caught myself actually talking to him.

The continual laughter tired me, and I dozed off, only to wake up and ascend from the catacombs for a second time. I was awakened by footsteps in the corridor and a sharp voice saying, "No, not here. Start on the third floor!" Then I heard doors banging and heavy objects being carried downstairs, and an occasional "Ah!" of relief, or someone saying, "Gently, gently!" I looked at my wristwatch. It was a quarter past ten, and I was surprised to hear furniture being moved at night in a hospital. It was no concern of mine, but it sounded a little ruthless. The sirens went, and I realized that they were moving not furniture but casualties who couldn't walk. I listened but could hear nothing. I began to feel slightly alarmed. Eventually it grew a little lighter in the room. I nearly dislocated my neck to look out of the window, and could see vertical white streaks moving about in the distance. These were the searchlights. So they were coming, and the searchlights were looking for them. I became more alarmed, but nobody came. I heard voices next door, and occasionally someone laughed; this time the laughter didn't sound so happy, but rather forced.

I listened and heard a faint murmur in the sky. I felt afraid, but I told myself that Munich was large and that the chances that they would bomb our neighborhood were small. Suddenly I felt a great longing for human company. I didn't call out, but it was hard to restrain myself. The murmur grew louder. I strained my neck to look out of the window again and saw some red and green lights in the sky. I could hear the Flak firing outside Munich, and once I saw a little spark in the sky which was the bursting of a shell. I had helped to fire ten thousand shells at aircraft, and they hadn't done much good, and that had been in daylight. Now they were firing by night, and I didn't think they'd hit very much. There were too many aircraft. At Herrsching we had sometimes heard them flying over at night and hadn't taken much notice. But we took a great deal of notice now.

The murmur grew somewhat fainter. These had been the Pathfinders, which guided the bombers to their target. The murmur grew louder again. Explosions started everywhere, and patients

ho lay in plaster, helpless and unable to move, started calling
t, and you could hear the voices of the nurses who had been
oking after them all day long and now had heavy work to do at
ght. The men who had not been fetched yet started drumming
a their bedpans, and one of them threw everything he could lay
s hands on at the door of his room. Eventually the door opened,
d a voice called out irritably, "Keep quiet, we'll deal with you
l in turn." After that it grew somewhat quieter, and then the
st bombs began to fall. My heart was beating so fast that I
ought that there'd be a snap and it would stop. I heard the
histle and the whine of the bombs, and then the heavy detona-
on, which roared like a train on the underground if it was some
stance away, or made an ear-splitting crack if it was close. I also
eard the patter of the falling incendiaries. It grew light in my
om because a house had caught fire. Then there was another
uge crash, the window panes flew out, and acrid fumes poured
. I wanted to shout, but my mouth was dry and my heart was
eating madly. I looked around and saw my uniform hanging on
e rail beside me, and my belt, with the pistol in the holster. I
retched out and grabbed at the clothes and brought the whole
t down. I managed to catch my belt before it fell to the floor. I
ok out my Radom, put in the reserve magazine, charged it,
sted the safety catch and the cock, and laid my hand on top of
e blankets, gripping the pistol. I was terribly afraid of fire, but
had a pistol, so at any rate there'd be no need to be burned alive.
Suddenly a whole stick fell around our school. The walls shook,
e nurses screamed, a wounded man on the stairs shouted, and
man's voice called out, "All right, all right, nothing's happened!"
hen there was more trampling of feet, and sobbing and scream-
g on the staircase; but they hadn't removed everyone from the
p floor yet. Something must have gone wrong somewhere, and
e warning had come too late. The wards were still full of help-
ss bandaged men, and bombs were falling and houses burning
l around.
Soon afterward the buzzing and humming in the air grew
inter, and my heart grew lighter. The tension went out of my
omach, and I lay back and admired the extraordinary reflection
f the fires on the walls of my room. There must have been a won-

derful blaze outside. But it was only a brief respite, because th
second wave came with high explosive bombs, baskets of incend
aries, and air mines. They did that to stoke up the fires made b
the first wave, make them merge into one another, and so obtai
a bigger effect. I lay there with the sweat cold and sticky on m
nose and brow. I brought the pistol a little closer and waited i
terminably for the nurses to come for me. Next door they calle
out for the nurses several times, but nobody came. They ha
removed the serious cases from the top floor, and now it was th
turn of the second floor.

I lay and listened to what was going on in the ward next doo
I felt sick from the acrid, burning smell that came in through th
smashed window. Next door they were very quiet, but suddenly
heard one of them praying. Somebody told him to shut up, bu
he went on praying aloud. The bombs started falling closer; w
were right in the track cut by the Pathfinders. I followed ever
single bomb on its way through the air. It would whistle or his
or sometimes whine, and every time I heard an explosion I fe
relieved. Then there was one which I heard whining only at th
last moment. The building twice shuddered briefly, and th
nurses' footsteps on the staircase ceased. I noticed at once tha
I could no longer hear their footsteps or their voices. There was
continual roar of explosions, and the smoke in my room gre
thicker. I heard someone next door shouting, "The wall's gettin
hot!" and everybody shouted, and the explosions and whining
grew louder, and then there was quiet next door. I felt the wa
next to my bed, and it was beginning to get warm. Shrieks an
shouts were coming from everywhere, and bombs went on fallin
all the time.

I don't know who it was who fetched me out. They came up
ladder and tied me to a stretcher so that I could be lowered pe
pendicularly. My stretcher was laid in a row of other stretche
in the street, and there I remained for the rest of the night. Fo
a time I watched the smoke from the Flak shells bursting in th
sky, and the red and green signal flares, but then it grew quiete
the last wave flew away, and the Flak stopped firing. The fire br
gade came with hoses and extinguished the flames in the burnin
building, and later we were loaded onto trucks and ambulance

and driven away. I'd lost everything—my letters, my personal belongings, everything. Only my pistol was still in my hand. This was the second time that I'd been picked up gripping my pistol. I lay for four weeks in the new hospital, suffering from a kind of shock.

I found out later what had really happened. Two days previously a trainload of amputation cases had arrived from the Eastern Front, and the men had been temporarily accommodated in the school building before being sent on elsewhere. The nurses had done their best. The man who lay next to me in the new hospital had been on the third floor, and he had been one of the first to be carried down to the basement. He described to me how the nurses carried the men down, and how they wept and shrieked when they got to the basement, and swore they wouldn't set foot outside it again. But they kept going back for more, until the stairs caught fire. Then they had to put the fire out before they could fetch any more. Then it happened. Two or three baskets of incendiaries fell on the building, and sixteen or seventeen of the girls were killed.

After four weeks I was able to leave my bed, and after another three I was given a fortnight's sick leave. I was also ordered to report to my military district headquarters in Berlin. During all that time no letter reached me; the mails must have been dreadfully disorganized. Only the nice little nurse to whom I had given a couple of cigarettes came and talked to me sometimes.

"I'm very sorry I didn't give you the whole pack," I said. "They were good cigarettes, they came from Switzerland, and they all got burned!"

VII

I arrived in Berlin in November. Clouds hung low over the city, and I went straight to our house in the Heerstrasse. When I walked in Kride started back as if she had seen a ghost. She was slender and beautiful again, though she had put on a little weight. She stared at me, goggle-eyed.

"Where have you come from, for heaven's sake? Where have you come from?" she exclaimed

"From the moon," I said.

"Aren't you dead?"

"Feel me and see!"

She felt me and then collapsed around my neck and wept. I found this all very remarkable, but she went on weeping for a long time, and I took her into the sitting room and sat with her, and eventually she recovered. The house was practically unchanged, except that there were no fish in the aquarium.

"Did you think I was dead?" I asked.

"Yes," she said. "They wrote from the Munich hospital and said you'd been killed by a bomb—a direct hit. Wait a minute!"

She jumped up and looked for her handbag. She found it, rummaged in it, and eventually produced the letter. It said I'd been killed in the air raid of such-and-such a date. They had actually found my pay book. There had been a direct hit on my ward, and death had been instantaneous. That's what they always say. It's all they can say. At the front they say it was a shot in the head and at home they say it was a direct hit by a bomb. It's humane and helps to maintain morale.

"Well," I said, "I'm still alive all the same."

She fell around my neck again and wept with pleasure.

"Does Johanna believe I'm dead too? This'll make her open her eyes!"

"Oh, Rodie," Kride said and started weeping again. "You don't know the worst yet!"

I felt at once that she had another piece of news to tell me, like that which had followed my father's flight into Stalingrad.

"After I got the letter I went to see Johanna," she said. "It was a terrible blow to her, she couldn't even weep properly. She might have been turned to stone. She said several times that it was her fault because she hadn't been to see you."

"But that's nonsense!" I said. "How could she say a thing like that?"

Kride said she had stayed with Johanna the whole afternoon and had tried to talk her out of the idea that it was her fault, and in the end she thought she had succeeded. In the end Johanna had become quite calm and had actually cried.

"It's good to cry, Rodie," Kride said. "It means the worst is over. It's true of most people that when they cry they're going to be all right."

"Well, if it was all right, what happened?"

She said Johanna had been quite calm and in the end had even stopped crying and saying that it was her fault. But after Kride had left she had gone back to her little nurse's room and taken a handful of sleeping tablets and a morphia syringe and lain down on her bed. When they found her she was dead.

She was given a Christian burial, though everyone knew she had committed suicide, but the hospital chaplain overlooked it because she had been such an excellent nurse. The story was put about that she had been overworking and had taken some sleeping tablets and mistaken the dose. She was buried in a cemetery in the Moabit district, and next day we went there and laid asters and dahlias on her grave. I wasn't able to weep. I read the inscription on the cross, for which the hospital nurses had subscribed. It said: "Johanna Selzer, born 7.9.1917 at Euthin, died 2.10.1943. R.I.P."

All I could think of was to wonder what "rip" meant, until eventually it dawned on me that it meant *requiescat in pace*— may she rest in peace. Was she resting in peace? Who could tell?

A few days later I went to the hospital and saw the matron. She was a little severe and contemptuous with me at first because I hadn't written, but when I explained about my shock she grew a little warmer and friendlier. She spoke very nicely about Johanna and told me how hard she had worked and what an example she had been. That's what they always say—it was a shot in the head, or a direct hit, or what a splendid person, and away with him. But all the same I liked hearing it. It did me good.

I wandered aimlessly around the city. On November 22 they came to Berlin too. Everyone thought that in that weather it was impossible, but they came all the same and found what they wanted. The Flak fired at random into the clouds and didn't hit anything, and they flew over the clouds and looked at Berlin through a little gadget and opened their bomb bays. Huge fires started in the center of the city, but we were out in the Heerstrasse, in an underground concrete shelter that had been built for the private residence of a gentleman who was a big shot in the

Directorate of War Economics, or something of the sort. That summer the building of public shelters in Berlin had been held up for quite a time because the supply of cement had been diverted to provide shelters for people who were indispensable to the war effort. This was quite right, after all, because there were plenty of people in Germany but only a few who were indispensable to the war effort.

The owner was a very friendly gentleman, and he admitted mothers and children into his shelter, which had two stories. The great man had a French walnut desk and a carpet in his workroom, and actually had a telephone. The reinforced concrete overhead was several yards thick, so that once you were inside you were perfectly safe. Kride was admitted because she had a baby, and I was admitted because I had only one arm.

Kride's baby had turned out to be a boy, and his name was Manfred von Borsin. He was a very odd baby and scarcely complained when he was removed from his cot, wrapped in blankets, and carried two hundred yards through the wintry air to the shelter. I grew very fond of him. When he took my thumb in his tiny hands I forgot about the war and my shock and everything else. I used to sit beside him and play a little game with him. Whenever I clicked my lips he used to raise his eyes and look at them. If he smiled while doing so, I'd won.

Meanwhile the bombs dropped outside, and the loudspeakers in the public part of the shelter announced where they were falling, where the waves of bombers were coming from, and in which direction they were going. It was all very interesting, like being at the movies. You sat there and listened, and it was, so to speak, another historic hour. But my hands were trembling from the shock.

Next day I wandered about Berlin and looked at the people. Many women wore trousers and had pieces of gauze fixed over their eyes with sticking plaster. Some were still black from the soot which filled the air and didn't disperse because of the clouds overhanging the city, and others had burns and holes in their clothing.

I saw streets where nothing had happened yet—and they were the unlucky ones because they still had it to come—and other streets that were heaps of rubble; these were the lucky ones because they knew what it was like. It rained a great deal that November; the rain drizzled down gently from the low, gray clouds. People had piled their furniture and all their belongings in the street, and the rain kept drizzling down, and the blankets and mattresses and sofas grew damp and eventually were completely soaked. I saw pictures standing in the street, and pianos and frying pans and all sorts of bric-à-brac, and I saw a little bronze bust of Hitler standing in the rain. It was about the size of my fist, and the rain was running down its brow and dripping from its nose. A lot of people noticed it but didn't say anything and walked on. It looked as if it had a cold.

The big crane I had once dreamed of was now really standing astride Berlin. What we had dreamed about in the good days had come to pass.

VIII

I went to military district headquarters, applied for an extension of my leave, and got it without any difficulty. All I had to do was see a doctor, who examined me briefly and recommended me for eight weeks' leave. I took the certificate back to headquarters, who sent me to my depot, where I was given my papers.

By this time it was evening, and I found myself in the neighborhood of the Schlesischer Station. I went inside and watched a leave train coming in from the west and then going on eastward. It was the Paris-Berlin-Warsaw express, on which I had traveled two years before. I saw men getting out of the train and meeting the womenfolk who were waiting for them. I noticed a Flak lance-corporal getting out of the train. He was a lean, bespectacled man of about average height, and it struck me that there was something familiar about him. I stopped and watched him talking to a girl. She was a fair, slender girl, with a sharp face, and she was crying and shivering in the raw wind. She scarcely spoke and sometimes she laid her hands on his face. The guard blew his whistle, the transport officer called out, "On board, everybody, shut the doors!" and ran importantly along the platform with his bag hanging around his neck. It struck me that he might be the little captain who had shouted at me two years before, and I believe he really was. He got into the train, and the Flak lance-corporal kissed his girl and got in too. She stood on the platform and waved to him as the train moved off, and the light from every compartment fell on her as it passed, so that she was alternately in light and in darkness. I looked at her more closely and recognized Johanna. I wanted to call out but couldn't. She kept walking slowly forward in the direction of the train, and by the time it had gone I couldn't see her any more. I saw this with my own eyes, and I went back to Kride in the Heerstrasse and told her that next day I was going to Yevgenia's.

"Then I'll be alone again," she said and sighed. "Oh, well! I'll go to Konrad's parents in Mecklenburg." Shortly after their marriage Konrad had been promoted to lieutenant-commander and transferred to Norway.

"It's a shame," she said later on. "There'll be no one left to look after the house."

"It's all the same to me," I said.

"But it's your house, Rodie."

"You can have it," I said.

I'd been sent a whole pile of papers by the lawyer—the provisional rights to dispose of my father's property—but I hadn't looked at them. I had a few thousand marks in the bank and could live wherever I pleased—at Kride's or Yevgenia's or with my old landlady in the Wörthstrasse. I had no responsibilities and no need of possessions.

"You're only joking," she said.

"I mean it," I said. "You can have the house. I don't want it. I've no family, but you have. You've got the child."

"Manfred's very fond of you," she said.

She had just wrapped him up with her long, thin hands, and he was lying there and looking at us seriously out of his big blue eyes.

"I'm very fond of him too," I said. "Besides, I saw Johanna to-day!"

"Are you mad?"

"No, I'm not! I saw her at the Schlesischer Station. She was talking to a Flak lance-corporal who looked just like me. When the train went she waved, just as she waved to me the last time I saw her. I'm not mad. I rubbed my eyes and pinched my arm, and I saw exactly what I've told you."

"You are mad," she said. "It's just as well you're going to Yevgenia's."

What she meant, no doubt, was that two lunatics would get on well together.

"You can keep the house," I said. "I haven't got the slightest use for it."

This time she didn't say I was mad.

Next day I went to Yevgenia's. In the meantime I'd found out that Ott-Heinrich Nissel had been killed six months after marrying Margarete. Yevgenia had heard the news as soon as she got home after visiting me, but she hadn't written to me about it. Perhaps she hadn't wanted to burden me with her sorrows. Perhaps she hadn't been entirely happy about the match. It had been a typical wartime marriage. A young man with decorations comes back from the front, meets a girl, goes back, gets leave to marry her, goes back to the front, and gets killed. Nissel had been an excellent soldier, one of the dry sort, ambitious, keen, and tough. But Yevgenia had said in a letter to Kride that after his wedding leave he had gone back to the front with a heavy heart. That was the reason. When they're married they've got something else on their minds besides the war; they make a mistake, and it happens. Yevgenia had mentioned that Margarete was at home, but wanted to go back to the women's auxiliary service. No doubt she had done so by now. I couldn't imagine that she could stand it at home.

During the journey I gazed out of the window at the white landscape and thought about Johanna. It was just as well that I was out of Berlin, because I had begun to see Johanna everywhere. My nerves were not right. I was very excitable, and sudden noises made my heart pound. I was a coward, and I knew it. But there was nothing I could do about it. I was a coward, not one of those iron men who revel in danger. But perhaps it would come back again.

At the last hospital I had lain for three weeks without talking. I had wept continually, my face had grown swollen and ugly, the doctors had given me sedatives and had set my leg properly. I had lain there listening for aircraft all the time, but we were outside Munich, and there wasn't much danger. The nurses told me afterward that in spite of that I'd implored them to carry me down to the basement every night, and that I'd grown frantic when the sirens sounded in the distance. They had had to hold me down to make sure my fractured leg didn't come apart again.

In the fourth week I had suddenly got better and had the feeling I was in another world, and I didn't get any more frenzies. But my hands still shook, and I had no inclination to write. I thought it would be soon enough to give them the news when I got to Berlin. I had no reason to suppose that in Berlin they believed me to be dead. Why should they? There were air raids somewhere every night now. Every night another town was raided. Hamburg, Wuppertal, Hanover—all the towns of the Rhineland were systematically burned and devastated. People died in the cellars like fumigated rats, but the war went on. They hung shields and banners on the walls, saying, "Our walls may break, but not our hearts." No, their hearts didn't break. People can die without having their hearts broken.

I started smoking a cigarette, and a ticket collector came in and said it wasn't a smoking compartment. I went into a smoking compartment and sat next to a fat man in Army uniform with gray shoulderpieces. He greeted me cheerfully and noticed my decorations and that I had only one arm, and offered me a cigar. It was an excellent cigar. He also had a bottle of liquor, which he offered me. I tasted it and said, "Vodka!" He asked whether I had been in the East, and I said yes. Was that where I had lost my arm? No, I said, I'd brought my arm back to Germany, where it had been cut off for me by a doctor. We both laughed, and he offered me another cigar.

Later he took down his suitcase and produced a cold roast goose. He offered me a piece of white bread and butter, and we ate half the goose and washed it down with vodka.

"No, we don't live at all badly in Poland," he said. "I'm stationed in a godforsaken hole on the other side of Warsaw, you know. The district commissar is an ass, but we keep the Poles hard at it. Ha! Ha! They have to work as they've never worked in their lives before!"

"Ha! Ha!" I said, helping myself to his vodka bottle. "That's something they won't like doing!"

"No, they don't like it at all, but they know what happens to them if they don't obey!"

He was another of the fearless ones. He wasn't afraid of anything. Later he told me about his Polish girl friend, who lived under the constant threat of being locked up if she let anybody know that she was his girl friend. Relations with Polish women were absolutely forbidden, of course, but everybody had them. If a girl made any trouble she was just "transferred." Ha! Ha! He winked at me as he said the word "transferred."

"Ha! Ha!" I said. "How they must love you!"

At this he took another gulp out of his vodka bottle and said that that was mentioned in the celebrated opera, *The Czardas Princess;* or was it *The Gypsy Baron?* "Polish charm is unsurpassed. . . ."

"Is it true?" I asked.

"Quite true," he said and showed me photographs of his present Polish girl friend, as well as of her predecessor, who had been "transferred." He must have been an important man, because he had brought enough provisions from Poland to feed an army.

"We must do these things," he said. "Otherwise we'd never win the war."

Of course this burly, jovial man on the staff of the district commissar was helping to win the war. When once it was won, nobody'd grudge him his good time with his Polish girl friends.

"After all, a man's a man! Ha! Ha! Help yourself to another drink from the bottle. What's the matter with you? Do you always tremble like that?"

"Shell-shock," I explained.

"Oh, shell-shock! I've got such a lot of stuff with me, you know, take the half-goose with you for Christmas. It's a present!"

He also presented me with a pack of cigarettes. Later on he got out and fell into the arms of a stout lady on the platform. They embraced and kissed, he picked up a small boy in a Bleyle suit and carried him, and called a porter. Then the train moved off. He actually turned and waved to me. Now I had half a goose for Yevgenia, as well as a pack of cigarettes.

It was getting dark when I reached the town where I'd spent my boyhood. Yevgenia was waiting on the platform, and a slender, attractive young woman was standing by her side. I blinked my eyes and recognized Margarete.

"Good heavens, Rurik, how bad you look! How bad! Poor boy, I know everything! Now you're coming to stay with me, and I'll look after you. . . ."

She went on talking for quite a time, while Margarete stood silently beside her. I wondered which of us would be the first to condole with the other. She was dressed entirely in black and looked thinner and more grown up.

"Hullo, Margarete," I said to her and held out my hand. She took my hand and bent forward and kissed me.

"Hullo, Rodie!" she said.

We walked from the station and waited for a tram. The town lay on a river and had a castle on a hill, as well as all the other things that an old German town ought to have. In the tram a boy got up and offered me his seat. I made Yevgenia sit down and stayed on the platform with Margarete and my suitcase. The boy said something to another boy and came up to us again and said he had a seat, but for me. He laid some emphasis on the fact that it was for me. These boys were very polite. They never offered their seats to old ladies, but always offered them to wounded soldiers. I thanked him and told him I preferred standing on the platform, but that it was very nice of him. He stayed on the platform too and asked me whether I hadn't gone to school in that town. I asked him how he knew. He said his brother had gone to school with me. I didn't remember his brother, but the boy seemed proud of knowing me because I had a couple of decorations and only one arm. You can't get that sort of thing out of them. It's in their blood, and there's no reason why it shouldn't be.

Margarete stood beside me the whole time, smiling and looking at me out of her dark eyes. Good heavens, how beautiful she's grown! I said to myself. Less superficially attractive than Josefine but more beautiful—more really beautiful.

I felt ashamed of my cheap uniform and wished I had one for walking out. The thing I was wearing was the best they had been able to give me when I left the hospital, and of course it didn't fit anywhere. The trousers were too long and the tunic too broad. I mentioned this to Margarete. The tram rumbled around a corner, and I fell against her because I'd just been pointing something out to her with my single hand.

"You're tipsy!" she said.

I explained that in the train I'd met a very nice friendly man from Poland, and that he'd offered me vodka and made me a present of half a goose. It was going to be my surprise for Yevgenia. She laughed and told me that when I'd written and said I was coming for Christmas Yevgenia had ordered a goose, and she, Margarete, had got a goose too, and now I'd turned up with half a goose, as well as being befuddled with drink from Poland.

"Not befuddled," I said. "He wasn't as friendly as all that!"

IX

That Christmas we all tried to forget where we were and what a world we were living in. We succeeded best in Yevgenia's kitchen, as well as in an upstairs room in her house.

On the first evening we sat in the kitchen and ate the Polish goose. In Poland they roast goose with mugwort, and it's delicious. After dinner we felt so comfortable that we had no desire to move to Yevgenia's showroom and light a fire. I said that next day I'd have to go and see the Nissels and report to district headquarters and get my ration cards. Yevgenia's sharp eyes had seen at a glance that my uniform didn't fit, and she said that first I must be smartened up a bit. I had to take off my tunic and trousers, after Yevgenia had adjusted them, her mouth full of pins and with a piece of chalk in her hand to mark the material. Margarete was sent out of the kitchen while I undressed. She said she'd count fifty and if I was still in my shorts when she came back, so much the worse for me. I said it would be so much the worse for her. She went outside and counted while I took off my trousers and put on an old pair of ski trousers that belonged to Kride; they fitted quite well at the hips but weren't long enough. Margarete came back and began ripping the seams where Yevgenia had marked them. Meanwhile her mother started sewing, while Margarete laughed and called me Herr Kride.

Yevgenia had raided all her old customers and suppliers and collected a number of bottles. We drank mulled wine, and I tried to remember the recipe for toddy that the Scotsman had given me in the Faroes. We didn't talk about my father or about Kride or about Johanna or about Ott-Heinrich Nissel—in fact we mentioned nobody who had lost his life in the war. It was like peacetime, except that it was really more enjoyable. In peacetime we hadn't known how jolly one could be and how much there was to enjoy in the world. That was something we only learned in the war. Every happy hour was like a gift. You said, It's just like old times. But it wasn't like old times, it was like the remembrance of old times.

I kept making cigarettes and putting them in Yevgenia's mouth, so that she wouldn't have to interrupt her work, and lighting Margarete's and my own cigarettes with the same match, for economy's sake. There was plenty of fire at that time, but matches were always short.

"Tell us something," Yevgenia said while she worked around my uniform with her big tailor's scissors and unhesitatingly cut away the material that she thought superfluous. "Do you think you've got nothing to do but smoke cigarettes and keep your tongue in your mouth?"

I said it would be better if she told me something. The only things I knew I preferred not thinking about, and apart from them I knew nothing but dirty stories.

"Then tell us dirty stories," said Yevgenia.

I knew plenty but I thought most of them too raw. In the end I told the story about the old major and the pants, and Yevgenia nearly split her sides with laughing. I'd always thought it an extremely funny story myself, and I was delighted that Yevgenia should enjoy it so much that tears came into her eyes and she repeated the point several times. I laughed a little too, but I had heard it and told it too often to be able to laugh as much as that. After a while I looked up and caught Margarete's eye, and Margarete looked at her mother and then back at me, and then we both burst out laughing because Yevgenia was laughing so much.

It was warm and comfortable in the kitchen with the two women ripping and cutting and sewing. Yevgenia had been tailoring ever since I was born, and I'd never paid any special attention to it. But that evening I was full of admiration for her clever fingers. She threaded a little needle with gray thread and sewed so quickly that your eye couldn't follow it. She never stopped to think and never got annoyed with the material. Sometimes she turned the material and pressed the edges between her fingers. That left her with a straight seam to sew, and she went on with her work again. Every now and then she leaned forward and bit off the thread with her healthy white teeth. If it snapped she took more thread, bit it, made a twist, and pulled it through the needle in the twinkling of an eye; and then she went on sewing again.

At first I'd thought my uniform was good enough as it was, and I rather objected to the whole of the first evening's being taken up with altering it. But after a time I began to enjoy the proceedings.

Margarete couldn't sew as cleverly as her mother and kept to the plain seams. We went on talking about the old days. Margarete talked about the time when she had been training for the Olympic team. She took one of Yevgenia's kitchen plates and showed me how to throw the discus. In return I told how to use a hand grenade to bring a saucepan of water to the boil. They would have liked to see a demonstration, but unfortunately there wasn't a hand grenade on the premises.

We were all so happy and excited that we didn't notice the time. Suddenly the sirens went off, and I noticed how it made me start. But, either because I had had so much to drink or because the two women were there, I didn't say anything, and watched them finishing their sewing. Then Margarete had to go outside again while I changed back into my uniform. Then we went down to the cellar, where we found Margarete lying on Yevgenia's bed. She said she was glad the sirens had sounded, because upstairs

it had been so stuffy that it would have made her feel quite ill. We
sat on a padded box and waited for a time. Then we heard the
humming of the aircraft and the Flak opening up, but they flew
on, and it grew quiet again. Margarete got up from the bed and
said that as there wasn't anywhere else to sit she was going to sit
on my knees. Yevgenia said she ought to be ashamed of herself, as
I only had one arm, but Margarete stayed on my knees, rested
her head on my shoulder, and said, "Good God, I'm tipsy!"

"You haven't had so much to drink," I said. "Just think of me
and the start I had on Polish vodka!"

"That's quite obvious," she said. Then she snuffled a little and
said no, it wasn't.

After an hour the all-clear sounded, and we went upstairs again.
Yevgenia said she was tired. She looked critically at my tunic,
made me take it off again, put in a few stitches here and there,
threw it down and said she'd iron it in the morning. She was too
tired to do it now, but she'd do it first thing in the morning.
Wasn't I tired too? Yes, I was tired too. We corked the bottles
and went upstairs, where my room was. Margarete was going to
sleep on Yevgenia's old couch in the showroom, Yevgenia was going to sleep in the cellar, and I was going to sleep on the second
floor. I asked why I couldn't sleep in what used to be the maid's
room, but Yevgenia said it was now her storeroom. She had hired
this room when she heard I was coming. She had been able to get
it because more and more people who could afford it were leaving
the towns of West Germany and going to Bavaria. The Bavarians
were by no means pleased about this, because they had felt from
the first that the war had been intended as a scourge for the
towns of northwestern Germany and not for Bavaria. But they
were the better able to put up with the situation because it was
only people with money who went voluntarily to South Germany. The others had to stay and get on as best they could in
the half-empty blocks of flats.

I said good night and went to bed. I hung my uniform outside
the door so that Yevgenia could iron it next morning. I turned
out the light and shut my eyes, but I couldn't go to sleep because
I heard them moving about downstairs. I heard Yevgenia's
heavy footsteps and Margarete's humming. I heard chairs being

moved about and the clatter of plates. Obviously she was clearing
up in the kitchen. I lay there and listened, and was surprised to
find myself not thinking about anything. In Berlin it had always
been difficult to go to sleep, and sometimes I'd left the light on
beside my bed so that I should know where I was even when I
was asleep, but here I felt quite comfortable lying in the dark and
seeing the light under the door.

Then Margarete finished her work in the kitchen and went into
the showroom. For a time I heard nothing, and then I heard Yevgenia shutting the showroom door and going down into the cellar. The cellar steps creaked, and then it grew quiet, and I dozed.
I was thinking of nothing, or perhaps about how pretty Margarete
had grown—quite strikingly pretty. I had held her in my arms
when she was still a baby in a torn shirt, and she had struck me as
a little uncanny even then. She was still uncanny—uncannily
pretty. I closed my eyes and thought of all this in a vague way. It
was very easy; it was more dreaming than thinking. This was the
first time for a long while that I'd felt at home anywhere. Once I
thought I heard the stairs, which were wooden and always creaked
at one point, but I didn't pay any attention.

I opened my eyes and saw a dark form in my room. I thought
this must be another of the things I'd seen in Berlin, and didn't
move. The form closed the door and came and sat on my bed. I
stretched out my arm, and it was Margarete. I was just going to
say something, but she held out her finger and said, "Sh!" She put
her finger on my nose. She laughed a little because she had missed
my mouth in the dark. I put my arm around her shoulders and
felt that she was cold. She had goose-flesh.

"I only wanted to see if you were asleep," she said.

"Is that all?"

"I wanted to know whether you like being here."

"Is that all?"

"I wanted to know if you—" She raised her head, listened,
and said, "Sh!"

"Who in heaven's name could possibly hear us?" I said.

"Yevgenia," she said.

"If Yevgenia came upstairs with her couple of hundredweight
it would be audible in the marketplace!"

She laughed, said, "Sh!" again, and listened.

"Oh, stop it!" I said. "What is all this play-acting?"

She didn't answer, and I was afraid I'd offended her.

"I'm so glad you're here," she said suddenly. I put my arm around her and drew her toward me. She rested her head on my shoulder and stayed there.

"I'm so glad that you're here," I said. She laughed a little.

"How funny it sounds, with your voice coming from underneath like that! Say something else!"

I said something else, and she laughed again. "It sounds frightfully funny, but I can understand you."

"It's Christmas in a week's time," I said.

"And then what?"

"Then Margarete will get a fur coat."

"That's not true."

"No, it isn't true," I said, "but perhaps Margarete will get something else that she likes."

"What?"

"That's a secret."

"I've already got all I want," she said.

"Is that true?"

"Yes," she said, "it's true, it's true, it's true!"

She didn't talk any more. She was young, and I could tell that she was fond of me. She rubbed her head against my neck; her hair was thick and rustled if you rubbed it between your fingers. She had big round eyes. Snow lay on the ground outside, the moon—or was it the stars?—shone on the snow, and when I opened my eyes I could see her black hair and her big round eyes. At night they always looked slightly astonished.

"You've got eyes like the dog in the tinderbox story," I said.

"What sort of eyes did he have?"

"There were three dogs," I said. "The first had eyes like soup-plates, the second had eyes like millwheels, and the third had eyes like the Round Tower."

"What's the Round Tower?"

"You know very well. The Round Tower's in Copenhagen. We saw it on the way to the Faroes."

"Oh?" she said. "I didn't!"

"Yes, you did. I pointed it out to you specially, because I knew you had eyes just like that!"

"You didn't know anything of the sort. The most you knew then was what sort of eyes Josefine had!"

"What sort of eyes has Josefine?"

"Goat's eyes," said Margarete.

"Goats have very pretty eyes," I said.

"Oh? They were pretty enough for you then, anyway! You and your Josefine!"

"She's not my Josefine. She's somebody else's Josefine."

"She's everybody's Josefine," said Margarete.

We went to sleep and woke up and went to sleep again. Next time I woke the red morning sun was shining through the window and Yevgenia was bustling about in the kitchen and singing. I woke up first and saw Margarete lying beside me, with her head buried in her arm, asleep. I stretched and listened to Yevgenia singing the "Red Sarafan" and bustling about with the crockery. I couldn't help laughing because the evening before Margarete had kept on saying, "Sh!" But perhaps she hadn't been able to think of anything else to say. That was the most probable explanation. I got out of bed and opened the door. My uniform was hanging on the hook outside, and it had been ironed.

x

It was a delightful Christmas. We didn't laugh all the time and weren't always gay. Only fools and people who have never experienced anything can be always gay. We'd had plenty of experience and knew there was a lot more in store for us, because the war was still going on. This was only a breathing-space, but it was Christmas, and it was a good breathing-space.

I went to the military district headquarters and was given my papers and a special extra ration of fifty grams of coffee because I could prove this was my first leave since returning from Russia. I counted as being on leave from the Russian front. There were also extra rations for expectant mothers, brain workers, those doing heavy manual labor, and the severely disabled. Each category got something different, and it was all very carefully worked out.

I felt full of admiration for the great and wise intelligence that calculated the respective needs of servicemen from Russia, brain workers, and expectant mothers. I couldn't find out on what principle the system was based. The man behind the counter had lost a leg at Uman. He had the Frostbite Order and a healthy outlook on things. He hadn't the slightest idea how the authorities worked out who should get what.

"A woman came here some time ago and demanded her extra ration as an expectant mother," he told me. " 'Excuse me, madam,' I said, 'but I see no sign of it.' 'Of course not,' she answered, 'I only qualified three-quarters of an hour ago.' Ha! Ha! Ha! Ha!"

I laughed and asked whether the story was true.

"Yes," he said, "it happened here in this very office."

I'd heard this joke a dozen times before, in the troop, in the hospital, and in the train. I didn't say so, but laughed heartily.

"You can have another sugar card," he said, "and the two tobacco cards. I've got extra ones, so I won't need to charge them to you."

I thanked him and left. At that time I was already so corrupt that I accepted whatever was offered me, without worrying my head about anybody who might have to go short as a result. I just took it. Anything by which I benefited just made me laugh.

I went to see the Nissels next door. They had both grown very old. It was stupid, I know, but all the same I couldn't help feeling rather guilty when I walked into their house. Old Nissel was sitting beside the radio, listening to the Sunday sermon. I sat beside him and waited till it was over. He shook hands with me and said what a fine man my father had been. He had had lots of tenants, but none of them had been like my father. My father had scrupulously looked after everything, had hardly ever had any visitors, and had always paid his rent punctually on the first of the month. He had been a really fine man. Nissel's wife came in and wept when she saw me. In the old days she had sometimes been jealous of her husband, but now she was only a sad old woman. They had built a house and made a garden, and what for? Ott-Heinrich had been killed in the Kuban. It was a useless house, a useless garden. I tried to tell them how sorry I was, but I couldn't find many words.

"Well," the old railwayman said, "you lost an arm too!"

"Better his arm than his head," said his wife.

I had had a remarkable encounter at military district headquarters. While I was waiting for my papers the door opened and in walked Friedrich Feldmann. He was a captain now. He looked more flourishing than ever and had the Iron Cross, second class, the Sudeten decoration, and a wound stripe. I stood in the corner and watched him talking to the sergeant behind the counter. I made no attempt to let him see me; on the contrary, I was very pleased that he didn't. He was so vigorous and forceful that the sergeant behind the counter nearly got up to talk to him, and anyone who has ever been to military district headquarters, where they don't even get up for generals, knows what that means. But there was something military about Feldmann; he'd always been a much better soldier than I. He'd come to see about gasoline coupons or tires or something, and the sergeant took a note and promised to send him the forms. Then Feldmann walked out as quickly as he had walked in. I couldn't help laughing a little. He was so important, so gracious, so impressive, and all about a few gallons of gas. When I'd known him earlier all you had to do to get gas was to go to a filling station and buy a few pfennigs' worth, but then gas hadn't been one of his worries. I wondered whether he ever felt afraid nowadays. No, I felt sure he never felt afraid. He was so resolute, and the resolute always get their way. They become field officers and get orders, decorations, gas, and tires.

"Who was that chap?" I asked the lance-corporal who brought back my papers after they had been stamped.

"The head of the garrison hospital."

"Has he been here long?"

"Three years," the lance-corporal said.

"How did he get his wound stripe?"

"Last year an incendiary bomb fell on the hospital."

"Really?"

"Yes, and he actually burned himself a bit. Ha! Ha! Ha! Ha!"

The lance-corporal told me that when Feldmann came here he

had been a lieutenant, but he had done very well for himself. He played Skat every night with the garrison commander.

I had no reason to bear the doctors any grudge. They had cut off my arm very neatly and mended my leg. I knew some who had been in Russia for three years and had come back without any decorations. But they must have seen for themselves how foolish they were, because no incendiary bombs were dropped on the Eastern Front.

So Feldmann had his little racket too. Everyone who had landed on his feet had his little racket at that time. Anybody who wanted to be something, anyone who didn't want to end up in a mass grave, had to have his little racket. I had had a very nice little racket of my own in France. So I had no reason to bear Feldmann any ill will.

That winter all the little rackets in Germany started going full steam ahead. Anybody who had a nose and could use his fingers to count up to five had his little racket. It provided security for the future. Anyone who was not satisfied to live for the day alone, anyone who had a sense of responsibility and a thought for the future, had to look about him and get busy with friends, connections, gasoline coupons, morphia, cement, or cigarettes. Racketeering was a feature of the modern world, and without a racket you belonged to the proletariat. Peasants, artisans, doctors, lawyers, industrialists, and merchants—all had their own rackets. The only people who didn't have a racket were the workers and the intellectuals. They would have liked to have a racket too, but the state kept too sharp an eye on them. The workers were searched at the factory gates to make sure they hadn't helped themselves to anything, and intellectuals had no say in anything at all because they were a luxury and were superfluous. It served them right. Once they had held almost undisputed sway in Germany, but that had been a long time ago. They had grown lazy and had capitulated. There was no more philosophy in Germany, no more distinction between right and wrong, though ethics was a subject on which the intellectuals had sharpened their teeth for centuries. The very conception of ethics had disappeared. State officials still existed for the purpose of carrying out baptisms and burials, but they were no more than a kind of celestial sergeant. They knew the regulations and rattled them off, and that was that. Those who wished to do things differently tended increasingly to disappear, and nobody missed them. The important thing in life had become one's racket.

That was the kind of thing I used to say to Yevgenia and Margarete when I came back in the evening. But Yevgenia didn't share my outlook.

"Oh, Rurik, it's always been like that," she said. "The strong have always slaughtered the weak. It is written: 'Unto everyone that hath shall be given, but from him that hath not shall be taken away even that which he hath.' "

"Then we'd better hang ourselves right away," I answered, "because we have nothing. And from us shall it be taken away!"

But she only laughed. "Have you really got nothing?" she asked.

"No, nothing," I said.

She glanced at Margarete. Old procuress, I thought.

There was frost and snow for a whole week. The nights were clear and starlit, and I used to enjoy going for walks with Margarete in the dark. We walked out of the estate and looked at the town, and once there was an air-raid warning. When one was outside a town and in safety it was the most beautiful sight imaginable. The searchlights were turned on, and their beams moved about the sky, but they needed a lot of luck to catch an aircraft. On these clear nights their range was enormous, and they picked up aircraft several times. Then the Flak batteries roared, and all the noises that were so horrifying and alarming when you were in a cellar were dramatic and exciting when you were in the open air. It was rather like watching a big film, with the flat countryside, the dark town, which you could hardly make out, and in the sky those squadrons of metallic birds with their apocalyptic humming. We never saw any of them shot down by the Flak, though every now and then the Flak used shells with green or blue bursting points. But the bursting points were so tiny and the sky so huge that it was practically impossible to see them. The planes throbbed away, heavy and impressive with their burden of phosphorus, metal, and dynamite, and it seemed incredible that men should be inside them. One was told that men were inside them, but I'd never seen anyone who took part in these nightly processions. At the time the German press was getting very excited because of the allegation that the British sometimes took their girls with them on these bombing expeditions. I don't know how they knew. Someone must have told them.

"If my great-grandfather had seen anything like this he'd certainly have gone out of his mind," I said to Margarete.

She was standing beside me, staring up into the sky and sometimes saying, "I think I can see one," but she couldn't see one; it was imagination. You could barely see them in the daytime, and at night you couldn't see them at all. It was hard to believe that they really existed.

When we got home Yevgenia had a hot meal ready. We warmed ourselves and then played games in the warm kitchen—halma or poker. We didn't worry about the air raids. A thousand years ago men would have crept under the earth if such heavenly hosts had appeared in the sky. Now one barely turned one's head to look. But a thousand years ago they had had the plague or the Black Death, which had been done away with in the interval. Perhaps that was the reason aircraft had been invented.

After a few days Yevgenia moved back to her sofa in the showroom, and Margarete and I lived in the upstairs room, and I began to forget about my shock and that I'd believed I'd seen people who were dead. Nothing could have been more soothing than living in a little town. Nothing could have been more soothing than Margarete. She had no ambitions and no illusions; she just lived for the day alone. All she wanted was a little affection, to open her big round eyes and to rub her rustling hair on something. Then she liked laying her head on her arm and going to sleep and waking up and being able to say, "Good, you're still there." Then she went off to sleep again and forgot everything. She had no philosophy, no ethics, no illusions about the world, no audacious hopes, no plans.

"You're immoral," I said to her. "Why won't you marry me?"

"Oh!" she said. "I've been through all that once, and what came of it? Nothing! Why do you keep worrying about the future? I go to sleep and forget everything, and then wake up and feel that you're still there and say to myself, Well, that's all right!

What more do you want? You must live every day as if it were the last."

"I know one day will be the last," I answered, "but I refuse to believe that every day's the last."

"You're a bit crazy," she said. "You're sweet but you're a bit crazy. You want to believe something, and because you want to believe it you really do believe it. You get an idea and like it, and you end by believing it; but it isn't true at all. Look around you; it's all deceit and illusion. What do you want to marry me for? What difference would it make?"

"Where do you get all this wisdom from?"

"Is it wisdom?"

"It sounds like it."

"I believe it's what all women think. Only men are sweet and crazy enough to believe in what they believe in. Women only believe in what really exists."

"And what really exists?"

"This," she said and kissed me.

This philosophy of Margarete's often made me feel old and done for. Whatever you may say against it, there's something in it. There's more in it than you see at first sight. It's the philosophy of our time. A whole generation lives on it, without worrying about the future. It's the philosophy that preceded all other philosophies, that will survive when all the others have perished. It's the philosophy of reality.

It was sometimes comforting and sometimes the reverse. It was something completely new to me, and I started a new life. I threw my old life away and lived with Margarete. For the time being I had no philosophy any more; the old ones had disappeared, and a new one hadn't yet taken its place. Margarete overwhelmed me with her philosophy. She was overwhelming and comic at the same time, like her philosophy. As a man, you believe in many things without loving them. You can be convinced of their truth without having any emotional attachment to them. There are men who believe in statistics, and others who believe in bacteriology or atomic physics or homeopathy or free trade or the doctrines of Karl Marx. At some point they have made up their minds to believe in the object of their choice, and that's the end of the matter. But this generation, which had grown up among bombs and propaganda, believed in one thing only, and that was the heart. So long as their personal relations with people were all right, everything was all right. The only thing they believed in was love.

I was ill when I went to Yevgenia's, but after a time I felt that I was ill no longer. I could chop wood with my one arm, I could sit still when the sirens sounded, I could switch off the radio when the news started. I grew well again without noticing it.

One day I looked at my leave pass and found that my leave was nearly up. Three days later I had to be in Berlin, to report to my depot. I tried again to persuade Margarete to marry me—not at once, I said, if she didn't want to, but in six months' time. But she shook her head. No, not now, and not in six months' time. "Come and see me whenever you like. You know I'm fond of you," she said. But she didn't want any plans for eternity and she didn't want any promises. Did I know today what I was going to think or feel tomorrow? She didn't want a husband who knew today what he was going to think tomorrow.

I spent two days arguing with her. They were wasted days, and afterward I had plenty of time to regret them. I went to the depot and was given a new job. Flak gun crews were now being formed of Hitler Youths and girls, and experienced gun-commanders were needed for training purposes. I was given the opportunity of extending my knowledge of how to fire at aircraft without hitting them, and in a fortnight I had acquired a vast store of technical knowledge.

I often wrote to Yevgenia and Margarete, and they wrote to me, at first together and later separately. Margarete rejoined the auxiliaries and was sent to a signals unit in Holland. When she had leave I went to see her. At other times we wrote.

Her letters were quite different from all the other letters I had ever had. Perhaps that was because we were so alone at that time and had nothing but ourselves. Her last letter reached me by tortuous ways in November 1944. At that time I was in command of an anti-aircraft train. The armament consisted of machine guns coupled in fours. Margarete's letter had been posted in Holland in the late summer. It said:

"I'm so frightened now and so lonely—if only I could be with you at your gun. They take women now, but it's useless for me to apply because they wouldn't let me leave my switchboard. I think of you, darling, and feel your head on my breast, and your hand, and I'm like fire and you're like ice—or are you the fire and am I the ice? I don't understand why all this is happening, why all this is happening to us. I no longer understand anything. Yevgenia told me the last time I saw her that when I was small you used to take me on your knees—I only had to stretch out my arms, and you'd take me on your knees at once, she said. I wish I were a child again. I'm often so terribly lonely, and I lie awake at night in the shelter with the others and feel your lips on me, particularly on my breast, and I feel your hand, and get quite crazy with longing. But I don't want to go crazy, darling, I want to lie by your side and feel nothing but tenderness and that you're beside me. I want to sit on the floor beside you and rub my hair on your knee and hear it rustling. Do you think it will rustle next time?"

I don't know exactly what I wrote back, but I was in much the same state as she was—we were all in much the same state at that time. The enemy was doing a lot of low-level flying, and we were kept very busy, and when they didn't attack us and flew on elsewhere we were very glad. Like everybody else, we were fighting for our lives. I never got an answer to my letter; the post was very disorganized. All I got was a postcard from Yevgenia, saying that she had no news of Margarete either, and that she intended to go to Berlin to get Margarete and Kride out. Someone had told her that Margarete's unit had been transferred to Berlin. She also wrote and said that a refugee woman from Rumania had told her that the Russians raped every woman they could lay their hands on. Sometimes they were shot for it by their officers, but never when the women were German. She wouldn't leave her daughters in Berlin. Berlin was a lost city; Goebbels was mad, and so was Hitler. It was an amusing postcard; nobody had read it, and I burned it immediately.

No, I could do nothing for Margarete. All I could do was travel about the country and shoot. One day a man came to our unit and revealed to us in the strictest confidence that a wonder weapon had been discovered against the bombers, a rocket with a magnetic war-head, which worked on the counter-flow principle. We were able to imagine the kind of thing that a magnetic war-head might be, but I never met anyone who had the slightest idea what the counter-flow principle was. We were still waiting for this secret weapon to appear when the Americans reached the Elbe and the war was over. It was a pity. With the counter-flow principle we really might have done something, if only we'd started with it sooner.

7 - Return

I left my Flak train on a Sunday morning in April. The others all left before me, and only a mechanic stopped and waited for me on the slope beside the railway line. The sun beat down warmly on the hillside, and he had unbuttoned his tunic and taken off his cap. He was a big strapping fellow, not too strong in the head, or he would have unbuttoned his tunic and gone off with the others earlier. But he said he wanted to stay with me. I had packed some things in a Luftwaffe rucksack—a blanket, washing things, some provisions, and cigarette tobacco.

"Give it to me, I'll take it," he said.

He took my rucksack and slung it over his shoulder beside his own, and we walked down a lane with hedges on either side. We came to a main road and stopped. We had absolute liberty of choice. We could turn either right or left. Alternatively we could keep going straight ahead, but the fields were damp and uninviting. Another possibility was to sit down where we were and have a cigarette, and that's what we did. There was a continual humming of aircraft in the air. We pushed our rucksacks and greatcoats under the hedge and smoked.

The Flak train lay a little over a mile away. It consisted of two platforms, each with four coupled machine guns, and a coach, which served as our quarters, in the middle. The evening before a man in uniform had come and taken away the engine. He couldn't have got very far with it, because we knew that all the bridges were blown. If they hadn't been blown we should have made off during the night ourselves. We told him so, but he wouldn't believe us and drove our engine away. During the night we had stood on the line, listening to the aircraft passing overhead, but they couldn't see us, and we didn't fire. I tried to get through on the telephone to all the usual higher formations, but the lines were all down. I could get through on only one line, and then an American voice answered. I told the men about this, and they said the thing to do was to clear off at daybreak and leave the train where it was. The Americans were all around us, they said, and by now the S.S. must have withdrawn to the Danube. I asked whether we should stay together or not, and they said we should. Then an argument started about where we were to go, and everyone had a different opinion. Some wanted to go north, where the British were, others wanted to go south, where fighting was still going on, others wanted to go west to the French or east to the Russians. Another possibility was to stay where we were and wait to see what happened. That's what I proposed, but the others all wanted to go home. One young lance-corporal said we were a lot of cowardly swine who ought to be court-martialed, and it was a pity there were no S.S. in the neighborhood, or we'd be taught the consequences of high treason. This young man had been with us for only six months. He had volunteered for some kind of special unit, but because of a mistake he had been drafted to us, and that rankled with him. The others wanted to beat him up, but I told him to go south and fight, if he felt like it. I don't know whether he ever got there, but he left during the night.

After we had sat by the wayside for some time the humming in the air grew louder. Three aircraft with rounded wings approached in formation at six thousand feet. They didn't see us, but they saw the Flak train. They flew over it, turned, flew over it again, and then came back toward us. We hid behind the hedge and assured each other that we weren't in any danger. Suddenly they started peeling off and diving down on the Flak train. We crept out from behind the hedge and heard them firing and heard the explosion of the bombs—six bombs. Then they flew low over the train again, and we crept back under the hedge. We heard them firing again, and then they flew away, and we crept out and smoked another cigarette. We didn't know where to go. There was no one to tell us. The mechanic sat next to me, smoking his cigarette.

"You can speak English, can't you?" he asked suddenly.

"Yes," I said.

"Can you speak American too?"

"It's the same," I said. He came from Mannheim and didn't know much about the world.

"Exactly the same?" he asked.

"No," I explained. "When an Englishman talks to an American, it's rather like a Mannheimer talking to someone from the Frankenthal."

He saw what I was driving at. "In the Frankenthal they talk a terrible jargon," he said. "You can hardly understand them. But at Schifferstadt they're still worse!"

"Is that where the good radishes come from?"

"Yes," he said. "I think Mormons live there, or Mennonites, or something of the sort."

We went on talking to pass the time and because we didn't know which way to go. In the end I stood up, picked up my rucksack, and walked off to the left. The road was white and dusty and worn from much traffic. During the night I had listened to the B.B.C. and found out that they were everywhere. I also listened to Berlin and heard a voice saying that everything was all right and that the new weapons were going to strike the enemy a terrible blow. In a few days, the voice said, Vienna would be German again; and Berlin would remain German. That was how I found out that Vienna was no longer German.

We walked the whole afternoon, hoping to get somewhere. I racked my brains, wondering what to do. After a time the mechanic insisted on carrying my rucksack again. We were in Franconia, in some godforsaken corner of Franconia. It seemed senseless to go farther on into the country, but even more senseless to sit by the wayside and do nothing at all. At last we came to a village with a majolica church roof. It was full of drunken troops. They told us that a mile and a half down the road there was a vault in the rocks full of wine bottles, so we made for it.

Just as we got to it a big truck drove up, containing men in uniform. They stopped opposite a hole in the rock and jumped out. Soon afterward a lot of people—civilians and men in uniform—began streaming out from the rock vault. They were laughing and cursing, and most of them had bottles of wine in their hands. They had been turned out by the men who came in the truck.

After a time some of the men came out with cases of wine. They called out, "Heave!" and lifted the cases onto the truck. Then they went back into the vault again. We climbed on board, called out, "Heave!" and unloaded the cases from the other side of the truck. We did this four times. Then they came out with another case of wine, and when they saw the truck was empty they started cursing. Next the man in charge came out and climbed onto the lorry to satisfy himself that it was empty, and then he started cursing too. Meanwhile we had filled our rucksacks with bottles of cognac from one of the cases, and we took our departure.

We climbed a hill, reached the top, and started unsuspectingly going down the other side. Suddenly firing started, artillery and rifle fire, and we were in the midst of a battle, with bullets flying everywhere and ricocheting off the stones. We flung ourselves flat on the ground and crept with our rucksacks into a hollow. We saw two American tanks two thousand yards away, with American infantry behind them, and to our left were young men in German uniform firing at them. They started attacking in short rushes, the Americans withdrew, and we crept back to the road along which we had come. It was a remarkable time, with men getting drunk on one side of a hill while a life-and-death struggle was taking place on the other.

We found another road, which led around the hill and on which there was no fighting. We spent the rest of the day and the night in a barn. The night was cold, we could see the stars shining through the cracks in the roof, but we lay warm and snug in the hay. It was good cognac—Renault, guaranteed twenty years old. We drank it appreciatively and used it to help down our sausage and Army bread. Next day we came on a wounded S.S. man. He told us that the day before the Americans had come back with reinforcements and driven them out of the pocket into which we had stumbled. About thirty men had been killed. We bandaged him and gave him a bottle of brandy. He was delighted with it and asked us whether by any chance we had seen his unit. It had been ordered to recapture Nuremberg at all costs. I asked who had given the order, and he said it was the Reifü.[1] That was the pasty-faced, bespectacled little man I had seen in my father's

[1] The Reichsführer S.S., i.e., Himmler.

house seven years before, who had explained to his secretary with
the aid of a cake-knife how to capture the Urals with the first
thrust and then advance into the heart of Siberia.

We couldn't leave the wounded man lying there, so we carried
him back to our barn. He grew feverish. He had received a glanc-
ing wound in the chest, but what he was most worried about at
first was that he had lost his unit. I found him some medicine,
and he had to swallow it with brandy because we had no water,
but he slept well on it. The stars shone through the cracks in the
barn roof that night too, but the wounded man groaned all night,
and at daybreak we went down to the valley and filled our water
bottles. Then we found a farmhouse, where we were given bread
and butter and milk, which we took back to our wounded man.
He was feverish for two days but then got better. They told us at
the farmhouse that the Americans had reached Munich. I wondered whether the voice from Berlin was still so confident about
the possibility of holding Berlin. On the third evening I left the
mechanic and the wounded man alone and went down to the
farmhouse. They were delighted when I put a bottle of brandy on
the table. They were poor people; the whole neighborhood was
poor. But they had a radio, and I tuned in to the B.B.C. and
found out that the Americans were outside Leipzig and had left
Munich behind, and that the British were at Rügen. There could
be no more talk of recapturing Nuremberg, which lay somewhere
to the north. The Americans had thrust forward on both sides of
us, and the war seemed to be over.

I told this to my two friends when I got back to the barn. The
S.S. man asked whether either of us had a knife, and the mechanic lent him his pocket knife. He went out into the moonlight, and for a time we heard him grunting and groaning. Then
he called out to me to come out, and I went out and saw that his
left arm was covered with blood.

"What's the matter?" I asked.

"I've cut out my blood group," he said.

The letter A had been tattooed on his left arm to show that
he belonged to blood group A. He said the Americans examined
all prisoners to see whether they had any letters or marks on their
arms, and it was said that all men with tattoo marks were sent to

special camps. He said he had no desire to be treated worse than
necessary, so he had cut out his tattoo mark. But it was bleeding badly, he said. Did we have anything to bandage it? I tied i
up with a first field dressing; he took a drink of cognac and told
me he had burned his pay book and his tunic that afternoon afte
I had gone away.

"Yes," he said, "the war's over now. Anyone who sees the hole
in my arm will be bound to think it's connected with the wound
in my chest, won't he?"

We said there was no doubt about it, that's what anyone
would think, and then we went to sleep, and two days later he
was better and we trudged on. He wore my greatcoat when he felt
cold.

We reached another village and found it empty. A man was
hanging from a street lamp, but otherwise everything was quiet
and peaceful. We knocked at the door of the inn, but nobody
came. Then the mechanic went in and came out again with some
beer. We drank and waited, but nobody came. Then I went in
and found a shed full of cows and goats, and a radio in the living
room. We switched on the radio and heard voices. First a German voice said that the war was over and that the unconditiona
surrender had been signed, and then two men spoke English. One
of them was Churchill, and the other I didn't recognize. We wen
on listening and heard a high-pitched, monotonous voice speak
ing a language that sounded like Russian. The announcer came
on and said the voice had been Stalin's. It took me a long time to
get over my surprise that Stalin should have such a high-pitched
voice.

II

That summer I was able to wander far and wide, all because
one of my arms was missing. We took the S.S. man to a hospita
and went on our way. More and more jeeps passed us. Some
stopped us, others slowed down and called out to us, but they al
ways let us go because I had only one arm. I had wrapped a piece
of bandage around the stump and wore my tunic over it, so they
thought I'd been wounded and let me go, and the mechanic too

We made our way to Central Germany and reached my old town. It was full of Americans. We had nothing to eat, so I bartered my wristwatch for a rucksack full of tins and looked for Yevgenia's house. It was burned to the ground, and so was the Nissels' house. There had been a battle in the town. A group of soldiers had entrenched themselves in the estate where we had lived and defended themselves with bazookas, and then fighter-bombers and tanks had come, and when the resistance was over all the poor devils who lived there had lost their homes. They had been built after the first war and destroyed in the second. Most of the people had lost not only their homes but sons and husbands too. After the first war they had tried to rebuild. They had married and built houses. For twenty-five years it had been all right. Then it was over.

There was no news about Yevgenia, no news about Margarete, no knowing what might have become of Kride. We wandered on toward the north. By this time it was summer. Sometimes we stayed with peasants, and we had acquired documents stating that we had been regularly released from the Army. We were given them by a German captain whom we met in a barn. He had released all his men and he released us too. He had the proper rubber stamps and the proper forms, and when he had completed them he said, "Well, lads, now you can keep your uniforms and ten years' pay and go home. You didn't imagine the end of the war would be like this, did you?"

We said no, we hadn't imagined it would be like this. We had expected another chance to march down the Unter den Linden and through the Brandenburg Gate and past the guard.

"Oh, well," he said. "It may all happen yet one day! Patience, only a little patience!"

He had very little hair left and limped badly. We asked him how old he was, and he was a year younger than I.

"You've aged early," I said.

"Oh, well," he said, "you don't look so very young yourself!"

He had been in every campaign, from Poland onward. He had been in the Army for two years before the war, which had broken out just when he thought he was going to be released. He had been a senior ensign, and in Poland he was promoted to second lieutenant. He had got no more promotion for a long time, and then he had been promoted to lieutenant and captain in rapid succession. He produced his pay book and showed it to us. There was a page full of decorations, including one that sounded like "Grand Cross with swords and crown of the heroic Michael." This was a Rumanian award. He said it was a miracle he had come through with a whole skin and now he was going to his mother. She was somewhere in Pomerania, where the Russians were, but he thought he'd be able to get her out. He'd find her a place in the west and then go and fetch her. His name was Eckermann, and he was very proud of it. "Yes," he said, "Captain Eckermann, released after eight years' service."

"Do you think you could put your name on my piece of paper?" he asked. "I meant to ask one of my men to sign it, but I forgot, and now they've all gone."

"Give it to me, sir," I said. I signed it "Major General Stamm."

He looked at it with satisfaction. "You really should have signed it 'Major General Goethe,' " he said. "That would have been very amusing. Eckermann released by Goethe! Ha! Ha!"

"Do you think the Americans would have believed it?"

"They might not, that's true," he said.

We went our several ways, and I heard no more of Captain Eckermann or his mother. He looked like the kind of man who would do what he set out to do. He was one of those simple souls who generally get their way.

For a time the summer was hot and dry, but then it became rainy. I lost my mechanic. He was picked up by the American Military Police and put into a demobilization camp, in spite of his release papers. I said I had to go to a hospital, and they offered me a lift to it. They were very friendly. They noticed my bandaged stump and felt under an obligation to help me, because they had whole skins. They reacted to my arm like all healthy people. In the end I managed to shake them off and went on wandering about the country. I went north in a coal train and looked for Kride. By a stroke of luck I ran into Konrad von Borsin in Hamburg. He said he had found his wife a little house in the Vierlanden. He was staying in Hamburg, looking for a job. He gave me the address, and I found Kride busy in a little kitchen garden, surrounded by beans, tomatoes, and cucumbers. She was wearing the same old buckskin gloves, and Manfred was playing on the grass. She looked younger and happier than ever.

"What's happened to Yevgenia?" we both asked in the same breath, and neither of us knew. Kride had gone from Berlin to Mecklenburg and from Mecklenburg back to Berlin. I had the impression that her parents-in-law hadn't been too enthusiastic about their son's marriage to a moneyless divorcée. She had stayed in Berlin until March. Then she had fled and gone northward with the boy and had got in touch with her husband through a naval liaison office. She told me all this while working in the garden, weeding, tying up tomatoes, and propping up bean stakes with the greatest efficiency. No, she had no news of Yevgenia, and no news of Margarete either. It seemed to me that she was not excessively concerned about her relatives' fate. She had her own home, her own family now, and all her energy was needed to keep her little racket above water. She had no time left over for sentiment.

I stayed with her for two days. It was remarkable how everybody had room for others in those days. I slept on a mattress under my old greatcoat, and nobody thought anything of it. It was actually quite comfortable in its way. We drank tea and ate things that Kride cooked. Sometimes I played with Manfred, who was two now. I had liked him when he was a baby and Kride had wrapped him up, but he wasn't to be compared to the Manfred that he had now become. I thought he looked exactly like what Kride's father must have looked like at that age, and Kride confirmed it.

"You're perfectly right," she said. "That's exactly what he looked like. I've got photographs of him, taken by the St. Petersburg court photographer. They're so alike that the resemblance would make you laugh. Unfortunately I haven't got them here."

I said I was perfectly prepared to believe her without the photographs, but I found it rather astonishing all the same. The child was so gentle, shy, and affectionate at the age of two.

"Well, perhaps he'll have a better life than we've had," Kride said.

"That's what all parents say about their children."

"I don't think my parents said it about me," she said. "When I was born everything was still in proper order."

"Oh, well," I said. "Perhaps they had their troubles too!"

"Now listen," said Kride. "You admit we haven't had much from our lives. What have we had? God knows I'd rather have lived in the nineties of last century! Then life was still worth living. When I think of the years through which we've passed . . ."

It was her firm conviction, which nothing could shake. I once tried arguing with her. I pointed out that there had been others who perhaps hadn't been quite so well off as she, but she wouldn't have it.

"So you believe all that rubbish too!" she said. "It's the fashion nowadays always to talk about those who are worse off. Of course there are always people who are badly off. But I think the best way of helping them is to see that you get on in the world yourself. I don't propose to stay in this cottage forever, for instance. Manfred must have brothers and sisters and must grow up in suitable surroundings. For the moment, of course, it's all right, but . . ."

And she went back to her garden and worked like a beaver among her vegetables, with gloved hands. Kride hadn't lost the war. I looked at her and felt certain that in a few years she'd have got back again to where she wanted to be. She was no philosopher but she had a sure instinct for the course of the world. She was ambitious, clever, and tough, and now she was in the prime of life besides. Even in these simple surroundings she was a strikingly beautiful woman. Any man allowed into her house couldn't help feeling it a privilege, not only because of her good name but because of her self-assurance.

"You mustn't take everything to heart so," she said to me later. "You mustn't take the world so tragically. You must take the world as you find it, and make the best of it. What do you gain by roaming about the world, not only looking all around you all the time, but pondering over all you see? I never ponder over anything. I think of the food I've got to lay in now, so that we'll have something to eat in the winter, and of the stock of wood and coal that we've got to get in. I've sent Konrad to Hamburg to get coal."

"I don't think there is any," I said.

"There's always some," she said. "The British bring it in from the country by train. The whole of Hamburg's living off the coal trains. They all jump on them and push overboard what they need. Konrad has a friend, he's a public prosecutor, a retired colonel. They've managed to collect a whole ton already, and when they've got enough we'll go in a car driven on wood fuel and fetch it."

That winter they had the most wonderful coal battles at Hamburg. On one occasion the municipality sent five hundred police to protect the British coal trains, but the wives of Hamburg used the big lumps of coal as missiles and put the police to flight. The police were unarmed, and besides they sympathized with the women because their own wives were among them.

I remember traveling by train from Lüneburg to Hamburg, either that winter or the next. Outside Hamburg people were waiting for the coal trains all the way along the line. I saw a small, fair boy jump down from a low bridge onto a coal train as it passed slowly underneath, and start throwing lumps of coal overboard to his parents, who were waiting on the track. I watched him for quite a time as we slowly overtook the coal train. A woman was looking out of the window next to me, and she was watching him too. Eventually we overtook the first coal truck, on which a policeman was dozing, with his truncheon beside him as a symbol of his dignity. The woman leaned out of the window.

"Wake up, you!" she called out. "There's a boy in one of the trucks behind, throwing coal overboard!"

The policeman pretended not to hear and passed out of view.

"Why did you want to give the boy away?" I asked.

The people in the compartment looked up for a moment, but then dropped their heads again.

"It's intolerable!" she exclaimed. "It's intolerable that people should simply be allowed to steal!"

"But what does it matter to you?"

"What does it matter to me?" she said indignantly. "It matters to me a great deal! After all, one must have order!"

The rest of the people in the compartment said nothing but just looked straight in front of them.

These years were exceedingly fruitful because they were so human. Everyone developed his own technique for coming to terms with life. There were some who just sat in corners glumly and starved, and there were some who walked upright and hungered gladly, like the saints and martyrs. But most people worked up their own rackets again—some little ones, because they had to start again from scratch, and others big ones, because they had started in good time, setting aside a few tons of cement or some trucks or one or two truckloads of war supplies.

One of the best rackets, as far as I could judge, was that of my friend Alfred Karawan. I thought perhaps that he might have been put in some particularly secure camp because he had been in the Field Security Service, but Alfred had calculated the times better than I had. I was sitting in the lounge of a hotel in Central Germany one day when he walked in, looking well dressed and well nourished. He didn't see me and disappeared again. I asked the waiter who he was and was told he was the town administrator. I went to his office and asked for him. He had a big office, with two secretaries in the anteroom. At first they didn't want to let me in, but I insisted on their taking my name. Karawan came out at once, of course, and was delighted to see me. The two secretaries then became exceedingly friendly and attentive, and one of them brushed the back of my tunic while the other asked whether I'd lost my arm in the war. No, I said, I'd lost it making cigarettes. We went and sat in his office, and he produced a bottle from his desk and gave me a drink.

"I really owe all this to you. If you hadn't put me into touch with Josefine, perhaps today I'd be—krrk!" he said, drawing his finger across his throat.

"Josefine?" I said. "Where is she?"

"She's got a hat shop in Lisbon," he said. "But let me tell you the story. I got her over the frontier to Southern France and kept in contact with her. She got information from me and gave me information which I passed on to the maquis, and six months before the invasion I went over to the maquis entirely. It was just the right moment. I stayed in France until the capitulation, and then came to Germany. They needed an intelligent administrator, and here I am! All right, isn't it?"

He had become slightly inflated and was very proud of having backed the right horse, but I'd liked him better before he became an administrator, when he was still a pianist in a bar. I told him so, and he wasn't in the least offended. It's extraordinary, but most people take that kind of remark as a compliment. They think, If I made such a good impression on him when I was a pianist, what must he think of me now I'm an administrator! They think you're jealous, and that's a comfortable feeling for anyone.

"I'll write to Josefine and tell her you're still alive. She's sure to send you a CARE parcel. Give me your address."

I told him I didn't have an address. At that time I still belonged to the upright and willing martyrs. Later I belonged to the sullen, hungry martyrs, and then I started building up my own racket.

III

During the period when I was a sullen martyr I wandered all over the country. At first I inquired everywhere for Margarete but in the end I gave it up. I met someone who told me that Yevgenia had died of inflammation of the lungs just before the end of the war. She was buried in a town called Halle and actually had a grave with a cross and a proper inscription on it all to herself. I went there and looked at the hill beside the cemetery where those who had died in hospital were buried. It was covered with tulips— great fat red tulips, tidily arranged, as only Protestant nurses know how to grow and arrange them. Yevgenia's grave was tidy, tidier than her life had ever been. It wouldn't have been nearly so tidy if she'd had to look after it herself. In view of all those tulips it seemed superfluous to lay more flowers on her grave. I sat down and thought of my old friend and felt glad that she had found peace. I wondered why she had died in Halle, of all places.

During that time I lived on what I had and had no ambition to live any better than the people I met on the road. The roads were full of people, streaming from one place to another, with their possessions loaded on pushcarts, perambulators, horses and carts, and old cars driven on wood fuel. The women wore trousers like the men, and everyone put on all the clothes he had, to keep out the cold. The cattle trucks on the railways were full of people going from one part of Germany to another. Some died of cold, others only got frostbitten toes or fingers. Sometimes the burgo-master or local administrator wouldn't accept these truckloads of humanity and sent them on somewhere else. Then they were left standing about until at last they found someone who'd accept them. These people had no racket at all but lived on the last breadcrumbs they had been able to bring with them in their pock-ets and suitcases, and if you took the trouble to talk to them they told you the most harrowing stories. Sometimes after listening to them I couldn't sleep at night. These things were happening daily and hourly before our eyes, and nobody took any notice.

There were also quite different stories, which were then re-echo-ing around the world—about the millions of Jews who had been gassed and then incinerated in Eastern Europe. At first everyone thought these stories were propaganda, but there could be no doubt that they were true. These stories had to be read and driven into people's heads, because they belonged to the picture of that time as much as the pictures of the fighting and the burning cities. There were some who refused to believe them even when they saw the pictures of the piles of corpses in the newspapers or the movies, but most people I knew realized they were true and hung their heads and said nothing, like the people in the Hamburg train. But while we looked at these pictures we knew that in the East-ern Zone of Germany the killing was still going on. We knew that the concentration camps which the Americans had opened with their tanks had been closed again after their withdrawal, and that new hordes of inmates were pouring into them night and day. It was a time full of bewilderment and horror, and at the same time of hunger for life, of greed and contempt, and there was no one who could see his way through the chaos. First there had been the chaos of devastated towns, and now there was the chaos of devastated souls, and this was the worse.

At about this time I went to one of the broadcasting studios and talked to one of their reporters about what I could do to find Margarete. He took down the particulars and asked who her par-ents were and what my relationship to her was. I said I was engaged to her, and that her father's name was Seidenbaum and that he lived in New York.

"A Jewess?" he said. "And you're engaged to her? My God, what luck!"

He meant it perfectly seriously. That was what he thought. I left my address and went away, but I never went back to find out the results of their efforts. Everything got turned into a racket. Some went to church and put money in the offertory box, and others proclaimed how loyally they had always stuck up for the Jews. Anyone who took any sort of job had his own racket.

Those first years were certainly not good years. But perhaps there was one good thing about them, and that was that everyone had a free choice about what to do with his life and everyone had to show himself in his true colors. We were the world's outcasts, and the roof over our heads was too small to cover us all. The strong and the clever, like Alfred Karawan, found themselves places in the middle, and the others had to do their best to find some shelter at the edge. Time had paused for a moment, and the pause gave people a chance to make decisions.

"You look awful," Kride said whenever I went to see her, but what she meant was, "How you've gone down in the world!" I never stayed with her for more than two or three days and then I went off again.

Konrad von Borsin had an office in a building in Hamburg. The first time I went to see him we were both dressed more or less alike. He had a table and a chair in his room, the walls were unplastered, and there was isinglass over the windows. I had some American bacon with me, which we fried over a little electric stove, and we ate it with bread which we soaked in the fat in the frying pan. He was delighted to see me.

The second time I went to see him there was plaster on the walls and glass in the windows. We smoked cigarettes and talked about the old days. I admired his new room. It was still very simple. You could still see the big dents in the floor made by the hexagonal incendiaries, and the room was nearly empty, except for a filing cabinet in the corner; but he had a telephone now, and he wore a collar and tie instead of a sweater with a roll collar.

After that I didn't see him again for quite a long time, but when I went again he had an anteroom as big as Karawan's, and a proper desk, an armchair, and a beautiful carpet on the floor. This time I stayed with him for only a quarter of an hour because he said he was terribly busy, he had the whole export-import trade on his hands. Wasn't there anything he could do for me? Wouldn't I leave my particulars and let him try to find me a job? Hadn't I talked it over with Kride? She had often talked to him about me. No, thank you, I said, I had no particulars to leave, I didn't want a job, and I was quite satisfied as I was. I was still wearing my old tunic, but Konrad had a new suit of English worsted, dark blue with a pin stripe. I thanked him very much and said I had only dropped in to see him.

"It was very nice of you, old man," he said. "Please drop in whenever you're passing!"

It so happened that I didn't happen to pass that way again.

I had a slight tiff with Kride. Three months earlier she had had her second child, and was going to have it christened.

"I want to christen him Roderich, after you," she said. "But you really must start doing something; you can't go on roaming about like this."

"Roaming about like what?"

"Like this!" she said. "You must get a job and get married and settle down."

"You should have married me," I said. "You were the first woman in my life. You were what the psychologists call an imago. You're my imago."

"Don't talk rubbish," Kride said. "Are you being serious?"

"No," I said.

"Why do you go on roaming about like the old Jew Nathan in St. Petersburg? Do you deal in old iron too?"

"Sh! Kride," I said. "I hope you're not casting any reflection on your husband's present occupation. Because he deals in scrap!"

"Yes," she said, "but wholesale."

She walked around the table and came and sat on the edge of my chair. Her gray eyes were close to my face, and she was rather irritated and upset.

"Do you know what you look like?" I said, to change the subject. "You look just the way you did in Naples when the small boy outside Zi' Teresa's told you you had big feet. Do you remember? Then Alfred Karawan turned up and nearly shook him to death."

"Good heavens, Rodie," she said. "How young we were then!"

We squabbled for a few more minutes and then made friends.

That evening Kride had a visitor. He was the gentleman from the Ministry of the Interior who had been among the guests that long-ago New Year's Eve in Berlin. He was now in the export-import business too. He wore a handsome gray suit, both tasteful and inconspicuous, and his head was full of figures about British groundnut production.

"Just look!" he said when he saw me. "What a sight for sore eyes to see a proper soldier again! I haven't seen one since Herr von Borsin gave up his uniform! How are you?"

I thanked him and told him I was very well. For a moment I thought he was a cynic. On that New Year's Eve he had regaled us with information about the healthy effect that war would have on German life because it would relieve the state of the burden of a lot of troublesome revolutionaries. But he wasn't a cynic. He was one of those simple straightforward people who always say exactly what is in their minds.

"What, in your opinion, is the effect of all the refugees now streaming into West Germany?" I asked.

"It's beneficial," he answered, frowning slightly and showing a few wrinkles in his huge forehead, which made him look like a big, peevish baby. "It's undoubtedly beneficial. I always say a thing can't be so bad as not to have a good side to it! The greater part of these refugees are very decent people, and it is only to be expected that the result of—shall we call it the restricted opportunities open to them?—will be to stimulate them to exceptional efforts. That will be the natural and inevitable result of the environment in which they find themselves. From the national economic viewpoint the result is that we have been provided with a reserve of workers who (a) have been immunized against the Communist virus and (b) will provide our own workers with sufficient competition to assure that wages are kept down to a level that will enable us to compete satisfactorily in the world market. . . ."

He quoted some examples in support of both (a) and (b). I thanked him and said that it was a great relief to me to hear this. I had always thought the refugees were very badly off, but I now saw that they were really very lucky to have been turned out of their homes.

"Well," he said, "to call them lucky is rather an exaggeration. But I shouldn't by any means go so far as to say it was a misfortune for them. Above all, they are filled with an enormous love of their old homes, and in that they must be supported, because it provides a natural bulwark against the advance of the East."

Next day, when I said good-by to Kride, I said, "Now you see the reason I don't know what to settle down to. Against that kind of cleverness I'm defenseless. It's the kind of cleverness that took us into Central Russia and brought the whole disaster in its wake. If only he'd restrict his cleverness to his groundnuts and not start applying it to human beings again!"

"You started the conversation," she said. "You started it by asking him his opinion."

"But don't you think he talks to other people in the same way? Don't you think he's convinced that he sees things as they are?"

"Of course he is," said Kride, "and that is how they are!"

"I don't know whether they are or not," I said, "and I don't want to think about them. I often suspect that what he thinks doesn't exist at all. The last time I heard him talk it was about the fundamentals of German life and the danger of a reaction in politics. Now it's the refugees who have got to act as a bulwark against the advance of the East. For whose benefit? For his! And they'll be stupid enough to do it, and he'll rub his hands because (a) we'll no longer have any revolutionary young people and (b) the pressure from the East will have been satisfactorily opposed. Then he'll sell his groundnuts impartially to both victor and vanquished. And if you imagine him in his underpants he's nothing but a revolting little fat man whom you in the east wouldn't even have allowed to decorate an office chair. Imagine him in his underpants!"

"I prefer not to," said Kride. "When are you coming again? We want to have the christening in four weeks."

"Have the christening when you like," I said. "I shan't come to any christening!"

"When will you come?" said Kride.

"When you're in a mess," I said. "When you're in such a mess that for once you're really desperate. You once had a chance of it, in Berlin, but then they built a deep shelter outside your front door, and nothing came of it again."

"Don't talk rubbish," said Kride. "When shall we see you again?"

"When I'm a millionaire!"

"That'll be a long time!"

"I'm afraid so."

"Are you being serious?" She laid her hand on my shoulder. "Tell me for once what you really think," she said.

"I'd certainly tell you if I only knew, Kride," I answered. "It's something I really and deeply want to do one day. But I can't. There are always so many pros and cons. I can always see a justification for everything, I do it every day. One can live in the way you do, and one can live in other ways."

"And how do you want to live?"

"If I only knew!" I said. "If I only knew!"

It was a trifle melodramatic. Kride kissed me and said I was to come and see her whenever I liked and as often as I liked, and there was no need to let her know in advance . . . and that above all I shouldn't think . . . and that she was dreadfully sorry that I was just going away like that again. I said I'd certainly be passing that way again, and left and dismissed Kride from my mind, and a few days later I felt surprised that I'd gone back there at all. They were on the way up, and there was no way up for me. I went on roaming about the country, watching how people lived.

IV

Two years after the war nobody knew any longer what he lived on. The clever and energetic ones found their way into the new government offices and made a living by allotting other people their rations, and as other people couldn't live on their rations they had to live on the black market. I met a man in the train between Hamburg and Munich who told me one could do big business in Italy with sewing-machine needles. We arranged that he should get the needles and that I should take them to Italy. Fifty pounds of needles is quite a lot, and not so easy to smuggle, but it was all organized. I met a man at Kufstein who guided me over the frontier to Austria, where I paid my way with American cigarettes, and another man, whose brother-in-law was in the frontier police, guided me over the Brenner. It didn't cost a lot, and for two packs of cigarettes he carried my rucksack up the steepest part for me.

"Yes, life's hard," he said when we sat down and rested in the morning in South Tyrol. "You'll get along easier down below. Do you speak Italian?"

"Like a Sicilian," I said. "I lived in Sicily for a year."

"No, I shouldn't like to live in Sicily," he said. "But if you talk Sicilian you'll be able to get along all right with the South Tyrolese in the valleys. Mussolini turned out a lot of Tyrolese peasants and replaced them with Sicilians. But only in the valleys. He left the Tyrolese in the mountains. You won't have any use for your Sicilian there."

"But I always thought the Duce was our friend."

"He may have been, but he took precautions all the same. He didn't want too many Tyrolese on the frontier."

I left him and made my way down into the Trentino, where I was met by a man to whom I handed over the needles. I never found out how the German supplier got his money, but he must have managed it somehow. I was given a huge pile of lira notes, as well as an Italian passport.

"You talk like a Sicilian," I was told. "Nobody'll suspect you."

I traveled south by way of Rome and Naples and met a lot of gay, friendly people on the way. The Italians had thrown in the sponge in 1943, and they'd only started in 1940 anyway, so they were better off than we were. Their life had gone back to normal, and they could even think about the Duce without rancor. I traveled past long walls covered with every possible kind of inscription. VV *Mussolini!* VV *la Casa Reale!* VV *Umberto!* A *basso Mussolini!* VV *Togliatti!* VV *de Gasperi!* A *basso il Commu-*

nismo! and so forth and so forth. Many of the inscriptions dated from the old days, but some were quite recent. Some were just scrawled with charcoal, and others were carefully painted. It was like a menu, the European menu. It had been just like that in Germany when I was seventeen, but there people hadn't taken the trouble to write everything out so carefully. In Germany you just drew a little cross or three arrowheads, and the passer-by understood. Words had become superfluous. If you disagreed with what you saw you just crossed it out.

In Naples there had been terrible destruction, particularly in the district where Elsie had lived. But her tenement house was still standing. The iron staircases and balconies were still there, though somewhat battered. But Elsie had gone. They called for the old woman with the crazy eyes. She looked at me, and I saw that she was blind.

"La signora tedesca è sposata," she said, and they all looked at me as if to say, Bad luck, old chap, you're too late.

"Whom is she married to?" I asked. "An Italian?"

"No, un' Americano," the old woman said. Elsie was married to a handsome American sergeant, a Negro. They now lived in a state with an unpronounceable name.

"Mississippi?" I asked.

She shook her head.

"Massachusetts?"

She nodded and said yes, perhaps that was it. The sergeant had driven a truck here in Italy and had a lot of money. He was the son of a clergyman in America. He was a very handsome man.

"How do you know?" I asked.

"Everybody said so," she explained. "Everybody said she was very lucky. He was five years younger than she, and whenever he came to see her he brought a whole suitcase full of food. The whole house lived on it!"

I went on to Reggio Calabria, thinking to myself that Elsie must now certainly be sending CARE parcels home to her people in Hamburg because she was always so kindhearted. Perhaps she had forgotten to mention who her husband was, and no doubt her people in Hamburg were glad and full of praise for their clever daughter, who sent CARE parcels home to the hungry. And all she had really done had been to run away from home twelve years before, for reasons that it was perhaps better not to inquire into. Perhaps her motives hadn't been of the noblest. But her enterprise and her taste for the picturesque had had a happy outcome. I remembered exactly the context in which she had used the word the first time I went with her to her flat. "What muscles you've got!" she had said, feeling my arm. It had been just flattery, of course. But now the arm had gone, and Elsie had a Negro husband and was sending CARE parcels home to Hamburg.

I took the train from Catania to Caltanissetta in the mountains, and from there went down to Girgenti. I took a taxi out to my uncle's. I'd thought of sending him a telegram, but then I'd decided to make it a surprise. When I got out of the taxi I was very disappointed. The lemon and orange trees were still there, but my uncle's house had been burned to the ground.

The driver said he had been very surprised that I had wanted to be driven there. Everyone knew the house had been burned down. It had been a punishment for the man who lived in it.

"Did someone set fire to it?"

"No," he said, "but there were German motor-torpedo boats in Porto Empedocle, and they were attacked by fighter-bombers, and one fighter-bomber was hit and set on fire and crashed on the house. It was full of petrol, and the whole house burst into flames."

"Was anybody killed?" I asked.

"The old lady," he said. "The old English lady who was married to the doctor. It was impossible to save her. There was just a crash, and the whole house burst into flames. Do you want to stay here?"

"What happened to the German doctor?" I asked. "Was he killed too?"

"No," the driver said. "He lives in a little house somewhere in Porto San Giorgio and paints. He's very poor because he can't touch his wife's money. It's in the bank, but he can't touch it because he's a *tedesco*."

"What does he live on?" I asked.

"The priest of San Giorgio gives him money, and the fisherman Battista has given him a little stone house that he built. He spends all his time painting pictures, but nobody buys them. In the old days, when he had money, everyone bought them, but now he paints and paints and doesn't even earn enough to pay for the canvas."

"Can you take me down to San Giorgio?" I asked.

"That will cost extra," he said.

We drove down to the village. I found my uncle in the little house that belonged to Battista, wearing a faded blue shirt and an old pair of fisherman's trousers. He didn't seem to be in the least surprised to see me. He was squatting next to a tripod over the fire, on which there was a pan with two tiny fish frying in it. I went down to the village, got more fish, a big *fiasco* of wine, and a bottle of olive oil. We fried the fish and didn't mention the fact that he had no money but that I had. Nobody in the village had recognized me.

"It's too dark to show you my paintings," he said. "I'll show them to you in the morning. I'm painting marvelously now! I've got an entirely new style."

"How did it happen?" I asked.

He looked at me out of his blue eyes and dropped his voice. "It was the theomachy," he said. "Do you still remember? It was the theomachy. Two days before they landed. She said to me, 'Thank heaven, now it'll soon be over!' Everyone was talking about the landing. 'They'll soon be coming and occupying Italy,' she said, 'and then they'll cross the Brenner into Germany. I pray every day for a quick victory.' I told her she was crazy. Sicily was only an island, and even if they occupied it what would they gain? They came every day and bombed the airfields and the harbors, and the Flak kept firing, and the air was full of bombs and shells. But we were safe in our house. There was no airfield in the neighborhood, and Girgenti was a long way away. That afternoon I went down to San Giorgio to see Battista. Suddenly the guns started firing. Six aircraft came over, and one began to wobble and come down. A man jumped out and fell into the water, and then we saw a cloud of smoke. I thought no more of it. The mountains were full of fires where bombs fell and aircraft crashed. Then I went back home, and the whole place was burned to the ground. Do you remember the theomachy? I told you about it once!"

"Yes," I said. "We had six years of theomachy at home. We had enough theomachy to last us for the rest of our lives."

He looked at me again out of his gentian-blue eyes. "I sit here and think and think," he said. "I want so much to find out what it all means. I want to paint a picture of it, but she won't let me. She always gets in the way."

He listened and moved his lips. Outside a ripe fruit fell from a tree, rolled a little way, and stopped. My uncle started and looked out of the window. There was fear in his face.

"That was she!" he said. "Did you hear?"

"It was an orange," I said.

"Do you think so?" he said in relief. "Sometimes I think it's an orange or a falling branch, but then I change my mind again and feel certain that it's she. Everybody's seen her. Go down to the village, the fishermen will all tell you!"

"Is that why you keep the door shut?" I asked.

I walked over toward the door, which he had shut as soon as I entered, but he got up and stood in the way.

"Leave it shut," he said. "I've no desire to see her. I've seen her several times already. It's not a pleasant sight. She was so terribly burned!"

"You're crazy, Uncle Martin!"

"Go down to the village and ask the fishermen."

"At least let me open the window."

He sat in the corner next to the tripod and gazed at me out of his gentian-blue eyes while I tried to open the window, which had stuck. He was a man of sixty-eight, but he was like a timid child. He had once called my father a humbug, but now he was a broken man.

The window was stuck so hard that it took me a long time to open it. When I succeeded the ledge was full of woodlice, earwigs, and other unappetizing creatures. I swept them away with my hand and looked out. The air was cooler and cleaner outside. Every now and then you heard a fruit or a twig drop.

"Did you hear?" he exclaimed several times.

"That was a lemon," I said, or, "That was the night wind." But he didn't believe me.

"Tell me, why do you stay in this godforsaken hole? Haven't you got any friends?" I said.

"I don't want to see anyone," he said stubbornly. "I want to stay here and think, and sometimes I try to paint what I see."

"And what do you see?" I asked.

He spoke long and disconnectedly. For a time I tried to follow, but then I gave it up. With us too there were more and more people who sought refuge in astrology or magic, or studying the Bible with a darning needle, or dangling rings over eggs. They simply had the feeling that previous methods had failed. I discovered that my uncle Martin was simply afraid of his wife. He always had been afraid of her. During her lifetime he had defied her, but now that she was dead he saw no way of defying her.

"She's there the whole time, with her cold, unapproachable eyes," he said. "She was perfect and faultless. And she had to suffer the fate that was meant for me!"

"What was that?"

"To be burned to death in the house. But she was burned to death in my place. It was my fault."

I told him he was mad. He didn't dispute it. No doubt people had told him so before. In the end we talked about other things, and he was sometimes quite sensible. Sometimes he actually had a kind of crazy wisdom.

"You'll see," he said. "The theomachy isn't over yet."

"No," I said. "You don't have to be a clairvoyant to be able to see that. It goes its own way, like everything that has once been wound up and that nobody stops. The whole world's full of it."

"The crane is a terrible bird," he said.

I looked at him in astonishment. "Why?"

"Oh, nothing, nothing."

I said no more, but he had said exactly what I had been thinking.

We drank and went on talking.

"Do you ever practice your medicine now?" I asked.

"No," he said. "I've given it up completely. It's pointless. You can't help people. You can't help anybody. I want to help the world with my pictures."

I didn't see how pictures could help a man with a broken leg, for instance, but that wasn't my business.

"How do you propose to set about it?" I asked.

"By painting what is happening. Not what has happened, but what is happening."

"Then paint Battista's wife with her fat belly. There you have the whole thing in a nutshell. Everything happens because people are born. And that's such an old story that there's no need to go on bothering one's head about it."

He said there was something in what I said, but it left out the connections.

"What connections?"

"Everything is connected with everything else," he explained. "Everything that happens is determined in advance by causal connections."

I went over to the window again and looked outside. It was a wonderful night, but we couldn't go out. We had to stay in this wretched hovel because he was afraid.

"I've never seen any causal connections," I said. "Everything's chance!"

"Chance?" he exclaimed.

"Yes," I said. "It was chance that my mother met Yevgenia, that we lived next door to her, and that my father married again. It was chance that I wasn't killed in Russia, that I wasn't burned to death in hospital, and that my fiancée believed I was dead and committed suicide. It was just chance! I happened to be traveling in a ship, sitting and reading, when a man came and asked me whether I was an art historian. I didn't want to say no, so I became an art historian. It was chance! I've always let things take their own course, and sometimes they've gone well and sometimes they've gone badly, but it was all the same to me. I don't see any necessary causal connections. If I'd been a Jew I'd have ended in a gas chamber, and if I'd been in the S.D. I might have put people in a gas chamber. True, the lines keep crossing and forming nodal points, but then they diverge again and go their own way. My father tried to change the course of history, and what came of it? We're worse off than you in Sicily. No one has ever asked me whether I wanted to do anything; I've always had to do it—sometimes because it was the law, sometimes because it was tradition, and sometimes because I was just told to do it. Anyway, I always did it. If I hadn't done it I'd only have done something else, and perhaps that might have been worse. I don't believe a cross in a cemetery decides whether you go to heaven. I don't know what benefit people get from national anthems. I don't believe in technical progress. I don't believe in causal connections. I only believe that things grow, and that the wise man lets them grow in their own way. Things have much more sense than people. I've seen our best brains at work, generals and directors of industries and economists and politicians, and all that came of it was appalling disaster. I see others at work and know that the same disaster is in preparation for them. I've had enough of your necessary causal connections, your predetermination, your fate, your providence. They're nothing but words, as worn out as an old stair carpet. There's no proposition that men don't end by turning into its opposite, just by continual repetition. I don't believe in anything except the big whales, who swim all together into a trap and die in it because they want to. They don't want to be parted from one another, and so they die. I've seen whales do that, but not men. Men call them stupid, and I think that speaks volumes. I've had enough of your pondering over the causes of things!"

He listened to the whole of this speech without attempting to interrupt.

"I've always thought myself a pagan," he said, "but in comparison with you I'm a pious Christian."

I stayed with him for about a fortnight. The news spread around the village that my uncle's nephew from Germany was staying with him. Battista recognized me and was delighted to see me again because we had once been friends and I had gone with him to the chapel. He had six children now, excluding those who had been stillborn or had died; and they all lived on Battista's nets and rod and line.

"Weren't you excommunicated for cutting up the candles?" I asked.

"No," he said. "The lady in the house sent the priest a bundle of candles—thick yellow wax candles that had been consecrated in Rome—so everything was all right."

"Lucky for you," I said.

He laughed and shook his head. "It doesn't worry me any more. I'm a Communist now! We Communists don't believe in the priests."

"I'm going along to the burned-down house tonight," I said. "Will you come with me?"

"*Mamma mia!*" he said. "Certainly not! The old lady walks! Many people have seen her—Marcello, and others too."

"But I thought you were a Communist and didn't believe in ghosts and superstition."

"*Mamma mia!*" he said. "It's true that the Communists don't believe in God, but they're not in power yet. They haven't proved that they can get rid of the old lady's ghost!"

I went to see the priest, as well as Luisa, who lived in a house at the end of the village. I told her I'd given the priest money for my uncle.

"You shouldn't have done it," she said. "There was no need to. The priest would look after your uncle anyway. You could have saved the money!"

"But that's very noble of the priest," I remarked. "My uncle used to plague him dreadfully."

Luisa still had the same grim, crazy face, the same steep forehead, and the same mop of black hair, in which streaks of gray were now beginning to appear. She couldn't help laughing at the stupidity of my last remark.

"*Madonna!*" she said. "The priest couldn't ask for a better object for his charity than your uncle. As long as he's got him he has an inexhaustible subject for his sermons!"

I didn't quite follow this line of argument, so Luisa explained.

"*Porco maggiore,*" she said impatiently. "Don't they have brains in your country? No? As long as your uncle goes on living in that little house the priest can point to him as an example of the consequence of wickedness. He preaches about your uncle every Sunday, and about the pitiful life he leads, and he describes how the devil torments him every night."

"But doesn't the devil torment him?" I asked.

"I don't believe it," said Luisa. "*Il diavolo è morto.* The devil is dead. I'm a Communist!"

On the journey from Rome to the Brenner I bought a newspaper and read about Giuliano, the Sicilian bandit. What a magnificent opportunity I'd missed! Obviously I'd gone to the wrong end of the island. Giuliano was a kind of modern Robin Hood and wanted to rid the world of evil by force. Oh well, everybody has his methods. I'd heard this sort of thing too often before. Evil can't be abolished. Perhaps if it were abolished there'd be no spice left in life at all.

I was guided across the frontier by a friend of the brother-in-law of the man who was in the frontier police, and had no difficulty. I traveled through Austria and returned to Germany by way of Kufstein and Rosenheim. I'd bought one or two little pieces of jewelry on which I proposed to live for some time to come. Fifty pounds of needles are a nice lot, and you get something for them. In Germany the government hadn't resigned yet, and people were either hungry or living on the black market. They sold carpets, bric-à-brac, Sèvres porcelain, old books, paintings, material for suits, hairbrushes, corsets, pieces of ivory, diamonds, and home-grown tobacco, which they treated themselves. Those who had nothing at all sent their wives, sisters, or daughters to the Poles who guarded the big camps. Nothing had altered.

At Munich I bought a ticket to Frankfurt. It cost as much as sixteen American cigarettes. In the train I sat next to a man who had taken up astrology. He told me that in the year 1972 we should be passing from the sign of Pisces to that of Aquarius. That meant the end of the Christian era; the new Messiah was already on the way. I told him I was born under Aquarius. Did he think that by any chance I was the new Messiah? He doubted it but said that all the same I was very lucky to have been born under Aquarius.

v

Nearly four years had passed since I had seen Margarete. During the war women had played a notable role. Before the war they had played a fairly notable role too, but after the war everything altered. Women still played a notable role, but, as far as they were concerned, we played no sort of role at all. We had no more uniforms—or rather our uniforms had become entirely unimpressive.

Besides, we had to wear civilian buttons on them. I had no trouble with my tunic, because the buttons were concealed in any case, and the regulations didn't apply to one's fly buttons, so I'd had to change only my greatcoat buttons. But in the trains and the shelters in which one often slept one naturally had to take the things off, and we didn't make at all a good impression.

How women managed I don't know, but they had a lead of several lengths over us from the start. During the first summer you actually saw women who looked very smart indeed. In winter they crept ruefully back into their trousers, but in the second summer there was a great blossoming of femininity, and during the third summer fashion papers actually reappeared. For a time I sold fashion papers myself, which enabled me to meet a lot of women. But after a time I gave it up. What a lot of things one started and dropped! In the long run all that mattered was food and drink, which couldn't be earned; they could only be wangled. Some did it by using their wits and taking risks, and others learned how to do it by the sweat of their brows and bitter experience.

During the whole of this period I had no news of Margarete and I thought she must have gone to her father in America. Anyone who could possibly manage it went to America—except the Americans, of course. All this time I thought of Margarete as one thinks of the dead. I had held her on my knees when she was a little girl running about in a torn shirt; I'd driven her about in a car, she'd often been a pest, and then I'd gone back to her and her mother, and the world had looked different. She had made the world look different. I didn't forget Margarete, but she must have gone to America, and she belonged to the past. I didn't blame her for going. At first I'd been rather worried about her and thought she might have been killed by a bomb. But she wasn't the kind of person who gets killed. She was so young, so full of cheerfulness and tomfoolery, and she was a discus-thrower, who occasionally swung her mother's soup-plates about. No, nothing could have happened to her.

At that time everybody in Germany needed an acquaintance who wielded rubber stamps. Living without properly stamped documents was very troublesome, because without them you couldn't get ration cards, express travel permits, and so on. Consequently everybody had an acquaintance who wielded rubber stamps.

The man who legalized me was an antique dealer. I met him in a café, and he offered me a job in his business. It was a pleasant job and enabled me to travel. He paid me a small salary and a good percentage. I accepted the job partly because I'd grown tired of buying my ration cards on the black market. The man's business was in the town on the Rhine where the house which my grandfather had given to my father was; the house which my father had later so ungratefully sold to move with me into another town.

I wasn't there very much because I spent most of my time traveling about, routing out antiques which I posted back to my boss. But I got myself a room in the town and registered with the police there, and once, when I came back from my travels, I went out to where the villas were and looked for my parents' house. I hadn't set eyes on it for about thirty years, so it was difficult to identify. But I had a few dim memories of eaves, crenellations, and balconies, and in the end I believed I'd found it. I stood and gazed at it for some time. It was early spring, and I looked at the beds and the borders and the bushes and the trees, and it all looked much smaller than in my time. I saw a small boy running about in the garden. He had fair hair and blue eyes. At the garden gate there was a brass plate with "Erik Clason, A.P.M." inscribed on it. The name sounded Swedish or Danish and fitted in well with the fair-haired little boy.

One cold rainy day—it must have been in the summer of the same year—I arrived back with a suitcase full of statuettes, vases, cups, and saucers, handed them in, and intended leaving again the same afternoon. The station was full of black-marketeers, pickpockets, pimps, and old men furtively offering packs of American cigarettes. I went to the ticket office to get myself an express travel permit. There was a queue of about fifty people waiting there already, and I decided that I'd never get my permit in time for the afternoon train but would have to take the night train. I joined the queue and slowly moved forward with it. Occasionally there was a slight squabble ahead of me, when someone thought that somebody else was trying to get in ahead of him, and at intervals a policeman turned up and told us to keep our places. On one of these occasions somebody called out, "Attention! Eyes front!" The policeman went away, and everybody laughed for five minutes over this witticism. The policeman did it only to show that he had some authority, though he was unarmed.

I noticed a woman a few yards ahead of me smoking an American cigarette. She was no longer young and was wearing an expensive fur coat. She was talking to another woman, who was standing in front of her. I couldn't see her properly because she was smaller and was entirely hidden by the first woman's fur coat.

A queue is a remarkable thing. Sometimes it's so noisy that you have to shout to make yourself understood, and then there's a sudden silence as if everybody were waiting for someone to say something. During the silences you could hear the noises on the platforms quite plainly, the tinkling of the trams in the street, and the rasping voice of the station announcer announcing the trains through the loudspeaker. Then somebody started talking again, and everybody else started talking too, and so it went on till the next dead point.

I stood there and moved forward when everybody else did. A queue is rather like a concertina. At times people stand rather far apart and at others they all start closing in until everybody's packed like sardines. When you've once got used to them you find that queues have a rich, secret life of their own, and you start feeling at home in them. Also they have their little excitements. The ticket clerk suddenly closed his window and hung out a notice saying that the issue of permits would continue from ticket window Number 17. The people at the head of the queue naturally saw the notice first and tried to get to the tail end as quickly and unobtrusively as possible, and then a mad scamper started to ticket window Number 17. The policeman arrived and straightened things out, and after a time everything was as it had been before.

After the queue had duly reassembled I could distinctly smell the American cigarette being smoked by the woman in the fur coat. Then a silence fell, and the woman in the fur coat said, "I hope I'll catch my train, Margot," and the invisible woman answered, "You've still got half an hour, Vera."

That was all, but I'd heard the voice, and it gave me an electric shock. I asked the man behind me to keep my place for a moment, and walked unobtrusively past the two women. I walked far enough past them to have time to see the woman's face on the way back, but I was practically sure even without that. On the way back I saw it was Margarete. She was wearing a small black hat and a violet kerchief inside her coat collar. I had often thought of her during the past years—of her strong, round shoulders, her untidy hair, and her face, with her eyes either closed or big and round and open, but now she looked much older and not at all like the old Margarete. She had a printed form in her hand and was looking at it. I stood there looking at her, and after a time the woman in the fur coat tapped her on the shoulder and whispered something. Margarete looked up.

"Good God!" she exclaimed. "Are you still alive!"

The face of the woman in the fur coat changed and became friendly. She thought I'd been staring rudely at Margarete, but now realized I was an old acquaintance. I went up to them and was introduced. Frau Verwaers came from Cologne, I was told, and that was where she was now going. Margarete was seeing her off.

I took her form and went straight to the ticket window with it. Normally I didn't like doing that. People had grown tired of seeing wounded ex-servicemen going to the head of the queue and sometimes objected. They objected now too, but I didn't care, because I wanted to talk to Margarete and get rid of Frau Verwaers from Cologne.

I got her express travel permit and rejoined them. We escorted Frau Verwaers to the entrance to the platform and stayed with her for a few moments out of politeness. Then Frau Verwaers disappeared into the throng, and we were alone.

We walked out of the station into the open space opposite the Hotel Breuker, forced our way through the lottery-ticket sellers, loafers, and dollar profiteers, and eventually reached a quiet corner. I had a great deal to ask her but I didn't know where to begin.

We walked side by side through several streets without talking. I had thought that when we met again we'd fall into each other's arms, and that she'd stand on one leg or show in some other remarkable way how glad she was to see me. It had become a kind of fixed idea of mine.

We walked through a lot of streets. She didn't speak, and I didn't know what to say. She had grown thinner, and I should have liked to put my hand through her hair, to find out whether it still rustled. But her face didn't encourage any such familiarity, so I didn't attempt it. Eventually we reached the villas overlooking the Rhine. It had stopped raining, the sun was peeping out through the haze, and we sat on a bench in a little square. It was quiet there, and you couldn't hear any trams or cars or men hawking their wares. It might almost have been in the country, except that we were surrounded by big villas standing in their grounds, with different colored trees—aspens, willows, and planes.

"I didn't think you were still alive," she said suddenly. "I wrote to you. Why didn't you let me know you were still alive?"

"I kept on writing to you till March, and after that it was pointless. What happened? I didn't get any more letters from you either."

She took off her glove, and I saw she was wearing a ring. I had sometimes thought that one day I should see her again, but it hadn't occurred to me that she might be married.

"Are you married?" I asked.

She nodded.

"Children?"

"One."

"How old?"

She didn't answer. The sun came out again and shone more strongly. A tigerish-looking kitten came cautiously, stiffly running across the little grass plot in the middle of the square, trying to avoid getting wet, and sat on a dark paving stone.

"I thought you must have gone to New York," I said. "That's what I've believed ever since the end of the war."

"I was in New York for six months. We got married and went first to New York and then to Sweden."

"Is your husband Swedish?"

"Yes," she said. "My name's Clason now."

I thought I'd heard the name somewhere before, but I couldn't think where. "Tell me some more," I said. "Are you happy?"

"Yes," she said. "What do you expect? I'm very happy. Perhaps in six months' time we shall be having another child, but I haven't told him yet. Heavens, Rodie, what a fright you gave me!"

"Like seeing a ghost, wasn't it?"

The kitten lifted its left paw and began licking it. After it had finished with its left paw it began on the right paw. Every now and then it looked around, and when the sunshine grew brighter it shut its eyes and remained motionless for minutes on end. Some people with a dog came from the street and sat on a bench opposite.

"I hope it hasn't done you any harm," I said.

"What? The fright? No, of course not. Only I've always been a bit frightened."

"Frightened? Why? Frightened of me?"

"Yes," she said and suddenly started talking.

"Our unit was transferred to Berlin, you know, and then the Russians came, and it was simply dreadful. If I hadn't met Clason I don't know what I should have done. He was the head of a Swedish relief mission and stayed in Berlin the whole time. He helped me and got me civilian clothes and put me in touch with my relatives in New York. He could do all that. You see, he—"

"Yes, but why were you frightened of me? I understand what happened, but you had no need to be afraid of me!"

"No?" she said. "Then that's all right. I've always believed that one day I'd see you again and that you'd— Incidentally you're terribly unshaven!"

"I was going to shave in the train," I said.

The dog suddenly caught sight of the kitten and went for it. The kitten was taken by surprise and didn't have a chance to run away. It rounded its back, hissed, and struck the dog's nose with its paw. The dog jumped back and howled. The people on the bench opposite looked up, laughed, and then went on with their conversation. The dog tried a few more assaults, but the stray kitten was skillful at self-defense. It rolled itself up into a kind of ball, and whenever the dog approached it sprang aside and gave it a blow on the nose or eyes with its five extended claws. Eventually the dog gave up. It sat down about three yards away from the kitten, watching it and licking its nose. Sometimes it let out a deep growl, and the kitten answered with a spit. Its hair was standing up like the spines of a hedgehog.

"No," I said. "You had no need to be afraid of me. Why were you afraid?"

"Oh, Rodie," she said. "It wasn't really you I was afraid of. Only suddenly I saw everything quite differently. I went to New York and heard them talking about the Germans. At first I didn't believe them, but when all those people were let out of the concentration camps, and the press was full of it, and everybody talked about it—"

"Yes, yes," I said, looking at the dog. It was picking up some courage again and was growling. Its hair was standing up on its neck and shoulders. The kitten was watching it out of the slits of its eyes and hissing. It kept its eyes on the dog all the time. It kept hissing and occasionally spat.

"I suddenly got quite a different view of things," Margarete went on. "Good heavens, Rodie, I was afraid of Germany, afraid of all Germans! I got married to get clear of it all."

"Yes, yes," I said. "And are you glad you got clear of it?"

"Yes," she said.

At that moment the dog leaped forward. The kitten struck out with its paw, but the dog caught the paw in its mouth and started dragging the kitten about. The people on the bench looked up and laughed, and the man called out, "Go for her, Harras, go for her!"

"Good God!" Margarete said, laying her hand on her body. "The dog'll kill her, Rodie. Do something!"

I saw a nice round stone lying in front of me. I picked it up and threw it. They were no great distance away, and it was a lucky shot. It hit the dog on the forepaw. The dog dropped the kitten's paw, howled, and ran toward its master on three legs. The kitten got to its feet, licked its paw, and limped away toward a bush. It walked on three paws only and kept on looking toward its enemy.

"Heavens, Rodie, that's just the kind of thing I ought not to see," said Margarete. "I hope it hasn't done me any harm. I didn't know you were such a good shot, Rodie!"

"That's something we learned," I said.

"Yes," she said. "But with guns, not stones."

"Oh, toward the end we used stones too. You've no idea! What does your husband do?"

"He's head of the A.P.M."

"What's that?"

"It stands for 'Association Philanthropique Mondiale,'" she explained. "It's a world-wide philanthropic association."

"So his profession's philanthropy," I said. "Is his name Erik Clason, by any chance?"

"Yes," she said. "How do you know?"

"I passed the house once. Is your little boy fair with blue eyes?"

"Yes," she said. "His name's Sven. Have you seen him? You must come and see us, Rodie. When will you come? Tomorrow? I've often talked to Erik about you. I haven't told him everything, of course, but he knows we used to live next door to each other and grew up together. Will you come and see us? Tomorrow, or the day after?"

"Of course I'll come. I'll come the day after tomorrow, in the evening. But I insist on sitting in the garden and having Japanese lanterns, and Sven must be allowed to sit under the table if he wants to, and he must be allowed to stay up as long as he likes."

"I didn't know you were so fond of children. How is it you know so much about them?"

I was just going to say something, but in the meantime an excited examination of the dog had been taking place on the bench opposite. The owner of the dog got up and came over toward us, with the dog behind him on a lead. The dog limped, and there was a grim expression on its owner's face.

"You threw a stone at my dog and broke its leg," he said to me. "I demand compensation. Give me your address."

I gave it to him. He wanted to see my identity card, and I showed it to him without letting it out of my hand. He noted down all the particulars—name, registration number, date, and all.

"I'm afraid this is going to be an expensive business for you," he said. "It's a pedigreed dog. Its value is beyond price."

The dog had sat down and looked as if it understood every word. It looked viciously at me with its light-green eyes. It seemed to know I had thrown the stone.

"Don't think I'm joking," the man went on. "Fancy throwing a stone at my dog!"

I pointed out that it had bitten the cat.

"A valueless, stray cat," he said. "They ought to be destroyed. They only eat the songbirds!"

"Was that why you shouted 'Go for her!' when the dog bit her?"

"Don't be impudent," the man said. "My Harras is nothing to joke about."

He walked back toward his friends and put his notebook into his pocket on the way.

We walked toward the villa. Margarete told me about her life. She was very happy, and it was a lovely villa, and in the summer they spent their holidays in Sweden on one of the big lakes. At Christmas they went to Sweden too, for the *Julklapp*. They had a country house with a huge fireplace, and when snow was on the ground they went in a sledge. Sven spoke a shocking jargon, half German and half Swedish, but she could understand Swedish now, and so she could understand Sven. She told me a lot about Sweden on the way to the villa.

"It's extraordinary that you should have noticed the brass plate outside our door," she said. "Do you notice the brass plates outside all the houses that you pass?"

"No," I answered, "only when they interest me. I admired the house, with its fine view over the Rhine, and in particular I liked the little boy. I should never have imagined he was your little boy. You've got black hair that rustles."

She glanced at me and laid her hand on her body. "Good boy, very good boy," Yevgenia had used to say when I sat Margarete on my knees or took her somewhere. Yes, Yevgenia had known how to get her own way with people.

"So we'll see you the day after tomorrow, Rodie," she said. "We'll have Japanese lanterns, and Sven will be allowed to stay up late. Do you know what he does? He sits under the table and stays there quite quietly, waiting for someone to pass something down to him. But his father doesn't like his sitting under the table!"

We had forgotten the incident in the little square. We were standing under the big wall outside the grounds, laughing and talking, when the man passed by with the limping dog. He looked at us malevolently.

"That'll turn out to have been an expensive game for you, Rodie," Margarete said.

"We'll see," I answered.

"Perhaps you should have been more careful. You shouldn't have thrown a stone and broken the dog's leg straight away!"

I laughed.

"Why are you laughing?" she asked.

"You see," I explained, "that's what you people always do. First you tell one to do something, and afterward you say one should have been more careful."

"It certainly hurt the dog," Margarete said.

"It hurt the kitten too."

"Yes," said Margarete, "but the kitten wasn't so valuable."

VI

On the way back I passed the bench on which we had sat. The afternoon's events seemed rather improbable and incredible, though not completely incredible. I wanted to make sure I hadn't been dreaming, so I went to the little bush, where I found the tigerish kitten lying on a branch and licking its paws. It spat a little when I picked it up, but I put it inside my tunic under my greatcoat and walked on down toward the Rhine.

The sky was now a delicate blue, the clouds had disappeared, and the water was dark green and lively, full of barges, cargo boats, and tourist steamers. The roads looked metallic, there were many cars on them, and the factory chimneys were not distant now, but very close and very big, and were pouring thick smoke into the air. I thought of the smoke at the Holzkirchner Station at Munich into which Johanna Selzer had disappeared; it had looked exactly like that, and I was surprised at feeling no emotion. My head was filled with something like the golden haze that had lain over the landscape in my youth. Occasionally someone stepped out of it—Yevgenia or Kride or Margarete, or the little man on the steamer who exclaimed, "It's over!" when he stared at the thick clouds that obscured the German coast, or Captain Jenkuweit, or the soldier who cut the letter A out of his arm—but they all vanished again, and only the kitten remained. It now started cautiously sticking its head out of my tunic and purring.

"Quiet!" I said. "Keep quiet! You've got no reason to purr. You're the last creature that's got any right to purr!"

But it looked at me out of its green eyes, in the middle of which were two black slits. Then it closed them and went on purring louder and louder. Quite a young kitten . . .